The

Winds *of* Autumn

A Marquette Legacy Epic Romance

The
Winds *of*
Autumn

Susan Rounds

SWANCOURT PRESS

ISBN 978-1-7343695-0-2 (paperback)
ISBN 978-1-7343695-1-9 (ebook)

Library of Congress Control Number: 2022911413

Published in the United States by Swancourt Press
Vacaville, California
swancourtpress.com

Book Design by Emily Snyder
Cover Design by Vanessa Mendozzi
Baroque Rose interior art © HiSunnySky/Shutterstock Images

THE WINDS OF AUTUMN
Susan Rounds, Author Publisher
susanrounds.com

Printed in the United States of America

Doubt thou the stars are fire;
Doubt that the sun doth move;
Doubt truth to be a liar;
But never doubt I love.

- WILLIAM SHAKESPEARE

PROLOGUE

Missouri, 1839

AHYOKA CRADLED HER swollen belly in her arms. The ache subsided, but winter's cold raged on. She looked down at her bare feet thudding on the frozen ground and felt the pain knife underfoot like arrow tips piercing her flesh. All the earth seemed covered in them. There was no escape. Swirls of white mist hissed from her lips and the groaning she could not silence. Yesterday, and days before, she faced the same unending torment, waiting for the freezing pain to give way, until the numbness set in.

Every step along the unbroken trail creaked in her bones, stirring sounds from her past of branches bending in the wind as it howled through the chestnut trees that grew in the land of her people. A memory she would never forget. If only she could forget the suffering.

She pleaded for rest. The soldiers would not have it. Two seasons had passed since the journey began in the mountains of Appalachia. Now the frost stung her cheeks and turned her tears into beads of ice. It was the time of the Cold Moon, but she felt no joy in its presence. Not in this place.

With bayonets prodding against their backs, the Cherokee tribe lumbered toward the great Father of Waters, like herds of grunting cattle. As they crossed its icy depths on the white man's wooden boats, sudden cries shattered the frigid air. The floating ice overtook the elders and swept them away to their deaths in the dark void of the Mississippi. How many more voices would be silenced before they reached Indian Territory?

Huddled by the water's edge, the survivors shivered and wept. Only the warmth of *Nuhda Iga Ehi,* shining in the sky, gave them solace. Ahyoka hid her face in her tattered shawl and tried shunning their voices, but it was her own agony she heard, a sickening sound that drove straight to her belly and the brutal beginning of her condition.

The end awaiting her filled her with fear. There would be no returning to the Enchanted Land, the place the white man called Georgia. The Great Leader, Andrew Jackson, had spoken his truth. "Leave your villages. You do not belong here anymore." Ahyoka did not belong anywhere, anymore.

Desperation forced her into the dead of night with a band of Cherokee fugitives. They escaped into the land of the Osage and the Missouria, hiding out of sight along the banks of the Gasconade River. Memories of the Enchanted Land surrounded them. *Nunna daul Tsuny,* the trail where they cried, was no more.

WITH the coming of the Cold Moon each passing year, Ag'nayan'ke listened to his mother's stories of their ancestral lands, and of the white man's betrayal. They emboldened him and gave him purpose. One day he would become a Cherokee warrior and wear the sacred eagle feathers. But as he grew, a fiery thunder quaked in his chest. He could not quell the burning question. Who was he? Around him, he saw a people he did not belong to. A people who did not look like he did. Then, under a darkened sky, echoed the words he wished he never heard.

Ahyoka's voice drifted through the buffalo skins. For the boy child, the hiding game he and the children played suddenly became a heartless game of truths. The guilt spilled from her lips of what the soldier called McDonal did to her. Ag'nayan'ke's hands pounded against his ears to silence her shame. It was too late. His burning question had been answered.

All he ever saw was devotion when his mother gazed into his blue eyes and caressed his pale skin. But the truth kept haunting him. Ag'nayan'ke, the tainted Cherokee. An incessant reminder to his mother of what she suffered. And when he watched the light disappear from her eyes, the emptiness in his heart festered into an unshakable anger. It was the only honor he had left to bear for the deed that could never be undone. For the stain the white man put upon the bastard child. Half-breed.

Chapter 1

Memories Left To Begin Again

September 1865
St. Louis, Missouri
THE RENWICK ESTATE

MARIAH PACED IN front of the glass doors framing the far side of her bedroom. Her footsteps rattled the door latch each time she walked by. She didn't notice the sound, or that she was the cause of it. Not a thought entered her mind, except one. Every step she took brought her closer to tomorrow—and the lieutenant. These past two months, he was all she thought about. All she hoped for. Her eyes grew wide at the sight of Mother's wedding veil hanging on the canopy bedpost. Soon, she would be the envy of every young lady in St. Louis. Soon, she would become the lucky lieutenant's wife.

If only Fanny could be here. They had so much to talk about. *I still can't believe you're gone.* Letting go of her sister was hard while the War of the Rebellion battled on. But worse, her sister's death made her face a kind of fear she never felt before.

A fear of the end. And with the constant threat of Confederate attacks on the city, she feared losing the life she'd known might be the end of everything.

Now, the war was over. Change had come. She stopped pacing the room. *I wish you had the chance to be married, Fanny. But I know you would have wanted this for me.* It was time to let go. Too many handkerchiefs filled with tears that said goodbye ended those happy days before the war. Maybe tomorrow could bring happiness back.

Her diamond sparkled in the sunlight and in her eyes as she toyed with her engagement ring. She batted her eyelashes against the glare, but it all became a milky blur. Her skin warmed in the sun. She sighed with abandon and set free all her cares. The tranquil mood lingered, until thoughts of tomorrow sunk in again. *All happening so fast.*

The light played tricks on her in the windowpanes. She couldn't make out the shadowy image but felt its presence in her room. Her breathing turned shallow, and her heart began to race. Only one man aroused such a rush of emotions, sending her gaze careening through the glass panes. When she looked up again, the image was gone.

That topsy-turvy moment left her flustered. Surely, unsettled nerves were to blame. Nothing else made sense. She thought to ask her mother, then changed her mind. Mother grew up an heiress to the Deneuve fur trading dynasty which controlled the entire Missouri River Valley these past hundred years. But her father's mounting debts ruined the family fortune. What did it matter if he loved his wife? Emilie Sophie Deneuve Renwick learned a lesson from her father about love. Marriage was for one reason and one reason alone. Money. Choices had to be made. Instincts had to be relied on. Mariah would have to trust hers.

A knock at the bedroom door had her scurrying about. "Who is it?" She didn't sound very calm. *Where's my lace fan?*

She dashed over to the dresser and peered behind her jewelry box. *There it is.* Teatime just ended, and she so wanted to enjoy the comfort of her afternoon dress. *I wish I could put it on now.* She snatched the fan and waved it in her face. All this fretting annoyed her. She already made the biggest decision of her life three weeks ago. There was no more worrying left to do.

A familiar voice chimed from the hallway. "May I come in?"

"Yes, Mother."

She tossed the fan back on the dresser and glanced in the mirror. Her pretend smile didn't suit her. But she kept it fastened on her face. Little good it did. Just as the door swung open, her mother's expression said everything. Mother had an uncanny way of seeing the truth in her eyes, no matter how hard she tried to hide it.

"I don't have to ask because I know the answer." A tease intended to lighten her daughter's mood lifted Mother's spirits higher.

"The answer to what?" Mariah tried acting casual with her remark, though she was never good at the art of deception.

"I can tell you're not yourself, but that's to be expected, don't you think?"

"I am quite myself. Why wouldn't I be?"

"Well, tomorrow will be a big day for you, so I know how you must be feeling." Mother drew near. "You're a strong woman, Mariah. You've always been, despite all that's happened in your life. Even when your father gave you and Fanny those ponies for your birthdays, you wanted to prove what a big girl you could be. I can see you haven't changed a bit."

Mother was right. She *was* acting strange about tomorrow. Her gaze drifted out the window. An air of unsettledness brewed in the sky. Far west of the city, grey clouds loomed above the Osage Plains. She'd lived in St. Louis long enough to know Missouri rainstorms could strike with a sudden fury. She took her chance and brought up another subject.

"A storm's coming." She looked at her mother. "Do you remember how frightened I used to get when the thunder roared?"

Mariah's need to talk about the weather made her mother smile. "Yes, I do remember, as if it were yesterday." Her mind fell deep in thought. "You and I both know all our yesterdays belong in the past. Tomorrow holds so much promise for you and Nathan. So much happiness." She gazed at her daughter in earnest. "I've told you before why your father and I were married. It was a marriage of convenience. And yes, we've grown quite fond of each other over the years. But it's not easy to find love when you're surrounded by affluence. Yet you have, and that gives me great joy."

Mariah let her guard down. Her mother's candor rang true. "The way you feel about tomorrow means the world to me." She sighed and shook her head. "I can't believe I'm getting married. I guess love works in mysterious ways."

During Missouri's worst of times, and the family's, Mother pushed her own feelings aside so she could deal with the day-to-day. All the more reason to rally her lady friends and help the less fortunate in St. Louis. Giving to those in need filled a void in her life, and let the healing begin.

With her hair gathered in a loose chignon and wisps of curls framing her face, Mother brimmed with pride as she floated across the room like a swan. A telling sign glimmered in her moon-grey eyes. Grief had said its last goodbye.

She took her daughter's hands in hers. "You're so grown up now, my precious Mariah Abigail."

Mariah gave a look of reassurance for her mother to remember always. "Don't worry. After Nathan and I are married, I'll still be me."

They both let out a gentle laugh.

Mother's loving expression reminded Mariah of her childhood when she and Fanny helped her make those delectable apple pies. The sweet aroma filled the house for hours on end. Two sisters together making memories to last a lifetime. A bit of flour smudged their cheeks and dresses as though they needed a blessing of sorts before they indulged themselves. How giddy they felt when they joined in and sung her praises. *Magnifiques tartes!*

In time, those cherished memories succumbed to brutal realities. The fabric of a nation had unraveled at the seams. But at war's end, Mariah found herself graced with a secret she needed to keep safe. This was her chance to give her parents the happiness Fanny couldn't give them. They would never need to know.

Mother leaned in and kissed her on the cheek. "If your sister were here, she'd be so proud of you."

Mariah touched the aragonite pendant on her necklace and wondered. Would the serenity be there that Fanny said she always felt when she caressed it? She watched her mother's movements sway dreamlike toward the door and take her there. And then she heard Fanny's voice. *Keep it close to your heart, my little sister. It will always lead you home.* Mariah saw the look of goodbye as Fanny pressed the stone into her hand. She held on tight and wouldn't let go, even when Fanny's hand turned cold.

Mother spun around. Her words rang out. "Heavens. I almost forgot to tell you. A message arrived from Nathan a short while ago. He won't be joining us for dinner this evening."

Mariah stood startled by her mother's remark. "Oh. I see." Her voice was edged with surprise at the news.

Mother gave her a coy smile. "I must say, I found his excuse rather romantic. He said it would be bad luck for the groom to see his bride-to-be the night before the wedding. Now isn't that the perfect thing for your future husband to say?"

A doting wink was the last image Mariah saw of her mother.

DINNERTIME was still hours away. The moment Mariah longed for arrived at last. She tugged her pearl hair combs. Her tresses spilled down her back. She nuzzled her toes in the Savonnerie carpet spread out beneath her feet. Her afternoon dress, a soft hue of yellow, gave her what she craved most—bare, unlaced comfort.

She stepped onto the balcony for a breath of fresh air. Wafting up from the garden, the scent of Mother's Damask roses greeted her. She peered over the railing. A surge of contentment welled up inside. Those curly pink blossoms were still there, ageless as ever, and a reminder of Missouri's autumn beauty and her childhood. *Some things never change.*

On this twenty-third day of September, a year after the Confederates conspired to attack the city and her home, those Damask roses became her anchor in a sea of constant change—a part of her life that desperately needed grounding. But this moment was not about the war, or memories of loss. It was about times to come.

A muffled sound echoed through the trees bordering the expanse of land between the Renwick and Valmont estates. The shifting breezes made eavesdropping difficult, but Mariah recognized those cackling voices. To be sure, Georgine and Edith were not dear friends, yet jealous acquaintances they turned out to be. How odd they were walking so close to the boundary of the estate. They never set foot outside for walks of any kind. She hid behind one of the Greek columns and steadied her breathing while she listened in.

"She—do anything—bed down a man. All she wants—get married—rub our noses in it."

Georgine's younger sister, Edith, blurted out her own secret. "Did you see—glaring—my breasts—theater balcony last night? Who cares—married—keep him sated. Mariah can't!"

Wicked laughter times two put the Valmont sisters in fine company. Each other's.

Mariah braced herself against the column. Their news left her in shock. Then her suspicions took hold. Were Georgine and Edith at it again, stirring up more of the same idle gossip they were so good at blathering about?

Their voices faded in the wind undulating through the grassy lowlands along the Mississippi River. The storm was closing in. Brooding clouds grew dark, almost beastlike, casting an eerie silence around her.

She thought of the wedding. Nothing was going to get in her way, not even Georgine and Edith's petty conniving. Their cruel words were just words, and she refused to believe them. *What could they possibly know about love?*

Back in her room, she caught a glimpse in the standing mirror of how a genteel upbringing could refine a Renwick woman. Etched across her delicate, fair-skinned façade lazed the politesse of Benton Park, a dignified composure instilled from childhood of the way a lady should behave, even under the direst of circumstances. But all that mattered was tomorrow. And new beginnings.

The clouds rumbled. A strong gust shook the doors and broke her thoughts. Rain unleashed from the aubergine sky and spattered against the window panes, distorting the maple trees outside and their branches twisting in the wind. She pressed her hand against the glass and watched the beads of water slide down. Like tears running down a child's face. A crack of thunder boomed in the heavens. She latched on to the drapes as the storm's fury weighed upon her, and an uncertainty that did not belong.

Chapter 2

For Better, For Worse

ATHAN EDWARD LAWTON, do you take Mariah Abigail Renwick for your lawful wedded wife, to live together after God's ordinance in the holy estate of matrimony?"

The reverend posed his question as if he asked it for the first time. In the Lord's house, vows of the bride and groom could not be taken lightly. "Will you love, honor, comfort, and cherish her from this day forward, forsaking all others, keeping only unto her, for as long as you both shall live?"

"I will."

Nathan listened as Mariah echoed her promise to him. With those two words, their world changed.

The reverend ended in prayer. "Guide them, that their love may be pure and their vows may be true."

An embrace pulled them close. Mariah brushed her hands over the gold buttons on Nathan's uniform. Her eyelashes fluttered at the feel of his raven hair teasing his starched shirt collar. The juxtaposition of black and white, of a man born to battle yet tender in his touch, lifted her heart to the heavens where they joined in a kiss filled with passion.

As their lips parted, Nathan whispered, "Here's to us, Mrs. Lawton."

Applause from the guests resounded inside Christ Church, except from Edith and Georgine. They both sat in their pew, hiding their china doll faces behind gilded fans that waved with such disdain, no suitor would dare come near them. All their gossip had been just gossip. But the charade carried on. Their eyes narrowed with envy, and words simmered under their breath, demeaning Mariah as inadequate for her husband's needs.

Warm air lingered in the afternoon and hinted of a summer's day in late September. Once they boarded the open carriage, Mariah gazed up at the steeple and fell mesmerized by the swaying bells. A sudden jolt from the horses startled her. She gripped Nathan's arm.

"Are you all right?" he asked.

She feigned a smile. "It's nothing. I'm a little overwhelmed, I imagine."

He nestled his hand in the curve of her waist. His eyes washed over her. From the moment they met at the officers' ball, they wanted to be together. Now they were husband and wife. Joined lips muffled a subtle moan. A rush of sensations engulfed Mariah. Oh, how he could kiss. When he drew back, his words left her dazed.

"Tonight, you will be mine, my love. All of you."

The church bells clanged in the belfry, and the guests waved farewell. As the sight faded from view, an absurd thought struck Mariah. The notion she lost her wedding ring turned her all gooseflesh with apprehension. She stroked her gloved finger to be sure. But her shivers wouldn't let up. The eerie feeling crept in again, just as it did minutes before outside the church. Nathan left her alone when he abruptly stepped away and spoke in private with one of the soldiers standing guard. A married woman without her husband. On her wedding day, of all days.

She settled back in the seat and reached for her handkerchief. *It's gone.* She plopped her hands into her lap and sighed. *I did lose something. A silly handkerchief.* Solving the mystery put her at ease, until she remembered the look on that soldier's face and the way he stared at her. She shivered again.

NATHAN cogitated. The wedding was over. His mind raced. The scent of Mariah's perfume still reeled in his head. All he thought about was her.

Five months ago, the War of the Rebellion ended. The Yanks won. Who the hell cared? The band of gold on his finger proved he picked the right side. Edmund Renwick, the Missouri Unionist, would've never given his daughter away in marriage to anyone called Johnny Reb. Acting the part of a die-hard Yank was a stroke of luck Nathan didn't expect. Getting married was the last thing on his mind.

The end of the war had him tasting victory when Mariah caught his eye. But in their binding kiss, this Renwick victory by far tasted the sweetest. If only his mother could see what became of him in this promised land of Missouri. Perhaps Ahyoka's spirit would find favor with her son.

> *Oh, sweet mother of Appalachia, sing your songs of joy to me. As I watch the ravens carve the mountains and valleys with their wings, and the sacred eagles soar high across the sky vault, sing to me of the Enchanted Land, the land of the Cherokee.*

The memory of his mother's voice tugged at his heart. Her songs lulled him to sleep every night. Forever, it seemed. He heard the wedding music playing again. Mariah's face shimmered pure as the Cold Moon snow. Like nothing he'd ever seen before, except in his mother's face. But Ahyoka's whispered words kept haunting him, and the pain of her past he had to silence.

GENERAL Winfield Scott gave the order to his brigade. Sergeant McDonal complied. They rounded up a band of Cherokees and hauled them off to the removal camp at Fort Butler in North Carolina. Ahyoka's family feared they would never go home. Though their hearts were burdened with sadness, the Great Spirit returned, as it had in seasons past, and ushered in the Planting Moon. But no seeds were sown, and no crops were gathered. For the Cherokee people, all that followed was void of meaning and purpose.

While the refugees waited at the fort, McDonal took Ahyoka away for questioning, and then had his way with her. Lucky for the sergeant, the general had orders to take those savages to Indian Territory. But he'd sooner hunt them down, like his Pa taught him to hunt racoons back in the Tennessee hills. He got real good at hunting down Ahyoka. She came in handy. Done turned the trail ride into a roaming whorehouse, until she got all pregnant. Just dirt now, that's all she was. No different than the rest of them. He didn't wait long. Ahyoka's poor little sister. So terrified of him. He coiled her hair in his hand and dragged her off at sundown. Marks of his anger scarred her face as her cries withered away. Ahyoka never saw her again.

NATHAN never told his mother the cutting words he heard her whisper through the buffalo skins, or how those words took hold of him. His destiny to be a great warrior, adorned with the sacred eagle feathers, was destroyed because of his father. Because of the white man. *You son of a bitch. I'd burn in Hell to make you pay for what you did to my mother. For what you did to me.* He imagined his mother's torment all over again. Her hushed words would not release him. Not today. Not ever.

McDonal smothered Ahyoka's body squirming beneath him. The taker had ensnared his prey. Willing evildoer. Vile. Possessed. He stared at her and crowed. But she turned on him. He flicked the spit off his face. You savage scum. Too bad he got mad. McDonal, the beast unleashed, out of control.

Her breasts bulged in his hands and in his mouth. He bit her nipples, making her scream. His groans mounted. Her flesh, laced with sweat, sweltered below as he tracked her down with his roused and ready weapon. Then, the perfect aim. He pierced her tight opening and thrust in deep while her lips burst open to wails of agony. A slap across the face. Shut up! Lust infected his loins. They spiked, about to rupture. He latched on to her hips and rode her like a wild animal until his body turned rigid, spewing the carnal seed inside.

McDonal didn't care if Ahyoka's soul burned with fire, or that she wanted to die. He dragged his tongue up the side of her face and licked her wet skin. It didn't take much to get him randy again. He groped for the leather strap behind her back. A helpless squaw, all tied up, made him crazy, real bad crazy. He could hunt down another one just as quick. But why bother? He laughed at her and stripped naked, and laughed again. Her sorry begging worked him up good. He rolled her over and glared at her bound hands, then watched himself take her again.

LIVING in two different worlds. Acting out two separate lives. That's what Nathan put up with every stinking day. A lingering kiss. Their vows were sealed. The band of gold suited him well. He replayed the scene over and over in his head as they walked down the aisle, arm in arm. Organ pipes droned a faint wedding melody, but all he heard was the voice of his mother calling out to him. *Ag'nayan'ke!*

In the eyes of every guest, Nathan saw his truth. The wicked deeds of the white man, resurrected. They were to blame for banishing his people. He was a half-breed because of them. All their money and conspicuous consumption riled him with indignation that seethed in his parting smile. He would make them pay. He vowed to make everyone pay. His day of reckoning had come.

CHAPTER 3

The Doubt Creeps In

MARIAH GAZED OUT the cottage window at the estate. This land belonged to her family and still took her breath away. Perched atop a rise on the hill, the mansion commanded a view of the grand Mississippi and stood like a majestic beacon, guiding riverboat pilots along the waterway as they navigated safe passage round Chatillon's Point.

Greek columns, painted white, fronted the mansion. Gargoyles loomed under the eaves, casting grotesque stares down at unsuspecting guests while lush carpets of ivy curved their fingered vines up the limestone walls. Near the cottage, a weeping willow tree arched over a winding brook that flowed downstream toward the great river.

Mariah made her way into the bedroom. Her thoughts wandered off to what awaited her and Nathan. His future as a military man suited him, but her father's connections in St. Louis might favor other opportunities. With the upheaval from the war leaving Nathan's plans uncertain, they decided to stay at the cottage for the time being.

A new life. A new husband. Benton School would be the same though. Since she found a passion for teaching, she never pondered the idea of marriage. There was a pressing need for her in the classroom after years of bitter conflict. As she recalled their hurried wedding plans, Nathan's approval of her work reassured her all was right. A quiet anxiousness came over her. The school year was about to begin, and the students would require her attention.

Enough daydreaming. I have to get us settled in. She straightened the pillows and smoothed the bedcover. The room felt serene in the morning light, yet its plain interior beckoned for a creative touch. What a splendid notion, letting the whimsy of her imagination run free. She smiled and slapped a bed pillow into place.

But her reverie was cut short when the floor creaked behind her. She whirled around and saw her husband in the doorway.

"Nathan—" She caught her breath. "I had no idea you were standing there."

"I know. I've been watching you."

He locked his arms across his chest and leaned against the door frame. His strong build tightened the fabric of his shirt. Each sleeve was rolled up just below the elbow, exposing his forearms that flexed in full view.

His stare sent Mariah's gaze tumbling down the front of her yellow dress. She couldn't think. Her mind went blank every time she looked at him. Then she remembered the meeting he arranged with her father. So why did he come here? Perhaps he stopped by to see if she needed any help. She glanced at him again. He stood there, waiting. Even in her unadorned look, with her hair gathered in a loose bun and a hand towel slung over her shoulder, he couldn't keep his eyes off her.

"You know why I'm here." Tension drummed in his voice. "I've waited long enough."

"I—don't understand." With her nerves all jumbled inside,

she didn't sound very convincing. How could she when she left him unsatisfied on their wedding night? Maybe his thirst was too much for her to quench. Something kept holding her back, and its grip felt stronger than ever.

Nathan stepped closer. "Then let me show you." His words barely held him steady.

He tugged on the towel. It fell to the floor. His fingers traced the curve of her neck and along the crest of her shoulder. He nudged her dress sleeve. A sigh escaped from her lips. Not a wisp of air remained in the room as she tried to breathe but forgot how. Her combs slipped from her hair, cascading her curls around her face. Whispered kisses dusted her throat, leaving her vulnerable yet aroused. She moaned. Suddenly, his hunger grew intense and confused her. She wanted to make him stop, but her heart pounded instead. Was love supposed to feel this way? There was no time for questions.

"Come to me. I need you . . ."

"Nathan—"

He held her tight. A whirlwind of feelings pressed against her lips and where his hand fondled her breast. Then her knees buckled. She threw her arms around his neck, and they collapsed onto the bed. He swept her on top of him, fusing his gaze into hers, while his hands moved down over her bottom and yanked up her dress.

She drew in a sharp breath. "No—"

How many times had a woman said *no* when he knew damn well it meant *yes*. He teased her lace neckline formed snug against her bosom. The sway of her breasts lured his tongue in between. He would do anything to unshackle her inhibitions and claim the essence of her. His rhythm caught fire, until her words doused him like a bucket of cold water.

"I don't want—" She turned away and couldn't speak.

He snapped her chin and glared at her. "What did you say?" His hand was shaking her face. "Are you telling me you don't want me? Well are you, Mariah?" He didn't wait for her answer. Anger burned in his chest. The sanctity of their marriage wouldn't even give him the rightful pleasure to take his wife. Then she made things worse by letting those tears well up in her eyes. And for what?

Her body crumbled at his side.

Of all the wartime battles he fought, he was sure he lost this one. He stood up and straightened his shirt but didn't bother to look at her. Without a word, he left the room.

The door slammed shut. A deafening silence closed in. Crushing guilt took hold of Mariah, and more, the humiliation she caused her husband. *What's wrong with me?* She covered her mouth. A rush of air roared through her nostrils. She felt like she was passing out. But if her hands gave way, the truth would be set free for everyone to hear.

There, there, Mariah. You had your chance to love him and let happiness come home again. Now you've thrown it all away.

Maybe Georgine and Edith were right. She didn't know how to love Nathan. She didn't know how to love anyone.

CHAPTER 4

Men And Their Money

Edmund was in his study, engaged in his morning ritual of strong coffee in one hand and a quick read of the *Missouri Democrat* in the other. He had no plans for shoving off to work until later in the morning but couldn't remember why.

The housemaid pounced into the room, almost shouting at the man of the house. "S'cuse me, Mr. Renwick. That man's come to see you."

Edmund slammed the newspaper on the desk. "Thunderation, Perdie. What man?"

His gruff voice reminded her she interrupted him. "It's the lieutenant—sir. Lieutenant Lawton." She teetered next to the door.

"Well, why didn't you say so in the first place? Send him in. And for God's sake, stop moving about like that. You're making me nauseous."

Perdie stepped backwards through the doorway and offered Mr. Renwick's invitation to the lieutenant, then turned on her heel and vanished down the hall.

Nathan craned his neck and tugged on his sleeves. He walked into the room. An air of clout surrounded him. His father-in-law looked every bit the smug banker, with his gold fob dangling from his gold watch he tucked neatly into his vest pocket. *Damned capitalists in their black suits.* He dismissed his observations. But he would have been amused just the same if Renwick's stock collar, overstretched to the hilt, suddenly snapped from around his neck. The man reeked of money, right down to the faint smell of fine coffee lingering in the room.

He clenched his hands behind his back. Standing face-to-face with the banking tycoon put him under pressure and back on the battlefield, outnumbered by a swarm of Rebel guns. He checked his temper. Their meeting this morning had his future at stake, and his reputation as someone to be reckoned with, but only if he stood his ground as an upstanding officer. A daring soldier who fought for the Union cause.

"Good morning, Mr. Renwick. My apologies for disturbing you."

"Nonsense. Good to see you. Have a seat." Renwick pointed to the chair with the coiled newspaper in his hand, then tossed it in the trash. "I'm the one who should be apologizing. Our meeting completely slipped my mind." He ambled over to his son-in-law and patted him on the back. "I think it's time you called me Edmund. You *are* part of the family now."

Nathan sat down next to the desk. He gave his full attention as Edmund plucked a cigar from the humidor and started rambling on about his grandiose plans to forge St. Louis into the great city it was before the war. All the idle talk had him nodding his head while he thumbed the corner of the mahogany.

Edmund's high hopes for his city left a scowl on his face. "That damn war sucked the life out of this town. Did you know St. Louis is the biggest city in the country, west of Pittsburgh? Now we're losing the race to Chicago." He huffed. "Well, not for long."

The banking industrialist and his fellow captains of industry believed in their metropolis, with its river of riches hauling steamboats and their cargo spoils into its port, like a mother bird feeding her young. There was no better place to live than in St. Louis, Edmund Renwick always said, and no better place to make money. Until the Confederates let their slapdash idea get trampled on the battlefield.

Renwick and his archrival, Robert Camden, never let the politics of war get in the way of their secret bet. And Renwick never liked losing a bet. Future Missouri prosperity would create the state's richest man, if he was a gambling man. In his quest to beat the banker at their high-stakes game, Camden built his steamboat operations on the Mississippi without Renwick's loans. But Edmund didn't need Camden's business. He had other plans.

"So how are you and the wife getting along?" Edmund pondered the awkward question and fell deep in thought. "The *wife*. The sound of it makes me feel old. My sweet daughter, a married woman. I still can't believe it." He shook his head and moseyed over to the window.

"We're doing well and making adjustments." Nathan didn't let on about any problems they were having. He curried favor with his father-in-law and knew his motives had everything to do with his fortune, and even more to do with his daughter.

"I know what you mean. The whole marriage business could be time better spent making money." Edmund chuckled. "Women are too complicated." His face tinged rosy pink as his voice reverberated in the room.

"I couldn't agree with you more. I'll do my best to take care of Mariah and respect her wishes."

Edmund looked at his son-in-law. A sharp tone edged his voice. "It's time we talked business. Your prestige as an army officer has served you well, but prestige is worthless unless it makes you money. Now that this confounded war is over, I want to know details about your plans. My daughter's well-being depends on it."

Nathan shifted in his seat and watched his father-in-law get all high and mighty pointing his finger at him.

Edmund had more to say. "Before I consented to your marriage, we both agreed your future as a lieutenant would not be adequate to provide for Mariah. You gave me your assurances. I expect some answers."

Nathan drew back. Old man Renwick was going to get some answers. For weeks, he mulled over this conversation in his head, orchestrating every word to get the right reaction from his father-in-law. The only one he would accept.

"I've given much thought to my military career and believe it's in my best interest to pursue as many options as I can."

Edmund faced the window while he ran the length of his cigar under his nose. He was a man of habit and cigars were one of them. But an invitation to take part in the custom hinted to a potential client that a deal was in the making.

"I lose patience when people start talking in circles. Straight-forward and to the point, young man. My time is short."

"Of course. I haven't discussed the matter with Mariah and would like your discretion with what I'm about to say. I'll let her know when my affairs have been settled."

He stood up and joined his father-in-law by the window. Neither of them spoke. Then he broke the silence with his jaw-dropping news.

"I have plans to move out West. The army has offered me a captain's command at Fort Laramie in Dakota Territory. The government needs control of the region to protect the westward bound emigrants. If I accept, I'll be promoted to major within six months." He expected a hasty retort. Edmund didn't say a word. "I realize both you and Mrs. Renwick may be uncomfortable with Mariah moving away from St. Louis, but I give my word I will protect her and no harm will come to her."

"I see . . ." Edmund's response sounded a thousand miles away.

"Once I reach the rank of major, I'm confident my plans will hold promise for future prospects."

Edmund snapped his head sideways and glared at Nathan. "Plans. Promises. I want details, damn it, and they better be good. I know more than anyone in this town that any gamble you take is a waste of time unless it pays huge dividends. Otherwise, you're nothing but a fool."

"I have no doubt, sir. The plans I'm referring to involve politics—and the railroad."

"Politics? The railroad? You've got some explaining to do, young man."

Calling him a young man started grating on Nathan's nerves. Out of the corner of his eye, he noticed Edmund's eyebrow arch, a sign that he piqued his interest. His father-in-law averted his gaze and lit his cigar. Grey swirls of smoke clouded the view through the window, but Nathan spied a figure walking by the brook near the cottage. It was Mariah. She left her hair down. Even from this distance, it glittered in the sun like flakes of gold. *Focus on the deal.*

He shifted his feet and stood tall at parade rest. "When the government organizes Wyoming Territory, they'll want an experienced military officer to be first governor. I have political alliances in the region ready to support my future candidacy."

Edmund nodded. "Political alliances are important. I have a few of my own. Business alliances, that is, and from Boston, no less."

Nathan held his tongue as Edmund puffed on his cigar, squinting through the haze. All the old man did was brag and to hell with anything he said. Didn't the paunchy banker just hear him talk about the territorial governorship?

Edmund carried on, roused by sudden vigor. "Do you have any idea how wealthy those capitalists are back in Boston? Waste money like it's trash." He eyed the humidor on his desk. "Good God, the lunatics even smoke cigars rolled in hundred-dollar bills. Damn near puts Missouri to shame. It's high-stakes gambling, if you ask me."

Renwick's big talk didn't fool Nathan. He had a hunch the banker smelled money, no matter how hard he tried to wipe that grin off his face. His father-in-law didn't let up.

"Could be I've got the winning hand this time. Could very well be."

The winning hand. What are you up to, old man? Had he underestimated Renwick's fortune? His mind raced. He had to plead his case.

"I admire your ambition, *Edmund*. You have my deepest respect." His voice grew sincere. "I want you to know, I'm determined to give Mariah the life she deserves. But my political career out West won't be enough. A new northern railroad is key. Our future happiness depends on it."

He peered out the window, not to enjoy the view. He left the moneyed man hanging, to ponder his future and its link to Mariah's happiness. Every word he spoke meant nothing if Edmund withheld his approval. He had one last thing to say.

"Plans are in place for the railroad line, but the government will need initial funds up front, as a show of good faith, before it approves the route. With your financial backing, I can make sure that happens." He drew attention to the wedding ring on his finger. "What I'm trying to say is, this is an investment I want to make, for my marriage and my wife."

He walked over to the chair and sat down. If this was the rise to a Rebel battle, the risk to an entire regiment hung in the balance. He never trusted one soldier to win the fight, but now he was entrusting one man to decide his fate.

Edmund dislodged the tube of smouldering tobacco from his mouth and pointed at the desk. "Help yourself to one of these fine cigars."

A glint sparked in Nathan's eyes. He opened the humidor and removed an aromatic brown cylinder. The feel of the cigar sent a surge through him.

"You're an ambitious man, Nathan. I like that. Use your ambition wisely and it will make you a rich man someday. Because of the risks I've taken with my clients from Boston, I'm afraid I can be of no help with your dubious venture. If your plans take hold, say in the next year or two, maybe some funds can be arranged then."

Nathan wasn't a man to flinch and show his hand when the stakes were this high, but his contorted fists almost punched Edmund in the face. *You bastard.* He bolted up from the chair. *Can't you see your damn money belongs to me now!* He squeezed the cigar until control found his voice. "That's a generous offer, sir. I am—in your debt."

Edmund waved his cigar in the air as if his entire board of directors just applauded him for the bank's latest profits. "Yes, yes. It's the least I can do for my son-in-law. I'm sure you didn't expect me to give you the entire bank." The old man laughed and followed with a quick rejoinder. "Work hard, my boy, and you'll get your reward."

Nathan had stomached enough. He stepped back to leave the room when his father-in-law pulled out his money clip, counted five large bills, and flashed them in his face like he was being dared to take them. He faked a look of surprise. The money vanished into his side pocket.

"That should do you some good, unless you smoke it." Edmund laughed again. Then his voice turned serious. "Mark my words. You've got my precious daughter as your wife, and she's worth more than all the money in the world. I'll hold you to your promise to take good care of her. Agreed?"

Nathan mumbled and shook his hand. A swift exit from the room had him barreling down the stairs demanding his horse. Waiting another second in the mansion infuriated him.

He bounded toward the stables, outraged that his rightful inheritance was taken from him. The forgotten cigar dangled between his fingers. He threw it on the ground and crushed it with his boot. Edmund's face lay mangled in the tobacco remains.

CHAPTER 5

Pilfer Your Soul

*T*HE STUDENTS KEPT calling her Miss Renwick, but Mariah didn't mind. Their forgetfulness helped her get used to the idea of being married. She was anxious to teach again and reclaim some semblance of confidence that waned of late. *Our marriage is still new and will take some getting used to.*

Chatter from the children brought her attention back to the classroom. They fidgeted in their seats, asking so many questions, bless their hearts, and more than she could answer. After sorting out the classroom rules, studies began in earnest followed by the students' favorite part of the day. Not a thump or a sneeze echoed in the room as she read stories about the frontier, and the Indian tribes who lived off the land, long before the pioneers arrived. Sadly, both sides had not found a way to share the place each wanted to call home.

As the rays of afternoon sun beamed through the classroom window, Mariah's face flushed from the heat. A figure, indistinct in the light, stood waiting at her desk.

"Miss Renwick." The young girl cupped her hand over her mouth and giggled. "I mean, Mrs. Lawton."

Mariah squinted through the glare. "Yes, Abigail. What is it?"

"Why is your face so red? And—and why do you keep spinning your ring on your finger?"

Abigail's direct questions had Mariah facing an awkward moment. She made light of it. "Well, I am looking forward to teaching my students again, including you. As for my cheery color, I imagine the sun has something to do with that."

"Oh. All right."

Mariah leaned into her desk and dropped her voice to a whisper. "I have a secret to tell you. Did you know we both share the same name?" She paused and watched a pair of eyes grow wide. "My middle name is Abigail, just like yours." The child's angelic face brightened the entire room, and her eyes glimmered ever more violet. Mariah saved the best for last. "That can only mean one thing. You'll be one of my best helpers in the classroom this year."

Abigail's voice squeaked with excitement. "I will be your best helper ever, Mrs. Lawton. I promise." She skipped back to her desk with a bounce in her step as her hair curls and ribbons swayed across her pinafore dress.

This first day of school was off to a good start.

Arithmetic exercises, word problem recitations, and Mrs. Lawton's spelling matches busied the students for the rest of the afternoon. Once the school day ended and the students left the classroom, Mariah gathered her school work and took one last glimpse at her syllabus. Then she plopped her hat on her head and was off.

The waiting carriage on the outskirts of town gave her time to enjoy the walk that lifted her spirits and helped organize her thoughts for the next day. Deep inside, she felt new again.

Just as she rounded Bellefontaine Road, a voice from behind called out her name. She looked over her shoulder and saw the family carriage approach, and her father leaning out the window, waving her down. The exhilaration of the outside air and her breezy thoughts screeched to a halt.

The coach pulled up next to her. She reached for her father's hand and stepped inside. If only she knew he had company along for the ride. Nathan's stare put her on edge. She didn't know what to say. But any second, Father would hint that his daughter wasn't behaving the way a Renwick lady should.

A faint smile formed on her face. "I'm surprised to see you, Nathan."

He took her hand and kissed it. "You've been gone the entire day, my love." He added a tender touch. "I've missed you."

Her father started going on about military papers Nathan signed. She paid no mind to his remarks. Then his words sunk in. *What military papers?* Nathan didn't say a word to her about his plans, yet Father already knew. She never doubted her father's sincerity, but he taught her well to notice it in others, or the lack of it. Instead of resolving the matter, she piddled in a back-and-forth game of awkward glances with her husband and a sense of relief whenever she noticed a passerby outside.

As soon as they arrived at the house, she kissed her father on the cheek, said her goodbyes and turned toward the cottage. But she couldn't avoid the inevitable.

Nathan tugged her arm. "Mariah. We need to talk."

She cleared her throat. "I see. Well, I have to put my things away first."

He let her go, and she was gone.

The scent of the meadow drifting over the estate was an enticing reminder of a place to escape for anyone yearning to be alone just now. Brilliant scarlet and yellow leaves rustled in the trees, waiting to be set free by the next gust of wind.

Mariah ambled out of the cottage and spied Nathan under the willow tree with his back wedged against the trunk. She averted her gaze as she approached, but when their eyes met, she blenched. His stare made her wonder what he was thinking. She had no time to ask. He set off and left her standing there while his figure receded in the distance toward the limestone bluffs skirting the shoreline of the Mississippi.

In an instant, she hurried after him, tripping over her dress. She clutched a fistful of fabric, raised the hem, and made haste. By the time she caught up behind him, her heart was racing. But as loud as it beat, she heard every word he said.

"We need to leave St. Louis. We'll be moving in early spring."

His demands struck her like a volley of gunfire booming in her ears. In the midst of catching her breath and sorting out the confusion, he lobbed another blow at her.

"I've accepted a transfer to a military outpost in Dakota Territory."

It wasn't just the arrogance in his voice, or even what he said that stunned her, but more how he stood with his back facing her.

"We won't be staying in St. Louis?" The notion of leaving home shook her to the core. "I can't believe I'm hearing this. And why on earth do we have to travel so far away?"

"I've been offered a captain's promotion at Fort Laramie. The decision's already been made."

She kept waiting for him to turn around and look at her. "What about my students, and Mother and Father, and—?" Her voice wilted at the thought of not visiting Fanny at the cemetery. "I realize the decision to stay in the military was yours, and yours alone, but you never discussed your plans with me before you made up your mind."

Would it have made any difference? Not by the way he peered over his shoulder and gave her a razor-sharp stare. "I had no reason to tell you about my plans." He walked away again, treading a path through the tall grass and leaving a trail in his wake.

With each step he took, panic set in. Mariah ran after him and maneuvered her way in front. She pressed her hands against his chest, demanding he stop this nonsense here and now.

"You can't take me away from my home, Nathan. You just can't."

He showed no regard for what she said and gave his answer. "I can. And I will."

Without warning, he grabbed her arms. The bayonet scar on the side of his neck flashed in her eyes, and so did that wild look she'd never seen. He came down on her, forcing his mouth against hers. She tried pushing away, but he snapped her hands behind her back and plunged them both into the meadow.

Her body writhed against him. "Don't fight me—Mariah. I'm not done with you—yet."

His swift maneuvering turned urgent. His game of virile patience was over.

The more she squirmed, the more intense he became. He pulled at her neckline and glared at her breasts. Lust roused through his loins. Raw lust of the unmarried kind. He splayed her arms above her head as his eyes darkened from blue to pitch black. His tongue swarmed over her peaks and firmed her nipples. He reacted to their arousal. She cried out. He didn't care. The pleasure was all his. Besides, he could be quick about it when he had to be.

He yanked up her dress with one hand and ripped open his pants with the other, void of all but the burning need to release.

Despite her struggling, he parted her legs and went deep. The sudden urge gripped him. But she was ruining the moment. He silenced her whimpers with his mouth like he was suffocating her. Another thrust, and he belted out a groan. A paralyzing wave shuddered through him. He took it to the end where he subsided from the frenzy, easing back just enough until the pressure ignited a second spark. He rode her higher. Higher. The need strained in his face. And then he released again.

A spent man had no cause for complaints when the taking was this good. Nathan satisfied himself. Nothing else mattered. Their marriage came to a mutual understanding of what love meant to him. Their rendezvous left a smirk on his face, telling Mariah, perhaps next time, she should fulfill her wifely duties more obediently.

Disbelief. Denial. The unthinkable happened. Mariah's world lay in ruins. The emptiness inside gave her the answer she didn't want to believe any more than the ache that smouldered below. To honor this kind of love was easy, unless those notions of true love kept getting in her way. She learned a hard lesson. But harder still, she had to reclaim her soul, or at least what was left of it. She had to find a way to go on.

CHAPTER 6

A Gift Given With No Demands

$\mathcal{T}$HE UNION DEPOT train station hummed with busy travelers. Mariah stared at the chaotic sight. The crowds reminded her of her father's travels before the war, when he took the train to Chicago and parlayed his negotiating skills into new business for St. Louis. Father boasted that Chicago commerce needed bank loans too, so why not from the State Bank of Missouri?

Odd as it seemed, with every luxury at her disposal, Mariah never traveled beyond St. Louis, except last year when Mother and Father whisked her aboard a train bound for Kansas City. The war had reached the banks of the Mississippi, a vital artery into the Deep South that twelve thousand Confederate soldiers were ready to die for. Only St. Louis stood in their way. Thank God the Union prevailed.

As she watched the flurry of activity, the noises unnerved her. She arrived early to greet a business client of Father's yet couldn't recall meeting Mr. Marquette the last time he visited the estate. But two years had gone by since she last saw the gentleman from Boston. She didn't even remember what he looked like.

She sighed under her scarf while she scanned the crowd. At least she heard the announcement and the platform where the train would arrive. *That will just have to do.*

The train slowed to a halt against the metal buffers. Passengers exited in every direction. She swung her head from left to right, as though she were gesturing in refusal of something, when a well-dressed man caught her eye. Unlike the other travelers getting off the train, he stood still. Perhaps he, too, was searching for someone. Mariah waved her hand and attracted his attention. He stepped off the train and approached.

"You must be Miss Renwick. I'm Julian Marquette. It's a pleasure to make your acquaintance."

Apropos pleasantries between strangers perhaps, but his brown eyes told her he knew exactly who she was. No sooner had he reached for her hand and kissed it than she pulled it away. A puzzled look framed his face, yet he smiled at her even so.

As tall as Mariah was, she lifted her gaze to take in Julian's physique. He was impeccably dressed in his suit. From his brown hair to his black shoes, he carried an air of self-assurance and a quiet strength that at once surrounded her.

His voice sounded unexpectedly sincere.

"You've changed since we last met." It was not her reaction he was pondering, just the sight of her standing before him.

His gaze made her feel uneasy, and his presence even more. She turned and bit her lip. *He must think I'm quite the lady behaving this way. Why did yesterday have to happen?*

She regained her composure. "I'm newly married, Mr. Marquette. My name is now Mariah Lawton. I do hope the change you referred to is for the better." The smile she gave him felt worlds away but not the hurt she felt inside. Every part of her cringed at the slightest look from another man. And then he spoke again.

"Indeed. More than you'll ever know. Please accept my best wishes for you—and your husband." He cast a momentary glance at the bustle around them.

Mariah's inner turmoil kept her from noticing the disappointment so apparent in Julian's face, and the regret in his voice. The passage of time always promised change, even when it was least expected.

They both became distracted and felt awkward because of it. Julian's smile made it all seem right again and gave Mariah the chance to ground her senses.

"My father planned to meet you, but he's not feeling well today. And since my husband, Lieutenant Lawton, had military duties to attend to, I came instead." Her direct tone did nothing to allay the sudden tightening in her stomach. Something unknown felt familiar.

As they left the platform, neither of them hinted the other was in a hurry. They walked through the train station and made their way outside where they boarded the carriage and sat across from each other. A snap of the leather reins lunged the carriage forward, narrowing the space between them.

"I think it's good fortune you and I have met again," Julian said. "I know it's been a while since I last visited St. Louis, but I feel like we've known each other a long time." He settled back in the leather seat and fell spellbound by her features. A hushed smile, unmistakable, formed on his face.

Mariah sensed the meaning of his words, then caught her breath. Nathan's hands were crawling all over her again. She suppressed the urge to shout out to the entire world how much she loathed her husband for what he did to her. She despised what she was doing to herself now. Her mind was trapped in her past.

"Good fortune perhaps, Mr. Marquette, but we really don't

know each other at all." It was a casual remark intended to keep their conversation from falling silent, yet its consequence gave her the chance to look at him again, and wonder.

"Please, call me Julian."

A gentleness echoed in his voice. There was no fear of him. Her instincts told her to trust him. He felt safe. He wanted nothing more than to be with her and take pleasure in her company. The compulsion to keep staring at him startled her. Was it wrong of her to behave so? Her gaze slumped into her lap. It was a sheltered place, contemplating the lace patterns on her dress, hiding from his thoughtful eyes. His kindness touched her, but she couldn't let him in.

As the carriage clattered along the cobblestone streets of Gravois Road, the commotion outside added a welcome distraction. Beyond the city's edge, the grassy knolls of the countryside came into view. The estate was just around the bend.

All at once, a thought struck Mariah with the ferocity of a bee stinging underfoot. Had Nathan's actions these past few months been a charade intended to fool her into thinking he cared for her? In those lighthearted conversations they shared, she took his personal attentions to heart, and he gave her such tenderness in return. What went wrong? She had no answers. When she glanced at the stranger she barely knew, she took comfort in his presence. A faint smile framed her face, this time in silent gratitude.

The carriage rolled through the iron gates, winding down the lane fringed with maple trees ablaze in red autumn leaves. "Welcome to the Renwick Estate. I'll have one of the staff help you get settled in. Dinner will be served at six."

Mariah's voice cast a faraway look in Julian's eyes. Her face, for so long a distant memory, shined radiant before him again. How could two years seem like yesterday? A whisper from his past took hold. A mystery he never revealed to her. One destined to remain a secret. He let it go.

As the carriage stopped in front of the mansion, he leaned in and placed his hand on the door, but didn't move. The scent of her perfume reeled his senses and dared him to look at her. He held fast, exploiting the moment where he felt her close, and remembered. *How I've missed you, Mariah.*

A tug of forces lit sparks between them and awakened an urgency they couldn't suppress, as they gazed into each other's eyes and felt the tension rising.

This time, Mariah didn't look away.

THE dinner hour had arrived. Father wasn't his old self and let everyone know how awful he felt. He put on his usual theatrics, so convinced was he that his misery would last for all eternity. Mariah watched him lumber down the staircase, grumbling at full volume, not caring who took notice of him. He was quite good at it, tossing his handkerchief over his face while he muffled a thunderous sneeze erupting from his mouth. His condition turned him into an absolute bear. She regarded his every move lest he unleash himself on their guest. Julian seemed too kind a man to endure one of Father's verbal tirades.

Once the men exchanged greetings in private, everyone entered the dining room where a sumptuous meal awaited the gathering. After dinner, Mother disappeared into the kitchen and returned with her dessert. Such a simple indulgence filled the room with praises.

Julian grinned and showered her with bighearted compliments. "Mrs. Renwick, the dessert is excellent. I remember your apple pie from my last visit and hoped you would indulge me again." A mere instant Julian waited until Mariah held tight to his gaze. "I think I should visit more often."

I should have visited sooner. I should have—too late.

Mariah gave her mother an affectionate nod. The hum of

dinner talk swept her up in an evening of conviviality that abruptly ended when Perdie appeared with a note tucked in her hand.

"A message from the lieutenant, Mrs. Lawton."

"Thank you, Perdie." Mariah's eyes darted across the table as she reached for the note. It was brief. "Nathan has been delayed and sends his apologies for missing dinner. He'll try to join us later."

Following the meal, the gentlemen engaged in their affairs behind closed doors. Later, Father excused himself and bid his wife and daughter good night. His weary look told Mariah he didn't feel up to mingling, so she engaged their visitor as best she could.

As they stepped out onto the terrace overlooking the garden, they gazed at the roses, aglow in the last rays of sun. Julian smiled and gestured with his arm. Mariah hesitated, then curled her hand in his embrace. How unprepared she was for the feeling. A skipped heartbeat made her unsteady. Holding on with two hands seemed the right thing to do.

They strolled along the garden path bordered with boxwoods and paused under the gazebo draped in wisteria vines. Evening's tide cast a soft light around them.

Julian braced his hands on the balustrade and peered into the distance. Mariah's gaze tiptoed toward him. The silhouette of his face stunned her. She took her chance and stared at him unhindered. Just as he motioned to speak, her attention shifted to the roses.

"I do have important business to discuss with your father. Traveling from Boston is too long a journey only to arrive and deal in pleasantries. I'm sure you can understand."

Reassuring her that he was just here for business shattered to pieces when their gazes met. It was there again, in that infinitesimal space between them, the subtle tremor of attraction, at once forbidden but about to collide.

"Business aside, I'd be a fool not to admit I've enjoyed our short time together—immensely."

His smile was true. His words touched, enough for Mariah to let go, and let him in. *They* had become more personal.

"I've enjoyed our time together too." Her smile faded. "Earlier today, at the train station, I didn't mean to be unkind to you. It's just that I—I haven't been myself lately."

She knew she was taking a risk she was unsure of, in front of a man she hardly knew, but she couldn't hide the hurt any longer. She had to trust someone. The feeling overwhelmed her. She closed her eyes and fell lost in the darkness with no way out. Then a caress on her chin shone a light in her mind, as bright as the whitest snow covering a wintry Missouri landscape. She looked up. Julian's gaze was upon her, and the truth that dwelled in his honorable eyes.

"If I can ease your worries in any way, Mariah, I will."

She held tight to his every word, and she believed him. Her lips parted and she said, "I know."

A voice thundered from behind.

"I didn't expect to find you here." Nathan stood on the garden path staring at them with a scowl on his face. "I hope I'm not interrupting anything."

He scrutinized Mariah and the two-bit rogue in the company of his wife. A no-good thief come to filch her affections. His past reminded him of what he learned as a boy child. Condemn others before they condemn you first.

Julian saw panic erupt in Mariah's face. She was desperate to escape. He stepped in front of her and offered his hand to the lieutenant as a kind of truce. Nathan refused. They both stood at arm's length. Neither one flinched. Nathan's stare launched a barrage of accusations that came at Julian full force. But his move backfired. Julian's stature had him looking down at Nathan, like he was daring the lieutenant to overstep his bounds.

Nathan's words cut him down just the same and made it clear their evening stroll was at an end.

"My wife has no business being here with you. Good evening, *sir*." He snatched Mariah's arm and marched her toward the mansion.

A husband and wife behaving this way left Mariah desperate to go back and offer Julian some sort of apology for her husband's actions. Then she thought better of it. Her arm was throbbing.

"Nathan, *please*. You're hurting me." She felt like a child the way he dragged her past the terrace stairs and out of view. Enough was enough. She wrenched her arm free.

His resentment flared. "I expect my wife to behave in a manner befitting a married woman and not cavorting around with the next man she finds available. Your conduct is unbecoming, Mrs. Lawton."

She stood flabbergasted, not by what he said but more by how he said it. His proper tone was deliberate. He was intentionally trying to mock her and the dignity of the Renwick name. A chill shivered through her bones as he paced in front of her, compelling her to stand at attention until he commanded otherwise. *Be strong.*

"I didn't mean to upset you. I was only trying to make our guest feel welcome."

He stopped in his tracks and glared at her. "I don't ever want to see you alone with another man again or you'll have me to answer to."

She took offense to his threatening words but thought it reckless to stand her ground by the way he pinched the tip of her chin. In a flurry, he stormed off, waving his hand in the air as though she were dismissed.

His anger trembled in her face. She looked back at the rose garden, then heaved her shoulders out of a slump and set her feet in Nathan's direction. When she reached the cottage, he wasn't there.

After she went to bed, she tossed and turned throughout the night until exhaustion won over. But sleep never came, only worries of what awaited her come springtime. In her heart, she prayed their westward journey would never happen. Nothing prepared her for this change in her life. She so wanted it to be a dream. Tomorrow would have to take care of itself. Whatever the outcome, she had to be ready.

CHAPTER 7

Finding Hope In Unexpected Places

S THE MONTHS passed and the stillness of winter set in, Mariah buried herself in her school work. But toiling away in the classroom didn't help her escape the emptiness inside. *Time can heal the heart, can it not?* Yet the love Nathan pledged to her—for better, for worse—already did its damage. If time could indeed heal the heart, it had thus far done nothing to change the truth.

The end of the school day brought about the usual quiet. Instead of preparing her lessons for tomorrow, she kept calling into question every decision she made. How could she see, through her starry-eyed gaze, that marrying Nathan may have been a mistake? He was a proud defender of the Union. What more did she need to know? Except he was not the man she thought he was. There were no answers.

A cloud of doubt hung over her, waiting in ambush if she faltered. But all the disappointment left Nathan to blame. Still, a feeling of guilt pressed at the back of her mind, trying to turn the blame on her.

There was no undoing what was done. She had to face reality or risk living the rest of her life shrouded in lies. She had to accept her life with Nathan. If Mother found a way to go on with her marriage, a marriage of convenience, she had to do the same. She didn't want to think about their journey come springtime. Her work needed to take on a new purpose and become her escape, though she quietly admitted it already had.

Stacks of papers and books lined her desk, like a walled fortress protecting her from unknown enemies lying in wait. Each passing day created too many homework papers to grade and too many lesson plans to compose. She didn't realize she may have burdened her students with more work of their own.

As the sunlight streamed through the window, deep thoughts blinded her from seeing a shadow steal across the room. She shut her eyes. Her hands pressed against her forehead, and her elbows burrowed into the desk. A world of worry weighed down on her. But then a voice murmured her name. She looked up in a daze. Was she conjuring up an imaginary world, or was he standing there, so close?

Julian . . . It's really you. She didn't notice how he was dressed. Only one thought raced through her mind. *I've missed you.* After he returned to Boston, she thought she would never see him again. She tried hiding her feelings, but the expression on her face said otherwise.

"Hello, Mariah." A tenderness echoed in his voice. "I didn't mean to barge in on you. Maybe I should call another time." He stepped back and started toward the door.

Mariah's sudden reaction had her leaping out of her chair. She fought to find the words, any words, to make him stop long enough for her to figure out what to say.

"Please stay. I was just—"

Nathan's warning in the rose garden rattled her. The jealous tone in his voice left Julian the intended target. Now her instincts took over, feeding her need, her only need, to keep Julian from walking away.

"I was just getting ready to leave and—well—I'd so enjoy having your company on my way home."

Julian hesitated. "I expect you're in a rush to meet up with your husband after a long day."

He dropped his gaze but then gave her that smile she so vividly remembered. She smiled in turn, enough to buoy his spirits for what he had to say next.

"I just arrived in St. Louis. Another bank loan needs to be arranged with your father. I was hoping I'd have the chance to see you again."

The ache between her ribs hung on to his every word. If she could, she would listen to his voice until forever. An upwelling of emotion let go her yearning.

"It's been so long since I last saw you."

She couldn't conceal how she felt, but regretted it and looked away. Her hands fumbled the papers scattered across her desk. She gave him more than she should have. More than her situation allowed. Yet his presence aroused an exhilaration within her she never felt before. She tried clearing her mind. Her eyes could not meet his.

"My husband left for Independence a few days ago to plan our journey for next spring. He's been busy making sure all will go well along the way." Her attempts at small talk were distracting at best.

She retreated from the desk and made her way to the coat-rack. Julian moved up behind her. She caught her breath. His closeness made her feel tipsy, like she was falling into his arms. He lifted the coat off the hook and draped it over her shoulders, easing his hands down her arms, not letting go, until he had to.

When she turned around, their gazes met and overflowed with words he wanted to say, and words she wanted to hear. They stood close, uncertain of their next move. It didn't matter. This moment had to be enough for both of them.

Julian took Mariah's hand and gathered it under his arm. "Shall we?"

Together, they walked outside into the cold blanket of winter. The new-fallen snow crunched beneath their feet. Their noses numbed in the frosty air that suspended the breath of their conversation while their rhythmic walk carried them down Bellefontaine Road. Two kindred souls moving as one.

A sudden halt interrupted their stroll. Julian glimpsed the Florissant Café, then winked at Mariah. A warm fire greeted them when they walked inside.

The noise of the café patrons swirled around them. They felt content savoring their silence with their hands huddled around mugs of hot tea. Mariah never cared much for the drink, but this time it tasted divine. Better than the best champagne she delighted in at the Renwick estate galas.

"So you and your husband are taking a journey next spring?" Julian steadied his voice as he posed the question. He knew the town of Independence meant traveling west—far west.

"Yes, we are. Nathan has accepted a military post in Dakota Territory. We'll be settling at Fort Laramie. It should be quite the adventure."

"I see . . ."

Julian's crestfallen words faded into thin air as he peered out the café window, searching through space and time for the moment, two years ago, when he first saw her. A furtive gaze was enough to fall in love with her from afar. She wasn't ready to find him then, but there was always tomorrow. And when tomorrow came, his love would be waiting for her. Now the end was near. He would never see her again, and she would never come to know how much his love for her had grown.

Mariah noticed the faraway look in his eyes. She chanced a longer glance and watched the firelight dance off his chiseled face. A wisp of hair curled down over his brow. His eyelashes blinked in slow motion. Every aspect of him was mesmerizing. Her elbow braced on the table as she rested her chin in the palm of her hand and drew a breath in and out of her mouth. His *mouth*. Those lips. So perfectly curved for giving pleasure. Undeniable pleasure. To imagine was easy. To take a taste would be . . .

She became distracted and didn't notice he was staring at her too. Their eyes crossed paths. Her hand thudded on the table and jolted her spine straight. She tried hiding her embarrassment, but the giggle already slipped out. They both laughed until the last drops of tea touched their lips.

After they arrived at the cottage, Mariah had no intention of saying goodbye. "If you don't have any plans for the evening, I asked the cooks this morning to prepare some beef stew. It will be far too much for me to eat by myself. I'd like it if you could stay for dinner."

Julian didn't hesitate. "Yes. Dinner with you would be fantastic. I'd love to."

He was grateful for her invitation. He, too, hated goodbyes.

But he couldn't deny how he felt and what could happen. His confrontation with Nathan told him to beware. Crossing the line would only jeopardize his relationship with Mariah. If she ever needed his help, he'd help her as a friend and nothing more.

He opened the door to the cottage and followed her inside. Fortuity found them standing close again. Two heartbeats collided and became one. Breaths halted in midair. He took his time, let it slow to a standstill, as he drew his hands around her shoulders and slipped off her coat.

Before they settled in, Mariah scanned the kitchen and turned back toward the door. "I need to fetch some biscuits in the main house. I promise I won't be long."

Later, she returned shivering from the cold with the bread basket tucked against her bodice. She uncovered the biscuits. A bready aroma filled the room. She was glad Julian started a fire.

They sat down at the table and shared their evening meal. Every glance, every gesture, sparked an intimacy between them. Even talking about the ordinary drew them closer together.

Mariah's curiosity had Julian sharing a bit about his childhood. He wasn't accustomed to drawing attention to himself and tried to end it there, but she wanted to know more about him. Perhaps just this once he could ignore his usual tendencies, if for no other reason than to take in the sight of her.

"My brother and I grew up in Cohasset. It's a small fishing village south of Boston, near the Atlantic Ocean." He paused, deep in thought. "It's the kind of place you never forget."

I'll never forget you, Mariah. The sparkle in her eyes bewitched him. She was there with him, reliving his past, as if she was carried back in time and became a part of it. The woman he wanted there all along.

"Cohasset will always have special memories for me." His nostalgic gaze spoke straight to her heart. "Very special memories."

Mariah sensed the mystery in his words and was drawn to them. A feeling of belonging washed over her. "I think I know what you mean."

How he wanted her to be more than a figment of his past. The affirmation in his eyes gave her all he could. Divulging his secret would destroy the time they shared together. Their fortunes had changed and left him no chance to lay bare the testament of his undying love for her.

Heightened tremors stirred between them, and more, the tremor of thoughts left unsaid. Still, their attraction had the power to tear them apart, and if given the chance, Mariah was convinced Nathan would show no mercy. The longing to embrace an impossible love withered away, like the tendrils of a dying vine trying to climb ever higher, yet knowing in the end it was all in vain.

But not this moment.

"When you love a place, it will always be home." Mariah's allusion of love for a place—or a man—lingered on her lips. They both yearned for that place. There was no denying what they felt. How could it suddenly end for them?

The silence was too much. Jumbled nerves. A skipped heart-beat. Those brown eyes. *Say something, or find yourself powerless to resist him.*

"Tell me—about your family." Her abrupt remark didn't sound very nonchalant.

Julian reined in the drumming in his chest. He couldn't think of anything to say with her dress rustling against his legs. A glimpse at the firelight collected his thoughts, but he made sure his feet didn't move an inch.

"For the most part, it was my father and my younger brother, Johnny."

His mind drifted back to Mariah's silent confession that revealed her true feelings for him. Their unspoken love could still be *their* love. It would be their promise to each other, for a lifetime. It was all they had.

"Johnny was a rule breaker and got into trouble a lot." Images from his youth flooded back. "I wasn't the perfect son. I just knew when to quit before our father scolded us. Being a preacher didn't mean he was forgiving."

He ran his fingers along the grain of wood on the table. Not once did he think this moment would come, together with her, sharing a part of himself because she wanted it this way.

Mariah had more questions. "What was your mother like?"

"I don't have many memories of her. She died when Johnny and I were young. Our Aunt Charlene lived nearby and helped raise us the best she could. We used to call her Cha Cha."

Amusing snippets of childhood exploits reminded Julian how long it was since he last saw his brother. Deep down, they were one and the same. Two men driven by their dreams. But Johnny's acts of defiance against their father went too far. He left home without a trace and never told Julian where he was going.

"Johnny gave Cha Cha plenty of trouble. As hard as he tried to get his way, she put him in his place. She knew what was good for him and kept him out of reach from our father's bad temper."

Bad temper. Mariah shifted in her seat and chased Nathan out of her thoughts. It wasn't hard to do when Julian flashed her a boyish grin that made his eyes smile. She leaned in, curious by his expression.

"What is it? Please tell me."

"I was thinking back to the time Cha Cha made her molasses candy. She never let a soul in the kitchen while she cooked, or else you were done for. It was just her way. But when the melted candy started to cool, she'd wait for the right second and pull it into long ropes. I couldn't resist." He acted out the dastardly deed as he spoke. "I'd sneak into the kitchen and grab hold of the sticky stuff and run around the house, chewing on it and making a mess. She got so angry with me. From then on, she called me Sticky. I never heard the name Julian again."

They both laughed. Mariah quipped, "Oh, to turn back time and be a child again."

Julian touched upon his favorite memories of building sand castles along Cohasset Harbor and digging for clams until sundown. Even with all his boyhood antics, he embraced the serenity the sea gave him.

"You've let me do all the talking, Mariah. Tell me about you." His voice carried the weight of his sincerity, for he wanted every memory she shared to become a part of him.

"Well, you must already know a bit about the Renwick family. I'm sure my father has hinted at one secret or two. He does like to talk a lot, especially with people he trusts." She kept her stories cheery but was taken by surprise when Julian broached another subject.

"I noticed a portrait in the library of a young girl. Is it a picture of you?"

Her expression turned wistful. "No, it's my sister. Her name was Frances. We always called her Fanny. She . . . died before the war from scarlet fever."

The old wound was still there and tugged at her heartstrings when she said her sister's name. It would be easy to run away and hide, but she didn't want to be alone in her room, or pretending to read a book in the library while she tried to shut out the world, and the pain. She put into words what she concealed for so long.

"I know it sounds strange, but I've never liked looking at that portrait of my sister. It reminds me of how much I miss her."

More than four years had come and gone, and not once did she tell anyone how much she missed Fanny. Not even Mother and Father. They were consumed by their own deep sorrow.

Revealing her feelings left her vulnerable. Her lips trembled. She covered them with her hands, but they trembled too. As much as she tried putting on her façade of poise and self-control, it all came undone in front of Julian. She closed her eyes and hid in that place of darkness she was before when they stood under the gazebo.

Julian gathered her hands in his and brought her back where she belonged. "I'm sorry, Mariah. I didn't know." Except for the crackling fire, the room was silent. He spoke again. "When my mother died, I was too young to comprehend the loss, but I remember how it felt to be alone."

Sharing Julian's company made Mariah feel right about wanting to share everything with him. She trusted him. His strong hands told her so.

A need welled up inside they both knew had been there all along.

Julian didn't want to let her go. Not now. In his awakened

mind, she was an angel, giving him every bit of kindness she possessed, as though she brought the heavens to his feet. He couldn't deny how long he yearned to tell her he was in love with her.

But what could he say to make her see how mad her husband must be? Nathan's plans amounted to a foolhardy scheme to cross the High Plains swarming with Indians and disease that would put her life in grave danger, if she even survived on the trail. He knew men like Nathan, greedy men, hungry for power and money. Men who were hellbent on destroying anyone who got in their way. Arrogant bastards. All of them. But it didn't have to end this way.

Tension rippled along his jawline. Mariah's fate was driving him to the brink. If he could just steal her away from all the insanity. If only the last two years never happened. If she let him, he could save her from all this. And he would, if she let him.

And then their hands parted.

The sensation from his touch sent flutters through Mariah. She placed her hands on the table, close to his. There were more questions she wanted to ask. "I imagine your work must be important for you to travel so far from Boston."

"The railroad business can be ruthless, and costly, but with your father's help, I've been able to continue a major railroad venture. That's why I returned to St. Louis."

Making it all sound like business only intensified his need. Her desire barreled right through him, just as it did two long years ago. He divulged the words he couldn't hold back.

"Truth be told, I would travel beyond the stars to see you again."

He cursed himself for lacking the restraint to bite his tongue and braced himself for her disappointment. She gave him nothing of the kind. Their attraction was real, and forbidden, but neither of them cared. He closed his eyes for an instant and captured the memory of how she looked. It was all he could take with him when he went home to Boston.

His smile was true. "I'd like to stay longer, but I have to go. Thank you for everything." As they both stood up, he saw the reluctance in her smile. They brushed arm against arm and walked toward the front door. He stopped and turned to her. "My train departs tomorrow. I don't know if I'll have time to call on you before I leave."

"I understand. It's been truly wonderful seeing you again."

A melancholy goodbye echoed between them, yet the look in his eyes told her he wanted to give her more than a fond farewell. He missed his chance before. Now he had no choice but to let her go.

He reached out and cupped her hand in his. "Goodbye, Mariah."

His voice surrounded her, like a coat of mighty armor, always at the ready to protect her if she ever fell into harm's way. She embraced it. He lifted her hand to his lips and kissed it. In a heartbeat, there would be nothing left of their goodbye.

Their fingertips tugged, and then slipped free.

A gust of air rushed through the open door and sealed their fate. With a tip of his hat, Julian disappeared into the dark of night. He was a true gentleman, to the end.

Mariah tried to stop thinking about him. Finally, she gave up trying. No matter what happened between her and Nathan, or how far she traveled, Julian would be with her, in her heart. She wanted him there. She needed him there, to help her face the unknown.

CHAPTER 8

A Heart Cries Out

OUNDS OF SPRINGTIME and the scent of the sweet air always lifted Mariah's spirits this time of year. But not today. So much had changed of late. Too much. Gone was the sensible woman who never let her family's fortune affect the way she thought. Gone, too, was the carefree woman who never worried a day in her life, until Fanny's death rattled her with an uncertainty she could not come to grips with. She lost sight of the woman she once was. If only she could step back in time and bring her sister home, all would be well again.

But the story of her past had already been written. It was up to her to make things right. Straightforward prudence instead of desire should have prevailed over her affections before it was too late. Too late to change course and be free of the bonds of a hopeless marriage. *How could I have been so blind?* She was living in a world that belonged to Nathan. It all seemed clear. Feelings of remorse for her sister's life, a life gone too soon, yet feelings of regret for her own life, a life entirely changed for the worse.

How could she meet with Mother and Father and tell them she made a mistake? Today, of all days, when tomorrow would be filled with goodbyes. Tomorrow, she would have to say goodbye to St. Louis, the only home she'd ever known.

No, there would be no admission from her that marrying Nathan was a mistake. Confiding in her parents would devastate them. What they went through watching Fanny die was burden enough to bear. This was not the time to trouble them with her problems. Besides, Father wouldn't have it. Not a word. The Renwick name would never be uttered in the same breath as the word *mistake*. Living out West, she'd have to find some way to fix the wrongs in her life. But deep inside, she felt the pang again. She was losing everything she held dear. Even Julian. A few poignant moments together—not enough to create a lasting memory—and then he was gone.

She scanned the cottage and wandered over to the kitchen window. The view outside of the purling brook once filled her with anticipation for the days ahead. Now, Julian's face appeared in the windowpane instead. He was saying something to her. She was certain he was. He had to be. Maybe it was goodbye. He never did say a forever goodbye on that cold January night. And he never did come back to see her one last time.

Why should he have come back? I'm a married woman. She had to face the facts, not a world of wishful thinking. Julian had every right to find his own happiness. Despite what she longed for, she had to let him go. No one could save her from her own misfortune.

A wave of emotion swept over her. She reached out her hand and touched the glass pane. "Goodbye, Julian . . ." His image faded from under her fingers, leaving only the echo of his name on her lips. She looked away and walked out the door.

NATHAN returned home for an early dinner with Mariah and her parents. The last place he wanted to be was at the estate. He was in no mood for conversation or putting on airs. His mind was focused on other matters.

Months of forging political connections brought him to this moment without even a whisper of his goings-on. But his impatience was eating at him, and it would be tested as soon as he faced the old man. One more day, the ruse had to carry on—the ignis fatuus of a soldier's duty and honor.

He dismounted his horse and spied Mariah sitting on a rock near the weeping willow tree. Its budding leaves cast a green hue against the late afternoon sky. He moved up behind her, riveting his eyes on her hair cascading down her back.

"Mariah." His jaw tensed when he said her name.

"Yes," she replied. Her placid voice mirrored the look on her face as it pointed toward the sun that her eyes shut out.

His impatience badgered him again. "Why are you out here in the sun? Don't you care what people think?" He didn't want an answer. A woman of her standing should know better. Her inattention to him roused his resentment. Not looking at her husband was a bad idea. Complicating his plans was worse.

He already impressed her folks and her friends by slipping a ring on her finger. All she was supposed to be was his key to the State Bank of Missouri. But her tight-assed father wouldn't even give him that. The scheme he cooked up just to make her his wife. And for what? But she caught him off guard on their wedding night. Took her innocence and stabbed the consummator straight through his lying heart. He never held a woman so delicate in his arms yet so afraid of his world.

That day at the cottage, he wanted to give her what he never gave a woman. He wanted to make it right, and make love to her. But she shunned him instead, like the half-breed he was. She wasn't any better than the rest of them. Everything would be different if she loved him then. *Damn her.*

"Your parents are waiting. Let's be done with it."

Mariah steadied her eyes on him. "It's not my parents who are waiting, Nathan. I'm the one who's been waiting. There's no need to be in a hurry now."

He despised her remarks. "Don't test me, Mariah."

"Well, it's true. You're hardly ever home anymore."

"Give me one good reason why I should be."

The words stung. Her face turned away from him as if he slapped her. He reached out to touch her but froze. He didn't want her silky hair getting tangled in his hand—and his heart. There was nothing more to say.

THE grand hall of the estate was the ideal setting for a farewell party, the likes of which the Renwicks never staged before. Any gala worth raving about demanded Mother's expertise, for this occasion had to be a joyous affair, even if her real motive for all the fuss was to avoid the inevitable. Mariah was leaving home.

Still, she had to stay busy and planning a party was what she did best. Clandestine use of the servants' entrance made for the perfect surprise that welcomed Nathan and Mariah to an entire gathering of friends and business associates. It seemed all of St. Louis had arrived to wish them well.

But Mother's reception stunned Mariah, and she was overcome by a sudden sadness with every last *hello* she spoke. For her entire life, she knew their names—Chatillon, Soulard, Laclede—families whose French roots had grown deep in Missouri. She felt a close affinity to them all these years. Their legacy, like her mother's, struck a chord that made her pine for what would soon become a memory. Soon, their voices would be saying *adieu*.

She restrained her emotions. But for how long? To behave

as though she were a happily married woman setting off on an adventure with her husband was more than she could bear.

Clamor from the guests grew louder. Her pulse raced amid the cacophony of gaiety and good cheer. She darted her eyes around the room. *I need to get out.*

Her elegance proved useful, replete with smiles which meant the opposite and nods of gratitude that concealed what she was really up to. Slinking along the foyer wall with her hand behind her back, she tracked down the nearest doorknob, wrestled the latch, and snuck inside. She was standing in the library, her safe place since she was a child. Her body relaxed against the door.

Commotion turned to silence. Vivid memories came flooding back.

Here, she took refuge after Fanny died. Here, she hid from the battle storm when the Confederates were closing in. Here, she stood again, hiding from a future that portended danger, and a husband she wished to God really loved her. This time, she did look at her sister's portrait, to say goodbye. *Dearest Fanny. Now I have to be stronger than ever.*

At the far side of the room, sheer curtains swayed in the evening breeze. She wended her way around the velvet settee toward the open window. Though the Damask roses weren't in bloom, she imagined their heady scent drifting into the room. And, she imagined Julian again, holding his arm and feeling his protection as they strolled together down Bellefontaine Road. Her heart rejoiced at the thought. It *was* a lasting memory. Her memory, to remember always.

Conversations out on the terrace sounded distant, but voices close by were distinct from the crowd. No sooner had her curiosity gotten the better of her than an eruption of laughter revealed two men outside the window. She slipped behind the heavy drapes and peeked around the fringe with a one-eyed glance. The breeze billowed the sheer curtains and gave a better view. No one else wandered nearby. She stared intently at the strangers.

In the growing twilight, the outline of their faces exposed little of their identity, but she recognized the Union blues. One of the soldiers started talking. The tone of his voice was a dead giveaway. She heard it before. Where? Soldiers on the estate grounds were a familiar sight during the war, with all the business Father kept on about Missouri's fate as a border state if its allegiance fell to the South. But the War of the Rebellion ended almost a year ago.

The soldier's chatter made her think of her student Abigail and how fast she always talked. Not as fast as he did. The gossamer curtains billowed again, drawing their conversation into the room.

"I know what kinda man he is Bailey. He trusts me with everythin'. Even his private affairs. But we ain't got time to be talkin' about that shit anyways. We gotta take care a business."

Bailey's voice had a slower rhythm as he thumped his comrade in the chest. "Not till you gimme the low down, Honeycutt. I wanna know about Lieutenant Lawton's *private affairs.*"

What private affairs? Mariah was shocked by the onslaught of innuendo about her husband, and more, by the name Honeycutt. She did remember his voice. On her wedding day. The corporal stood guard near their carriage outside the church. Nathan stepped away and spoke to him while she stood alone, waiting. Brief commands were given, but all she heard was Honeycutt stutter the word *moonlight.* Then he stammered to the lieutenant, "Ye-ye-yessir."

How odd, she thought. Now his speech rang clear.

CORPORAL Honeycutt's loyalty took Nathan by surprise. It was no secret between them that he saved the corporal's life at the Battle of Bayou Fourche before they captured Little Rock. But it was a fluke. An accident. The butt of his gun ricocheted into the back of a Confederate assassin behind him, sending the Rebel's bullet through the corporal's left shoulder instead of straight between his eyes.

Honeycutt carried his limp appendage as a reminder to his commanding officer that he'd repay his debt with utmost discretion to the lieutenant's affairs. Honeycutt never questioned any orders he was given, but he had a hunch what could happen if he crossed the line.

MARIAH'S suspicions ran rampant. She was so mystified by Honeycutt's presence at the estate, she didn't pay attention to what they said next. All she heard was her heartbeat pounding in her ears.

Bailey yanked his forage cap off his head and whacked it on his leg. "Well, I'll be damned. I figured the lieutenant liked his drinkin' and gamblin', but gettin' real friendly with the ladies don't seem right. Besides, how's he gonna keep his *private affairs* private when you and I already know what he's up to?"

"Damn it, Bailey. Ain't you got nothin' between your ears? Just keep your trap shut. If the lieutenant finds out I told you, I'll be pushin' up daisies from six feet under. Anyways, I sure feel sorry for the missus. If she ever found out, she'd be in a real bad way."

Bailey nodded as Honeycutt gave him the signal to clear out. "I'll scout the area out front. You keep an eye out back here, then follow my trail. We don't got much time." He scuttled off toward the courtyard with his left arm swinging like a clock pendulum.

The voices vanished. A tide of air moaned through the window, nudging Mariah closer to the edge of the abyss. Another inch, and she'd tumble headlong into a nightmare. Her fingers throbbed in a death grip on the drapes that kept her from collapsing on the floor. All she could think of were those long nights she lay awake in bed—alone. So many nights while her wedding ring spun in circles round her finger.

It can't be true. Not this. She retreated from the window, but not one muscle made her do it. Her body felt possessed by another aspect of herself. Gone was the old Mariah and the words she just heard. Gone was the hopelessness and misery she felt. How easy it was for the new Mariah to slip into her skin. She fit perfectly.

Not a thought crossed her mind as her dignified composure guided her out to the grand hall to mingle and make merry with all of St. Louis. Pouty lips gave way to a simper, leaving her alter ego ready to move in on him. This was the way a lady should behave, even under the direst of circumstances.

She didn't need to deny the truth of her husband's infidelity, or pretend it was a lie. All was well again in Benton Park. All was well again with the new Mariah.

Across the crowded room, she spied her husband and cast him a teasing look. He struggled to make sense of her as she slinked up beside him and coiled her arm under his. She felt giddy and so relieved to be free of the notion that true love was all she ever wanted. It was simply a matter of how she looked at things, and how her alter ego already did her a world of good. A life of duplicity, after all, could double her chances of survival.

CHAPTER 9

Light In The Dark

WORDS SPOKEN FROM a mother's heart. Words Mariah never forgot. *You can find strength in the unlikeliest of places.* After losing the eldest daughter her mother had given life to, finding strength in any place seemed impossible. Yet in the face of her mother's sadness, Mariah concealed hers. *This, too, shall pass. This, too, must pass.* But grieving had a mind of its own and left nowhere to hide except in the shadows of someone else's. And there, Mariah stood fast and became the place where her mother found the strength she needed to carry on.

In all those years while other hearts needed tending, Mariah never came to terms with Fanny's death herself. Leaving St. Louis yesterday opened her eyes to more than new surroundings. She saw with greater clarity the precious gift her sister gave her. Life had to be lived each day. There was no time for regrets. Looking back, it was Fanny who became the unlikely place where Mariah found her own strength, the kind that could transcend the highest mountains and traverse the lowest valleys of life's changes, so she could carry on too.

As the train chugged through the Missouri countryside, the rhythm of the railcar could have lulled Mariah to sleep. But on this train bound for Independence, the growing distance between her and St. Louis left her desperate to hold on to anything familiar. Seeing the vistas unfolding before her, she hoped time was all she needed to get used to her new life. The thought was little consolation for her sentimental mood. Staring at her husband only magnified how she felt.

His blue eyes looked cold as he sat with his arms crossed, shutting her out. The image of the dashing Union officer who whispered her name through his kisses was just a memory. If the passage of time did nothing to lessen the sting of infidelity, the return of elusive love seemed all but lost. She so wanted to forget the secret Honeycutt divulged that night. It changed everything.

She fought back the tears welling up in her eyes. She hated crying in front of Nathan. He made her feel weak. Why couldn't he make her feel cherished and loved? What had gone wrong between them? The stark truth was as plain as the distant look on his face. *Nathan never loved me. Not now. Not ever.*

Her eyes dared him to come play her two-faced game again. He was so good at it, masquerading as a man of honor who beguiled her with his ways, enough to make her see only the man she wanted to see. The man who made her believe she could give him her love freely—until he took it from her. She cursed the Renwick name under her breath, and all its prestige, and all that damn money Nathan married into.

She, too, was getting good at his game. The loving wife would stand by her man no matter what happened, but it would be on her terms. In the confines of the train, she braced herself for the unknown.

Nathan locked his stare into hers. "Is something bothering you?"

She ignored his tone as her fingers drummed in her lap. "Yes. Quite."

"Well, don't look at me." He shifted his gaze out the window.

"Don't you care to know what's bothering me?"

"If I did care, would it make any difference?"

She leaned forward and pressed her point. "If you did care, maybe our marriage might be more acceptable to both of us." The heat rose in her face. Their conversation was long overdue. "I don't know what's happened since we've been married. It's gotten worse between us—" Her voice broke off.

He sat there without looking at her, as if she didn't exist, not even in the recesses of his wanting mind. She perched on the edge of her seat and curled her fingers into fists, demanding his attention.

"Are you listening to me, Nathan? Something is *missing*."

Just then, he grabbed her arms and demanded *her* attention. A swift tug, and he had her down on her knees, trapped between his legs. The ire in her eyes fueled his need to quell her restlessness and put an end to her little game. In the midst of her tizzy, she didn't give him much resistance.

He kissed her hard but savored her longer than he expected, pushing his urge deep to lie her down right there in the railcar and make love to her. Love her tender. Let her forget what he did to her. Let her feel the good in him he fought like hell to hide. He still remembered the innocence in her kiss. No woman ever gave him that. An ache settled in his chest. She was wearing him down, telling him to give up the fight. Playing with fire was a fool thing to do, but the devil didn't care when every touch of her lips tasted of mind-bending sweetness.

He couldn't control the shaking in his hands. He was coming undone, and she was letting him, until his provocation made her slap him in the face. Dazed, he let go of her breasts and flashed her a smirk while he moved his hands round her back and gave her one tight squeeze of her pert bottom.

"Is that what you were . . . *missing*, Mariah?"

He teased her long enough to know he could still have his way with her, whenever he wanted, whenever it suited him. He'd never tell her how close she came to setting him free.

PIONEERS swarmed around the legion of covered wagons huddled at Courthouse Square. The sight was a familiar one in Independence. Men, women, and children toiled at loading supplies and belongings into their wagons. The emigrants, all but strangers to one another, seemed frantic. Harrowing tales from the overland journey were spreading among them, and one more than any—the tale of the Donner Party.

Fate found them trapped in the Sierra Nevada mountains by an October snowstorm in 1846. The wretched souls were buried deep in snow for an entire winter and starved to the bone until half were dead. Every springtime since then, Independence went mad with a fever that goaded the pioneers west without a moment to lose.

But any wagon trains heading out late on the trail faced other dangers, long before they reached the mountains. The hot days of summer already sabotaged their plans as they traversed the High Plains with its grasses dried up, leaving little for the cattle and horses to graze on. A land so parched became their greatest threat if a raging fire swept the prairie. They had good reason to be frantic.

After the train arrived at the depot, Mariah stood on the platform watching Nathan walk away. His last words told her what to do and made it clear she was on her own. He had a wagon boss to find and a wagon to load up. But his hasty departure left her facing a stark reality that engulfed her full force. *I don't want to be alone here.*

A passing farm wagon wasn't a horse-drawn carriage, though the ride kept her from trudging through the crowd of people on the road. As the wagon rumbled to a stop in front of the hotel, she made her way inside and took a room upstairs at the end of the hall.

She opened the door. The bleak interior bowled her over. In one corner of the room sat a chair with a broken seatback. Against the wall stood an old sideboard with a cracked pitcher and wash basin on top. The bed, framed between two box windows, was nothing but a heap of lumps. She stepped closer and pushed down on the mattress. It crackled and smelled of straw. The thought of sitting on the bed didn't rattle her as much as the thought of sleeping on it. She traipsed over to the chair and eased down on the seat, ever so slow, afraid she might break it. All she could do was stare at the floor.

Minutes passed. Her anxiety grew.

She left home only once before during the war. Now she found herself on the threshold of a journey that would take her across a wild frontier. To teach her students about life out West was one thing. To be at its doorstep was another. *I can't believe I'm living this life.* Nothing prepared her for this.

The unwelcome companion she'd come to know tracked her down. Fear was itching to pay her a visit, and it was pounding at the door. She bolted up and paced the room. The walls were closing in. She had to get out.

Commotion on the boardwalk had her stumbling into chaos. Her coat was clutched in her arms, and she couldn't keep anyone at bay. A breeze kicked up and made her shiver. She bundled up and set off, not caring which direction, but had no idea where she was going.

The storefronts were all a blur. The faces were too. Across the road, piano music streamed from the town saloon. The sounds were overshadowed by voices behind her bellowing propositions. She glanced over her shoulder. Two men were grinning at her. Their teeth were stained the color of tobacco. She cringed and picked up her tempo, slogging left and right through the mob with a stomp in her feet that warned everyone to get out of her way.

All at once, the crowd vanished. She was standing on the outskirts of town. A view of the sky hinted sundown was near. Up ahead, a road bordered by trees narrowed in the distance. The notion of wandering off out there seemed more agreeable than the dread of turning back. But no matter which direction she went, she'd feel just as lost, like a ship adrift at sea with no anchor.

Veering from the road, a winding path led to a farmhouse surrounded by a meadow and a rail fence. What was it, quite sudden, that made her think of her sister, and riding Willow and Daisy Jane? She scurried toward the homestead and caught a better glimpse.

Those Shetland ponies reminded her of the ones Father gave her and Fanny on their birthdays in October, two weeks apart. One bay and one chestnut, and both magical in her world, where a giggle and a neigh made for the best of conversations, and the best of friends. Those memories left her longing to be home again. *Oh, Willow. My precious Daisy Jane.*

The cold crept in. Her hands called out for warmth. She shoved them into her pockets and closed her coat in front. As her chills subsided, she felt her fingers twiddling a piece of paper in one of the pockets. Curious, she pulled it out, unfolded it, and read the words.

My Sweet Mariah,
*   I must write quickly before you return to the cottage.*
The heat from the fire feels warm against my face, but the
burning in my heart began long before tonight. You are,

and always will be, the only woman I will ever love. If I am destined to leave this world a lonely man, my heart will not be, for you will always be with me.

I know we cannot have what isn't ours to share together, but time can change things if one is patient, and I promise you, Mariah, I am a patient man. For you, I must deny the impossible or we shall never see each other again. I wish I could be with you to protect you, but that is not my place.

The memory of your beautiful smile, and your touch, must be enough. For me, you will always be.

Always,
Julian

The words seared into her being. His secret was hers.

She could have buried her face in her hands and wept over her hopeless situation. But she didn't. Old words written on a piece of paper, long forgotten. But they weren't. Every whisper of air that brushed over her told her she already faced the end. But she hadn't. The note resting in the palm of her hand had no power to change her circumstances. Julian could no more save her and undo her marriage than he could rescue her from this town and the looming journey out West. It all seemed so impossible. She had her obligations after all. Obligations and expectations. But Renwick blood coursed through her veins and flowed thick with determination to fight for what she wanted. And for the first time in her life, she knew exactly what she wanted. Not for Nathan, or her mother and father. Not even for Fanny. To believe a future with Julian was somehow possible, she had to deny the impossible too. For both of them. She trusted every word he'd written and believed he would someday lead her home, to be with him.

As she pressed the note against her lips, she held tight to his promise, forever etched in her soul. Julian was there again, standing close, drawing her winter coat around her. And when she turned and their gazes met, his eyes told her what she now understood. Julian loved her. Every moment they shared gave her an indomitable strength. She would never be alone again.

The road back to town stretched ahead of her. It was time she embraced her destiny and faced Nathan with all the resolve she could muster. She headed for the town saloon.

Chapter 10

Into The Unknown

THE SMELL OF WHISKEY churned Mariah's stomach and grew stronger as she closed in on the saloon. Grating piano music and a sea of curse words spilled out onto the road. She covered her ears, but that didn't help mask the odor. No sooner had she reached the boardwalk than a cowboy burst through the swinging doors tumbling past her. Another cowboy careened behind him. They staggered to their feet, wiping trails of blood from their faces. To think this was the beginning of her adventure to Fort Laramie. She almost laughed.

A few steps further and she'd be inside the brawling place. But voices chimed in her head and wouldn't let her feet budge an inch. How pointless it would be if she walked into the saloon on false pretenses. What if Nathan wasn't even there much less seeking a pleasurable distraction? Just having those perverse thoughts filled her with guilt.

An accidental eavesdropping of a soldier's idle talk was hardly proof of her husband's infidelity. Corporal Honeycutt could have been lying. But Nathan planted the seed of doubt long before they left St. Louis. If only she could take back her life before she met him, and before the war and Fanny's death when all was simple and predictable. Standing here in a town that cared nothing about her own vanishing independence, her life was anything but predictable. And the truth she sought was about to be tested.

She pushed open the swinging doors and entered the saloon. Stares ambushed her from every corner. She panicked and spun around. A slew of eyes blocked her path. Racket erupted behind her, rasping the daylights out of her nerves. The piano man kept banging on the keys and wouldn't let up. Ting, ting. Ting, ting. Her heart beat as fast as the music. Thump-thump, thump-thump. All the taunting drove her to the brink. *Make it stop. Make it stop!* She gritted her teeth and growled, blocking out the noise. She had dirty work to do, and it needed to be done quick. Then she could get out of there.

Facing the crowd, she set her sights straight ahead. At the back of the saloon, gamblers huddled around poker tables, making their wagers and whooping it up. One of the tables looked out of place. Two dance hall girls were toying with a friendly sort. The cowboy slouched in his chair with his legs and arms tangled in their web. They couldn't keep their hands off him. A high-stakes game was playing out, but it wasn't poker.

At another table, she spied a soldier waving a tawny bottle in the air. His leg mimicked a makeshift chair as he propped up a saloon girl, eyeing her bosom like he wanted more. He planted a kiss in her plumpness. She pushed away and brought her lips to his ear. He grinned, then glanced upstairs and back at her. The ladies kept the boys drinking their whiskey and buying more, but an invitation from the likes of the lieutenant was hard to come by.

The ruckus in the saloon muffled the denial in Mariah's voice. She lunged at the bar and dug her fingernails into the wood, holding on for dear life. A twitching moustache flashed in her face. The bartender stared at her. His mouth was moving, but she couldn't hear a word he said.

He yelled at her again. "This saloon ain't the place for a lady wantin' a drink."

She fetched her breath and tried to think of what to say. Then she yelled back. "I don't need a drink. Give me a glass. An empty whiskey glass!"

The bartender gawked at her more confounded than before. He offered her the tumbler. She grabbed it and peered over her shoulder, pinpointing her target. Each step toward the poker table deepened her anger as she watched his lips sidle up that slender throat.

She slammed the glass on the table. Nathan jolted back and saw his wife glaring at him. He tossed the saloon girl aside and dragged his sleeve across his mouth while his other hand gripped the whiskey bottle like he was trying to crush it. He squirmed in his chair. The weight of Mariah's stare robbed him of control he always claimed as his own. She had him trapped in a corner and he had nowhere to hide.

"Isn't it time you bought your wife a drink, Nathan?" The guts that came with those words took Mariah by storm. *Damn you!*

He tipped the bottle into the glass. The whiskey spilled over the rim. She picked up the drink and guzzled every drop. His jaw unhinged. She banged the tumbler on the table and wiped her lips with the back of her hand. This wasn't the woman he thought he knew.

"I can see you're entertaining someone, so I won't keep you from your *affairs*." She looked daggers at the saloon girl and back at him. "I'll be waiting for you in our hotel room when you're done."

She stomped out of the saloon onto the road. Shouts thundered behind her. Nathan grabbed her arm and whirled her around. Pain streaked to her shoulder. She was getting tired of the way he manhandled her.

"Let go of me."

He chided her through clenched teeth. "Don't you ever embarrass me in front of anyone again." He latched on to her other arm and shook her. "Do you hear me?" God, how he reeked of liquor and perfume as he struggled on his feet.

Mariah had never tested her husband's limits before, but he was testing hers now. She roared back. "All you did in that saloon was embarrass yourself. As for me, my conscience is clear. If this isn't the kind of marriage you want, don't expect me to change it. I pledged to be your wife and to keep my vows true, and I plan to do just that. Now take your hands off me."

She broke free and left him standing in the road.

Nathan's penchant for booze gave him trouble plenty of times. He liked trouble. As for his way with women, he considered his charm a natural gift to be used for mutual benefit, lest it be wasted. But the urge to bed down a woman couldn't suppress his greed. He needed Mariah. Not her love. Her trust. He'd behaved badly toward her the last few months, too obsessed with forging his future out West that he forgot he had a wife. And too tempted with distractions. He'd have to make amends.

But the two-bit cheat she caught in the saloon left him no chance to excuse his past actions. His ruse had to go on. Besides, somewhere in his heart he'd find a way to apologize to her. *Apologize? For what? For giving a damn about you. Keep walking away, Mariah. Take hold of the hate. Hate me more than you've ever hated anyone before . . .*

He spat in the dirt. He shouldn't have grabbed her and shaken her like a rag doll, or raped her in the meadow like his son-of-a-bitch father did to his mother. The guilt raged in his gut. He craned his neck and heard it crack, then raked his fingers through his hair. There was some business to tidy up. He headed back to the saloon.

With his hero's welcome from the war, and his encounter with that St. Louis banker, Nathan saw his chance and took it when he wooed Renwick's daughter. Never mind the old man's empty-handed offer. He was still the devoted son-in-law whose lucky streak gave him a wife riddled with one opportune weakness. Her dead sister.

Mariah's loss set her on a path to find happiness again. Giving her hand in marriage proved to be her remedy and the perfect ploy for his plans. In time, she'd bleed Renwick money when her new life demanded it. A meager soldier's wages would never be enough.

Despite the unknowns on the trail to Fort Laramie, Nathan made certain Mariah's father assumed what he came to believe. His son-in-law was the dutiful husband who swore to protect his wife and give her the kind of life she deserved. A life that underhandedly smacked of betrayal.

The dawning light. A new day. A chance to follow the dream. For so many pioneers setting out on the Oregon Trail, hauling their wagons full of belongings, this day was a new beginning and one filled with hope for a better life.

Nathan found his man, a wagon train captain named Silas

Bingham. Keep the emigrant party small and hire a seasoned trail boss, and they'd reach Fort Laramie without delay. But the overland journey could take longer if the wagons broke down, Indians attacked, or disease started killing folks. The threat of those obstacles left Nathan no time to squander.

His pulse quickened when Bingham shouted for the convoy to move out. The smell of the wild plains downright smelled like the territorial governorship. He inhaled another breath.

As daylight waned in the afternoon hours, the distance the caravan traveled convinced Mariah that weeks had gone by. Nathan told her to ride on the wagon. She'd be trouble if she didn't and wouldn't survive walking on foot. Sitting up front opened her eyes to the frontier ahead, but she held a death grip on the seat just to keep from falling off. Her body shuddered as the wagon wheels lurched over rocks and into ruts carved in the ground.

Silas rode alongside her. He never budged, much less said a word. He'd seen her frail kind before. Those women had no business being on the trail. A few days out and she'd fall to pieces, or be one of the first to get killed or die from the cholera. The way he saw it, he didn't much care what happened to her. His job was to get the wagon train to the Willamette Valley in Oregon in five to six months' time, and he planned to do that, with or without her.

By day's end, they reached the Shawnee Mission in Kansas. Once Silas halted the caravan, Mariah couldn't stop quaking from the ride. Aside from the first day's hardship, not once did she lose sight of the only face who wasn't a stranger. But Nathan ignored her. She didn't expect his attention after their encounter at the saloon. Still, an occasional glance would have been comforting. By the looks of it, he was too busy parading his horse up ahead to even notice her. She blotted him out of view as she winced at her sore buttocks.

Everyone started setting up camp for the night. She wanted to help but was overruled by a power far greater than she was. Without a thought, she crawled into the back of the wagon, curled up next to a pile of blankets, and drifted off into a deep slumber.

CHAPTER 11

The Fates Be Damned

THE TRANSCONTINENTAL RAILROAD still boggled Julian's mind. In time, he was convinced it would transform the country's destiny. Two iron rails of track spanning a vast wilderness from Council Bluffs, Iowa to Sacramento, California. He scanned the blueprints spread out on his desk for at least the hundredth time. His adrenaline pumped for the hundredth time too. Without the railroad, every corner of America languished as a piecemeal nation. Once the railroad was built, he envisioned a rapid succession of states joining the Union. A country of states united would mean unimaginable industrial growth.

But his partners with the Union Pacific Railroad couldn't silence the cries of their investors sitting in the boardroom, ready to breathe down his neck about the latest construction breakdown. Every meeting made him think they were trying to take down the operation. For him, the railroad's success was the only logical outcome. Failure was out of the question. Why the hell didn't they understand that?

A morning telegraph confirming another delay in lumber

shipments sent a tense vibration across the room. All eyes were on him, their railroad architect, promised deliverer of their future profits. As much as he disliked dealing with these captains of industry, the Transcontinental Railroad needed more than his brains to get built. He'd just have to put up with it. *Focus on the meeting.*

He sat down next to his boss. Charles Dunnigan played the game with these men the same as he did. Make one guarantee after another. But the slightest miscalculation on his part, anywhere on the line, and they'd pull their investment out of the project. All of it. That threat hung like a noose around his neck.

There was no panacea for the recent lumber setback. Shipments from the Ozark Mountains were out of his hands. And he sure wasn't counting on finding any timber on the barren wasteland of Nebraska Territory. Delaying the meeting another week would've given him more time to work out a solution. He shouldn't have let his distractions get in the way. A rushed feeling came over him at the sudden thought of Mariah, but it ended the second he looked across the table when the onslaught began.

"You've done a better job since you took over from Durant, but now we've got a lumber shortage staring us in the face. That's inexcusable. Young bloods like you never think things through."

Henry du Pont spoke his mind. He made his usual trip from Delaware to attend the meeting. With the war over, his black powder explosives company needed westward railroad expansion, no matter his doubts about Julian controlling the country's riskiest venture.

The criticism had Julian biting his tongue. "I understand your concerns, Mr. du Pont. Your investment is at stake. But accusing me of not—"

His response got cut off. John Fritz at Cambria Iron Works pressed his point. "It's no secret the country's still bleeding from the war. But damn it, Marquette, without my iron rails coming out of Pennsylvania, you've got no railroad. And I won't jeopardize my company just for you and your Harvard credentials." His face flushed when his tone pitched higher. "With the government nearly broke, Missouri money's all you've got now, and I sure as hell won't leverage any more of my assets until you put this mess to rights, or else I'm—"

Julian interrupted. "Rest assured, Mr. Fritz, my men will keep pounding track to the west. As for the lumber shortages, I don't anticipate problems for much longer. You have my word."

Then du Pont chimed in again. "You're damn right there won't be problems for much longer. Not if I have anything to say about it. But this quagmire you've gotten us into is halfway across the country. I don't see how you aim to fix it, considering your word isn't worth much to those of us sitting in this room."

Dunnigan could see a powder keg of egos ready to detonate if someone didn't stop their rant before it was too late. He spoke out of turn and gave Julian a first line of defense from the capitalist mob.

"We've had enough meetings over the past year to know that Julian has found solutions to every problem the railroad operation has thrown at him. With all due respect, I'm confident he'll do it again."

Heat radiated through Julian's shirt collar. All the talk was wasting time. He shouldn't have ignored his construction boss in Omaha City who warned him weeks ago about the lumber slowdown out of Arkansas. *Why didn't I pay attention to Casement?* He boxed himself into a corner and had to find a way out. But the last thing he wanted to do was let the meeting drag on. He opened his collar and tossed his string tie on the table. The back of his neck was on fire.

"I appreciate your vote of confidence, Mr. Dunnigan." He stood up and walked to the front of the room, eyeing the map on the wall. "We all agree the lumber problem needs a quick solution. Up to now, we've been accessing timber down in the Ozarks, but with the steep terrain, hauling wood to the railroad line has been slow." He pointed out the mountain range straddling Arkansas and Missouri. "Getting timber out of the mountains has been our Achilles heel since we first broke ground with the track in Omaha City."

Fritz threw aside the latest report on the railroad. "We're well aware of the situation."

Julian ignored him. "The lumber shipments were never a problem when my men were laying a mile of track a day. Now they're laying two to three miles a day. The lumber crews can't keep up." He switched course and braced himself. "Let me explain how we've been harvesting timber in the Ozarks."

A collective groan reverberated around the room. No one wanted to hear the boring details again which offered no solutions. Julian was pushing his luck. He had no choice. They demanded answers, and he needed time to figure out his options. But what did he know about rough-sawing trees and skidding logs out of the woods?

He rattled on with any scrap of minutia that filtered into his head. The longer he talked, the longer he stared at the map. No need to face a bunch of angry men ready to lob insults at him again. Then it hit him. *The map.* The answer was glaring right at him. True, it would be unreliable information at best. Pure bull otherwise. But all they wanted in the first place were outrageous reassurances.

More timber. He had to find another swath of terra incognita to solve his pressing problem. All points on the map left one solution.

"We'll get more lumber from the north. From Minnesota. Use the Rock and Big Sioux Rivers to barge it south to the Missouri River, and on to Omaha City."

A wave of silence filled the boardroom. The matter was settled.

As the sky turned to dusk over Boston Harbor, the candlelight cast a dim glow across Julian's desk. Looking out from the second story window, he felt his mood changing with nightfall. It had been a long day. His mind drifted off to Mariah and the time they spent together. He sighed. *God, I miss you.* His dream to build a railroad seemed so easy, when doing nothing to try and save her seemed hard as hell. Each time he blinked, images flashed in the window of the brutal trail ride she was enduring without him.

The creaking chair grated on his nerves. He was on edge of late, worried if she was safe. But the more he brooded over her fate, the more worked up he got. He slammed his fists on the desk and stopped the chair's movements. Nathan's grip on Mariah took hold of him. He couldn't set her free. And each passing day reminded him that time was running out.

THE Dunnigan Estate was one of Boston's finest homes. Julian's invitations had become more frequent with his new partnership in the railroad. But he engaged in more than business during his visits. Since he made the acquaintance of Dunnigan's daughter, they were seen together on several occasions to be considered friendly with one another.

Annabelle made it no secret she wanted more than shared pleasantries between them. Julian's money had nothing to do with her feelings for him. She had every luxury a woman could want, and was spoiled and proud of it. To claim Julian for herself would be a conquest like no other, as if the entire Roman Empire was lapping at her feet. Tonight, at the Dunnigans' customary Beacon Hill party, she tasted her sweet chance.

"Daddy, you did invite Julian to the party, didn't you? I'll be upset if I don't see him this evening. Besides, you know I find all your other guests boring to talk to." She laughed. "In fact, I find them utterly boring to look at."

Her rant seemed unimpeded by her mouthful of food as she sat at one end of the dining table, nibbling the delectable breakfast roll into a tiny morsel. She tidied up the last crumb with a dainty lick of her fingers.

Charles never interrupted her unless it was a moment like this, when the cup of tea sealed her lips. "Yes, I expect Julian will be coming tonight."

He had other motives for inviting his partner that any father would understand. Annabelle needed a husband. He saw her in Julian's company time and again, and knew she had an alluring eye for his affections. She'd need a bit of taming, to be sure, but he was convinced Julian was the man to do it. Of course, there were other shortcomings a prospective husband had to overlook with his daughter, and long-winded chatter was one of them.

"Well, I'll be certain to wear something . . . revealing. I wouldn't want Julian to think I'm not worthy of his company. Now would I, Daddy?"

She sank back into the velvet chair, stroking the armrests with her hands, and gave her father one of those smiles that hinted she'd be up to no good.

CHAMPAGNE flowed freely as did the accolades for the men building the railroad. This was no ordinary affair at the Dunnigan Estate. When Charles set the scene for a grand company party, it signaled another milestone for the Transcontinental Railroad. And tonight was no exception.

The railroad bridge crossing the Missouri River between Council Bluffs and Omaha City had just been completed. Railroad lines coming from the eastern seaboard would, in time, connect to the transcontinental line via the railroad bridge. All eyes were on California and pushing the railroad west.

Charles relished evenings like this. They didn't happen often, and were overshadowed by the business at hand, where the risk of finding new bank loans was met with an equal fear of defaulting on them. The financial credit pouring in from St. Louis was his biggest gamble yet. If it wasn't for Julian, God knows where his fortunes would be now. In the ditches, no doubt.

The weight of America's future rested on Julian's shoulders, and he carried that responsibility with a near obsession. Charles needed no convincing who his eventual successor would be for the railroad. Any of his other partners would prove capable of overseeing his controlling interest when the time came. But Julian's dedication reached far beyond his own private ambitions. He wanted this railroad for the people.

Excitement hummed in the reception hall as champagne glasses clinked in a toast and dedicated the new bridge.

The crowd cheered. "Hear, hear!"

Julian kept his eyes down while he sipped from his glass. He didn't want to be singled out for a job he liked doing alone. But his boss wouldn't have it and made him the man of the hour. He cleared his throat and swigged the last of his champagne. All the attention made him uneasy. Just then, Annabelle came to his rescue. A tug on his arm had them stumbling onto the balcony into the backdrop of Boston's city lights.

Chatter from the guests faded. Annabelle's ruby dress took center stage. She made a graceful turn in front of him. Surely, he admired perfection with the enormous railroad he was building. If any woman could get his mind off that beastly thing, she was the one. From those curls accenting her creamy bust to the glint in her emerald eyes, she had him at her mercy.

Before Julian could say a word, she was corralled in his arms without him lifting a finger. She placed her hands on his evening jacket and felt his chest move when he breathed. *My perfume pleases you, doesn't it, Jule darling?*

She purred as if she lost her voice. "I thought you might be in the mood . . ." He leaned down and listened closer. ". . . for some quiet company. I hope you don't mind mine."

All at once, she planted a fast kiss on his lips. Oh, the satisfaction it gave her using her little tricks to draw him in. She'd never admit she was plotting all day for this moment, with his manly taste pressed against her crimson. Why was he acting like nothing happened?

"May I compliment you on how elegant you look this evening."

His polite comment annoyed her. He wasn't bending to her charms. "Julian, please. We're not strangers, you know. I think it's time we talked more *intimately* with each other." She imagined the pleasures she'd find underneath his tailored suit as she slid her fingers around his collar and teased him with a coy smile. "You do find me attractive, don't you?"

"Of course I do. What man wouldn't?"

He took a step back. She stepped forward, leaving not a breath of space between them. The scent of his shaving lotion curled her toes. He smelled like a real man. Every strapping inch of him.

"I don't care about other men. I only care about you, and settling down, and getting married. And—well—I think I just might be the perfect wife for you to settle down with." She didn't mince words when it came to what she wanted. She showed him what she meant. Her finger curved around his lips while she parted hers.

The way she carried on had Julian tensing his jaw. It wasn't going to be easy to back out. Her auburn hair told him to beware. He gathered her hands and drew them together as though she were praying all of a sudden.

"I have no desire to be married, Annabelle. My work is too demanding. I'm sure you can understand." He saw the disappointment in her face. But he had more to say. "As it is, I need to leave on another urgent business trip. I'll be gone from Boston for quite some time."

Her eyes narrowed. Her suspicions mounted. She snatched her hands away. "You're going to St. Louis again, aren't you?" She took offense. "I don't know why you spend so much time in that shantytown. Whoever *she* is, I doubt she's worth the trouble. You obviously don't know a perfect woman when you see one."

Annabelle had never felt the sting of a man's rejection. Julian might as well have ridiculed her in front of everyone. Her other suitors would be on their knees begging for her affections. Julian was denying her greatest triumph, and all he could do was stand there with a deadpan look on his face.

Her body quaked. She coiled her fingers into fists, contorting her ladylike manners into a tantrum. But his maddening indifference to her passionate response left her wrists writhing in his grasp. How dare he treat her this way.

"Release me at once."

With no warning, her fussing screeched to a halt. She cast him a helpless look and wilted under his strength as if she became obedient to him. He took pity on her and kissed her hand. His consideration was too much. She slapped him across the face, then turned on her heel and stormed off the balcony.

The depth of that woman's convictions made her hard to forget. Julian thought it strange Annabelle spoke of Mariah without even knowing it. But the business trip he told her about wasn't going to take him to St. Louis again. He was heading west to Omaha City to fix the construction breakdown on the railroad. His general partners agreed it was the right thing to do.

With his trip only a day away, hunting for timber in Minnesota was the last thing on his mind. He had bigger problems to deal with, and they would, by design, take him urgently close to the Oregon Trail.

CHAPTER 12

Finding Purpose

ARIAH'S HEAD POUNDED like a drum. Riding for days on the trail convinced her she needed to get off the wagon, but she hadn't mustered the nerve. This world she was living in left her without a clue of what to do, except what Nathan told her. *Stay put. Don't touch the reins. Don't talk to anyone. Get out of the way.*

As the caravan slowed to a stop and the air cleared from the choking dust, she slithered down the side of the wagon and planted her feet on the ground. Solid ground. She brushed herself off and took stock of her surroundings.

Some of the travelers were staring at her again. She sighed. Just another constant reminder she wasn't one of them. From the way she dressed to how she spoke, even her complexion still gave her away as a privileged woman. But she was tired of being different.

A wave of vertigo swept over her. All the jouncing from the day's ride had the earth heaving around her. She leaned against the wagon wheel and latched on to one of the spokes. The unsteadiness subsided and gave way to a sense of calm that freed her mind to thoughts of home and when she was a little girl.

Oh, the fun she had all those years ago, stealing into the kitchen with her father, all dressed in their Sunday best for their make-believe time. Her favorite dessert made of velvety ladyfingers and creamy custard tempted her in plain view. Anything so delicious as Charlotte Russe was surely named after a British princess and a royal czar from faraway Russia. It only seemed fitting to play the part while father and daughter prepared to feast on an extra helping or two. *Shall we have a taste, Charlotte Russe? Yes, we shall, Czar Alexander. Then let us spy our scrumptious cake and eat up every single crumb!*

How silly it seemed, cherishing her nickname. But despite the sweet memories of the life she once lived, all she wanted was to find her place alongside everyone else in the wagon train. To walk like they walked. To fit in and be one of them. At least for as long as her feet could hold out.

Each day on the trail became a battle to preserve her strength, and to keep from going mad. Her aching muscles, and the emotions she bottled up, left her asking why she dragged herself into this living hell. Apart from the harsh realities brought on by a godforsaken land, she faced another awakening. She couldn't banish the thought. It glared right at her, as if the sun wasn't blinding enough already.

In the confines of her life in St. Louis, she couldn't imagine the cruel irony that bound her and Nathan together. But she saw it now while she watched his horse break away from the wagon train and evaporate in a cloud of dust.

For him, every minute of the trail ride heightened an urgency to reach Fort Laramie. She felt the same, only for a different reason. The struggle to keep their marriage intact was paramount, not for the love fading between them but for her own survival. Hundreds of miles of wilderness lurked ahead. Facing those dangers with her husband could protect her from peril.

What other choice did she have? To turn back and go home was unthinkable.

Mother and Father would never find out about her hardships, or that her marriage was in vain. For them, she had to be the light following their family's tragedy. She couldn't give up. It wasn't Fanny's choice to cause her parents so much pain, but it was Mariah's choice to keep her anguish to herself. Forever if need be. To accept failure was not an option for her or for Nathan.

By sunrise, the wagons were hitched and supplies loaded up. The pounding rhythm of the oxen was afoot. A voyage that began as an adventure for the pioneers had whittled down to backbreaking work, and a daily test of their courage against unknown threats on the trail. But their power to endure came from each other in bonds of friendship and a helping hand, enough to face a new day.

After reaching their next encampment, Silas set out doing his usual tasks. Mariah had grown accustomed to his routine until the last campfire was put out. Beyond his tough exterior dwelled a hardihood she took to heart since they first rode side by side on the wagon. Though he ignored her and kept to himself, she came to regard him with kindness. He reminded her of her father. How she needed his help to find her bearings and figure out where they were going. Knowing that could shed light on where Nathan had gone.

She caught up to the wagon boss and blurted out her frustrations. "Silas, where are we? I need to know—" She coughed through a dry throat. "How much farther do we have to travel?" Her voice strained. She didn't let up. "*Please* tell me where we are."

Silas saw all sorts of folks on the trail, but he didn't know what to make of Mariah. He took his time while he stood there staring at her. Then he gave it to her straight.

"Just crossed into Nebraska Territory. Makin' good time I

reckon. Rock Creek Station's where we're settin' up camp to-night. Need to stock up on supplies before we head out come sunup."

Every time he glanced at her, he couldn't shake the image in his head. From dawn till dusk, she kept tripping over her frilly dress and got it all tattered and dirty. Then she put that sorry look on her face like she was ready to pass out. He gave his rambling thoughts a good mulling over when he chimed in again.

"I ain't pryin' or nothin', ma'am, but you don't look so good." A chewed piece of straw hung out of his mouth as he squinted from under the brim of his hat. He waited for her reply, and waited a tad more.

Mariah's gaze drifted between his face and the blur of boots shuffling around them. The stare he gave her hinted it was her turn to speak.

"I . . . yes, I'm sure I've dressed more elegant than this." She wiped her forehead in the crook of her arm and peered down at her shoes and back at him. "Quite frankly, my feet are *killing* me."

He didn't expect her confession but heard it anyway. Her troubles didn't seem to break her spirit though. A fight brewed in her eyes like he never saw before. He figured she was set on yelling her fool head off. Or maybe she was getting choked up. He couldn't tell. After a half dozen land crossings between Missouri and Oregon, not much surprised him on the trail, and Mariah's type was the most predictable.

Lines creased his brow. He yanked the stub of straw from his mouth. The thought didn't sit well with him, knowing death preyed upon the weakest. But she proved him wrong. She didn't belt out a word much less shed a tear. That fiery look told him her confession was all he was going to get.

"Not much we can do except walk or ride, otherwise this

wagon train won't make it to Oregon. No two ways about it."
He glared at the sky. "We're losing daylight. Gotta get to work."
He tipped his hat and bid her good night. "Evenin', ma'am."

He wasn't about to get soft on anyone, specially city folk,
and most of all with Mariah. Driving the convoy west gave him
enough problems without having to deal with her frail nature.
As the sun hovered low on the horizon, he scouted for a place
to picket the horses before dark.

Everyone started their evening chores after the day's ordeal.
Their treading boots had covered miles, inching them closer
to journey's end. But all the sweat and toil left Mariah out of
sorts. She could barely stand up and tend to her piddly tasks.
Her fellow travelers forged ahead, still full of vigor, while she
lagged far behind in grand miserable fashion. Greater forces
wore her down.

The trail ride became this beast of a thing, overwhelming
her with a tide of aching limbs and consuming all her rational
thoughts, except one. She had to get to Fort Laramie alive. Yet
unbearable exhaustion took its toll, and with no end in sight,
she grew more frustrated. If she could just slip into the wagon
again and fall asleep, like she did the first night. But help was
needed lighting the fires and cooking the meals. She had to
do her part. Besides, the pain from her blistered feet already
fought against her fatigue and won.

A circle of wagons formed around the families gathered at
their campfires, dining on the likes of beans and a bit of fatty
bacon and cornbread, all washed down with copious amounts
of coffee. Mariah couldn't get used to the meals, or the taste,
or the smell. Another adjustment she had to make to her new
way of life. High expectations for fine dining, there were none.
It was just a matter of filling the stomach.

Dusk settled in. She all but gave up trying to light her
campfire. Nathan hadn't come back, so there was no sense in

waiting for help from a husband who wasn't there. She plopped down in front of the random bits of wood and crossed her arms in protest. A voice rose up behind her.

"Deary, let me help ya with that."

The woman crouched next to her and rearranged the kindling. She placed the smaller twigs over the tinder and the larger pieces on top, then struck the flint to the mounded pile. With a deep breath, she blew out a stream of air until a flame ignited under the chunks of wood.

She gazed at Mariah. "The name's Stella McKellican, just so ya know. I've been watchin' you since we left Independence. Ya look ta be too fine a woman ta be out here on the trail." Her accent sounded strange, but her red hair took some of the mystery out of it.

"Thank you for your help, Stella. I'm Mariah Lawton." She sighed, feeling the heat from the fire warming her tired frame.

Stella had more to say. "It'll be a spell before ya can do any cookin' on yer fire, deary. Now git up off yer arse an' come see what I've got for ya over yonder."

Mariah wanted to stay put but felt obliged, and even curious, to find out what the Irish woman was talking about. She followed Stella to her wagon. An unexpected gesture had Stella handing her a couple of dresses and a bonnet, along with a pair of manly looking boots.

"It's time ya started dressin' like the rest of us. Ya might not fancy them woolen clothes, but they be keepin' the wind from blowin' right through ya. And, just so ya know, I'll not be expectin' anythin' back either." With her hands planted on her hips, she gave Mariah a look that said she meant every word.

Images of an Ohio family unfolded as Stella's two children huddled around the campfire, gobbling up helpings of beans and a hard biscuit or two. Mariah smiled at the sight of the little ones.

Her hunger pangs drove her back to her campfire where she

tried her hand at cooking before it was time to turn in for the night. Stella's invitation to dine with them was kind, but she needed to claim her own victory for once, without help from anyone else. How glorious it felt conquering this one battle.

As the quiet of night flowed over her, she thought of nothing. The feeling didn't last long. A sudden idea, full of inspiration, lifted her spirits. She wanted to tell Stella right away, but it would have to wait until morning. Sleep had come calling again, and it was determined to stay.

CHAPTER 13

A Chance To Right A Wrong

*T*HE ACRID SMELL of burning oil drifted over the train platform. Grating metal screeched from the locomotive's undercarriage as it lumbered to a halt at the Council Bluffs train depot. Billowy white clouds of steam hissed skyward against the dim light of an Iowa dawn. The weekly train from New York, connecting from Boston, just arrived.

What a sight to see for the denizens of the town who basked in the excitement while they scratched their heads. A railroad line coming here? Nothing but desolate land surrounded the crossroads, and only the hardiest souls called the place home. For them, holding on to the few possessions they had in these parts was tough enough, never mind holding on to their town's identity. Some highfalutin politicians wrote a charter in 1853, banishing the name Kanesville for Council Bluffs. But what the locals lost in a name, the train made up for with its dizzying presence.

Before long, pioneers swarmed the town in droves, some chasing down a dream about gold out West. They didn't much care about the town's identity or the folks who lived there.

Council Bluffs was just another name for another nameless place they'd never call home. But they'd been coming for a long spell, riding in from the east and navigating up the Missouri River from the south. And they were still coming.

Day in and day out, steamboats docked along the river-bank, unloading those gypsies and their possessions for the overland journey on the Oregon Trail. Not even the bluffs bordering the township could stop them. But the town with no identity had no railroad line traveling west, and that obvious fact gave the place a bad name. Council Bluffs was at the end of nowhere.

Then, everything changed. The Iron Road was coming. The building of the Transcontinental Railroad, all the way to California.

THE train whistle shrieked but didn't stir Julian out of his trance. As hues of pale purple tinged the morning sky, the glow from the conductor's lantern bared his reflection in the train car window. Staring at his likeness showed him what he hadn't sensed before. His face was tied up with worry and his jaw was clenched tight.

He threw his head back against the seat. That telegram still riled him. Before he left Boston, he wired Edmund Renwick to contact his boss with any loan matters while he was away inspecting the railroad line. He didn't expect a plea for help as a reply.

Standing on the train platform, he glanced in both directions and headed north into town, on the lookout for a livery stable and a horse. With any luck, an Arabian like his stallions back home could handle the long ride across Nebraska Territory, and beyond if need be.

His eyes burned as he squinted into the rising sun. Missing

out on an entire night's sleep wore him down. He had no one to blame but himself for getting all worked up thinking about that telegram.

Renwick's words were not those of a high-powered banker courting a future client. The man was worried about his daughter. Over a month had passed and still no tidings from his son-in-law or their whereabouts on the trail. But Renwick's news proved him right. Nathan had no intention of looking out for Mariah. Renwick's last words left no doubt. *Can you help find my daughter?*

Up ahead, a row of ramshackle buildings skirted the road and marked the boundaries of the town. A general store. A land office. Even the undertaker and saloons gave a sense of protection from the wilds. But Council Bluffs wasn't much different from those Hell on Wheels railroad camps riddled with gambling, drinking, and brothels, except for the marshal's office and the jailhouse. For that alone, the townsfolk were grateful they had the law on their side, or at least the appearance of it.

Beyond the Pacific House Hotel, Julian spied the livery stable. He stepped off the boardwalk and tracked the dirt road. The crowds boggled his mind. So far west. So far from anything. But he couldn't dodge the stares. Maybe he looked too spruced up and didn't belong out here. Maybe a frontier town had no place for a law-abiding city man like him.

He could feel it. Every breath he took weakened his moral fiber and gave power to a vigilante notion he couldn't shake off. This was new territory he was up against. Some kind of justice had to be waiting out there to save Mariah from the nightmare she was dragged into by her husband. The more he thought about Nathan, the more incensed he became. *I need to get a gun.*

An empty stomach started working against him. He searched for a quick remedy. The black Arabian stallion he claimed at the stable hadn't been ridden much since the war and didn't want a rider. He walked the horse to the nearest eating house and darted inside where he guzzled two cups of coffee and feasted on a plate of hot grits and boiled eggs.

His telegram to Mariah's father said he'd try and drum up any information he could find out about her. He didn't tell Renwick the plans not even his railroad syndicate knew about. What the hell was he thinking? He had no plans, except to get on a train and head west.

The image haunted him. Her face. All he saw was her face. Trying to forget her was like telling himself to quit breathing. But he had to beware. Nathan couldn't be trusted. Still, his kind would be easy to find. All he had to do was follow the stench.

With his hunger sated, fatigue settled in fast. He raked his fingers through his hair and grabbed the reins from the hitching post. A soft muzzle nudged his hand. A reminder, maybe, that his lack of sleep had skewed his thinking. The distance he put between himself and Boston convinced him to keep going and stop for nothing. Deep down, he was getting careless. But word would get back if he didn't check in with his construction boss. Dunnigan hired Jack Casement in the dead of winter when progress on the line came to a standstill.

Damn the inspections. Mariah's closeness danced on the edge of every tide of warm air drifting over him. It was all the reminding he needed to find her. If Nathan didn't send a telegram to her father, chances were good he wasn't even traveling with her. And if Mariah was alone, she was in more danger than he thought. He needed to get moving.

Across the river, he headed for the provincial railroad office in Omaha City where he met with Casement and hashed out the details for new lumber shipments out of Minnesota. The meeting and a wire to Dunnigan took the better part of the day but gave him the assurance he needed from Casement who was his critical link on the front line. Their handshake set him out of the office toward the tracks.

Sunlight sparked off the bands of iron spanning the prairie to the west. He stood awestruck at the sight. A rush of excitement tightened his chest. He felt like a wild horse ready to run free. The McClellan saddle was broken in and would make for an easier ride. He didn't expect it to unleash a flood of memories from back home, riding his horses along the rocky beaches in Cohasset.

But the last few nights he woke up in a cold sweat. What if he couldn't find Mariah? Taking a gamble into the unknown with no way to calculate the outcome was risky business and uncharacteristic for him. He was losing all sense of time and place out here on the frontier where Boston felt a world away and Mariah felt so close. Now her fate rested on the back of his steed. *This will be a long hard ride for both of us. Help me find her, Chakote.*

He rode off into the wind across the open plains. Pounding hooves charged him ahead. Hours passed as he sped toward the sun ticking downward in the sky. A visible sign of every measure of daylight that vanished. Darkness. An unforeseen nemesis. A greater obstacle to finding Mariah than getting shot at or facing a stampede of buffalo. The race against time didn't give him much in the way of comfort thinking about it.

He stopped and rested Chakote, then swigged from his canteen and adjusted his leather chaps. He figured he could make do with his cowboy's rendition of a suit and tie. A cotton shirt and black vest, topped off with a hat and red bandana cinched around his neck. He wasn't so sure about the bedroll strapped behind him. Both saddlebags bulged with food rations and extra canteens of water.

The itch to get going came on strong again. He tugged on the reins, guiding Chakote in a circle, and scanned the panorama. With a quick jab, he spurred his horse and pushed on. That raider of daylight hadn't moved in on him yet.

As one day on the trail blurred into the next, the end of the track line came into view. Riding at a steady gallop, he gave one last look over his shoulder. The size of the railroad amazed him in a way he never imagined from the confines of his office. Line after line of iron rails had been hammered to the crossties with German and Irish strength and the might of Freedmen forging it westward. The sight of the Transcontinental Railroad reignited his vision of an America united into one nation on the precipice of greatness itself.

Staring ahead at the empty horizon didn't lessen his unease about the coming days or weeks, and if he'd even find Mariah alive. What if disease or a stray bullet already left her rotting on the trail? He whipped the reins against Chakote's back. *Stay alive, Mariah. Stay alive . . .*

The sun dipped low in the sky. Day's end was near. He tipped his hat back and rubbed his stubbled chin, then peered across the terrain for any sign of the Oregon Trail. Losing daylight was the least of his worries now. The wind had kicked up. He smelled trouble in the air. Dark clouds rolled in and warned this was no light rain shower he'd be up against. He had to find shelter. Fast.

Chakote barreled into the rising squall as spurts of rain pelted Julian's face. He tasted the rainwater on his lips. It was getting harder to see in the distance, and he couldn't spot a place to hide. A jagged bolt of lightning ruptured the sky. The rumble of thunder spooked Chakote. He lurched his head sideways like he was trying to jerk the reins from his master's hands.

"Whoa, boy! Take it easy. That's just the clouds talkin'."

Julian stroked the horse's neck, settling him down, and drove his spurs into him again. Rain beat against their backs and distorted the lay of the land, but he could still make out an object at the bottom of a ravine, northwest from his current position. For the past few days, he followed the Platte River and didn't veer once since he left Omaha City. Drenched to the bone, he broke away and made a run for the wagon.

As he approached, a nearby creek bed full of rainwater burst into a gushing stream. He dismounted and tied the reins to the brake lever, then grabbed his saddle and belongings and ducked underneath the wagon. Waiting for the storm to pass was going to take a while.

All the rain coming down gave him time to fill up the canteens. He opened the flasks and dangled the leather straps from the wagon tongue. Lucky for him, the tongue broke off from the axle, forcing the emigrants to abandon the wagon. Huddled under cover, he planted his head in the groove of his saddle and chewed on a strip of dried beef.

Another thunderbolt ricocheted in the clouds. Chakote reared up, flailing his hooves in the air. Days like this had the horse wanting to be unbridled and running free.

Flashes of staccato lightning split open the sky. Hail poured down and hit the ground, crackling like lard sizzling on a hot griddle. Pellets of ice covered the land in white as if it snowed all of a sudden. Julian covered his ears and recoiled from the noise. The sound was deafening, but he liked it. He let go and welcomed the uproar storming from the heavens. Out here, in the middle of the open plains, he took in the hard ways of the cowboy, and he liked that too.

This windswept land has a voice all its own. It can speak to you in ways no human can. Merciless will it be, yet stunning in its beauty. But to hear its voice stirring around you is not enough. Take heed, and listen.

As you look upon the land, you cannot grasp its splendor unfolding majestic before your eyes. See it, and be awakened. Breathe deep. Savor its earthen scent. Only then will you come to know the essence of this place.

CHAPTER 14

To Be Wicked Forever

ARIAH WAS TIRED of the taste of dirt that coated her mouth and made her gag. But she got real good at getting rid of it. She let a pool of saliva form in her mouth, then spat out the dirt and wiped the drool on her sleeve. Oh, how she could impress the ladies of Benton Park with her elegant mannerisms as she stumbled over rocks and clumps of brush strewn along the trail.

Those thoughts expired when she took another step. She winced. The blisters on her feet rubbed against the inside of her boots. Relief, there was none. Just finding another distraction. She glanced down at her hands and shook her head in disbelief. They looked old and worn as she turned them over, back and forth. One rough hand touched the other. They were tanned yet sunburned still.

The memory of being a lady evanesced with each passing day and was a stark reminder of what she couldn't face. Her life in Missouri was gone. She felt afraid since those memories were all she had left. This wasteland destroyed the Mariah she'd known. A woman overwhelmed by a frontier that devoured its prey and relished the anguish they suffered before they died.

Scenes of brutality surrounded her. She gazed beyond the trail and saw scattered mounds of earth along the river. How tragic, she thought. Dirt tombs of dead emigrants, piled high, as if to keep the water from flooding its banks. What a pitiful end for them and their dreams. But she saw unburied bodies too. A chill shivered through her. The frightful images severed her last strands of hope which kept her determined to finish this journey in one piece. This land paraded its dead in front of her, waiting for her to weaken and become its next perfect victim.

Another step had her ready to scream. She swore bees were stinging her feet. And to think all she wanted was to walk with the other travelers and be one of them.

Her cracked and bleeding lips, for so long swollen, smelled of lard. It was a fair trade. The grease kept her lips supple and relieved the pain. If only her feet could find favor with the likes of no boots. Walking became unbearable and the discomfort inescapable, yet the daily ritual carried on. Trudge ahead. Trip and fall. A grimace for good measure. Wipe the tears off the face. Repeat.

But not every tear had been wiped away. Here and there, one trickled down her cheek and over her lip. She licked the droplet. It tasted brackish. No matter. Her body took anything she gave it, even a teardrop or two. Nothing would be wasted out here.

AT high noon, the wagon train reached Fort Kearny. Nathan was at the garrison waiting for them to arrive. He cornered Silas and had a brief word with the wagon boss.

The pioneers took in the sight of their first army outpost on the trail. A safe oasis that offered them rest and a place for replenishing their provisions. And a chance to send a letter back home to a loved one they left behind. But more, their respite gave them precious time for repairing the wagons before they rode the longest stretch of the overland trail that would take them into unknown territory.

After leaving the fort, the caravan meandered along the great Platte River. Beyond its fertile banks sprawled a vast champaign of sweeping grasslands as far as the eye could see. The pioneers had reached the land of the High Plains. Plentiful water abounded, but so did swarms of nagging mosquitoes. An annoyance they paid scant attention to when eagles soared overhead or they faced a lone wolf who braved into camp. The wilds had startled them with the unexpected.

By week's end, an abrupt change altered the terrain. Silas and one of the men rode off and scouted the trail up ahead. A fork in the river confirmed what Silas guessed. Two branches flowed in opposite directions. The North Platte headed into Dakota Territory, and the only way across the Rocky Mountains—over South Pass. Where they were positioned would take the wagon train the wrong way, far from the Oregon Trail along the south fork of the river into Colorado Territory. Silas sent the man back to the caravan with orders for everyone to set up camp. The convoy of overloaded wagons would cross the wide and dangerous river come morning.

The decision to stop early didn't sit well with Nathan. His patience had worn thin. He set off and tracked down Silas. Suspicions about the wagon boss were eating at him while he was forced to wait at Fort Kearny for the wagon train to arrive. Silas halted the caravan after some of the families took ill with typhoid fever. That excuse rankled Nathan. He lashed out at Silas for not pushing ahead on the trail.

"Ever since we left Missouri, you've been runnin' this wagon train like a mama's boy." He maneuvered his horse next to Silas and ripped the reins from his hands. "I don't like no mama's boy pussy footin' around and makin' me wait."

Silas retaliated and spurred his horse. The mount reared up, tearing the reins from Nathan's grasp. Silas bolted toward him but was stopped cold when Nathan drew his gun and pointed it straight at him.

"Don't test me old man. I'm supposed to be in Fort Laramie by now, and you're messin' up my plans."

Those images of Silas pandering to his wife were twitching his trigger finger. The wagon boss stuck his nose in everything she did. Unloading supplies from the wagon. Hauling scrubbed clothes back from the riverbank. Silas crossed the line and needed to be taught a lesson. He gritted his teeth as the cocked gun wobbled in Silas's face. Then he lowered the revolver and jammed it into his holster.

This wasn't the first time Silas had a gun shoved into his mug. He reacted the way he always did when he encountered a threat on the trail. He stared down the lieutenant, daring him just this once to pull the trigger. Nathan didn't shoot him, but he could have. That crazed look in his eyes told Silas to beware.

When both men rode into camp, Mariah noticed something was wrong. Nathan stomped toward her in a hard line with his eyes narrowed and his hand on his pistol grip. A terse remark left her humiliated as he mocked her appearance. He didn't even touch her, shunning her like a leper. She was shamed by her own husband, and her heart rekindled the memory of how to ache again.

Her saving grace these past days had been Stella's children. She felt overjoyed by their presence and her new place in their lives. Stella agreed to let her teach lessons to Jessie and Martha. Had they lived in St. Louis, they would have attended Benton School, though their free-spirited ways might have been difficult for Mrs. Lawton to contain within the walls of the school house. No, they needed to be out here in the open air where nature had a free spirit all its own.

But the trail ride was wearing them down, and she worried how they would hold up in the coming weeks. For now, they took a liking to their frontier schoolmarm, and she discovered a fondness for them that filled the emptiness inside.

The usual clanking of pots and searching for campfire wood kept everyone busy. Mariah sensed the children's eagerness to please and take gratitude wherever they found it, and she was delighted to give it to them.

Neither Martha nor Jessie flinched when no firewood could be found and they harvested buffalo chips instead. The odor repulsed Mariah. At least the manure didn't smell once it burned. That was small consolation for losing her appetite. But she had to eat to keep up her strength, and not even the foul stench was going to get in her way.

After the evening meal and a short lesson in geography, Jessie and Martha scampered back to their camp for the night. Mariah wandered over to another campfire and listened to stories some of the men were recounting.

"I tell you what, Jake. I can taste the sweet grass of Oregon this very minute, as much as I can feel the hand of death on my shoulder. That wagon train we passed today means trouble. Cholera's been spreadin' real fast since we've been ridin' through Nebraska Territory."

Tom Akin knew Jake Coon's problems weren't much different than his. Both men sat with their backs pressed against a wagon wheel, staring at the twisting flames lighting up their haggard faces.

Jake nodded. "Yeah, what I saw today made me wanna turn around and head back to Ohio. We been lucky so far. A'course, our luck won't last forever. And when the cholera hits, there'll be a whole lotta bodies to bury, that's for sure."

Tom blurted out the grim truth. "Heck no. You saw it plain as day. There won't be no time to do any buryin'. No, sir. No time at all."

Nathan stood back watching Mariah's reaction. Ribbons of firelight danced on her face and stoked a fear that opened her eyes wide. Her chest heaved as she cupped her mouth like she was going to vomit. He guessed she'd seen enough, smelled enough, and had enough of all the talk. Any more dead bodies and she'd be pushed over the edge. Her terrified look told him plenty.

But fear already did its damage, paralyzing Mariah. She locked her sights on Nathan. *I can't bear this any longer. I don't want to die out here!* Her silent plea implored him to find his place at her side and offer her the comfort of his hand, or just a petty considerate glance. Something. Anything, to keep her from losing all faith in him. It wasn't right for him to behave this way. The others must be wondering why he was even married if he couldn't even act the part.

He stood there with his arms crossed. A glint of gold sparked on his finger. She waited. His eyes gave nothing back. No compassion. No empathy. No love. Maybe he hated her. If that was his final gesture, maybe she didn't care. She couldn't care. Her hands stifled her choking breaths. It was too much. Her mind snapped, and she fled into the dark.

Silas stood night watch as one of the sentries and guarded the circle of wagons while he tried settling down the horses and oxen stirring in the makeshift corral. Most nights the wind quit blowing after sundown, but not tonight.

The animals grew restless. Their ruckus cloaked a nearby sound. Sitting against a rock, Mariah found a place of shelter where she could hide and be alone. Her cheeks felt moist as she wiped a lifetime of tears from her face. Tears shed for her dying sister, and for her mother who only wanted her to be happy and live the life Fanny never had. And tears for her father who, through his own hubris, believed in Nathan and all his proud promises. All his proud lies. She wept louder.

What if her own pride put her in this predicament because she was dead set on forging ahead, even if her husband cared more for his own ambitions than he did for her? She could have turned back and given it all up, and admitted defeat. Somehow defeat found her anyway, out here in this deserted land where she couldn't be more alone.

Julian felt worlds away and was just a memory now. With every day, she craved his strength more than ever, as though he were Atlas set to sweep her off her feet and carry her to safety. She pulled the tattered piece of paper from her bosom. The darkness concealed its message, but she memorized every word he wrote. Every word that came from his heart. *You will always be with me. Always, Julian.* She clung to his promise all this time. Yet holding on to the impossible had become hopelessly impossible.

She hugged the rock and sobbed against it. Finding comfort in this most wretched of all moments seemed foolish. But there it was, cocooned in her arms, stone hard and void of emotion, bracing her up to keep her from falling into unending despair.

The pool of tears masking her eyes didn't hide the gloom surrounding her, or the boots thudding toward her. Startled, she pushed away from the rock, trying to see who was standing there. The face hovered over her. It was Silas.

He lifted his night watch lantern above her head and got a better look. "What in blazes are you doin' out here in the dark, Mrs. Lawton? You know it ain't safe bein' away from camp."

Silas always talked tough with her, but even that heart of gold behind his burly exterior couldn't save her. "I don't care if I'm safe. I don't care about anything. Nothing matters any-more . . ."

The odds of getting bushwhacked on the trail kept Silas vigilant day and night, but he never saw the reaction coming from

Mariah. She hightailed it off her rump, threw her arms around his neck, and buried her face square in his chest. He never heard such sadness pour out of a woman's heart. No sooner had he set the lantern down on the rock and consoled her than his left shoulder hurled back and his body coiled like a snake. A fist slammed him in the jaw. Damn, he didn't see that bush-whacker coming either. But he sure as hell saw Nathan grab hold of Mariah's hair and snap her head back. She tumbled to the ground.

"You keep testing me, old man. Next time I see you touchin' my wife, I *will* pull the trigger."

Nathan dragged Mariah back to camp without another look at the man who messed with his woman. They kept their distance and walked along the perimeter, out of sight from the others.

As they rounded the back of the wagon, he stared at her and swallowed hard. Traces of blood stained the side of her mouth. A knot twisted in his gut. He didn't mean to hurt her, but she defied his orders to stay clear of every man who walked the face of the earth.

"You look a mess. Go clean yourself up and stay in the wag-on tonight. I don't want anyone asking questions."

His remarks lit her temper on fire. She ripped her arm from his grip and yelled good and loud. "Are you afraid someone will think you're a wife beater, *Lieutenant Lawton*? Is that what you are—afraid?"

She panted in a frenzy as the anger sucked her breath away. But tasting her own blood made her feel faint, until Nathan slapped her across the face. She was getting out of hand.

Chapter 15

The Devil's Plains

*J*ULIAN PEERED INTO the distance through the glare of
the midday sun. Staring at the same flat terrain with no
trees had a way of dulling a man's mind. Make him go
soft in the head if he didn't keep his guard up. He rubbed his
eyes with his bandana and blinked away some of the trail dust.
At least he could see all the way to the horizon and spy any
trouble before it got too close. The kind of trouble a fast gun
could outshoot or a fast horse could outrun.

But this wide open country stirred up another kind of
trouble. Warnings from the crews working the track line had
reached him back in Boston about the freak weather gone mad
every springtime. Brooding clouds would appear out of nowhere. Towering thunderheads darkened the blue, unleashing a
fury of storms that ripped through the sky. Dodging hailstones
was like dodging a spray of bullets. A lightning strike could
knock a man out. Both could kill him. If those storms raised
enough hell, they'd spiral into a deadly tornado, a twisting
mass of violent winds obliterating everything in its path, like
an overland hurricane. That threat lurked in the back of Julian's

mind no matter what day it was. There was no place to hide out on the devil's plains.

He squinted hard. The flatlands weren't all bad luck. Made it easy to spot a settlement this far away. Might be emigrants homesteading the prairie. Didn't seem likely though. Army barracks, he guessed. It had to be Fort Kearny. Endless days riding alone across Nebraska Territory gave way to a sense of relief. Maybe he'd have the chance to talk to someone besides his horse.

Chakote kicked into a gallop and headed toward the outpost. The sight of the fort had to be a welcome one for the pioneers heading west. It was a welcome sight for Julian.

But his life back in Boston never felt this solitary. He battled company men to build the country's biggest railroad, with years spent analyzing construction costs and manpower needs, and government maneuvering for critical land grants. His work became a near obsession and forced him into a kind of seclusion, leaving no time for anything, or anyone. But he wanted it that way. He needed it that way, to forge the dream into reality. With not a soul around for miles, for days, and far too much time to think, this isolated mission he'd taken on was far different.

Closer in, he saw soldiers milling around the fort. Too few to do any good if the frontier post needed defending. He slowed Chakote to a walk and kept the dust down as he approached.

A walled garrison with armed sentries was what he expected to see, not a bunch of scattered buildings and a stockade too small to hold more than a dozen horses. By the looks of it, Fort Kearny wasn't much of a fort at all.

Late spring brought warmer days and all the rain he encountered of late. He looked down at his boots caked in mud and shook his head. No doubt his present state of attire would've had him banished from Beacon Hill. As he wiped the remnants of trail dust off his face, he didn't much care about Beacon Hill or Charles Dunnigan, or his board of directors. Venturing this far west fed a fire that made him more restless with each passing day. He needed to quench the flames or he'd regret it for the rest of his life.

He headed to the supply store. Asking a few questions might get him some answers. Just then, a soldier clad in a frayed uniform walked outside, bracing a small barrel on his shoulder. He caught up to him.

"Pardon me. Any idea where I can find the fort's commanding officer?"

The soldier gave him a wry grin. "You're in luck, mister, 'cause I'm headin' over to Captain Murdock's quarters right now." He shoved off.

Julian nudged Chakote. Maybe the captain had some news about Mariah or Nathan. Someone could have seen them at the fort. He craned his neck and took in the surroundings, and the face of every stranger he thought might give him a clue.

Despite the rugged terrain and the fort standing in its midst, this land felt right to him. He came to know it in a way he never imagined. The smell of the prairie grass and the ground drenched from rain was reminder enough he hadn't been so alone after all.

He inhaled a breath through his mouth and tasted Mariah's closeness. Had she even made it this far? Getting a lead from Captain Murdock on her whereabouts was a long shot. Asking about the lieutenant could drum up more information.

The saddle groaned from his shifting weight. Another day's ride was over. He got so used to the rhythm of his horse on the trail, he didn't notice Chakote's gait slowed to a near crawl. A pang of guilt hit him, seeing the band of sweat edging his saddle. He dismounted and peeled off his gloves and stared into the horse's jaded eyes.

"You've done well, my friend, but I haven't been much of one to you." He stroked Chakote's mane with an apologetic look on his face. "Take it easy, boy. I'll walk from here."

He led the horse by the reins and tracked the soldier's path along the wagon train thoroughfare. As they approached a row of barracks, the soldier veered right but his gaze turned left. Near the blacksmith shop stood a guardhouse and a powder magazine, and beyond, a caravan at the edge of the fort. *A wagon train.* He riveted his eyes on the travelers, searching. His shoulders slumped. Strangers, every one of them.

The soldier skirted past a fence where he stacked the barrel under a lean-to. He double backed and marched to the front door.

"You best wait out here while I notify the captain of your arrival."

Julian nodded. The soldier's tone seemed better suited for a high-ranking officer than a city dweller like himself. He wrapped the reins around the hitching post and waited a spell. Then the soldier stuck his head outside and waved him in.

He ducked under the door frame, took off his hat, and scanned the room. Life looked rough at the outpost for troops in the United States Army. Nothing but a dirt floor and sod walls. Rank afforded the captain a big chair where he sat at a desk with his hands locked behind his head. His tired uniform didn't fare any better than the soldier's, but his polished black boots clamored for attention.

The officer stood up and made his introductions. "How do, stranger. I'm Captain Murdock. Private Durgan said you wanted to see me."

Julian squared his shoulders and tendered his hand in a welcome gesture. "Good to meet you, sir. I'm Julian Marquette."

"You don't look like most folks passin' through here. Somethin' tells me you got more smarts than you'd ever be needin' out in this territory. Where you from, Marquette?"

"I'm from back East, near Boston." All the idle talk had him tapping his hat against his leg. He got to the point. "Don't want to take up much of your time. I'm looking for someone who might have traveled through here. His name is Lawton. Lieutenant Lawton." Just saying Nathan's name made him mad. But losing his temper wouldn't get him any closer to what he came for. He gripped his hat with both hands. "Any chance you can help me out?"

The captain's eyes lit up at the mention of the lieutenant. "Good God. Everyone at the fort knows about him. Crazy son of a bitch. Had to break up more than one fight between him and my men." Murdock had more to say. "He liked that damn whiskey too much. Gonna get someone killed if he don't watch out."

Murdock's comments proved Nathan was at the fort. But how long ago? Julian had to find out if a lot more riding was ahead of him. Murdock was right though. The lieutenant could get someone killed, even his wife. *Stay focused. Find Mariah.*

A CAPTAIN'S promotion awaited Nathan at Fort Laramie. So did his rendezvous with Colonel Moonlight. Those talks in the dead of winter with Moonlight's political friends in Omaha City was no accident. He made his promises and agreed to their demands. They didn't need to know his father-in-law left him empty-handed. Still, all bets were off if he didn't ante up and make it worth their while.

Once the bureaucrats in Washington organized Wyoming Territory, they'd have their man picked for the job as the new territorial governor, and a keen supporter of the northern railroad line. A man they met in Omaha City.

Politics and hush money made for the perfect greased handshake. A congressional vote was on the line. But Moonlight's game was paying off too. He had his eye on Nebraska statehood. Its first governor needed to be a respected bluecoat, a protector of the white man's peace and its ever-expanding democracy. A man who had the makings of another political crony.

CAPTAIN Murdock walked around his desk and squinted at the Easterner. By the look on Julian's face, he figured something was on his mind. Telling him the lieutenant was a crazy man didn't seem to sit well with him either.

After hearing Murdock's news, Julian almost punched a fist through his hat. "So the lieutenant *was* here." He rattled off one question after another. "Do you know when he passed through? Two days ago? A week? Two weeks?"

Murdock recalled the scuffles Nathan started at the fort. "Heck, I'd say not more than a week ago. Haven't had a fight break out since he left." He glanced at the private. "What do you think, Roscoe?"

"Yessir. Sounds about right. I was cleanin' up a barrel of bourbon that busted open outside the supply store when he headed outta here with Silas and the wagon train. Good scout, that man Bingham."

Murdock slapped Julian on the back and smiled at the mention of Bingham's name. "Damn right he's a good scout. No matter what he puts his mind to, he never quits till he gets the job done. Always liked his way of doin' things." He left Julian hanging while he bragged about his old friend.

He'd been stationed at Fort Kearny not longer than six months when he first heard of a scout who knew the Oregon Trail so well, many said he could ride the two-thousand-mile journey blindfolded. They were friends in Virginia and parted ways after the war broke out.

Murdock saw a lot more fighting than Silas before he took

his new post at Fort Kearny. What he found at the garrison was no match for what he battled at Bull Run. Fears of wild Indians attacking the fort and the wagon trains, and cutting down every white man in sight turned out to be untrue. The day the caravan left the fort, Silas told Murdock the emigrants were worried more about the cholera.

Julian didn't hear a word Murdock said. He was distracted, thinking how close he was to finding Mariah. *The wagon train left a week ago.*

His mind whiplashed to late winter and when he last saw her. More than two years slipped away since she first walked into his life. He missed his chance to woo her then. He had his reasons. Justifications that added up to losing the only woman he ever loved. What a fool he'd been.

The evening at the cottage. Their intimate conversation. Sharing her company left a storm raging inside him. He tried to resist the nuanced gestures she gave him. Any indiscretion would leave her to blame. Now he'd come this far. He couldn't jeopardize the only chance he had to save her. But he had to find her first.

He whacked his hat against his chaps. His gaze flashed between the captain and the private. "Either of you recall seeing a tall woman with dark blonde hair and blue-green eyes? Was she traveling with the lieutenant?"

Roscoe paid no mind to his questions. "A whole lotta those wagon trains pass through here, and a whole lotta people. Gets to where ya can't tell one group a folks from another." He stretched his neck up to Julian's face, on the verge of telling a secret, then rubbed his jaw and let it slip. "That supply store's got a telegraph office, ya know. Good thing for the lieutenant, I guess. Henley told me he was sendin' off some kinda important telegram 'bout money and railroads or somethin'."

Julian tugged on his bandana and fired off another question. "Was the name Renwick mentioned at all?" Maybe Nathan sent a wire to Mariah's father once he got to Fort Kearny. But what did money and railroads have to do with anything?

"Naw. Can't say Henley said that name. Didn't make a tar-nation bit a sense though when the lieutenant told him to write down somethin' about the moonlight. Henley laughed at him and near got his face torn off. He said the lieutenant lit into him like fire on a bear's ass. All the folks in the supply store kept starin' at him 'cause he was yellin' up a storm."

The news stumped Julian. Names ricocheted in his head. He knew the players in the railroad game. Crocker and Hun-tington with the Central Pacific. Pomeroy with the Santa Fe. Roscoe's tale didn't add up. Then the shine off Murdock's boots broke his thoughts. A sinking feeling in the pit of his stomach warned him Mariah could be in danger. He had to find her before Nathan went too far.

Roscoe's mind wandered off. "Hey, Marquette. You know the woman you're askin' abou—"

Julian cut him off. "Did you see her?"

"Like I said, lots a folks pass through here. Can't say as I saw the lady you're lookin' for." He grinned. "Take my wages for a month if I could get a look at a sweet woman like that. Make it two, and I could show her a real good time." He snorted and wiped his sleeve under his nose.

Wild stories were hard to come by out in the middle of the barren plains. But anybody who ran into the lieutenant always had a tale to tell later. Wherever he went, trouble didn't take long to find him.

Julian heard enough. He needed to get moving. Murdock offered him one of the barracks to spend the night and get rid of the trail dust. He accepted the chance to get cleaned up but said he needed to reach the lieutenant and deliver an urgent message. He didn't tell Murdock about the cargo he was planning to take back. Precious cargo he had to find before it was too late.

CHAPTER 16

A Trail To Nowhere

"DON'T DO IT! It's too dangerous!"

Nathan ignored Mariah's panicked words, and the obvious truth. Trying to force the oxen down the sheer slope was risky enough, but towing a heavy wagon from behind would be pushing his luck. They'd crossed the south fork of the Platte River on their own, without help from Silas or the other men in the wagon train. Nathan was set on doing it alone. In all his misguided certainty, he dismissed Silas as far too slow and too useless, and broke away from the caravan to reach Fort Laramie without delay.

The typhoid fever outbreak was a sorry excuse to make him wait at Fort Kearny for the wagon train to arrive. He didn't care if those families ever made it to Oregon. They were a waste of his time, and he ran out of time.

Glaring down the steep ridge and the obstacle it posed made him fume. He swore under his breath this impasse was just another attempt to destroy his crusade. There was no one left to blame except God Almighty himself.

He climbed up the side of the wagon and shoved the reins

into Mariah's side. The power of his stare choked her with fear. "Do what I tell you, or you'll have *me* to answer to when we get to the bottom of this damn hill." He mounted his horse. "I'll guide the oxen down. You keep hold of the reins."

But the beasts stood their ground against the sharp descent. The wagon teetered on the bluff. Nathan maneuvered his horse between the two oxen and pulled on the yoke beam while his yells rang out across the valley below.

"Use the whip! Now!"

Surefire fury boomed in his voice and made her obey. Her spine jolted straight. Terror paralyzed her. *I don't want to die!* Images flashed before her eyes. *Fanny. Mother and Father. Forgive me. Julian, I never told you that I love you. Dear God, help me—*

She snapped the whip. A violent lunge ripped the reins from her hands. The heavy beasts barreled down the hill as the wagon careened into the abyss. Through the whirlwind of dust, Nathan's figure burst in front of her, and then vanished.

The wagon pitched, hurling her body into the air. She screamed and tumbled backwards through the canvas opening, tossing about like a bucking horse trapped inside a corral.

Without warning, the wagon stopped. She dug out from underneath the blankets and boxes and peered out the back of the wagon.

"No—" What she saw filled her with fright. "Nathan!"

Midway up the slope, he was lying facedown on the ground. His body looked as lifeless as a dead man's. It couldn't be. After all they'd been through? She stared in shock until her mind caught up to what her body already set out to do.

Scrambling over a storage chest, she snatched a blanket, jumped out of the wagon, and clambered up the hill. She dropped to her knees and froze. *Think, Mariah. Think!* Even if every bone in his body was broken, she had to move him. She dug her boots into the hillside and draped the blanket next to him. Her hands trembled, and her voice cracked.

"Nathan, can you hear me? *Please* say something."

He didn't budge. A faint groan would have hinted he was still alive. The hurt he caused her these many months past didn't matter now. She placed her hand on his hip and the other on his shoulder and rolled him toward her onto the blanket. Grasping each corner, she heaved against the force of his weight.

The morning sun pressed down on her back. All sense of time blurred, leaving only the task at hand and the rhythm of her movements. Pull. Breathe. Pull. Breathe. At the bottom of the hillside, she slumped to the ground, drained from exertion. Behind her, the wagon was some distance away under a small grove of trees, and beyond, a spring flowing into a pond. She looked at Nathan's body and thought the worst. What if she was dragging a corpse? She shuddered and got back on her feet. Despair was chasing her down. She had to keep moving.

Each step robbed her of the strength she had left. Her dry mouth felt like a stampede of horses ran through it. Closer in, she heard a gurgling sound. *The pond.* Her life in St. Louis had given her every comfort, but all she craved now was water. A few drops of water.

She tugged on the blanket, grunting through clenched teeth. "You can't die—Nathan. I won't let you—"

Fatigue left her disoriented and her senses too jumbled about. Her feet felt detached from her body, and her muscles ached until no feeling was left in them. Then the sun's heat subsided. A mantle of shade sheathed her back. She was standing under the trees. A godsend. She reached the wagon.

The blanket fell from her hands. She stumbled to the pond and collapsed at its edge, plunging her face into the water. A surge of bubbles churned to the surface. She flung her head back, gasping for air. Wet strands of hair stuck to her face as she cupped water to her mouth and quenched her thirst.

She hurried back to Nathan's side. Her eyes swept over him. Not a tremor or even a whisper of pain. She leaned down and listened for his breathing. It was no use. The water spilling into the pond masked the sounds she tried to hear. But if she touched his skin, she would have her answer. The thought petrified her. *I can't. I just can't.* Fanny was there again, lying on her deathbed. Her hand cold as stone. Mariah shivered. She had to do it. Even if his body was cold, she had to know.

Her hand touched his. It felt warm. In a flurry, she dashed to the wagon for some clean cloths, then filled a bucket with water from the pond. Gently, she wiped the dirt off his face and cleaned the cut on the side of his forehead. But when she lifted his shirt, her heart sank. Bruises. Across his front were dark bruises, a sign his internal injuries were ones she couldn't mend. She wrung out another cloth and wiped his chest.

He groaned.

Her body recoiled. "Nathan, I thought you were—"

She couldn't say the word but felt its desperation turning time into her worst enemy. Hour by hour, his fate rested on her shoulders no matter how little she could do for him.

A spasm twitched his head. At least his neck wasn't broken. That was slight consolation if he was hemorrhaging inside. She cringed at the thought and made haste, collecting twigs and branches for a fire. As the flames burned steady, she kept watch and dared not let those demons take hold, but fastened her hopes on just one. He had to make it till morning.

By sun's first light, her worries turned to relief when she heard him moan. She stoked the fire and heated a pot of water. A quick rummage through the wagon uncovered some hardtack for her to eat. Next to the box of dried biscuits, she spotted a bar of soap and a towel. The scent reminded her to escape to the pond later on.

Nathan's boots were a struggle to get off and caused him more agony than she wanted to give him. She was relieved he started to come round. But as the day wore on, his heightened awareness must have sensed the trauma. By afternoon, she was at her wit's end.

Waiting for Silas to arrive with the wagon train was pointless. There would be no help coming from them. Much time was lost on the trail, trying to beat the fever, though she guessed Silas knew only a miracle would have kept them outrunning it. At least they left Independence early enough to reach the Willamette Valley before winter set in. How unimportant the journey seemed to Fort Laramie since this turn of bad luck could be the end of it all.

Still, it troubled her to face no other possibilities. Being alone meant she had to find another solution. Another way out of this mess.

The tincture. Mother gave her the medicine before she left home. Dr. Collins prescribed the sedative in case the need arose to help Mother sleep. In the days before Fanny died, Mother was fading away right along with her daughter. A few drops put the inevitable out of her mind, enough to get through the night.

Mariah combed one of the chests and found a small box containing the vial and a bottle of her perfume. She peeked inside. Thank goodness the bottles didn't break when the wagon tumbled down the hill. Not much of the tincture was left, but it was something. She tipped the vial into the corner of Nathan's mouth and massaged his lips together, hoping against hope the sedative would work.

All the turmoil since yesterday kept her from noticing the birds chirping high in the trees. As she gazed up at the sight, the blue sky blinded her with its brilliance. If there could ever be heard the sound of complete serenity, she embraced it. The tincture worked. Nathan fell asleep.

A wave of calm came over her, and so did exhaustion. She

was tempted to crawl into the wagon and doze off. Instead, she gathered the towel and soap, together with her hairbrush and a clean dress, and wandered over to the pond. She peeled off every stitch of clothing and tiptoed into the water.

Moans of repose exhaled from her lips. Her nakedness tingled. She took a deep breath and submerged in the water. In a rush of exhilaration, her face erupted through the glassy surface, sending a cascade of water down over her bosom and her hips. Endless miles of riding the trail flowed out through her pores. Standing waist-deep in the pond, she traced the portion of soap over her skin and tossed it onto the bank. Her hands swirled the saponaceous lather through her hair and all over. Delicate ribbons of foam encircled her breasts when she succumbed to the water again.

As she dried herself off and donned her dress, she felt like a new woman, so refreshed. She scrubbed her clothes and wrung them out, then hung them from a tree branch and brushed her hair dry in the breeze.

Contemplating her whereabouts on the plains left her pondering her situation and how dangerous it had become. There was no one to protect her if she faced any threat, even if that meant an encounter with Indians. She was trapped and had no choice but to wait for the wagon train to arrive—unless *they* arrived first.

This was not the time for panic. Nathan needed her. She thought of Jessie and Martha and prayed they were safe. More than anyone, they deserved to reach Oregon and begin a new life. They were too young to die out in this wilderness.

A powerful gust rose up off the plains and almost pushed her over. The treetops started swaying, and the leaves chattered in chorus, creating a deafening noise below. Her thoughts seemed to have summoned the heavens. Dark clouds engulfed the sky, alerting her of a storm headed toward camp. Her hair whipped around her face, and mounting dust caught wings of its own, riding the wind in every direction.

But the approaching storm didn't startle her as much as a distant figure on horseback sidestepping down the hill, not far from where the wagon made its downhill tracks.

She latched on to the tree trunk. Fright coiled around her throat. The wind kept tugging at the hem of her dress, like it was pulling her toward danger. A crescendo of foreboding warned her the end was near.

The masked man closed in. His horse stomped its hooves and reared its head against the power of the storm, with its flaring nostrils drinking the wind. Mariah dug her fingers into the tree trunk. A flash of sanity hit her head on. She saw no point in trying to run. If he pulled a gun on her, she'd be as good as dead.

The intruder dismounted and steadied his hat. He stood close enough to see the terrified look on her face and realized her fear was because of him. He stepped toward her and took the red bandana off his face. Amid the swirling dust, he found her aquamarine eyes and called out to her.

"Mariah—"

Just saying her name again was enough.

But what Mariah saw was impossible—an illusion manifesting itself through the dust in the wind—unless she was losing her mind. She pushed back from the tree and stood an arm's length away. If madness had taken hold of her, she would have still believed it untrue. Yet she could not mistake his eyes, the stormy brown of his eyes, drawing her in and loving her, and telling her she was safe.

Thunder cracked overhead. Neither of them heard it. There was too much to say but no time for words, only their embrace as they fell into each other's arms. Not even the incipient tempest could tear them apart.

Mariah buried her face against Julian's chest. "I can't believe it's you. It's really you—"

Julian hugged her tighter, to the point of delirious. And there he felt his lips caress her hair. He had to be dreaming. Hell had to be a far better place than the life he was living without her. His senses lit on fire. He drew her face up and met her gaze. So much had changed. They knew this was different.

Their breath coalesced and felt warm against their lips. And then they touched, and kissed *their* kiss.

Julian's need swelled as Mariah gave way and let him taste her plea for more. He pulled her closer. Her belly pulsed against his. Through the thin fabric of her dress, he felt her breasts pressing against him.

Mariah quenched his kisses with all her might. The man she knew she could never have was holding her in his arms, giving her the passion trapped in his heart for so long. Her fingers slipped through his hair, for the first time. Oh, how she dreamed of this moment.

"My sweet Mariah—" Julian's words rumbled between their kisses as he cradled her face in his gloved hands. "God, I've missed you." His chest heaved with a hunger. He couldn't quell the urge inside. So much time passed since he last looked into her eyes.

The words she moaned pushed him to the edge. "I want you. Only you . . ."

Their lips tasted of desire, so long suppressed, for the sake of propriety, and for him, for the sake of his railroad. Now their time had come and its intensity eclipsed every emotion they ever felt.

Raindrops started falling and trickled down their faces, parting their kiss long enough for them to gaze into each other's eyes and savor the sweetness they just shared.

They held each other close in one embrace. Julian couldn't let go. Mariah's body molded perfectly into his. Perfectly. He memorized every part of her he touched, and every part that touched him.

Their nascent love affair had just begun when the look in her eyes all at once turned to shock. It startled him. She pushed away, casting her hands against her cheeks and leaving him dazed at her sudden reaction. And then she ran away.

CHAPTER 17

A World Away From Home

*J*ULIAN WATCHED MARIAH run toward the wagon and vanish behind it. His heart pounded through his chest, out of humiliation, or wounded pride. No woman ever set free those pent-up feelings he unleashed on her. And all she could do was run away from him? He felt like he'd been punched in the gut. After all these months, fate brought them together, and in its own twisted way, ripped them apart.

Once before, he did the respectable thing and let her go. Now he couldn't. He tasted her love, and it intoxicated him. But in all his masculine boldness, he stumbled and fell hard. He wanted to be her hero, to be the knight on that black stallion who came to save her. What he found was the truth he couldn't face. He let her get too close, and she let him know she had no place for him in her life. She didn't need a hero.

Always the gambler who never folded when the stakes were high, he just lost the bet of his life. Two years had come and gone, and this is where it got him.

He tried keeping those visits at the Renwick Estate strictly about railroad business, but they were more than that. Then he violated every code he believed in by gambling his heart away with a woman whose passion turned his world upside down.

It was easy, pretending to listen to Mariah's father talk about politics and banking while they sat in the parlour quaffing their brandy. And easy to let his gaze wander outside the room into the grand hall. An occasional nod assured Edmund he had his full attention, until Mariah's perfume drifted into the room and made him unsteady. A subtle glance revealed her perfection. Her face bright as sunlight and her lips waiting for his kiss. Damn, he wanted her. But his railroad left no room for another. It was a safe place to be, sitting in the parlour watching her, without her watching him.

Standing alone with the storm bearing down, he saw how reckless he became surrendering to her love. He deserted that safe place. To love her meant more than living a life without her. They shared something he never felt before. There was no denying he would never be the same.

A clap of thunder jolted his horse. He snatched the reins and tied Chakote up to a tree branch. All the hoof stomping didn't do much good. He was in no mood to run him down. Shifting winds flung sand into his eyes. He jammed his fist against the tree trunk and cursed. The outburst cleared his head, leaving him sure of one thing. Whatever happened, he wasn't going to let Mariah out of his sight.

He followed her path beyond the trees. As he rounded the wagon, he froze in his tracks. His eyes fixated on a body lying on the ground near the campfire. He was wrong thinking Nathan abandoned Mariah. By the looks of it, he was out cold, unless he was dead.

A wagon stranded out in the middle of nowhere, with no help for miles around, didn't leave much in the way of contingencies. He had a clue of their whereabouts from his encounter with a caravan after he crossed the fork in the Platte River. The wagon boss told him to be on the lookout for a grove of trees at the bottom of a ravine. *This must be Ash Hollow.* But if Nathan was in trouble, Fort Laramie was another nine or ten day's ride.

Mariah's attempts at moving her husband spurred him into action. He rushed to the campfire. "I can help."

She nodded. "He's injured."

"I'll carry him."

He lifted Nathan over his shoulder and brought him to the back of the wagon, then hoisted him under the canopy into Mariah's waiting arms. She covered him with a blanket, placing another under his head. Just as Julian climbed inside and huddled next to her, the sky ruptured in a downpour and drummed against the canvas. All they could do was wait for the storm to pass.

Seeing no visible wounds left a puzzled look on Julian's face. "How did he get hurt?"

"He tried to guide the oxen down the hill, but they spooked his horse. It happened so fast." The accident replayed in her mind. "They nearly trampled him to death . . ." Her breath expired.

Julian didn't feel any pity for the man whose life was in Mariah's hands. Only time would tell if things got better or worse. All he wanted was to comfort her. He drew his arm around her back and gazed at her. As much as she couldn't let go of Nathan's fate, he couldn't let go of her.

"I'm sorry about your husband."

He took her hand. She held on with both. But they were shaking, like her voice. "When is it going to be over, Julian? When?" Her body sunk into his side as if she were reliving the entire journey yet couldn't bear the memories of it.

"It's all right. I'm here now." His words warmed a place on her forehead where he breathed in the scent of her skin. "No matter what happens, we'll get through this—together."

"I can't believe you found me . . ."

He held her hand tighter, imagining the taste of her lips

again. So close. Her soft hair soothed him. In the midst of the rain pelting down on the canvas, a calm ensued. She sighed. But then she reacted the way she did before and pushed away from him, overcome by the guilt only a married woman could feel for letting another man console her.

He sized up his thoughts with the facts.

"We're losing daylight. Not much traveling we can do now. Come sunup, we'll take the trail to Fort Laramie." He scanned the inside of the wagon. "Should be enough here to get him stabilized for the ride before we head out."

His concern meant the world to her as her eyes met his. She caressed his hand and let him know he could take over and be her protector. A smile framed his face. He'd take that over a hero any day.

With each task, Mariah found new purpose. She dug through the boxes for some bandages and wrapped them around Nathan's abdomen. A few extra blankets gave him a cushion around his body while a barrel of flour and sugar cocooned him on one side. Julian shifted the two large clothing chests, one to the front and one to the back, balancing the weight in the wagon bed for a steadier ride over rough terrain.

The sky quieted down, leaving a patchwork of vermilion clouds tinged in orange after sunset. Mariah lit a candle and placed it on top of one of the barrels. Little time was left to eat and get some sleep.

Julian jumped out of the wagon. She looked at him, worried. "Where are you going?" The candlelight cast a faint glow on his face.

"I'll sleep by the campfire tonight. Change into some dry clothes. I don't want you getting sick. We've got a long ride ahead of us."

Under the wagon, he noticed a small pile of branches, enough to start a fire and keep it burning into the night. He untied his bedroll from the saddle and set up his usual sleeping arrangement.

In the shades of twilight, he spied a soft flicker under the canopy. His eyes riveted on the silhouette of Mariah's figure. Her movements kept him spellbound as he watched her raise the hem of her dress, revealing the tender curves of her body, from her legs up to her hips, and up to her bosom, and then off. A mere second, her breasts quivered and disappeared under a thin curtain of fabric. Without even trying, she was testing his willpower like she wanted to break him. He threw his saddle on the ground and roamed into the dark.

At daybreak, he hitched the oxen to the wagon and saddled up his horse. He couldn't shake that image of Mariah from his thoughts. All those miles crossing Nebraska Territory, he kept a cool head because Chakote let him speak his mind. And last night was no different.

Starting out on the trail left them no time to lose. Nathan's chances of staying alive could be slim to nothing. Mariah sat ready in the wagon as Julian snapped the whip, setting the oxen in motion. The beasts leaned into the yoke, heaving forward and lowing deep while their hooves pounded the hardpan.

By late morning, a peculiar sight appeared in the distance, forcing a stop to the wagon. Julian squinted above the horizon. Long threadlike strands undulated in the sky, due north of the wagon's westward path. Closer in, a sudden burst of lanky grey birds ascended in graceful unison above the grasslands edging the North Platte River. Their sprawling wing spans astounded him. He called out for Mariah to look outside.

Together, they watched them dance skyward, ever higher, and sensed they were in the presence of a singular wonder. The birds climbed toward a distant flight of Sandhill cranes Julian first spotted. A sea of speckled red caps crowned their heads, and their spindly black legs and white cheeks, dusted like powder, mingled with the faraway echo of a multitude of blaring trumpet calls. It was a sight to behold, starkly breathtaking amid the bleak surroundings, and one neither Julian nor Mariah ever saw before. Not even Boston or St. Louis could transcend such beauty, with all their hustle and bustle and fabricated noise.

Yet the desolation of the overland trail was quick to remind Mariah that her husband's condition was deteriorating. One look at him pushed her hopes deeper into doubt. He woke up, clutching his stomach. Pain contorted lines on his face. His once mystic voice groaned as if death was at his doorstep.

She opened the bottle of tincture and tipped it into his mouth. *It's empty.* She panicked. *What do I do now?* His agony overwhelmed her. She cracked.

"Stop the wagon, stop!"

Julian yanked the reins. "Whoa, there. Whoa." He ran to the back of the wagon, fearing the worst, when Mariah dove into his arms.

"There's no more sedative. I can't stop the pain—" Her mind spun out of control at the unthinkable. "He's too far gone—" She lashed out. "I can't save him—"

Julian tried settling her down. "Mariah. Listen to me. You're doing all you can to help him. But if we don't get to Fort Laramie, he might not survive. We have to ride on."

No matter what he said, she wouldn't let up. He hugged her tight but that triggered her anger which rose up full force and made things worse.

"He's going to die, I know he is!"

She'd reached the brink of hysteria. For her, there was no solution to Nathan's predicament. Death might be days or hours away. All she could do was watch him suffer.

She glared at Julian with unbending eyes, telling him she was ready for a fight. He gave no resistance, only his unwavering constancy, so she could hold on and they could face this fight together. And in his gaze she understood what he was telling her all along. *Trust me, Mariah. Believe me. Love me.*

Then it came, all the love—her love for him—in a flood of emotion pouring out from her eyes. In that moment, something happened which defied explanation. Mariah knew it *was* possible to love Julian, to love him unconditionally, even if they could never be together. He would see her through the rest of this journey, come what may. His strength would be enough to see both of them through.

The heat of his embrace sparked her senses. The memory of his kiss intensified. She leaned her forehead against his chin and surrendered the weight of her worries, letting him take his stand between her and the unknown.

"We'll make it, Mariah. I promise you. We'll make it."

His promise took on greater purpose. Julian had Mariah's husband to think of, and time was running out.

As the days dragged on, another force worked against them. Fatigue strained the trail ride beyond the unbearable. One wagon. Two souls. Another courting death. But no other soul around to save those who needed saving. And no way to escape those hounding thoughts.

The wagon forged ahead, bound for the border of Dakota Territory, while the day's heat grew more intense. Julian squared his hat down low over his brow in a duel against the blinding sun, fixing his line of sight just above the oxen horns. Hours crept by. Beads of sweat trickled into his eyes, blurring his vision. He swabbed his face on his sleeve and tipped his hat up. The approaching milepost startled him.

Shooting into the sky, like a sword ready to commence battle, stood Chimney Rock. The three-hundred-foot spire rising up from the flatlands was a spectacle of nature. An anomaly not seen before anywhere on the trail. Julian heeded the warnings from Silas to be on the lookout for the landmark. From there, he knew how far they needed to go before they reached the fort. *Five more days.*

They stopped for the night and broke camp at dawn.

The terrain bucked the wagon as the wheels traversed the cavernous ruts thousands of wagons carved through the mud. When the trail gave way to patches of smooth ground, Mariah hung on to every second of calm the land gave her.

Nathan's bouts of unconsciousness became more frequent. But each time he woke up, his eyes told her he hadn't forgotten who she was. Holding on to that kind of hate must be worse than the suffering, yet it was enough to rekindle her worries. His look of rage caved in to grunts before his mind shut down again.

In a state between sleep and death, Nathan hovered perilously. Fear was there again, waiting for her. She dreaded the next time he'd wake up, when she'd feel the power of his stare crushing her to a pulp.

Through the canvas opening, she took in the breadth of Julian's shoulders, and the red bandana cinched around his neck. Her heart fluttered. He was her one and only, the cavalier and cowboy of her dreams. As she watched his strong hands steady the reins, she felt the tug of his embrace again. Her breath caught. Julian was by her side. A world away from home. Without him, her life would be in danger. Still, it was up to her to take on the task at hand, the task that needed tending. She was the wife of an army lieutenant. It was her duty.

She gathered the wet cloth and squeezed a few drops of water into Nathan's mouth. He needed hydration, what little she could give him. But he defied her at every turn. Rousing from his stupor, he ripped the rag out of her hand and threw it at her.

"Don't touch me. I don't need your . . ."

The words drained him. He passed out. She uncoiled her fingers bunching her dress and opened his shirt. The bruises looked darker, and his stomach had distended. Internal swelling made her think the worst. She wiped down his chest and covered him up, but would not speak the word she heard once before, after Fanny said goodbye.

CHAPTER 18

Into The Bad Lands

*T*HE INDIAN WARRIOR spied every hideout in the towering bluffs. It was wise to make oneself invisible on the hunt. Bear Wolf had learned the ways of the Lakota Sioux from his father, Chief Conquering Bear, and became a skilled horseman and buffalo hunter on the plains, a sacred place the white man had been crossing with his wagons.

He stood upon the rock formations looming over the valley below. In his mind's eye, he saw each jagged edge in the sandstone rock and every notch in its surface. Even in the dark of night, his cunning stood vigilant. Moving his powerful figure along the rocky ridge, he scouted the valley of the North Platte River with his sharp eyes. Whether the hunter or the hunted, chances of survival improved if one took advantage of high places.

Two women from his tribe exchanged gestures with a tall white man who rode alone into the canyon between the bluffs. Bear Wolf sensed no threat, yet waited a moment longer to be certain. He scanned closer. The white man was in need of something. But he was foolish to leave a wagon stranded so far away.

MARIAH stood in the shallow end of the river and filled the three canteens dangling from her neck. The hem of her dress dripped beads of water that flared out from her circular movements each time she spun around on the lookout for Julian's return. He'd been gone a long while, but in the heat of the midday sun it felt like an eternity.

As the wind soughed through the prairie grass, she listened intently to every sound. Nathan's groans, emanating from the wagon, magnified her anxiety. This was no place for a woman to be alone.

With their supply of water running low, she traipsed back and forth from the river, emptying the canteens into the water barrel. She kept one canteen full and climbed under the canopy. Nathan gave her less grief when she trickled the water into his mouth. Any hopes for his recovery were dimming. His will to live had all but abandoned him.

Since they left Independence, the barrels containing their food supplies weighed down much of the wagon's load. The smoked bacon required one barrel alone for storing the meat, packed in bran, to keep the sun from melting the fat. There was no getting rid of needed rations.

Mother's silverware sprang to mind. Not heavy enough to matter and too sentimental to let go of. She stared at the two rosewood chests laden with her finer clothes and pursed her lips. *Ballroom dancing and afternoon tea at Fort Laramie?* How misguided her notions had been. She dragged the heavier chest to the back and shoved it out of the wagon. A lighter load might quicken their journey. At least the oxen would be pleased with her prudent judgment.

The clothing chest made for a comfortable place to sit as she pulled her sunbonnet on her head and shielded her eyes from the sun. She welcomed the breeze cooling her skin. Pondering the distance left to reach the fort, she sat inattentive to her surroundings.

In the shadow of the bluffs behind her, a cloud of dust erupted off the plains. Through the billowy haze raced an Indian brave on horseback charging toward her. The rising rumble of hooves alerted her to danger. She turned around and bolted up. The warrior closed in. His long black hair gleamed like obsidian.

All the lessons she taught her school children about life on the western frontier were from the confines of her classroom. Now she faced this land in the flesh and with a heart that pounded as loud as the hooves.

The sight of the warrior terrified her. *Oh God. He's going to kill me.* She should have heard him coming sooner. The thought incensed her. *I don't even have a gun.* Caution and keen hearing honed her senses since the start of the trail ride. This time, they failed her.

Her sweaty hands stuck to her dress, and her boots felt rooted in the ground. *Sweaty hands.* She remembered the wind cooling her skin, but the direction it was blowing kept the sound of the warrior's horse downwind from where she sat. It was too late.

She turned to run when a voice shouted her name.

"Mariah!"

Fright blinded her from seeing Julian riding behind the Indian brave. Two women on another horse followed farther back. The warrior dismounted and staked his claim in front of her. She panicked. Julian lunged at her and grabbed her arm. His look told her to trust him. But every bone in her body kept telling her to run as her eyes flashed between the man she knew and the man who made her fear for her life.

She gasped. "What's happening? Why are they here?"

The warrior's stare pierced like a knife. His daunting figure quaked the ground under her feet. Stirring at his side, his spirited horse reared its head and stomped its hooves until a command was given and the defiance stopped. The brave turned his gaze, scanning the plains. His chin jutted out. Proud. The trail of the white man brought tales of savages that fed the fears of those who believed but did not know. His voice thundered to make them understand.

"Lakota Sioux not fight. White man come. Want help."

Bear Wolf resented the aid the Sioux women offered the white man. Yet their token of goodwill was the way of his people. Still, he would never forget how his father had been shot in the back, not just by white men, but soldiers. The killing of Chief Conquering Bear started a war in 1854—a wasted war that began endless violence.

He set his eyes on Mariah. "You. Speak now."

His powerful presence frightened her. Questions kept swirling in her head. Why was Julian with these Indians? And why did he want their help? She was petrified of them. Fear could do strange things to the mind. Bizarre thoughts ran amok.

Julian had been searching the area for another route to Dakota Territory when he encountered the natives in the canyon below Scotts Bluff. The trail along the river was blocked up ahead by a swath of rugged bad lands, cutting off their route to the fort. Luck had him stumbling upon these strangers who were more familiar with the land in these parts than he was. If he could just convince Mariah they were no threat. But he wouldn't let go of her until he was sure.

"I asked them to come. They may be able to help Nathan." He felt her arm give way, a sign that she understood why these outsiders were in their midst.

She looked at Bear Wolf with her hands clenched at her side. "My husband is badly hurt. Can you help him?"

Bear Wolf shook his head. "No. No pejula."

Mariah furrowed her brow. The Sioux women approached and dismounted their horse. A thought struck her. *Silas.* He gave her some sage advice in case the caravan ever needed help from the Indians. Those Lakota and Cheyenne words he taught her took on a new purpose.

She dashed to the wagon and climbed inside, then ran back clutching her diary. Flipping through the pages, she spied phrases of greeting and exchanging names, and for sickness or the fever. She turned another page and spotted the word.

"*Pejula.* That means medicine. He said no medicine." The Sioux women walked toward her. Could they help? She glanced back at her diary. "Wa . . . si . . . chu." She pressed her hand against her forehead. "I think that's right. Wa . . . sichu. Owa sicha."

If she said a man was wounded, why did their faces erupt in smiles? One of the women pulled out a small leather pouch from behind her buckskin covering and patted it with the palm of her hand.

"Han. Wasichu, owa sicha." The Sioux woman's eyes opened wide. An eagerness echoed in her voice. "On'glak . . . capi. Hitunkala . . . nakpala." She opened the pouch and revealed some herbs.

Mariah's look of gratitude had them leapfrogging into action. They heated a pot of water, then crushed and steeped the herbs, making a warm tonic. Nathan grimaced at the taste but swallowed without a fight. One of the women scooped out the pungent mash settled at the bottom of the pot. She smeared it across his stomach and over the cut on the side of his face, above the scar from the Rebel's bayonet.

This last effort seemed futile if he didn't survive. Mariah refused to think about death. Hope lifted her spirits, and she clung to it with every breath.

While the Sioux women focused their attention on the wounded man, Bear Wolf was nowhere to be found. Mariah marked his movements when he returned to camp and left again, steering his horse in another direction. His actions went on until he searched a great distance across the range for what must have been the buffalo. Their multitudes once roamed the land but were vanishing with every change of the seasons. Thousands of emigrants in need of food on the Oregon Trail were partly to blame. Many days and many more braves had to hunt them now.

Dusk draped the sky, forcing the Sioux natives to set up camp with the travelers. By morning, it was clear the route the expedition would take.

"Maka Sichu. Follow river, not good."

Bear Wolf pointed to the south, away from the river. His gestures described a ridge of high terrain they'd have to cross. Julian recalled the bad lands he saw the day before. He nodded to Bear Wolf.

The Sioux women said their goodbyes and took their horse in a canter to the north. Mariah watched their figures shrink in the distance, then shifted her eyes to Bear Wolf. She still did not trust him and feared he sensed her apprehension by the way he stared at her in silence. Yet he stayed with them and gave the signal to load up. He waved his hand, guiding the wagon in the direction of Mitchell Pass.

Julian felt uneasy without the river for his compass. Heading south instead of west had him wondering if they'd ever reach the fort. The sheer uphill climb kept him fixated on the trail and navigating the wagon through a long narrow gap. The slightest sway, left or right, and the wagon scraped against the walls of rock.

As they lumbered toward the summit, the air was getting thinner and breathing was labored. Hours limped by under the strain of the hot sun. By late afternoon, they crested the pass. A shout from Bear Wolf halted the wagon.

Mariah peered out the canvas opening. "Why have we stopped?"

Bear Wolf reined in on his Mustang. "Follow path. You go now."

He drew an arc in the air, warning their encounter with the river would come at the end of the Mitchell Pass descent. Julian tipped his hat and turned the wagon northwest. Bear Wolf watched until he could see them no more.

From his vantage point atop the summit, he scanned the lofty bluffs and the immensity of the flatlands stretching to the distant horizon. All was silent but for the brisk wind, weaving through the river valley below. The sound carried the voice of the spirits on its wings, telling him to hold fast to this sacred land the Sioux had been given by their creator. A sacred land lost could only foreshadow the demise of his people.

The wagon trekked beyond the mountain pass as the sure-footed oxen moved slow and steady, traversing the unstable bedrock. On the downhill slope, the widening trail leveled out to fertile terrain, and their first sign of the river.

Julian adjusted his bearings and focused his mind on getting back on course. But all the jostling over the summit shook some sense into his thoughts about his job in Boston. He figured Dunnigan was expecting a telegram from him. One that was long overdue. Telling his boss he came this far to save a woman he was in love with would make him the laughingstock of the entire Union Pacific board of directors. He'd have to drum up an excuse by the time they reached the fort.

What excuse? He knew he'd been too reckless in his actions. His hands twisted the reins. Maybe he liked being reckless, and to hell with everyone else. A snap of the whip shut out thoughts of the railroad. Ash Hollow was on his mind. And that kiss. He needed to tell Mariah how he felt. He needed to show her.

No sooner had the noise of the creaking axles brought him back to the trail than Mariah called out for him to stop the wagon. He yanked off his hat and gloves and raked his fingers through his hair, letting the breeze cool him off.

Down by the footboard, he grabbed one of the canteens and peered inside the wagon. *Damn.* Every time he looked at her, she kept nudging him to the edge, like she was daring him to make his move. He dragged his sleeve over his brow and glanced at her again. Those words they knew could never be spoken burned in their gaze.

He opened the canteen and offered it to her. "I thought you might be thirsty."

She smiled and reached for the flask. Her hand touched his and weakened his grip. That restless feeling ambushed him. The look in his eyes told her he wanted to give her more than a taste of water. He guided the canteen to her lips and held it steady while she drank. When she eased away, a strand of liquid slid down her throat and beyond her neckline. He tightened his grip.

There was no point in hiding the truth standing between him and the woman he loved. Anyone with half a mind could tell Nathan was as good as dead. Out here in the wilds, instincts rode roughshod, leaving no place for chivalry, for it was long dead too. To survive, one needed to take, and the taking was so easy, and the moment so right.

Tension flexed along his jawline. He tugged on the canteen. Mariah drew closer. So did he. Close enough to brush the wisps of hair away from her face. She surrendered to his touch. Her hands sunk into her lap. The sound of her voice soothed his restlessness.

"How can I ever repay you for all you've done for me?" Her eyes meant every word she said.

He leaned in and kissed her cheek, and whispered, "You already have." Gazing at her, he said, "I'll always be here for you. For as long as it takes, I'll be here."

Then he faced the trail and drank deeply from the canteen that just touched her lips. A pull on the brake lever set the wagon in motion. Fort Laramie was waiting.

CHAPTER 19

The End Of The Trail

IT COULD HAVE been a mirage, a place that didn't exist, since for hundreds of miles in every direction nothing did exist. The tedium of the trail had a way of creating distortions in the mind. But not this time. Signs of life erupted on the barren landscape. It was Fort Laramie.

The outpost hummed with the brio of a city back East. Horses and wagons crisscrossed the garrison while soldiers and emigrants milled about. The flurry of activity buoyed the newcomers off the Oregon Trail. It was a sight unlike any they'd seen since Fort Kearny. For the pioneers, their journey was not over, but for Julian and Mariah, Fort Laramie was the end.

Mariah took comfort in a renewed sense of hope she hadn't felt since the Sioux women cared for Nathan in the shadow of Scotts Bluff. Her spirits rose higher as the fort's doctor approached the wagon and ordered the soldiers to transport the lieutenant directly to the hospital. She didn't need to explain to him that his new patient had serious injuries. She could tell by the look on his face.

DESPITE bouts of unconsciousness and the incessant agony, Nathan sensed a change of routine, and an incredible stillness beneath him. His willpower exploded. *The fort.*

This was not the time to concede defeat, but to spit in the face of death like he did countless times during the war. He cut down enough Confederates to know the white man's poison coursing through his veins bled out of every Rebel he massacred on the battlefield. If he had the chance, he would've cut down every Yank just the same.

He could taste it again—the fight—the biggest battle of his life to beat the white man at his game and take back what belonged to him. Ahyoka's spirit would come to see that her son was worthy to be a full-blooded Cherokee.

MARIAH refused to leave the hospital. She had to hear the doctor say the words she prayed would promise a recovery. Not a year passed since their wedding in St. Louis, and now this. When was it going to end? What had gone so wretchedly wrong?

Abandoned heart. Abandoned home. Abandoned life. The pages of her future were not even written, but her fate was already sealed. It would be easy to blame others, to blame circumstances that put her here, yet choices were made along the way, and she alone chose to make them. For better. For worse.

Somehow forgiveness found its way into her heart. But she would never forget Nathan's spite, his hurtful words, and his virulent act claiming her for his wife. As the doctor disappeared down the hall, silence converged around her, like the lull before a storm. Painful memories made forgetting painfully impossible. True love was all she ever wanted. All she hoped to give a man. An honorable man who only wanted to love her back.

> *Julian . . .*
> *How did you find me?*
> *Why did you come?*
> *I looked at you in disbelief but denied the impossible.*
> *You are my protector, till forever.*
> *In my heart you'll always be.*
> *Your lips tasted of desire.*
> *I couldn't breathe. I didn't want to.*
> *Looking for a sign.*
> *Desperate to turn back time.*
> *I yearn for the love you can never give me.*
> *Even now . . .*

THE end of the line had come for the railroad magnate. Julian did what he set out to do. He had no business comforting Mariah at the hospital. Just the business of building his railroad.

He headed for the telegraph office and dispatched a wire to Mariah's father posthaste, telling him he found his daughter and that she was safe. But sending a telegram to his boss with an update on his whereabouts had to wait.

As he paced the boardwalk outside the building, he mulled over the terrain on their ride into the fort. Something about the lay of the land didn't look right. Call it a hunch, or feeling too beat up from the trail, but he couldn't figure it out. Was it the new fork of the Laramie River that veined the grasslands? Maybe the outlying hills to the west, a sign of the end of the High Plains. Or just the jumbled piles of rock studding the rising plateau.

Then it hit him. The excuse he needed for coming this far had been staring him in the face for miles. *The gap.*

Before he drew up the maps for the train route, he relied on reports from mountain men scouting Dakota Territory. They marked an area west of the fort called the Black Hills which forced him to move the track line farther north through the Powder River Valley. But when he drove the wagon into camp, he spied a narrow gap in the Black Hills, and beyond, flat terrain. A shorter route for the railroad.

He could hear his boss already.

You must be joking. Change the fundamental path of the railroad line? That'll stir up government meddling and drive up costs. Bad idea, Julian, unless you have a damn good reason.

Julian didn't have a good reason, and he sure as hell didn't want to rile his boss. At least Dunnigan wouldn't question why he came this far.

Building the railroad was a messy business. Company rivalries had turned cutthroat, pitting the Central Pacific and Union Pacific against each other in their quest to link the tracks between Council Bluffs and Sacramento. Bragging rights were on the line for the company that laid the most track. But Julian was convinced the Transcontinental Railroad would get built because of it.

The people's railroad. The truest measure of a nation's promise. For the people of America.

If only Julian's ally could see the unfolding of the country's greatest feat. He kept the letter in his desk that President Lincoln sent him two weeks before he was assassinated.

On April 1, 1865, the president wrote, "If I can leave one legacy from my presidency, it will be the Transcontinental Railroad, and its track of iron rails tethering our fragile nation together, from east to west, into one common purpose again."

With the future of the United States at stake, someone had

to have the guts to see the railroad project through. Someone who didn't give a damn about the glory. Julian vowed to keep his promise to the president until the job was done.

As he leaned against the portico post outside the telegraph office, he scanned the fort's surroundings. The rising heat warned of a hot summer ahead. He tugged the brim of his hat below his brow, then rolled up his sleeves and nudged his fingers into his pockets. His forearms flexed in the sun. He let out a breath. The grueling trail ride was over. Nothing but idle time left now. He cleared his head for some rational thinking that was long overdue, a task he hadn't put to much use since he left Council Bluffs. He stood there for a spell, feeling the warm zephyr breezing off the plains. All too fast he realized he was in no mood for rational thinking.

The quiet dinner at the cottage pulled him back into the past, and the unspoken words he and Mariah never shared. And then Ash Hollow happened. Those memories sustained him, and he felt them magnified a hundredfold in their embrace. As he framed her face in his gloved hands and beheld her perfection, he was certain she couldn't be a figment of his imagination. When they kissed, that wall collapsed. He couldn't stop. But it was a mistake. A reckless lapse of judgment on his part. He traveled the High Plains to find her and protect her. To leave without her and keep on loving her had to be enough.

A gust of wind swept over the fort with an urgency on its wings, telling him he'd soon have to head back home to Boston, alone.

He sauntered along the edge of the garrison and got a feel for the place. Its lack of fortified walls reminded him of Fort Kearny, though he heard enough accounts from Captain Murdock that Indians never attacked the outposts.

The grounds were quiet. He headed to the corral for a check on his horse. As he walked behind the mess hall, voices echoed near the back door. He gave a sidelong glance. Two women had their eyes on him. They watched his every move while they brushed their tousled hair away from their faces, preening themselves at random.

"Howdy, stranger."

"Hey there, cowboy."

He tipped his hat and smiled. They sighed as he passed by. Around camp, a handful of ladies had their pick of the men. But Maggie and Kate never saw a cowboy like him. A stranger whose strong build and long stride played up his swagger something fierce. That Easterner looked as rugged as any cowboy in these parts, and more of a man than they'd ever seen out West.

Julian ignored the attention. For a second, he swore he was back in Boston. Dunnigan's daughter never made it easy on him. Trifling with the heart seemed to be Annabelle's specialty, and he indulged her to protect his railroad and stay in the good graces of his boss. But thinking about Boston didn't matter. Mariah did. One look was all it took to bring the railroad magnate to his knees. *To hell with doing the right thing. The respectable thing. To hell with it all. I want you, Mariah. I wanna make love to you.*

With no trail left to follow and no destination driven to reach, Julian's thoughts consumed him, and he let it happen unabated. A rocky outcropping beyond the fort caught his eye. He saw his chance. When evening fell upon the encampment, he'd make his escape with Mariah and quench every drop of his thirst. He'd give her all his love until morning came. *No more waiting.* He squinted into the blinding sun and walked the long route to the corral.

THE fort's commander arrived at the hospital demanding to see the new patient. Colonel Thomas Moonlight had no tolerance for dealing with civilian doctors, most of all, Dr. Riddler, and that cocky tone he bandied about.

"I gave him some pain medication a few hours ago, Colonel. He needs to rest and can't see anyone. You'll have to come back later."

Moonlight stood tall and lanky, with a penchant for throwing his weight around, what little he had. "It's no surprise, Riddler, you and I don't like each other." Not addressing the doctor by his title was deliberate and intended to insult the man. "Since that damn war stole all my best soldiers, including my doctors, I don't have any choice but to put up with you."

Their confrontation outside the lieutenant's room had them staring each other down, waiting to see who would give in first. Moonlight had no intention. "That said, get out of my way."

His brow puckered. Why didn't the doctor heed his orders? He was the officer in charge, for God's sake. *You're just like the lieutenant.* He clashed with Nathan's insubordinate behavior in one too many battles he led during the war. No sooner had he ordered a retreat than the lieutenant did an about-face and rushed the troops back into the winning fight.

But what the colonel lacked in battle tactics he made up for with his vanity, a man so enamored with himself, he believed his decisions were always right and his judgment always sound. His victories claimed as his alone. Anyone who contradicted him was the real imbecile, including Riddler who hadn't budged an inch.

"How long are you going to keep me waiting, *Doctor?*"

Riddler crossed his arms and huffed. "Fine. Ten minutes. No more."

Moonlight entered the room, stopping at the foot of the bed. He glared at the lieutenant. Why wasn't he awake? *Inferiors never show any respect.* He moseyed toward the window, riveting his eyes on the hutch against the wall. The intricacy of the carved wood fascinated him. He pulled off his glove and fingered the scrollwork. *I'll arrange to have this brought over to my quarters.*

On the hutch rested a metal tray lined with surgical instruments. He plopped his folder on top and chuckled to himself. His officer's quarters could be the most lavish of any accommodations west of the Missouri River. Another worthy anecdote he could brag about. Never mind that he ordered routine inspections of the Oregon Trail, east and west of the fort, for any possessions the pioneers tossed out of their wagons to lighten their loads. He had full control of his entire garrison and kept his image as polished as the buttons gleaming down the front of his uniform.

He strode back to the bed and yanked the other glove off his hand. Impatience stoked his temper with every passing second. He whacked his gloves on the bedrail.

"Damn it, Lieutenant. I don't have all day."

Nathan's eyes rolled open at the sudden jarring against the bed. A blurred figure appeared in front of him. His mind fixated on the lack of pain around his stomach. Relief overcame him, and he drifted back to consciousness with ease.

"Lieutenant Lawton. It's been a while since Omaha City. Good to see you again."

"Likewise, Colonel." Nathan pulled himself up in bed and raked his fingers through his hair.

Moonlight wasted no time. "I believe we have some business to attend to regarding the future of Wyoming Territory. Do you have the needed funds we agreed on?"

Nathan never did like Moonlight's starched way of talking. He found his question premature. "You're getting ahead of yourself, sir. The funds won't be available until my promotion papers have been signed first."

Moonlight grinned. "I'm one step in front of you." He walked over to the hutch, flipped open the folder, then grabbed the document and waved it in Nathan's face. "Congratulations,

Captain Lawton. We'll reserve the formal ceremonies of your promotion for another day, shall we?"

"My thoughts exactly. We've got more important business to deal with. First off, the peace treaty. You and I know, without a treaty between the Sioux and the white man, the bureaucrats in Washington won't organize Wyoming Territory. Until that happens, there's no chance for future statehood. We need to push for the peace treaty now." Nathan felt a surge of power with every word he spoke. "Aside from the Sioux and Cheyenne, every stinking Indian tribe in the region has been rounded up on a reservation. It's only a matter of time before it happens to them."

Moonlight nodded but sensed an abrupt shift in their conversation, as though he was outranked by the lieutenant who was acting like some kind of general. Still, he had every confidence in the man's ability to mastermind their plans. He let Nathan go right on talking.

"You've come through with my promotion, but you better make damn sure the money's in the right hands. I want guarantees. If I don't get the territorial governorship, the deal's off." He gritted his teeth and softened his tone. "Let's get a new peace treaty signed so both of us can get our own civilian promotions. Agreed?"

Moonlight concurred wholeheartedly. "Agreed."

Months of waiting kept Nathan's plans tossing and turning in his head. Now he'd reached Fort Laramie. His time had come. His crusade had begun. He liked the sound of it already. *Governor Lawton.*

The hero from the War of the Rebellion could do no wrong. Edmund Renwick, the patriot, saw the lieutenant as the effectual savior of his banking empire from the hands of the Confederates. For his valor, Nathan deserved the governorship. So what if his Union glory was a farce from the start, blinding old man Renwick right down to his sorry-ass soul. The ignorant bastard let him walk right on in and claim his daughter, no matter the sins he left in his wake.

Moonlight's grumbling snapped him out of his thoughts.

"Don't count your promotion too soon, Lieutenant. Dealing with these savages has become the bane of my political ambitions. Our last meeting was a dismal failure."

Nathan locked his eyes on Moonlight. He had no time for talk of losing one's ground. "You might outrank me, Colonel, but when it comes to buyoffs, I hold the cards. You better tidy up your mess with the Indians so our politicians in Washington can vote their conscience. Do I make myself clear, *sir*?"

Tolerating incompetents riled him. He stifled his temper and held his tongue. There was too much at stake to let the colonel get under his skin. Those key votes from Washington would favor his appointment as the first Territorial Governor of Wyoming, and give him control over the route of the northern railroad. But he couldn't deny his link to Moonlight existed solely because of the colonel's connections. Granted, Moonlight could sway his own political future. So be it. Rumors of Nebraska statehood promised the election of a new governor, and that suited the colonel just fine.

CHAPTER 20

Goodbye Is Never Enough

PRIVATE KETCHUM WAS assigned the task of unloading the wagon and escorting Mrs. Lawton to her new residence at Quarters A. Unlike the rows of barracks adjacent to the parade grounds, Quarters A was a small house with a veranda surrounding it on three sides. Senior officers were given the finest accommodations at Fort Laramie.

Mariah stepped onto the porch and walked inside. As she looked around the front room, she felt confined. Living in a house and sleeping on a bed was going to take some getting used to again. How mixed up her life became since she left St. Louis.

Earlier, she roamed the garrison but couldn't find the fort's commanding officer to make her introductions and tell him about Nathan's injuries. Even Julian seemed to have vanished, leaving her without any sense of direction. Then reality sunk in. Her long journey was over.

She wandered into the bedroom and dug into the clothing chest Private Ketchum hauled in from the wagon. One by one, she hung her dresses on the wooden pegs in the armoire and placed her undergarments on the shelves. The woolen dresses Stella gave her looked a far cry from the ones she brought from home. Feeling the coarse fabric brought back the ordeal from the trail. A wave of angst swept over her. She had nowhere left to go. It was time she faced her new life out West—the life of a married woman, very much alone.

A knock startled her. She walked into the front room and opened the door. Private Ketchum stood there with his shoulders drooped.

"I'm real sorry, ma'am. The barrel a flour was way too heavy."

Behind the wagon, the powdery wheat lay strewn across the ground. Ketchum promised a quick cleanup, but Mariah's tired expression told him she didn't care.

"It's all right. Whatever you can salvage can be brought to the mess hall with the other rations."

He looked down at the box clutched in his arms, then glanced at her with a stumped look on his face. "When the barrel busted open, I found this at the bottom. I thought you might be wantin' it."

Her low spirits, masked by her weary face, left her with no inkling of what to do with the box. She pressed her hand against her forehead and sighed. "It's been . . . a long day. Just put it in the bedroom near the armoire."

After Ketchum left the house, she thought back to Independence and her attempts at checking the wagon supplies before they headed out for Kansas. But the memory was all a blur, clouded by the passage of time, and more, by a lightheaded feeling. *I need to get something to eat.*

The last rays of sunlight cast shadows across the parade grounds as she trudged to the mess hall. She frowned at the idea of walking into a madhouse full of soldiers huddled in a feeding frenzy. A place not befitting a woman who wanted some peace and quiet now. Hunger overruled her doubts. She opened the door and stepped inside.

Memories of the saloon in Independence struck her head on. Eyes darted at her from every corner of the room. All she could do was stare back. It was like a shootout with no guns. Whatever they wanted, their looks told her she had it to give. *Leave me alone. Quit staring at me.* She spotted an empty table near the door and sat down, fixing her eyes straight ahead.

Any regrets for setting foot in the mess hall came too late. A barrage of taunts left her trapped in a corner. The door was right there, but she couldn't get out. Her body froze from the onrush. She clamped her eyes shut, protesting under her breath for the noises to stop. If all the uproar was their way of giving her a hearty welcome to the fort, they did a fine job of it.

A bang on the table snapped her eyes open. She glared at a pair of hands splayed in front of her, scuffed and grimed with dirt. Whoever she was up against had her dreading the worst.

The hands inched toward her. The voice chafed against her face.

"Hey, purdy lady. I've been waitin' a long while to see a fine woman like you show up in this hellhole. I think I might be dreamin'."

Mariah flashed her eyes at the soldier. His smirk made her cringe. She sprang to her feet, but he pulled her back down and squeezed her wrists so tight the blood throbbed in her fingers.

Her writhing goaded him. "You sure are a feisty woman." He lunged over the table and shoved her against the wall.

She shrieked. "Get away from me—" His stale breath turned her stomach.

Sharkey Quitman had a reputation around camp for causing a ruckus, but he didn't take too kindly to being interrupted when he was in the thick of it. He ignored the figure bursting through the door, demanding he release the woman.

"You heard the lady. Now *back off.*"

The voice sounded like a no-good thug trying to cut in on

his prize. He narrowed his eyes at the stranger. "I aim to get what I want, mister. So why don't you just piss off."

Sharkey relished the scared look on Mariah's face and the hold he had on her, and those sweet apple dumplings behind her scanty dress. Damn, he could almost touch 'em. A sure-fire hot streak rammed down his pants. He grabbed her by the neck and moved in on her.

"Gimme a taste a that ruby saucebox, sweet thing. Big man Sharkey ain't got all day now."

Julian swung around the soldier's backside and drilled his hands into his shoulders. Sharkey hurled sideways and crashed into a table.

"If you touch her again, I'll have your hide. Only next time, I won't be so nice about it. Understand?"

The private staggered to his feet and tripped toward the door. Julian let him pass. But he didn't see it coming. Sharkey spun around and hit him with a right cross, knocking him to the floor. Blood trailed from the side of his mouth.

Sharkey, who stood twice his size from side to side, spat in his hands, rubbed them together, and started punching the air. "I guess you picked the wrong man to fight with, mister. Is that all you got in you?" He sneered and looked at his comrades. "Hey, boys. Ain't this the yellow-bellied tenderfoot from back East we been hearin' about from Maggie and Kate?"

Wild laughter bellowed across the mess hall. Everyone chanted for *Sharkey! Sharkey!*

He didn't let up. "You're just one, weak, sorry son of a bitch who can't even put up a good fight. Ain't that right boys!"

The chanting grew louder. "Sharkey! Sharkey!"

But his boasting had him blinded. Julian faked a roll onto his side like he was done for, then hooked his boot behind Sharkey's and yanked it forward. Sharkey teetered. A second later, Julian barreled into his gut, slamming him against the wall. The private belched out a grunt and doubled over. Julian heaved him up straight and finished him off with a fist to his jaw. His head snapped back, and he dropped to the floor.

The mess hall turned quiet, as if a church full of congregants were praying for the Lord's intervention. None of the soldiers looked like they had any plans to take up the fight. An exodus left the mess hall deserted.

Julian glanced at Mariah. "Are you all right?"

She nodded. "Yes. Are you—?"

"Not here. Let's talk somewhere else." He guided her outside, around the back of the building.

She stopped and gazed at him with a worried look on her face. "You're bleeding. Let me help you."

He shrugged. "It's nothing."

"I want to help. It's the least I can do."

She lifted the hem of her dress and tore a piece of fabric from the lining. Gently, she dabbed the blood. He winced but held steady while she tended his wound. Standing close, he fell lost in her aquamarine eyes.

Her question rocked him.

"Can we go for a walk?"

"I'd like that." He could tell something was on her mind.

They wandered along the Laramie River on the outskirts of the fort. No words were spoken between them. Mariah stepped to the river's edge and dipped the cloth into the water, then wiped the last trace of blood away. The bruise on Julian's cheek was a reminder of what he did for her. She cooled it with her hand. He winced again.

"Be still," she whispered.

Her voice mesmerized him. The pain disappeared. Her dress brushed dovelike against him. He gathered the fabric in his hands and held on. The end awaiting them bowed gracefully to this moment as they shared their forbidden love through eyes of devotion.

Julian didn't need to ask Mariah where she wanted to go.

She hinted with her eyes when she looked beyond the fort toward a rocky hillock. Each step they took sounded of time ticking away, but all he thought was that his chance had come to be with her.

She interrupted the silence. "No matter where I've gone and what I've done, trouble seems to follow. And somehow, you've been there to protect me."

They walked ahead toward the hills until they reached the outcropping. She left his side and braced her hands against a boulder, trying to ground herself and her scattered thoughts. Staring at the open plains, she fought to put into words how she felt since that autumn day when they both stood under the gazebo. Every fiber in her being resisted him, but she let him into her heart anyway, not knowing he would give her the strength she needed to carry on.

She turned around, hesitating. "I know you'll be leaving to go back home to Boston." She couldn't face the truth. Not yet. "A lot has happened between us. There's so much I want tell you." She had to show him she still believed in the impossible. Her resolve formed a smile to warm his heart. It was the least bit of gratitude she could give him.

Julian's voice rumbled to her core. Maybe for the last time. "Words aren't enough, Mariah."

They had nothing left to hide. Their love, soon to be lost, now bid its farewell.

He stood before her and cradled her face in his hands. His touch made her hold tight as she uttered the words he'd written on that piece of paper.

"I know we can't have what isn't ours to share, but I will never forget . . . your kiss."

Their final moments called out for Julian to share his love with Mariah, and risk it all for the woman he would never see again. Their last goodbye drew ever nearer, and they felt its heartrending presence when they suddenly embraced.

Mariah wept her eternal love song against Julian's masculine build as though she would never stop. And she would never see his emotion welling up, his misty eyes a telling sign of his undying love for her. He could have loved her then with all his heart, but the ache inside overwhelmed him. This was the end.

He hugged her boldly in his arms and protected her with his manly armor. His face disappeared in her silky wonder, where he closed his eyes and inhaled its honeyed scent until his lungs burned. The forbidden words he kept secret for so long slipped achingly from his lips.

"I love you. God, how I love you."

There was nothing more to say. Nothing more to do. Only to remember, and hold on.

CHAPTER 21

The Beast Within

AGAINST THE DUSKY SKY, the faint light from the lantern flickered on the parlour walls. The room was filled with fine furnishings but none Mariah called her own. None that would ever make her feel like she was home again. Given time, she hoped this place might give her a reason to go on and make some sense of her new life. Perhaps caring for Nathan could be that reason, and give him a chance to care for her again too.

It was hard to think. In the distant hills, in Julian's arms, she longed to stay there forever. She had walked back to the fort alone. He wanted it that way. There would be no more tears to look upon, just their memories of being together.

When she welcomed his first glance more than two years ago, she was unaware of his intentions. Her single-mindedness only saw what overshadowed her life. A broken family. A bitter war. Her dream of becoming a teacher did make Mother and Father proud, and gave her a chance to mend her life, until Nathan came to call.

Their perfect marriage rekindled happiness, and along with

it, blind love. A masquerading man he was. Impostor extraordinaire. Devious manipulator of the heart. A man who convinced her she was incapable of loving anyone when she couldn't love him. What she was blind to, besides Nathan's alleged love, was the love hidden in Julian's heart all those years ago. She had missed her chance and didn't even know it.

As time passed, and Julian returned to St. Louis, she couldn't even remember him when they met at the train station. So much time slipped away. Then a fire ignited within her, blazing with a passion she never felt. She tried to keep things simple and avoid complications, and heartache. Now the heartache was more than she could bear.

How she wanted to believe the wisdom of her mother's words. *The passage of time is the greatest healer.* If time did have a way of healing the sorrow in a woman's heart, Mariah was certain it wouldn't happen to her. Too lost in her own sadness at the thought of Julian leaving tomorrow, she heard his voice again, professing those forbidden words. The secret he never revealed to her at the cottage, fearing its destructive power if he did, had fallen from his lips. Julian loved her.

She collapsed into the chair, bumping the arm against the table. The lantern wobbled back and forth, lulling her into a trance she didn't want to escape. Each moment she spent with Julian was there again. His smile. His touch. She drew her arms together and imagined his embrace. Every scrap of memory she had would not release him. *I'll never forget you.*

What Julian did was the act of a valiant man. He crossed the High Plains and found her and brought her to Fort Laramie, knowing his journey back home would be alone without her.

Nathan owed his life to Julian, but he'd never admit it. He despised the man. How ironic. She had no other explanation. His cruel words. His lust for women. The violent hand that struck her into submission. All of it meant he despised her too. If Dr. Riddler promised a full recovery for her husband, they would be together sharing the same house, and the same bed.

Exhaustion overwhelmed her. She trudged into the bedroom. Her emotions twisted at the sensation of intimacy, reminding her of the married stranger she'd soon be with again.

The weight of Julian's goodbye was too much. She toppled onto the bed and buried her face in the covers. Her suffocating breaths numbed her to the core while the beat of her heart echoed hollow inside. She turned her head, lying there breathless and bleary-eyed, seeing a wall painted white. A blank canvas full of emptiness.

Her gaze sunk to the floor and to the wooden box smeared in flour residue. For the longest time she stared at it, as if possessed by a force that all at once made her question what she was really looking at. She sat up on the side of the bed. The memory of being home washed over her. She'd seen the box before. A long time ago.

She knelt down and unlocked the two gold latches. The feeling of being up to no good spooked her. She snatched her hands away like she just touched fire. Childhood secrets started dancing in her head. Her mind willed her hands, inch by inch, toward the box again. The lid tugged against her fingers and thudded against the wall.

Her body recoiled. She gasped at what she saw inside. Money. Newly minted bills all banded together in small bundles. It was no accident the box ended up at the bottom of the flour barrel. Someone must have put it there.

Too many questions left her mind swirling in doubt. But this wasn't the first time she aroused suspicions about her husband. Now she faced a part of his life he kept hidden from her. A part of his past that filled her with dread. There had to be a reason.

She canted her head and read the inscription scrolled under the lid. *Edmund Atticus Renwick*. Her heart sank.

In her mind's eye, she was standing in her father's study, peering at his locked safe. She saw the frown he always gave his little girl when she pestered him about what was inside. But why did he close the door to the room whenever strangers came to call? He made it clear the locked safe was off limits to everyone but himself. Father's private business was just that—private. Dire penalties for snooping kept her at bay until the day her father met with a business associate and forgot to close the door. She peeked into the room. The safe was open. A box with shiny latches hid inside. Discovering Father's secret convinced her the box was full of treasure. If only.

She shook her head in protest, denying what her eyes could not. An ominous feeling crept in. The box didn't belong here.

But Father might have given Nathan the money. He might have arranged it all. A simple answer to a problem she didn't need to worry about. An explanation that would keep her believing there was still a shred of good in everyone.

She picked up one of the bundles, fanned it with her fingers, and guessed its value at two thousand dollars. Four rows of three. *Twenty-four thousand dollars before my very own eyes.* She threw the bundle back into the box and slammed the lid shut. Voices in her head came to her rescue. *There's nothing to fret over, Mariah. Just put it out of your mind.* Sitting on the floor in a strange house, in the middle of an army outpost, out in the middle of nowhere, she so wished that were true. *Put it out of my mind? I must be out of my mind to even think such a thing.*

Searching for a motive left her facing one certainty. She had to confront Nathan and find out the truth. Why didn't he tell her about the box, and why did he hide it from her? Had Father given Nathan the money, or not? The questions rattled her. The bad dream was real. She couldn't wish the truth away. Stolen money. All of it. Stolen. And her husband—the thief.

She tossed and turned throughout the night. By morning,

she was a wreck. As she stared at the ceiling looming above the bed, she imagined Nathan lying next to her. The thought made her feel worse. She once believed her marriage was the right choice, but that notion turned out to be utterly wrong. And the excuses she concocted to defend her husband's honor couldn't fend off the darkness closing in.

Not a glimmer of hope was left. No mending of broken vows. The magnitude of this moment lay hidden inside the box, and the question chasing her down. How could she ever rebuild her life with Nathan if he was hellbent on destroying it? Finding the money by accident changed everything.

She sprang up in bed and threw her fists in front of her face.

"This madness has to stop—"

She didn't wait for the tears to flow. She had nothing left to cry for. Her anger mounted with every breath, heaving her out of bed with the force of cannon fire. And then she screamed until her ear drums nearly burst.

"No more!"

The words thundered against her lips and put an end to the misery cutting a chasm through her heart. A place she once believed would someday be filled with love. Who was she fooling? *Someday never comes, and it never will with Nathan.*

She rummaged through the armoire and found her favorite dress. The yellow one with the revealing neckline. She wore it the day Nathan came to the cottage but was denied his pleasure for reasons she didn't fathom until now. *I have never loved you.* It was so easy to say. There was no more guilt. Only the truth.

The front door slammed shut. She rushed down the steps and stormed toward the hospital. Soldiers marching their drills blocked her path across the parade grounds. She skirted the commotion and took a roundabout way, walking faster and faster. Then she ran.

She tripped up the stairs and stopped on the landing. Her heart pounded. She caught her breath and tugged on her dress.

Gazing down her front, she liked what she saw. Even her necklace drew attention where she wanted it. A dab of perfume was perfectly placed below the aragonite pendant.

Inside the hospital, all was quiet. She paced the hallway from end to end, but Dr. Riddler was nowhere to be found. Waiting to ask permission to see his patient magnified her unease. She needed to talk to Nathan this very minute. She had to know. She had to uncover the lie.

At the end of the hall, she swung open the door and froze. The look on Nathan's face formed a knot in her stomach.

She feigned a smile. "You're awake."

"So I am. Have you come to offer your *condolences*?" His tone was always genuine when he mocked her.

Lying there, he looked as relaxed as ever, without a care in the world. He pulled himself up and braced his hand behind his head, admiring the view. Mariah eased closer. Her fingers skimmed along the bedside and up his arm to his collar where she unbuttoned his shirt, giving her hand easy access. His reaction to her fondling made her push him to the edge.

"Condolences? On the contrary, Nathan. I've come to please you."

With arousing precision, she leaned over him, ever so slow, and beguiled him with her tumescence. She felt his breath against her bosom as his eyes flashed from blue to pitch black. His look hurled her back to the meadow, and the pain. She panicked. *I can't do this.* But her alter ego already moved in and slipped into her skin. Oh, how her purring made him crazy, real bad crazy.

He squeezed one of her breasts. The other hand followed, mimicking its mate. That smirk he gave her put him in control, until she slid her hand up the inside of his leg and made him groan. She came down on him and kissed him hard, with no shame, then pulled away, leaving him scorched with hunger by her femme fatale maneuver. Spiked with need, he drew her breasts together, eyeing her cleavage with his open mouth. She corralled his hair and guided him in.

Her moans taunted him. "It's been so long . . ."

He tongued her skin, tasting her perfume, and nudged the lace on her neckline. His urges soared at the sound of her voice pleading with him to tear off her dress.

Then her words exploded in his face.

"But tell me first—if you stole my father's money."

Mariah always underestimated her husband's reaction to things. In an instant, his temper would flare in a fit of rage at anyone who stood in his way. Liquor had been his excuse, but he behaved equally bad when he was sober. This time was no different, and she was just as unprepared for his outburst.

The beast had awakened. Her head whipped sideways from the force of his hand, stinging her cheek like shards of glass. She lurched backwards and grabbed hold of the chair. She had to stay on her feet and out of his reach. But she couldn't escape his biting words.

"You never learn to shut up, do you?" Nathan clutched his stomach and swung his legs over the side of the bed. "As for your father's damn money, let's just say he owed it to me."

She ignored the throbbing in her cheek and shot back. "Owed it to you? For what?"

"For putting up with *you*."

Mariah felt the fear again, her fear of him and what he might do to her. But his vitriol fanned a fire as her newfound anger lashed out, ready for the fight of her life.

"You're a no-good thief. That's what you are. A lying, cheating thief!"

The door loomed beyond the foot of the bed. She was trapped.

"Well, a woman who marries a lying, cheating thief like me is nothing more than a whore."

His words cut to the bone. She couldn't stop the hurt from

reaching her heart, for there dwelled the truth she came to find. "Call me whatever you want. I'm through with you and your lies. I'm going home, and I'm taking my father's money with me."

Nathan growled through his teeth. Outrage seethed in his face. The greatest threat against him had become his wife.

He lunged at her, cursing like a mad man. She ducked under his grasp, but his hand grazed the side of her throat. Her necklace snapped. The aragonite pendant vanished into thin air. She bounded toward the door and dashed out of the room.

He yelled after her. "If you touch my money, I swear I'll kill you! Nothing's going to stop me. Do you hear me? Not even you!"

She ran down the steps of the infirmary. A glance behind her stoked her fears and kept her running ahead as she darted her eyes in every direction. She spied Chakote tied up by the corral and veered toward him. Beyond the fence, Julian walked out of the barn with his saddlebags slung over his shoulder. Her heart jumped. She still had time to stop him.

"Julian!"

The sound of her voice and the sight of her running toward him caught him off guard. They already said their goodbyes. But the terrified look on her face warned him of trouble. She almost ran past him. He spun around and whisked her into his arms, sending the saddlebags hurtling to the ground. Her bosom heaved against his chest. She couldn't speak.

"Mariah. What happened?"

Her breathing raced and her body trembled. "Something's wrong—terribly wrong. I'm scared—"

Wherever she'd been, panic followed her. "Is it Nathan? Did he try to hurt you?"

"He—" She gasped for air. "He stole my father's money. Thousands of dollars. I found out by accident and confronted him. When I told him I was taking the money home, he went mad. He said he would kill me—"

They'd run out of time for more talking. What had to be done had to be done fast.

"Listen to me. I need you to go back to the officers' quarters and pack up your things. I'll deal with Nathan. Once I've hitched up the oxen, I'll meet you—"

A shockwave shuddered across his face. His stare froze into her gaze. The torment engulfed him. Another blow struck again. His eyes shot skyward, and his back arched violently while his hands tried hopelessly to cling to her. The weight of his body strained against hers. They collapsed on the ground. And then his face slumped into her lap.

Mariah stared at him in horror. Had another nightmare hunted her down? Or had death, the unwelcome visitor, come to pay its final respects?

"Oh God—no. Julian— Don't leave me. Please don't leave me!"

He was lying there with blood oozing from his back. Every drop was taking the life out of him. A cold body left for dead now. The light of his brown eyes—gone.

Insanity spiraled into chaos.

Mariah looked up and saw terror head on. Nathan stood between her and the hospital. His left hand clutched his gut and his right hand the Colt revolver, pointed straight at her.

He snarled, full of rage. "This one's for you, *my beloved wife*."

Tears streamed down her face, but her screams fell silent as she stared down the barrel of his gun. Just the squeeze of the trigger and it would be over—obliterated—as if she never existed, along with the man she loved, the man she had always loved.

Fright marched in, disjointed and blurred, numbing her body into a stupor as an act of mercy before the bullet struck.

Out of nowhere, a voice shouted from beyond the fray. Was there another demon come to finish her off? The revolver switched direction and aimed at the other target. Gunshots rang out. Another bullet pierced the ground, spattering dust in the air. Nathan staggered and dropped his gun, then tumbled back and hit the hardpan.

Mariah reacted like a crazed animal, driven by instinct and no common sense. She bolted to her feet, mounted Julian's horse, and rode toward the rising sun, and toward home.

Chapter 22

To Live Or Die

ALL WAS LOST. Where the sky once blazed a brilliant blue, only a world of darkness reigned. East of Fort Laramie, the Oregon Trail disappeared. Not a sign was left of the telegraph line. The meandering strands of the North Platte River that guided the emigrants from going astray evaporated without a trace.

Mariah swore she was losing her mind. Pandemonium blinded her and corrupted her thoughts. The look on Julian's face chased her down and would not release her. His agony was all she could see, and it shrouded her in the worst nightmare she'd ever known. *Run, Chakote, run!*

She rode into the wind with the reins clenched in her quaking hands as images flashed before her, dragging her back to that place fraught with death. The men in her life were both dead. In an instant, gone. Nathan's bullets destroyed the man she wanted to love forever. But she would never know Julian's love, and he would never know hers. Staring at his bloodied back, inside she died too. Tears blanketed her face, and nothing could stop more from falling. Tears spurred by a barren heart that could endure no more. *Run, Chakote, run!*

And then the clouds came, billowing white overhead. Goaded by the winds, they grew dark like the world around her. In the distance, a pack of horses kicked up a wall of dust. She sped toward them into oblivion, fleeing from death, leaving it far behind, and the man she lost.

Julian was never coming back. Nathan's venomous hate cut him down, plunging her into unending despair. But every mile that passed beneath her, taking her away from all the horror, she denied it ever happened. She became a fugitive from the truth.

Summer's heat rose skyward and bloated the rain clouds until they ruptured. The tempest showed no mercy as it roared across the plains. Shifting winds beat against Chakote and alerted Mariah to the Cheyenne warriors barreling toward her, yapping like a pack of coyotes set for the kill.

The ground shook under the stampede. Deafening noises shattered the air. In the frenzy, a force swept up behind her, jolting into her back. She lurched in the saddle, on the edge of falling off, when a pair of arms snatched her waist and held her so tight she choked on her screams.

Streaks of lightning splintered the sky and electrified the braves. They converged on the white woman who put herself in harm's way. An easy target whose scent they smelled as they closed in on her.

The reins vanished from Mariah's hands. She was caught in a fierce embrace. Another evil tracked her down and left no escape, except surrendering to the last glimmer of light. Her life.

Chakote heeded his new commands and turned them north toward a hilly enclave hidden from their current position. Pitting warrior against warrior, the speed of a cunning horse would decide who captured the forbidden fruit. Chakote once proved his worth to his old master, and he proved it again. The wild Mustangs were no match for the Arabian stallion as his long, sinewy legs outran them all.

The rumble of hooves faded away, but Mariah kept a death grip on the pommel. By the time they reached the hideout, she was soaked to the bone. A crack of thunder split open the sky and spooked Chakote. He reared up, bucking his riders to the ground. The last moment Mariah remembered was a thud against the back of her head when she passed out.

THE faint tang of burnt wood hung in the air and permeated Mariah's nostrils. She grimaced, but not from the smell. Her head pounded like a drum. In the dark, all she heard was the rhythm of her breathing. All she saw was cloaked in black. Her eyelids grew heavy. She fought to stay awake as she tried moving under the weight that held her down. The strain was too much. She drifted off.

Light flickering from the fire stirred her awake and gave shape to a form looming above her. She blinked through groggy eyes at the face of a ghost with no voice but whose presence she felt riding Chakote in the storm. The figure crouched beside her and fixed his gaze on her.

Bear Wolf had been watching Mariah since he returned from the hunt. Her look sparked a glint in his eyes. She was foolish riding alone on the plains. But he saved her life. The Great Spirit would find honor in his deed and grant him what he desired the first time he saw the tall woman with the straw-colored hair.

Her fiery courage startled him. She tussled under the mammoth buffalo skin, clawing her way out. He lunged at her and grabbed her hips, pulling her back onto the bed.

She gasped. "Let go of me—"

Her fists pelted his chest, but his muscles deflected every

blow. He thrust her arms above her head and glared down at her. Even the heat from his body carried the power to keep her trapped. So did the fringe of his raven hair brushing against her cheek. She panicked. The yellow dress. She was still wearing the yellow dress. Would the warrior who possessed the might of three men leave her body in ruins? She couldn't quiet the heaving in her bosom as his voice thrummed against her lips.

"No fight. No more." His words shook the earth like the stampede they outran. His stare made her obey.

She nodded. "No fight. No more."

He let go and retreated to the campfire.

The relief Mariah felt didn't stop the throbbing in her head. She muffled the ache in her voice with her hand. Showing any sign of weakness in the presence of her captor could make things worse. Yet fear and exhaustion already took their toll, as did the weight of her mistake that made her a captive against her will.

Out of the corner of her eye, she spied Bear Wolf facing the fire. His brawn glowed in the burning light and summoned a kind of power over the flames rising higher out of the pit. Her body trembled, draining what energy she had left. Then his figure dimmed. The shadows returned. On the brink of unconsciousness, a shiver tingled along her shoulder. She moaned.

The Sioux warrior never touched a white woman that way before.

A blanket of stars draped the sky as Bear Wolf stood beneath the celestial canopy, gazing up to pay homage to the Great Spirit who gave balance to the universe. Wakan Tanka did not speak to inferior warriors, but Bear Wolf felt the spirit's presence at night when silence covered the land and his hatred for the white man became shrouded in the infinite darkness.

He had no suspicions of the sleeping woman with the pale skin. She was not to blame for the death of his father, or those who raided their ancestral lands and claimed it as their own.

But she belonged to them and would never understand the struggles of the Sioux. For all the white man had taken from him, he vowed to take something back. In time, she would learn his people's ways.

THROUGH cracks in the rock formations, slivers of sunlight pierced the cave. Mariah saw the place where Bear Wolf kept her hidden. She rubbed the back of her head. It still ached. But her hunger pangs gave her more grief than her head did.

Her mind whiplashed to her clash with Bear Wolf, and the last glimpse of him huddled by the campfire. The sensation on her shoulder sent a chill up her spine. *What did he do to me while I was sleeping?* Her hands reached under the buffalo skin and palmed her dress. She sighed, then scoured the hideout. He was gone.

She prowled her way to the cave's entrance but halted in her tracks and glared at her bare feet. They weren't going to get her very far. The scent of cooked meat drew her to the fire. She didn't care what it was, only that it filled her belly.

By the glowing embers, she dropped to her knees, snatched a chunk of meat from the skewer and devoured it. Just as she grabbed another mouthful, a thud made her recoil from the feast. Her boots appeared next to her. She froze at the sight of another pair of shoes next to them. Moccasins. *His* moccasins. She looked up, with the meat pressed against her lips, and steadied her eyes on him. Bear Wolf's presence wasn't going to stop her. Not his stare or his silence.

She rose to her feet and shoved the charred morsel into her mouth, chewing it slowly. Deliberately. In one swallow, she demanded, "You can't keep me here. I won't stay."

He jutted his chin up. "You will stay."

She clenched her hands in defiance. "No, I will not."

"I say you will."

He stood firm with his arms crossed. In protest, she turned her back on him, testing his fire. He retaliated with a grunt. She spun around and darted behind him, but he caught her waist and pinned her against the wall of the cave. Her body writhed in fits of anger, trapped by his muscled frame. Their impassioned gaze had Bear Wolf demanding control, and Mariah release, locking them in a tug of war that left only one way out.

Exasperated, Mariah succumbed to Bear Wolf's strength. "I will not fight you anymore."

Bear Wolf felt her words touch his face, and felt the storm within her still warm against his skin. He eased his grip, holding her close. His voice rumbled above a whisper. "Ishda wiyun . . . peji mahpiya." He brushed his thumb above her cheekbone and said, "Eyes color of grass and sky." Her spirit burned bright. She belonged among the people of his tribe. He spread his shoulders wide and gestured. "You come. We must go." He stepped back and turned away.

In a burst of sheer willpower, Mariah's last fighting breath had her dashing out of the cave as barefoot as before but more determined than ever to find Chakote and run away. To hell with everyone telling her what to do.

The spartan plains stretched out ahead of her. An expanse of desolation paralyzed her footsteps. She didn't recognize anything. *Which way should I go?*

Images from the fort reeled in her head. Scenes overshadowed by her encounter with Bear Wolf. A volley of gunfire rang out in her ears. A pool of blood seized her heart. The face of death crushed her with grief and left her maddening world in shambles. The nightmare found her again, and she crippled under its weight as her wails echoed across the land and buried hope in its grave.

There was no place to run. No escape.

Bear Wolf heard her cries and moved up behind her. For him, those sounds were not so easy to forget. He had seen the light pass from his father's eyes, and he remembered. His hands came to rest on her shoulders where he turned her toward him and shared in her sadness. He reached down and took her hands and let the memories of his grief hold tight to hers.

All his strength he gave her as she laid her head upon his chest and wept profoundly for the one she had lost. The memory of the white man he spied in the canyon wakened in his mind. The man who showed no vengeance in his eyes and only sought help for another.

He leaned in and breathed his knowing words through her sundrenched hair. "You cry for white man who is no more."

Mariah felt his intended meaning and knew he understood.

"For many moons, sorrow for my father was great. Now I hear his voice among spirits. So will your sorrow be. The spirits will make it so."

She gazed up at him and let him brush away her tears, and let his hand rest there upon her cheek as her eyes clung to his compassion. From that war-torn pedestal, Bear Wolf stepped down and swept Mariah into his titanic arms. And she took solace, a lingering solace, in the earthen scent of his skin and found the courage he gave her for what lay ahead.

Their embrace did not end for the longest of times, for their need was absolute, and her grief was great. Mariah's life force had to find its own destiny, and find its own peace. Bear Wolf held her close, so she would not forget, that he would always be there to defend her in the sacred land of the Sioux. And, he would always be watching.

CHAPTER 23

Facing The Truth

DELIVERANCE FROM MARIAH'S past would be difficult, if not impossible. Fear was for so long that unwelcome visitor. Its disguises were many. Fear stole her innocence and sealed her fate as the omen of fearful things to come. And they had. When the insanity would end she didn't know, but she was convinced it all began the day she met Nathan.

He taught her fear with the words he spoke. Showed her fear when he hurt her. And he made her fear for her life when she stared down the barrel of his gun. How she hated him, even in death. Yet she hated fear even more, for it lived on inside her and made her afraid of facing her future. A future without Julian. Every end held promise for a new beginning, did it not? But those were empty words now. Words that had no meaning. With no purpose in her life, fear would find her again.

As the horses traversed the sagebrush blanketing the rolling hills, Bear Wolf guided Mariah back to the place she recognized. The Oregon Trail and the North Platte River. She heaved a sigh of relief. The landmarks weren't home, but they gave her comfort even so. There was no fear of the familiar.

Up ahead, they reached the junction of the Laramie River. Mariah had to travel the last stretch of the trail alone. Bear Wolf had his reasons for staying out of sight of Fort Laramie. The fort's leader, the one they called Moonlight, killed two of his Sioux brothers before the white snow of winter covered the prairie. It was a public hanging that proclaimed the colonel's superiority among his people. The Sioux braves had made a fair trade with the Cheyenne, returning a white woman and her child to the outpost as a sign of goodwill for keeping the peace with the soldiers. For their deed, they were hanged.

Bear Wolf reined in his horse and gestured for Mariah to ride on. He watched her soft figure recede in the distance and curve around a bend in the trail. And then she was gone. He turned his Mustang to the north and rode into the wind.

As Mariah approached the garrison, she fought back the impulse to turn around and bolt. More than fear, death lurked ahead of her. *Dear God, help me get through this.* Closer in, the corral came into view, and the cemetery.

Chakote slowed to a halt a few yards from the hospital and waited for his rider's signal, telling him which way to go. Mariah sat in the saddle with a blank look on her face. She didn't know what to do, or even why she came back. *There's nothing left for me here.*

A chorus of voices rang out in her ears. She looked for the sounds calling out to her. "Mrs. Lawton! Mrs. Lawton!"

Jessie and Martha ran toward her with their hands flailing in the air. Their faces beamed at the sight of their frontier schoolmarm. Beyond them, Stella watched with big eyes and a smile that matched. Mariah looked toward the barracks and spotted Silas huddled by a group of wagons. He was too far away for her to make out his reaction, but she was sure he recognized her.

Seeing everyone from the wagon train had her heart flut-
tering. She slid down off the saddle and greeted the little ones.
Their innocent hugs filled her with joy, as did Martha's concern
for her.

"We didn't think we were going to see you again. I'm glad
you didn't get lost." She cradled her yarn doll in her arm. "It's
been an awful long journey, hasn't it, Mrs. Lawton?"

"Yes, it has, Martha. Too long." She looked them over, marveling at the smudges all over Jessie's face and Martha's not-so-
white pinafore. They hadn't changed a bit. She pinched their
cheeks and hugged them again. "I'm so happy to see you both.
I hope you've been helping your mother and not forgetting to
do your schoolwork."

Jessie nodded. "We have, Mrs. Lawton. Mummy said we've
been hard little workers. She promised us a treat at the sutler's
store. We can't wait—" They both skipped away, grinning from
ear to ear with their voices singing out. "Yippy! See you soon!"

"Indeed. Be good children now!" She waved goodbye.

Chakote snorted and shook his head, tugging the reins in
her hand. She squeezed the bridle and leaned against him,
steadying herself as she walked toward the wagons. The four-
legged beast was all that stood between her and the corral.

She approached Silas. He turned and walked the other way.
She called after him. "Silas, wait—"

He looked over his shoulder, so as not to be rude when he
spoke. "How do, Mrs. Lawton." He cut short the pleasantries.
"Beggin' your pardon, ma'am. I best be goin'. Wagons need to
be worked on. Cattle need tendin'."

She blurted out her feelings. "It's so good to see you. I was
worried you might not make it." He kept quiet, but even his
silence comforted her. "Well, I wanted to tell you I'm glad you
and the others are safe."

Silas gave no answer, just a shifty look in his eyes, like he
stole something and had to leave camp real fast before he got

caught. A puzzled expression framed Mariah's face. She reached out to him again.

"It's time I told you. I should have said it ages ago." She stepped closer. "Thank you for everything you did for me on the trail."

Silas spun around. His face contorted in disgust. "You wanna thank *me*?" He almost busted up laughing. "You of all people." He jammed his thumb into his chest and cursed to high heaven. "Damn it, Mrs. Lawton. I'm the one who killed your husband! You oughta be tellin' me to go straight to hell."

Hatred had a way of haunting a man when he despised himself, and Silas loathed every worthless bone in his body. More than when he pulled the trigger. Spilling the truth right in her face made him want to puke.

His blistering words severed Mariah's nerves and left her on the verge of collapsing. Silas Bingham murdered her husband? She couldn't relive those moments again. But her wounded heart cried out for healing, and it would only come to pass when she rekindled the nightmare. She had to, if not for herself, then for Silas.

The reins fell from her hand. "I know what kind of man you are, and you're no killer."

He paid no mind to her nonsense. She had him figured all wrong. He needed a punch in the face and all the damnation she could rain down on him. Inside, he felt he had it coming. His head drooped, masking the secret that he never killed a man before. He deserved to be punished for his crime. His miserable soul didn't need saving.

Mariah saw the suffering in his face. She reached out and hugged him in the same way she would have hugged her own father, so she could show him how grateful she was for what he'd done.

"I'm sorry you had to do it. If you didn't, I would be—" Her voice cracked. "You saved my life."

With all those notions muddled up in his head, Silas didn't know what to think. But he felt it, the absolution of his sin by the woman who didn't die at the hand of her husband because of him. They held each other until the pain and the shame of it all released him.

Mariah gazed at him in earnest. "None of us could have done anything to keep it from happening. Nathan brought death upon himself."

Silas cleared his throat. "I know. It just happened so fast. Seein' him pointin' that gun at you left me no choice."

He recalled how untested Mariah was after the wagon train left Independence. He thought her flimsy as a flower blowing in a spring breeze and would have gambled his hard-earned wages she wouldn't last a week on the trail. Looking back, he'd have been holding the losing hand.

Chakote nudged Mariah's arm with his muzzle. She stroked the soft fur and took a deep breath. "I'd—I'd like to ask you a favor."

Silas scrunched his brow and tipped his hat. "I'm glad to oblige. Is there somethin' you need help with?"

Her request would sound illogical no matter how she said it. She hoped the words would come out right. "Can we walk together . . . and take the horse to the corral?"

He didn't quite know what to make of her question. She handled the stallion with ease up till now. He figured she had good reason, so he didn't ask why.

Mariah handed him the reins. They turned and faced *that place*. Their walk was slow and steady. Nothing out of the ordinary. Just a stroll to the paddock. But she clung to his arm, petrified with fear.

Silas gave her a sidelong glance. Something was scaring the living daylights out of her. Then it hit him. Like the butt of a rifle slammed against his head. All he was thinking about was his own guilt. He killed the man who hired him to drive the wagon train west. The man who was this woman's husband. The terror he saw in her face before he shot the lieutenant looked the same now. She was reliving the madness that saw her husband killed before her eyes.

He stopped short of where Mariah had found herself fearing for her life. "Are you sure you wanna keep goin'?"

She stared ahead. "Yes. I have to."

Each footstep was a struggle. Her body moved with the weight of a corpse, inching her closer to where the torment began. She halted near the corral fence. It wasn't intentional, crushing Silas's arm the way she did, but she couldn't stop hers from shaking.

A wave of anguish splintered her voice. "He's really—dead." She said the word as if it were her own dying breath.

Her stomach twisted into a tangled mess, and her heart heaved in protest, for she could no longer deny the tragedy when everything went wrong. How could such brutality take the life of a good man? There were no answers.

"I'll walk alone to the cemetery, and say my goodbyes." She looked at the wagon boss and stood ready to face the end. "Thank you for your kindness."

Silas took off his hat and scratched his head. Quite a few paces back, they already passed over the spot where he shot the lieutenant. Just then, he called to mind a part of the trail ride. "After the caravan crossed the south fork of the Platte River, a man rode into camp lookin' for your husband. I can't recollect his name."

Mariah blinked through watery eyes. "Was it Julian? Why are you telling me this?"

"Well, he ain't buried over at the cemetery. Doc Riddler's been workin' on him since yesterday. He ain't doin' too good though."

Cutting words not befitting a man of Silas's character sliced deep to the bone. Was she being tricked into believing his lie was the truth? She threw herself in front of him and snatched his arms. Her face seethed with anger as her gaze burned into his.

"How dare you lie to me. I was there with Julian. Nathan killed him—in cold blood!"

Silas stood flabbergasted at her sudden change in mood. She wasn't behaving like any hysterical woman in shock over a senseless killing. She was fuming with a kind of rage he'd never seen. He grabbed her arms and made sure she understood his every word.

"Mariah. You gotta hear me out. I was there too, and that man Julian ain't dead."

How could she believe him when nothing he said was true? *I saw his dying face!* She couldn't think. She couldn't speak. But glaring at Silas made her sure of one thing. She despised liars.

"If you're lying to me, I swear I'll—" She lashed out. "For God's sake, tell me the truth!"

They both stood there with their arms all knotted together, frustrated as hell. What else could Silas say to prove he was giving it to her straight? But the silence she shoved between them was deliberate, in case he needed one last chance to come clean and flat out tell her it was a cruel joke. The woman so downright lost and turned to stone would surely understand.

Silas never made it his business asking the emigrants in the wagon train why they wanted to take a two-thousand-mile journey plagued with death and disease, much less face a bunch of troublemakers on the trail. From the first day he met the lieutenant, the man stood out from everyone else. His temper put the entire wagon train in jeopardy. And his wife. Silas figured the lieutenant wasn't even married, the way he left her huddled alone by the campfire night after night.

But no man had a right to beat his wife or threaten to kill anyone because the wagon train wasn't traveling fast enough to suit his needs. That was the first time Nathan pulled a gun on him. The second time he did proved to be his last.

As for the stranger who rode into camp, Silas figured Julian had some unfinished business of his own with the lieutenant. Staring into Mariah's eyes told him he had just one answer he could give her for the man she thought was dead.

"I'm tellin' you the truth, Mariah. You gotta believe me. They took 'em both right to the hospital, but your husband didn't make it."

His last words had Mariah dashing to the infirmary. She tripped up the steps and burst through the front door, careening to a stop. Seeing Julian resurrected from the dead seemed ludicrous. The unbearable agony contorting his face was still branded in her mind. The blood. All the blood. Life itself was drained from his body. Death had marched in and conquered him.

She yelled down the hall. "Dr. Riddler!" No one answered. "Where on earth is that man?" Waiting another second had her wringing her hands. She rushed pell-mell from one door knob to the next, hunting for proof.

At the end of the corridor, the doctor emerged from the shadows. "Mrs. Lawton, is that you?"

She bounded toward him and halted in her tracks. "Where is he? Tell me where he is."

Dr. Riddler gave up trying to find her and inform her about the shooting. He didn't know why she showed up now. A frown creased his brow. Telling her would be unpleasant.

"I'm sorry, but I have bad news. Your husband died yesterday. His condition was too critical. I couldn't save his life. Please accept my sincere condolences."

Mariah was at her wits' end. She tossed her hair from her face and pressed a hand against her forehead with the other square on her hip. "Yes, yes. I know he's dead. What about Mr. Marquette? Is—is he dead too?"

The doctor shrugged at her response to her husband's passing. "Follow me, and you can see for yourself." He retraced his steps down the hall to the last room on the right, where the lieutenant was recovering after his arrival at the fort. He opened the door.

Mariah stared in shock at the sight in front of her.

Dear God. It can't be. Julian—

Disbelief. False hope. The truth was only a few steps away.

Mariah's reaction to the patient expressed something personal between them. Something profoundly revealed. She padded toward the bedside as the door clicked shut behind her. Julian was lying on his stomach with his body covered by a white sheet. She tried putting into words what her eyes beheld, and she could finally comprehend.

"It's true . . ."

Her knees thudded on the floor. She cupped Julian's hand in hers. It felt warm to the touch. Blood pumped life to every corner of his shattered body. His face was turned toward her. His eyes were closed. Sleeping. She brought his hand to her lips and kissed it, then breathed deep and inhaled his scent. There was no more doubt. Not even the impossible. Julian was alive.

CHAPTER 24

It Is Meant To Be

ORT LARAMIE WAS once a world filled with melancholy. A dismal place that symbolized what had gone wrong in Mariah's life. Now it changed to one of purpose and possibility. The fort would never be her new home, but she was going to stay here for as long as it took until Julian recovered. He had to, after all this madness.

Dr. Riddler didn't give her any details about his patient, only the two bullets shot into his back. "There's no cause to get your hopes up. Mr. Marquette's condition is extremely unstable."

"Can't you operate on him to remove the bullets?" Mariah asked the question outright. She had no time for mincing words.

The doctor looked perturbed by her insinuation. "Mrs. Lawton, I am quite capable of performing the most complex operations, but this primitive hospital doesn't provide much for a skilled surgeon. I don't like the results any more than my patients do." He crossed his arms. "If Mr. Marquette were under my care at the New York Hospital, I could give a prognosis that he might survive. I can't make those kinds of promises here." They walked into his office where he finished his commentary. "To put it bluntly, in this facility I run the risk of serious complications if I operate. But there are equal risks if I don't."

A pronounced pause upended his analysis. He didn't tell her what he really thought. He was fed up with finding death or amputation the only options, whether he operated on his patients or not. *It's a damn fine waste of my talents.*

Images of those bullets lodged in Julian's back sent a chill through Mariah. She sat down in the chair, brooding over his plight. The doctor had given his reasons. Just cutting into a man could be the end.

"If the bullets aren't taken out, what then?"

Riddler paced behind his desk. He summoned caution with his choice of words, as though his professional medical opinion was all he had left at his disposal to make up for the sorry surroundings.

"Based on where each bullet entered his body, the upper bullet may be resting behind his heart. If the bullet isn't removed, it could migrate and disrupt the heart functions. This poses a major risk, not to mention the threat of infection." He stopped pacing and stared at her. "There's another complication I think you should know about. The upper bullet is located near his spine, so paralysis may occur. In other words, he may never walk again." He squinted hard, in case he missed something, but her face showed no reaction to that ungodly word.

"And the other bullet? What about the lower bullet?"

"In the time between when both shots were fired, Mr. Marquette must have lurched from the first impact, since the lower bullet penetrated his body at an angle. When I cleaned the area, I felt a slight bulge under the surface of the skin. That's a good sign. With his bleeding under control, a shallow incision may be enough to extract it."

Mariah's spirits perked up at the altered timbre in Riddler's voice. He sounded like he'd already slain the dragon and won the fight. "Will both operations be done right away?"

She waited for his answer while he settled into his chair. Her impatience mounted. The suspense of not knowing what he was thinking had her heels clicking on the floor. All he needed to say was *yes*. The thought churned over and over in her mind. One man's life was in another man's hands. But all she believed was possibilities. Nothing mattered except that Julian lived.

"Mrs. Lawton, it's none of my business why you're concerned about Mr. Marquette's condition. As it is, I need to wait until Dr. Johnson arrives here at the fort. His assistance is crucial for the surgery near the heart and spine. In the meantime, I'm preparing to operate on the lower—"

"Another doctor's coming to Fort Laramie?" Tension rose in Mariah's voice at the prospect of a new physician weighing in on a dangerous procedure that could leave Julian paralyzed, or worse.

"I sense your apprehension, but Dr. Johnson is a competent physician. We worked together in New York City before the war. Fort Laramie will be fortunate to have us both here during the transition."

"Transition? What transition?" The words snapped out of her mouth.

"I sent a telegram back East a few weeks ago about my replacement, since my assignment here at the fort is almost over. I found out Dr. Johnson will be taking my place." He leaned into the desk. "Lucky for Mr. Marquette, he'll have the benefit of two skilled surgeons to remove the upper bullet. The operation will require both of us if it's going to have any chance of success."

Too much was at stake to make sense of it all. Mariah had no control over decisions that weren't hers to make, except her need to act at once and do whatever she could to help out.

"Well, there's no better time for us to get to work than

now." She blurted out the remark so fast, she surprised herself by what she said.

"My apologies, Mrs. Lawton, but did I hear you say *us?*"

"Yes, you did. It's no secret your hospital attendants are just soldiers who'd rather be fighting Indians than nursing the wounded. When you're ready to operate on the lower bullet, I'm sure I can help you as well as any one of them can."

An unusual arrangement, to be sure. The doctor was well aware of the shortcomings of his hospital staff and could use a good hand at his side when the time came to perform the surgery.

"Very well. But you must follow my explicit instructions. Before we begin, we need to minimize the presence of bacteria, otherwise we risk contamination. I won't allow you near the patient unless you've used the scrubbing room first. Understood?"

"Understood."

"Let's get to work then, shall we?"

Each moment filled Mariah with a newfound purpose. Every command the doctor gave her, she executed without hesitation. She marched over to the mess hall and ordered the kitchen cooks to boil pots of water. The surgical tools required sanitizing and water was needed for scrubbing down. Sharkey rounded up another soldier, and they hauled the supplies to the infirmary.

A quick change into a clean dress from the officers' quarters had her dashing back to the hospital. She washed her hands and arms with hot water and soap, then sterilized the surgical instruments and made sure enough cloths and gauze were on hand. It was the least she could do for the man who showed her their love was worth fighting for. Now she could show him he was right all along.

The more dangerous task lay in the hands of the surgeon, a man Mariah had to trust as he punctured the skin and probed for the bullet.

"Open the carbolic acid and sterilize the incision."

"Yes, Doctor."

Her eyes riveted on the patient. Julian's musculature took her breath away. The contours of his back sent a surge to her fingertips. She fumbled the bottle. It clanked against the metal tray. She tightened her grip and dribbled the carbolic acid into the open wound. A deep exhale released the strain in her hand. That peaceful look on his face made her think nothing happened, until she glanced at the bullet holes, and the blood.

"More gauze. I need more gauze." Riddler steadied the scalpel while Mariah dabbed around the incision. He peered closer. "I can see it. A clean shot. No bullet fragments. Hand me the forceps. I need to— Damn."

She panicked. "What's wrong?"

Julian groaned. His body started writhing.

"He needs another dose of ether. Quickly."

She doused a cloth with the anesthesia and covered Julian's nose and mouth. A minute passed, and his body went limp.

"Well done. Once I remove the bullet, pour the carbolic acid directly into the wound."

Mariah set the bottle of ether back on the hutch and grabbed the antiseptic. "I'm ready." All she thought of was Julian's reaction to the acid had he been conscious. She cringed.

The laggard hands of time prolonged tension in the room until the clink of the bloody slug on the tray signaled the operation was over. Mariah dribbled the carbolic acid into the incision and watched the doctor suture the skin with the needle. She soaked a patch of gauze, placing it over the wound.

No sooner had Dr. Riddler finished the surgery than Private Ketchum pounced into the room. "Doc, we got a couple wounded soldiers down the hall. They just came in from the Powder River Valley. Looks like they tangled with some Indians."

"I'll be right there. Mrs. Lawton, can you finish up here?"

"Yes, of course."

"Change the dressings often and keep them soaked with the antiseptic. Do the same with the upper bullet wound. The last thing this man needs to battle is a deadly infection."

After he left the room, Mariah washed and sterilized the surgical instruments and discarded the blood-stained cloths and remnants of gauze. Her eyes fixated on the wound and any movement Julian made. She didn't want to miss the first sign if anything went wrong. But the bleeding worried her something fierce. She feared it might never stop.

The need to be doing instead of thinking kept her focused while she cleaned the metal trays and readied more strips of gauze. She stayed by his side as the afternoon sun peeked through the corner window.

There wasn't much time for all the turmoil to sink in. Mariah recalled standing in the same room, telling Nathan she was leaving him and taking her father's money back home. Now she watched over Julian and prayed he would live.

Around them, all was quiet. In that silence, sleep and death could be one and the same. She pressed her hand against her bosom and felt it rise, up and down, and felt her lungs fill with air as though she were trying to breathe for him. Through all this insanity, his pain would be hers. She leaned down and kissed his cheek.

"I'm here, Julian. I'm here with you, for good—"

Her voice expired. *I can't bear to see you die again!* Fear was waiting for her. She just had to let it in. Or shut it out. In his face, she saw her answer. If those bullets were not destined to kill him, he had to survive. His will to live was fighting for both of them. His battle had to be her battle too. Only then would she triumph over fear and let nothing stand in their way.

A memory flickered in her mind. The wintry day at the Florissant Café, and the warmth of the fire surrounding them. How she wanted the moment to last. To not say goodbye. She never imagined Julian would risk his life to find her and keep her safe. The odds were against him from the start, and he had nothing to gain in return, for they could never be together. But with their last goodbye in the hills outside the fort, the words that spilled from his lips were everlasting.

She brought her face close to his and felt his heart say his time to die was not meant to be. Only his time to live. And she believed him.

THE sins of Nathan's past left a trail of tragic consequences. In the aftermath, the wreckage of violence was over. Seeds of hate withered away, yet other consequences remained.

With Captain Lawton a dead man, the plot to buy political votes jeopardized Colonel Moonlight's appointment as Nebraska's first governor. But Moonlight had bigger problems. Another bungled army attack against the Indians in the Powder River Valley was the last straw.

Mariah paid scant attention to Private Ketchum's news about the colonel who was demoted to sergeant and heading to Fort Kearny at once under the command of Captain Murdock. After too many unauthorized attacks against the Sioux that undermined what few fragments of peace remained between the natives and the white man, the army saw fit to bring in a new leader. Mariah understood one certainty all too well. Change will come. In time, change must come.

BY early evening, Dr. Riddler finished tending the wounded soldiers. The skirmishes created the usual commotion at the hospital, followed by a wave of calm. He ordered Private

Ketchum to escort Mrs. Lawton back to the officers' quarters so she could get some sleep.

Mariah protested, insisting she remain at Julian's side in case his condition deteriorated. It wasn't like her to squabble with the private as they left the infirmary, unless she had good reason. For her to be with Julian every moment was reason enough.

"I guess I'm more tired than I thought and could use some rest."

Ketchum understood. He was fighting his own fatigue. "I know just what you mean. But Doc's doin' his job the best he can, and he ain't exactly goin' anywhere right now."

Mariah needed to hear those words. "You're right. I should have the good sense to let him do his job then. If anything happens, please come tell me right away."

He nodded. "I sure will."

"Well, good night."

"Good night, ma'am." He stepped off the porch and headed back to the hospital.

She walked into the house, and without bothering to undress, plopped onto the bed and fell into a deep slumber.

Late the next morning, the day's heat settled over the fort. If not for the warm air drifting into the room, the entire morning would have passed her by. She tossed and turned and tried falling back asleep when her mind roused. Thoughts of Julian engulfed her, like a downpour roaring through a canyon in the middle of a summer storm.

Lazy girl. Get moving!

She sprang out of bed and opened the armoire. It was empty. All her clothes were gone. She whirled around and saw them scattered on the floor. A puzzled look framed her face. But there was no time for pondering the mess. She had to see Julian.

Dashing to the dresser, she filled the basin with water and

washed her face. Her skin dried in the warm air. With each stroke of her hairbrush, she thought of the money she discovered and everything that happened because of it. How her life changed so suddenly.

The money. A sense of foreboding crept in. Her eyes darted to the floor. The wooden box was still there. She beelined across the room and hurled the lid open. A curse twice placed upon her made her gasp. Father's money was gone. But hunting down the thief didn't matter, or Nathan's devious plans. The stolen money didn't matter either. Julian did.

In her haste setting off for the infirmary, she realized she hadn't visited the cemetery. *Why should I? I'll only find misery there.* Seeing Julian again set her heart racing. A new day had come, and another chance.

She entered the hospital room. Dr. Riddler greeted her. "Good morning, Mrs. Lawton. I see you've had a good night's rest."

"Yes, I have." She glanced at his patient. "How is he doing?"

"The blood from the incision coagulated, so the bleeding has stopped. If the wound doesn't get infected, it should heal with no further complications. He's also managing the high level of trauma which bodes well for the next operation."

Riddler offered no smile. His prognosis told Mariah he was optimistic. She would take that in lieu of a smile any day. His parting remark about Dr. Johnson's coming arrival had him exiting the room.

A foolhardy wish, but Mariah wanted validation, just a glimpse from Julian's eyes giving her the proof she was looking for. Proof he was more alive than dead. He had to be, to battle the second bullet.

In between dressing his wounds, she rocked back and forth in the chair. Her eyes and ears kept a hold on him. She watched for any movement and listened to every sound. The rhythm of his breathing. The upward motion of his back when his lungs filled with air. An awakening in his face that wasn't there the day before. His will to live was getting stronger.

She pulled the rocker next to the bed and kept tempo with her feet. Inhale. Exhale. Inhale. Exhale. A small journal she found on the bookshelf rested in her lap. The title, *Healing with God's Bounty,* made her imagine Julian's body whole again. She fanned the pages through her fingers, then placed the journal on the hutch. The hours passed. Her eyelids grew heavy. She dozed off right where she wanted to be—by his side.

All was serene in her dream where she floated among the clouds, looking down at the gentle waves ebbing and flowing along a shore. Beyond the banks, an expanse of trees and grass bordered a home which at once felt familiar to her and grounded her feet. She was not alone. A rustling near the garden path drew her eyes to a man walking toward her. She couldn't see his face but sensed in his presence that she knew him. His voice was transcendent when he reached out and called her name.

"Mariah . . ." He whispered again. "Mariah . . ."

She stirred from her dream and opened her eyes. Julian's hand was touching hers. She looked up. All doubt vanished. His brown eyes were gazing at her.

"Julian—" The murmur of his name against her lips once echoed despair. But no more. "I thought I lost you forever." She raised his hand and held it to her cheek.

And there, her caress sparked a balefire that raged down to his core. He couldn't hold back the yearning. "Lie with me."

Her pulse quickened. She peeled away the sheet and eased her body beside him. He curved his hand around her back, sealing their embrace. But the pain surging inside punctuated the exhilaration between them. He blocked it out—resisted it with all his might—for he had waited so long to feel her next to him, unhindered.

They were mesmerized by each other's touch as sensations

explored the once forbidden. The heat of their breath urged them closer, until they fell headlong into a kiss. *Their* kiss.

How they wondered what this moment would be like, since it once seemed so impossible. No words were spoken. None needed to be. Their kiss was heaven-sent. All too fast, Mariah felt Julian's lips release her as he drifted back to sleep. She lingered in his limp embrace and quietly kissed him once more.

CHAPTER 25

A Time For Letting Go

A HOSTILE LAND, AUSTERE and unforgiving, offered only hardship for the pioneers. Along the trail, death preyed upon the weary until their willpower surrendered and they faced the end. Still they came, despite the odds, seeking their own promised land.

Oxen hooves and tattered boots forged ahead to a distant place, a mirage even, of someone's own brutal making. But in each emigrant's soul raged a fire, an unstoppable desire to find a new home, a new life, and a wellspring of hope. To believe in the struggle was their battle cry. A voice inside refusing to fall silent, lest the dream be allowed to wither and die.

More than a thousand miles once stood between Julian and Mariah. St. Louis and Boston felt worlds away. Yet a remote outpost seemed hardly the place to find true love, in the wake of a killing that could have seen them both dead had Silas not pulled the trigger.

Mariah refused to leave the hospital. She didn't want to let go of the feeling of lying next to Julian. Then voices erupted in the corridor and startled her. She leapt to her feet and smoothed her dress into place.

The door opened. Two men walked into the room single file. Her stare wasn't meant to be rude, just a way of steadying herself while she reeled in her senses and pretended to ignore the wounded man.

"Mrs. Lawton, how is our patient coming along?"

Before she could answer, Dr. Riddler moved to the bedside and diverted his attention away from her. But she was far more watchful of the stranger as her eyes scoured him from head to toe. *He must be the new doctor.* She wrung her hands together, trying to shrug off her impression of him. He was an outsider. Someone she didn't trust. The silence in the room magnified her suspicions.

Dr. Riddler turned to her. "My apologies. This is Dr. Samuel Johnson. He just arrived at the fort."

Smiles were exchanged, but the pleasantries were cut short when both men huddled over the hospital bed. Mariah's scrutiny of Dr. Johnson left her wondering if he was really a doctor. He couldn't possibly be with that boyish face of his. And his hair, all slicked back and rounded behind his ears. His spectacles did give him an air of expertise and calmed her mind somewhat. As for the suit he was wearing, he looked altogether overdressed out here on the prairie, teeming with all manner of the uncivilized.

But she couldn't ignore how much he reminded her of Julian when he stepped off the train in St. Louis. A confident man, and very much in charge. What mattered now required utmost precision with a skilled hand as she watched him examine the upper bullet wound.

Dr. Johnson's comment was brief. "The clinical limitations here will hamper the surgery. We'll need to discuss the details before we proceed."

"Yes, I agree." Dr. Riddler continued. "There's a high risk of disrupting the leg and heart functions."

The sting of their remarks pushed Mariah back against the window. She didn't want to hear any more of the medical talk. But she had to know what would happen to Julian.

She cleared her throat. "When will you do the second operation?"

Dr. Riddler glanced over his shoulder, narrowing his eyes at her. He didn't like having his concentration interrupted. "Once we've finished our examination and decided on a course of action, we'll perform the surgery tomorrow. Any further delays will not bode well for Mr. Marquette."

"I see . . ." She pressed a hand to her forehead as worried thoughts set in, putting her on edge.

Dr. Johnson peered above the rim of his glasses, noting Mariah's reaction. He approached. "Rest assured, Mrs. Lawton, he's in good hands. We'll keep you informed of his condition."

His words did comfort her, but the fear still lurked beneath her veil of self-control. In this place, she did not want to face the unknown.

THE last sliver of sun hovered above the horizon. Its burning rays were tempered by the end of another day. Mariah ambled past a group of wagons congregated behind the barracks. The haggard looks of the emigrants hinted they just arrived off the Oregon Trail. Some of the travelers crouched along the banks of the Laramie River, plunging their faces into the water. A chill pricked her skin as she recalled the toils of the overland trail and its meager moments of rest.

She wandered about the compound. There was a lot more waiting to do before the next surgery, and more time for her imagination to run wild with images of the first operation. The scalpel slicing through skin. All the blood oozing out. A clank on the metal tray left the bullet lying in a pool of crimson. Tomorrow, the cut would go deeper. What if something went wrong? An accidental slip of the knife could strike the last blow and pierce Julian's heart.

Her breathing stuttered. No, she never did have a knack for waiting, not the impulsive little girl who always clamored for her parents' attention while she outdid Fanny at every turn. Now she had someone else to think of. She had to be strong. *This is our battle. Together.* It was time she started believing in their future. But that wouldn't happen until she said goodbye to the past.

She turned the corner behind the sutler's store and walked toward the cemetery. The plot of land had no fence surrounding it and was far removed from the buildings which made up the fort complex. Without trees or walking paths, the cemetery was not pleasing to the eye, considering a cemetery was not a pleasing place to be anyway.

The dreaded thought struck her. Nathan's body lay buried there in a makeshift grave. She eyed the mounds of dirt. Crisscross twigs of gnarled wood formed grave markers with the last name of the deceased etched in a vertical line. She walked by the gravesites, reading each name, and froze next to the one she recognized. *Lawton.* She caved under the weight. Her knees thudded on the ground. The anguish wrenched open a floodgate of memories. Naïve memories. Bitter memories.

MARIAH's wedding dress glistened white as winter's first fallen snow. Her heart hid no secrets, and her promise was eternal. At the altar, they joined hands. Anticipation brimmed in their eyes. Nathan stood before her in his imperial blue, daring and full of pride. His vow to cherish her and forsake all others resounded in the church for all to hear and to see, forever sealed in their binding kiss.

The feigned loyalist to the Union cause always championed his own and never gave up the fight, no matter the cost. Nathan was a hero from the War of the Rebellion, but the white man's contagion coursing through his veins branded him an insurrectionist, to the end.

MARIAH looked down at her wedding ring. A circle of gold. Never-ending. A love to last just as long. Their marriage gave her all but that, and in its wake left her a widow. The heat rose in her face. Memories hunted her down. She set free her fury, and her resentment grew.

You . . . used me.
You cheated on me.
You nearly destroyed my life
and the life of the man I love.
What did you ever know about love?
You only thought of yourself.
You selfish bast—
Damn you, Nathan!
Damn you!

Her muffled cries were overheard by the woman standing behind her. Stella rested her hand on Mariah's shoulder.

"There, there, deary. It'll be a spell before yer heart's rid a the man." The comfort of her presence did little to stop the tears from streaming down Mariah's face. "I don't mean ta be rude or anythin', but Nathan was a vary wicked man. Ya be much better off without him. Simple as that, I say."

Her words were honestly spoken, yet Mariah's anger felt like it would rage on without end. She stood up and wiped her tears with her trembling hands. A deep breath ensued, and the crying stopped. She had grown accustomed to the habit. Nathan always thought her weak when she cried.

Stella never had the mind to meddle in anyone else's affairs. She had little time enough for tending to her children much less herself. Living a hard life without a husband took its toll. But her sanguine complexion, mirroring the color of her hair, evoked a fiery spirit that drove her to embark on a journey to her family's new home in Oregon.

An upwelling of gratitude echoed in Mariah's voice. "You and the children have been my saving grace. More than you'll ever know."

Both women looked at each other and both understood how complicated life could be, trying to be a woman yet having to fight like a man to do it. They hugged one another as kindred spirits, both aware of the pain of death.

THE pioneers gathered around their campfires, telling stories, good and bad, of the hardships they endured. Despite the dangers, an eagerness filled their voices about the days ahead and what they would find once they reached the Willamette Valley.

For now, their time at Fort Laramie was a godsend. The closest thing to being home for them. Here, they rested their weary bones, found supplies for their wagons, and escaped the rhythm of their routine on the trail.

Mariah didn't say a word. She was too intent on feasting on chunks of bread Stella baked in the mess hall. The smell of the scorched and unsavory kind wouldn't be missed, and gnawing on hardtack gladly forgotten. Maggie and Kate welcomed the change Stella brought to their daily work of humdrum soldier meals. A little womanly chatter in the kitchen added excitement to the task at hand.

Jessie and Martha sat by the campfire, nibbling on their mother's pumpkin pie. It was a sight Mariah never thought she'd see, and it brought a smile to her face. The hug she gave the children gestured a momentary farewell as she grabbed a lantern from the back of the wagon and strolled to the corral.

Dusk fell upon the camp, dimming the wilderness. In the distance, a rocky promontory etched jagged lines across the sky. A man's likeness stood out against the stark backdrop. His forearms rested on the fence, and his boot braced on the lower rail. He looked as though he were in contemplation and had found no better place to be.

Mariah swished her dress, hinting someone was approaching. "Hello, Silas."

He peered over his shoulder and tipped his hat. "Evenin', Mrs. Lawton." A piece of straw hung from the corner of his mouth.

His ceremonious remark made her frown. She drew up next to him and cast him a sideways glance. "Silas, *please*."

He stared ahead and persisted with the formalities. "Finest time a day has surely come upon us."

"Yes, I suppose it has. But fine or not, *Mr. Bingham,* you and I have known each other far too long to be talking so polite."

Silas shrugged and pulled the dried stalk of grass out of his mouth, letting it fall into the shadows. All he could do was act like the simple man he was, and he spoke no different. "Considerin' all that's happened, it's the least bit a respect I should be showin' you."

He said what he wanted to say, what needed to be said, in his own way. Mariah understood. They both had time enough to sort out the tragic events of that day. But the healing would not come so fast. Faces in pain, and faces filled with vengeance.

Guns set to kill and to keep from killing more. Lives shattered in an instant. For Silas, only guilt remained.

ONE day, it was going to happen out on the trail. Now it had. Pulling the trigger was ugly for Silas, worse than the whipping hand of his father. How he tried not to be like him. His father's violent deeds grew out of one human flaw. Anger. And that fact never changed.

When he was a man of twenty, all he wanted was to leave Virginia and make a new life for himself. Away from the walls of iron furnaces where Elijah Bingham never saw the light of day slogging away in the blazing heat. His father was nothing but a machine, devoid of compassion for his son. For him, a life toiled *was* a life lived. Not for Silas. The tinge of melancholy haunted him for the son he swore he would never have. His father's legacy of anger had to stop.

A drifting homestead out on the plains felt gratifying and the way he liked it. A wild yet peaceful place where he kept his promises and did what had to be done for those looking for a better life—a life he already found worth living.

Then the lieutenant hired him. He respected the Union officer and held him in high regard, until his disguise exposed a man no different than his father. An angry man who used violence to get his way. He avoided Nathan at every turn and stood sentry at night to calm his mind. But the anger that consumed Nathan kept hounding him too.

The wagon train pushed on, day by day, as Silas struggled to contain his need to see justice done to the man who saw fit to beat his wife.

THE pungent scent of sagebrush, heavy in the air, reminded Silas how unforgiving the Oregon Trail could be, and how unforgiving he'd been to himself. It was regret he felt for the man who chose to put himself above everyone else and was willing to kill an innocent woman to do it.

As the growing twilight obscured their view of the corral, Silas and Mariah sensed an earthly stillness settle over the land. A kind of hush that could quiet fears and ease the burdens of the past. In that stillness, the lantern cast its warm glow against the darkness, an embracing light giving solace for two souls who needed it.

Silas spoke in a low voice. "We'll be headin' out day after tomorrow. Makin' good time I reckon. Should reach Oregon by September."

"I see." Mariah curled her arm under his and held on. Deep down, she believed Silas was a good man. She needed to enlighten the wagon boss about what he'd really done. "I think it's time I told you." The man she came to trust, more than the man she married, deserved to know. "You've given me the one chance I thought I lost. The chance to love someone for the first time in my life."

Silas felt his boot thud on the ground. He sure as heck hoped the light from the lantern showed the confounded look on his face. Then her words sunk in, and his eyes grew wide. His regret took on a new purpose. There were others to think of now.

"You mean that Easterner, Marquette?"

Mariah's face shone brighter than a hundred lantern lights. "Yes, Silas. That Easterner, Marquette."

Past events irrelevant to Silas at the time came round again in his mind. "Well, I'll be damned." He heaved a breath as if he finally solved the riddle. "When Marquette rode up to the wagon train after we crossed the river, I figured maybe he was tryin' to settle a score with your husband." He tipped his hat back and rolled his eyes. "Can't imagine anybody needin' to settle a score with the lieutenant."

Looking toward the west, he listened to the tufted hair grass rustling in the breeze. This land, belonging to no man, gave him a comfort like kinfolk and a presence of mind to straighten out his affairs when the time came. And now it had.

He gazed at Mariah and asked another question. "You mean to tell me that man came all the way from Boston just to find you?" He didn't wait for an answer. He had a hunch from the glimmer in her eyes. "He must have been plum crazy doin' what he did."

A grin puffed up his moustache as the pieces of the puzzle fell into place and revealed how much a part he played in the game of fate. And then the simple man spoke his simple truth.

"Heck, Mariah. He must be plum crazy for you."

CHAPTER 26

The Brink Of Oblivion

AYS COULD HAVE been weeks, even months. For Julian, time had no meaning. His last glimpse of consciousness expired when a blow slammed him in the back and knocked the air out of his lungs. An inferno ruptured inside his body, severing his senses. A tunnel of gloom was sucking him in and stealing the light as he clung to the sight of Mariah's face. But she was slipping away. And then his world tumbled into black.

In the infinite darkness, nothing existed. No shapes. No substance. No awareness. Had he reached purgatory, bound for the kingdom come, or was he descending into the realm of Hades, never to return? No, not the netherworld where the dead dwelled forever. Not if sounds lurked in the shadows.

A muted voice floated above him. A soft lilt. So familiar. Mariah. She was in that other world. But he was trapped and couldn't get back.

Then, out of the murk shone a faint light. Amorphic figures shifted through space. He tried to tell them he wanted out. ". . . awake. Need to stay . . ."

A cloth muffled his mouth. The gut-wrenching stench plunged him back into the void, detaching his mind from his body, and with it, the pain. He spiraled downward. A mortal lost. Adrift in a sea of emptiness. Not even the arms of Morpheus could find him, for there were no dreams to take comfort in, not even the nightmare of his passage to Hell.

Glints of light punctured the dark. Disjointed fragments took shape. They sparked images that lit up his mind, and the awakening of a singular thought. His life didn't end. Mariah's voice was there again, dragging him up from the depths to show him the way home. He was alive, and his suffering made him stronger.

As the fragments linked together, complete thoughts fell into place. He knew he was in the hospital and what put him here. Gunshots ricocheted in his head. The deathblow struck. One higher. One lower. His back lunged forward, and a rush of air hissed through his teeth like a fire-breathing dragon. A shockwave shuddered through him. Then he collapsed on the ground.

Another sound pierced the air. He heard it before he blacked out. What happened? He tried focusing on the splinter of memory that was missing. The anguish was too much. He gave up. His brilliant mind made him the architect of the greatest railroad to be built, but now it failed him miserably.

Movement shuffled around him. The voices returned. They added a new dimension and an awareness of time passing. He did not try to make sense of the commotion, just that it continued.

The light reappeared and stung his eyes as hazy images came into view. A rocking chair. A hutch against the wall. Sunlight sparkled on the floor below the window. What was it? The shimmer of gold. Mariah's necklace.

He heard it again. The bone-crushing racket. A third gunshot rang out. And another. A new synapse triggered more images of those unanswered moments.

The first impact. His head recoiled violently. Behind him, the lieutenant was holding a gun in his hand. Then the second slug drilled into him, searing through his back. Two bullets, but he was still alive. The cold-blooded murder backfired. A stroke of luck. A miracle. Now he knew the face of the man who tried to kill him.

Too many more questions that needed answers demanded more strength than he had to give. Whatever happened altered the course of events. Otherwise, he'd be dead, and more than likely, Mariah too.

The door latch clicked. Once. Twice. Prying hands shifted his head to the side. Metal clanked against metal. An acrid smell filled his nostrils and shot a line of pain straight up to his skull. When would the insanity end? He was getting sick of it. All of it. A shattered man ripped apart between agony and the tenebrous dungeons of Hell. In a flash of fading consciousness, his willpower gave way, ready to make a deal with the devil.

And then he remembered the taste of her lips.

THERE was no defining moment, no exact dividing line separating tranquility from turmoil. The change left Julian at peace and his body relieved from the torment. His sleep was deep and sustained.

A balmy air drifted over him as he rested undisturbed, until a chill pricked his jawline and stirred him awake. He opened his eyes. A vaulted ceiling arched above him. Beyond the foot of the bed, a sheer curtain rippled in the breeze. The room felt strange to him.

Near the window, candlelight flickered against the wall and illuminated the blue dress she wore. *Mariah*. Her silhouette stunned him. He dug his elbows into the bed and pushed himself up. Ache and desire churned inside. He gazed at her willowy figure, down to her bare feet, where she traced the tip of her toe up her ankle, painting an imaginary line that sent a tingle up his spine. Every move she made was so unintended. It electrified him. He felt restless and more alive than ever as he watched the water droplets plink into the basin each time she dipped the cloth in and out. When she twisted it, his senses snapped.

Mariah turned to him. His gaze startled her. She drew up to the bedside and sat down. The sensation of the cloth gliding over his chest made him collapse on the bed. So cool to the touch. But it couldn't quell his raging fire.

She stood up. In one motion, he grabbed the cloth from her hand and tossed it on the night table. A quick tug eased her body on top of him. The feel of her figure pressing against him pushed his urges sky-high.

"Kiss me, Mariah. I need to know this isn't a dream."

She set free her passion so he could taste the wonder of her lips and believe her touch was real and not a delusion shrouding the pain. The urgency in his kiss sent sparks to her fingertips and emboldened her caress. This moment they wanted was once nearly destroyed. The heat of their bodies intensified their need.

"Julian, I've missed you—"

He held nothing back as their kisses went deeper and ignited a fevered rhythm that kept him fighting for every breath. "God, it's been so long—"

His hands skimmed over the curve of her bosom where he tugged at her bodice and revealed her chemise. His eyes lit up, seeing her nipples tense against the fabric. His touch triggered her sweet reaction and made her weaken in delight. Her moans told him all he needed to know. Her pleasure was his.

The words spilled from his lips. "You're beautiful. All of you."

She caught her breath. "Is this really happening?"

He slowed his pace and rumbled, "Yes, my love. It is."

One by one, he uncoupled the three tiny buttons and watched her breasts slip free. So perfect. So aroused. And so ready for him. He cupped them in his hands and teased each nipple with his tongue. Her body arched, and her breathing strained. Never had she felt such a heat smouldering between her legs.

Sounds of suppressed hunger grew uncontrolled between them. Julian resisted the pain scorching through his back. All he wanted was to show Mariah how deeply he could love her. He clung to her gaze as he guided her hand across his stomach, and down lower. In her eyes, he saw the way she responded to what she touched. Teetering on the precipice, she swooned.

For them, it was no secret their eyes always spoke the truth. They could no more hide it than deny it existed. And Julian couldn't hide the truth now.

Devastation poured out of his eyes. The ecstasy vanished.

Mariah cried out. "I'm hurting you—"

He saw her face fill with guilt and cursed himself for making it all go wrong. Then the anger took hold, nearly choking him. *I can't feel anything.* He pounded his fists on the bed, refusing to believe what happened, and the damage done from a vigilante's bullet. The nightmare found him again.

An imperceptible stirring under the bedcovers brought Mariah to his side. He threw his arm over his face, unable to withstand the shock that he failed her. The exhilaration of sharing their love all but abandoned him. He was less than a man now. A man no longer worth having. Useless words could never make it up to her.

A soft kiss brushed his cheek. He gave nothing back. How could he? He had nothing left to give. Something died inside, and it left him powerless to change his fate. His bleeding heart let Mariah go, away from where he ached for her to be—in his empty arms.

CHAPTER 27

A Reason To Go On

*N*o ANSWERS WERE GIVEN. No questions were asked. Facing a condition with no cure left Julian with no options, and that didn't sit well with the railroad man who leveraged risk every day for better options. A prisoner in his own body, he beat himself down with his thoughts. *My life's nothing but shit now. Gone to hell. Every worthless piece of it.*

The turn of events stunned Mariah as much as it did Julian. The dangers he faced had all been because of her. And by some miracle, he was still alive. Until the day she took her last breath, she promised her undying love to the man who battled against the odds and risked his life for her.

By early morning, she left the officers' quarters and fetched some coffee and grits in the mess hall. She returned later and found Julian awake, sitting bare-chested on the edge of the bed. Her eyes drifted down to his pant line but then darted to his face when he looked at her.

"I've brought you something to eat. You need to regain your strength."

"I'm not hungry."

She offered him the cup. "At least drink some coffee."

"I don't need any damn coffee."

She flinched at his remark and placed the grits and coffee on the night table. Out of the corner of her eye, she noticed the broken water pitcher scattered on the floor next to the dresser. She ignored it and changed the subject.

"Let me take a look at your bandages." She spoke as if nothing happened between them. "Doctor's orders."

A burst of anger erupted before her eyes. Julian flung his hand across the night table, sending the tin plate of grits and coffee cup hurtling across the room.

"I don't need you or any doctor barking orders at me!"

His temper mounted. He braced his hands on the bedpost and tried standing up. His body lurched. He snatched her arms, forcing his weight down on her. They both staggered and fell to the floor. The desperation in his face turned to fight as he rolled onto his back and pushed up against the bed. He blundered it earlier when he tried to reach the dresser. This time, he maneuvered his legs with his hands before he moved in any direction.

The sight of him struggling had Mariah feeling helpless. She denied the word and would not speak it. All she could do was watch him grapple with the side of the bed. Every attempt left him slumped on the floor. She tried putting her hands around his chest, but he pushed her away.

"Leave me alone. This is my fight, not yours."

He shoved his legs alongside the bed. His swearing growled deeper, like a fire being stoked straight up from his belly. He grabbed the bedpost, twisting his body as he inched up. A rousing grunt, and he lunged on top of the bed.

Mariah stood up and made her way to the dresser, then opened the bottle of carbolic acid and soaked a few strips of gauze. She placed the gauze and a coiled bandage on the tray and carried it over to the bed. There was no need to hurry or make demands. She sat down beside him, waiting. He gave in without protest. Gently, she cleaned his wounds and wrapped the bandage around his torso.

As much as Julian tried ignoring her touch, her caring hands soothed him. But her closeness was more than he wanted. The bitterness lingering inside him had no place for her.

"It's not enough, Mariah." He fixated on his legs.

"What's not enough?"

"I'm not enough—for you." His eyes shut out the appendages dangling over the bed.

"How can you say that, after all we've been through? You mean more to me than anything."

She uttered every bit of truth she believed. But it had to be *their* truth. *Don't give up on us, Julian. Not now.* Yet his actions told her the curse already took hold and tainted the heart of the man she feared she was losing again. She so wanted to be in his arms. He awakened a passion in her she didn't know existed. A love she longed to give him, even if they couldn't share it fully.

Tension in the room strained the space between them. Mariah retreated from the bed and placed the tray back on the dresser. She returned to Julian's side, hoping he'd look at her and see the compassion in her eyes. He stared straight ahead. He did not want to see what lurked there. He did not want her pity.

"You don't deserve a cripple. That's what I am now. A useless cripple." The word raged in his mind throughout the night. Its power cut deep and robbed him of his chance to love Mariah the way he wanted to love her.

"I don't care if you can't walk. You're alive, and nothing else matters."

Still, he did not look at her. She turned to him and framed

the side of his face with her hand, gazing at him in earnest. "Listen to me. We can't change the past, but we can get through this together. You have to believe me. *Please* let me in."

He heard every word she said, but he was dead set on wallowing in his own misery. Why should he let her in? All he had to give her was the life of a broken man dragging around a broken heart. Fate dealt him a heavy blow, and its poison corrupted the very essence of who he was.

HIGH noon brought a flurry of commotion to the outpost. The fort's new commanding officer, Major James Van Voast, accepted his assignment after a brief induction ceremony on the parade grounds. He had no time to squander. Some of the troops admitted on the quiet they missed Colonel Moonlight's leadership, but the dire situation confronting Van Voast that afternoon had him fuming at the colonel's incompetence.

Pressure from Washington brought him to Fort Laramie. Opposition from the Sioux Nation for a new peace treaty was almost certain since Moonlight bungled talks with the tribal leaders in early spring. Army violations to the Fort Laramie Treaty of 1851 were staring Van Voast in the face. He was on tenterhooks and knew this was the army's last chance.

The upcoming meeting with the Sioux tribes was intended to reassure them of the Great Father's promise to make amends, though his sharp tongue proved to be without honor. If both parties could come together and heal old wounds, talk of a new treaty and a future of peaceful coexistence might be possible.

A sense of unease swept over the garrison. News spread that the tribal chiefs were approaching camp, not to battle with bows and arrows, but to battle with words. Fort Laramie had long been a strategic outpost on the High Plains and stood its ground as a protector of emigrants on the Oregon Trail, and a force of military power in the region. Without the fort, the white man's progress would be put in jeopardy.

Van Voast ran the risk of traveling alone to meet the high chiefs from the Ogallalla, Brule, and Minneconjou tribes where he offered his personal invitation for them to come to the fort. He pleaded his case that the Great Father wanted peace as much as they did. But the army's push to seize their sacred hunting grounds in the Powder River Valley would throw the white man's promise back into his own lying face. Van Voast needed some kind of guarantee so they could walk away from the gathering, holding their heads high. Problem was, he had no guarantee. And time was running out.

JULIAN grew more frustrated as the afternoon heat wore him down. He felt marooned in a world where he didn't belong. The bedroom walls had closed in. He stared at his legs spread out on the bed with no mind of their own, limp and forgotten by the rest of his body. His desperate straits had him trapped. He was fed up.

A knock at the door snapped him out of his thoughts. He should have called out and invited the visitor in, but he didn't feel like it. He was stewing good and hard and was ready for a fight. Beware the sorry sucker who was stupid enough to walk in on him. He had nothing to lose. Half his body already fought its own battle, and lost.

The visitor chimed from the front room. Julian recognized Riddler's voice, having heard the man more than he saw him of late. Just as the doctor appeared in the doorway, he hammered him with the weight of his stare.

Riddler flinched. "My apologies. I didn't mean to barge in on you." He furrowed his brow. "Your surgeon isn't exactly who you wanted to see, is it?" He grew accustomed to that reaction from his patients. Acting like old chums was never part of the deal. But the man from Boston lost a lot of blood from both operations and needed a good looking over. "Well, I haven't seen you since after the surgery, so it's time I examined your wounds. From my first glance, I'd say you're making progress."

Julian swore he was just insulted. "What the hell are you talking about? Progress, my ass. I can't walk because of you."

The news surprised Riddler. "I see." He crossed his arms and entered the room. "That's unexpected news." His mind retraced each step of the operation, but he reached the same conclusion, leaving him with no answer. "I don't know what to tell you. Dr. Johnson and I considered the surgery a success."

"Well, if you ask me, you botched it up bad."

Riddler's conscience started eating at him. He riled enough of his former patients who faced the trauma of amputated arms or legs. Now this. He clenched his jaw. The news of Julian's paralysis pissed him off.

"You had two New York surgeons working miracles under the circumstances. And we only had two options. Either we removed the bullet, or you died."

Julian tossed him a blank look. He had no words to counter, not even for the physician who helped save his life. His emotions, like his legs, became paralyzed too.

The doctor saw no point in carrying on the conversation. "Let me take a look at your wounds."

Julian charged and stopped him short. "Why bother? I'm already a *cripple*."

"I won't deny that, but until I examine you, I can't form any opinions about your condition or what it could mean for your recovery."

He stepped toward the bedside and waited. His patient grumbled and sat up, dragging his legs over the side of the bed. He inspected the two concave lesions on Julian's back, nodding at the thick scabs formed tight over the wounds. Then he poked the bottom of his right foot for any sign of movement.

"Can you feel this?"

"No."

He jabbed the other foot. "Any sensation at all?"

"I can't feel a damn thing."

"Well, for the time being, I suggest you make use of a wheelchair to get around the compound. I'll have one brought over from the hospital. Otherwise, you're stuck here in bed."

Julian glared at his flaccid legs, seemingly disconnected, as though they didn't belong to him. The dreaded question kept haunting his thoughts. He had to ask. "Doc. I need you to tell me straight. Will I ever—walk again?"

Riddler understood the impact his answer would have on his patient. If he didn't choose his words with utmost care, they could have devastating consequences for the way this man was going to live the rest of his life, and if he would choose to live it alone or not. No matter what he said, his words had to speak the truth.

"Paralysis below an injury is always a risk. In your case, Dr. Johnson and I had to cut through muscle tissue to get to the bullet before we extracted it. Rest assured, the wounds will heal, but any nerve damage is out of my hands. No surgeon can fix that."

Julian wanted a straight answer, and he got one. There was no sense in fooling himself. No sense in dwelling on it. It was time he set his sights on other prospects. "I guess I should head back to Boston and move on with my plans."

Riddler took Julian to be a man like himself, a man who didn't want to stay in this hellhole out on the plains any more than he did. He looked at his patient and grinned. "Well, I'd say our timing couldn't be better."

Julian's mind was trapped in the past and the life he might've had with Mariah. Then the doctor's remark sunk in. "What are you talking about?"

"You're in no shape to travel alone, and I need to return to New York. My time is up here at the fort, and not a moment too soon. Now that Dr. Johnson is in charge, my contribution to medical science in this territorial prison is at an end." He stepped into the doorway and turned around. "Based on your condition, I think we should hit the trail by the end of the week. What do you say, Marquette?"

The impromptu idea conjured up no objections from Julian. "I guess I could use the company." He nodded. "By the end of the week then."

Mariah's name wasn't mentioned, and Riddler didn't ask. He saw it happen before during the war, only worse. Soldiers who marched into battle full of fight, not giving a damn if they got maimed but later wishing they died instead. What they were left with was unspeakable. Severed legs and arms. Lead bullets that shattered bone and lacerated tissue, leaving gaping wounds the size of a fist. Those soldiers ended up with more than broken bodies. They lost their identities and loathed the creatures they became. Once self-pity took hold, love had no chance of surviving. All that remained for them was an empty life. Alone.

Private Ketchum shoved his head through the open door and hollered into the front room, right into Riddler's face. "Hey, Doc! Ya there?"

His expression turned to shock when he spotted Julian sitting on the bed. The last time he saw the Easterner, he was being hauled on a stretcher to the infirmary, all shot up and covered in blood. Since his first day assigned to the fort, he never saw a man with deadly injuries come out of the hospital alive, much less with all his parts still intact. In this place, every soldier downright called that a miracle.

He glanced at Riddler. "Major Van Voast asked me to come

lookin' for Marquette. Word around camp's got the major wantin' to find out what he knows about the railroad that's comin'. Wants to do a little talkin' with him, I reckon."

Julian flashed back to the world he left behind before the nightmare began. He cursed himself and the bitter man he became. The man who gave up.

The Transcontinental Railroad. The people's railroad. How could he have purged it from his mind? His life's work, forgotten. *Hell no.* He had a railroad to build. His body failed him, and he failed Mariah, but he still had the brains to finish the job he set out to do. To build the Iron Road.

He swallowed hard. His future would be different now. He couldn't change the past. As much as he regretted the bad turn his life had taken, it wouldn't be right for him to stand in Mariah's way. It was time she made plans he couldn't be part of anymore. It was time to start thinking with a clear head. All he had left was his dream to build a railroad across America. He wasn't about to let that dream die too.

CHAPTER 28

Thundering Skies

AVING A PREACHER for a father had been a scourge for Julian and his brother Johnny. After their mother died, they found no comfort for their grief, just anger from their father, as if he blamed them for her death. They were too young to understand his actions, the man so undone by his loss that he turned his grieving against them.

Too blinded by his own vanity to see the harm he caused, their father stood high in his pulpit, hiding behind his veneer of the Divine, bellowing hellfire in his sermons to those who couldn't contain their own anger. But his preaching only brought more hurt.

Julian remembered his punishment—the Hand of God his father called it. He hated watching his brother endure the same. And Johnny took it personal. A son was, after all, supposed to look up to his father, except Johnny had a real problem looking up to a hypocrite. How could a father take his anger out on his own flesh and blood and let his pride overshadow the damage he'd done?

It wasn't pride that cursed Julian now.

He squirmed in the clunky wheelchair. Moving half his body felt strange. His senses did too. Like they were making up for what had shut down. From where he sat on the covered porch, random scenes and noises drew his attention. Details he wouldn't have noticed before.

On the far side of the barracks, he spied the guardhouse. A soldier abandoned his post. Around back, Sharkey stood with his boot propped against the building, taking a swig from his pocket flask and waving it in the air. Near the mill yard, he heard the faint tap of a blacksmith's hammer. Each clang echoed two seconds apart. He looked up. Hoisted high above the parade grounds, the flag rippled in the breeze. A gust of wind blew in, and the fabric snapped. Flecks of sand scurried in wavy lines across the porch, stinging his face. He turned his head and caught a whiff of stale coffee wafting up the steps.

His line of sight stretched west beyond the fort. Thin clouds of dust curled skyward behind a line of wagons traversing the outlying hills. The caravan was headed in the direction of South Pass, a gap high in the Rocky Mountains. A gradual rise in the earth where towering peaks didn't exist, as if they were dynamited to smithereens.

Julian thought back to the plans and maps he drew up, along with the maze of paperwork the Union Pacific had to navigate, and how all those efforts gave an irony to his dream. Without the discovery of South Pass, there would've been no push to travel west, and no dream to build a railroad.

His mind wandered off for a bit and let him forget. Not much left to do except watch the day go by. But he was tired of all the distractions. That restless feeling kept hounding him. Sitting in the wheelchair made it worse. Why didn't he hear back from Ketchum or the major yet? Guess nobody wanted to talk to the man wasting away in a wheeled contraption. He was getting good at feeling sorry for himself, enough to drill a couple of fists into his legs and force some kind of reaction out of them. *Not a damn thing.* His hands didn't let up. Maybe they'd set fire to his temper and get his blood pumping so fast he'd fly out of that wheelchair and take his life back.

A bead of sweat trickled down his sideburns. Every bit of air he sucked in was a fight for what strength he had left. There was no way out of this mess. God, he despised being a cripple. No sooner had his conniption shriveled up in the stagnant heat than Ketchum and another soldier came marching toward him. The private looked peeved himself.

"I tell you what. Bein' a striker ain't all it's cracked up to be. The major's got me bustin' my tarnal hide all over this fort doin' his stuff." Another bale of words flew out of his mouth with each step he took up the stairs. "Hell, all I'm doin' is women's work. Fetchin' meals. Cleanin' up his quarters. Runnin' telegrams back and forth. Fine soldier I turned out to be. Ain't seen a lick of fightin' since I got here."

Julian didn't hear a word he said. He dragged his sleeve down the side of his face and lit into the private. "About time you showed up. Taking your own sweet time, is that it? I didn't think you were coming at all." He stopped his rant when Ketchum looked at him like he was just court-martialed. "Son of a—" He shook his head. "That was uncalled for, what I said. I don't know why—"

Ketchum shrugged. "Naw. I had it comin'. Besides, all my belly achin' can't hold a candle to all the hell you been through." He turned and waved the other soldier up the steps.

They both hovered over the wheelchair and braced their hands against the sides. Julian caved under the weight of their stares, crushing him with humiliation. His mind unhinged and rekindled the memories of his father. The Hand of God was at the ready, waiting to beat him down again and obliterate all he accomplished—all his life's work—until nothing was left but an insignificant man. Not even his father's preaching of the

Divine could save the useless cripple when self-pity already left him rotting inside.

He was done doing it alone. Better get used to the idea or let self-pity devour the only shred of decency he had left. His dignity. He just wasn't sure he cared anymore.

Together, the soldiers lifted the wheelchair and carried Julian down the stairs. Ketchum's voice sounded urgent all of a sudden. "Gotta get you to post headquarters lickety-split or the major's gonna be cussin' up a storm."

The wheelchair jounced across the hardpan, tracking along the Laramie River. A sharp turn yanked Julian's head sideways. What was all the hurry about? And why did the major want to talk to him about the railroad? He leaned back to ask Ketchum when he caught sight of a figure at the edge of the fort. Mariah was standing in the middle of the cemetery. The wind swirled through her hair, scattering dirt across the pile of graves.

He couldn't deny the obvious. Now he was certain. Nathan was dead. The shock of it all must have brought Mariah to his bedside that night. He didn't know she was so vulnerable. Whether he hated her husband or not didn't matter. Nathan's death urged her toward him out of loneliness, not love.

Ketchum turned the corner of the building. Julian tightened his grip on the wheelchair, but he couldn't hold on to her. She was slipping from his grasp. He shouldn't have pushed her away. Was he out of his mind? He felt the one-two ping in his back again that rammed the air out of his lungs. Those bullets were enough to change a man. Make him a quitter if he didn't quit already. *I can never love you this way, Mariah. You deserve more than a cripple like me.*

AND then they came, wearing their feathered headdresses and buckskin loin cloths, and their tanned leggings, riding atop their Mustangs with their chests adorned in hair pipe breastplates. Dust whipped off the High Plains and around their powerful steeds as Fort Laramie appeared before them. The Sioux tribal chiefs commanded the attention of everyone at the fort, not because an order was given, but out of respect for the Indians who lived there long before their own kind arrived.

They were guided into the Big House, built of adobe, where the warriors could not smell the scent of the buffalo, or see the sun rise above their sacred hunting grounds, or listen to the Great Spirit summon the rain down from thundering skies and fill the rivers with its water. And they could not sit upon the ground with the strangers who talked of peace, but still did not know how to make peace with the Lakota people.

"It is an honor to welcome the Sioux Nation to Fort Laramie today." Major Van Voast's words reverberated across the room as fragments of light etched lines through the tiny windows, casting shadows on everyone's faces. "I speak on behalf of the United States government, and offer my gratitude to the leaders of your great nation for allowing us to honor your people and your way of life once again, by coming together for our one common purpose. To seek a lasting peace."

The major's announcement voiced the gravity of the meeting to his fellow army negotiators. They all stood at attention behind the long table, staring in silence at the natives standing on the opposite side. Van Voast realized too late the arrangement was a mistake. Two adversaries facing each other with a wall of wood wedged between them. The gathering had all the makings for a confrontation.

Van Voast looked striking in his dress uniform, with his broad shoulders lodged inside his blues and specks of gold trim accenting his sandy hair. His sweeping moustache gave him an air of flamboyance as one not to be taken seriously. Those who did underestimated his reputation for enacting swift retribution on anyone who turned on him. He could cut a man down by glaring right through him.

This wasn't the time to aggravate the tribal chiefs. They didn't come to the fort with open arms. The last treaty they signed with the white man turned into empty words. Finding no honor in the Great Father, and left with no choice but to defend their land, Chief Red Cloud refused to come and sit at the table, and talk again.

The Sioux chiefs waited until the major motioned for them to be seated. Chair legs skidded across the floor and disrupted the silence. Van Voast hesitated, then sat down. Any last hopes for delaying the talks were long dashed. And any hasty assurances he promised could cost him his rank, or worse, an unprovoked attack.

How was he going to break the news to the natives? He had no way to defend the army's actions when they blazed the Bozeman Trail across the Sioux's prized hunting grounds in the Powder River Valley. The Fort Laramie Treaty they signed in 1851 instructed the army to protect it. Now he had to tell them the Iron Horse would soon cut its tracks straight through the heart of that sacred land.

The civilian interpreter, Antoine Janis, began the introductions.

"We offer you peace, Tah-Shun-Ka-Co-Qui-Pah, known as Man Afraid of His Horses, from the Ogallalla band of Sioux."

The formalities were necessary and but a small gesture to earn their trust.

"We offer you peace, Ma-Za-Pon-Kaska, Iron Shell, from the Brule band of Sioux."

Antoine continued, introducing Heh-Won-Ge-Chat, One Horn, from the Minneconjou band of Sioux, and Two Bears and Red Horse, from the Yanctonais band of Sioux.

One lone headman in attendance had yet to be introduced when the door swung open and a figure wheeled into the room.

The headman's eyes narrowed and then opened wide as the pale light unveiled the face of the white man. He bolted up from his chair, knocking it to the floor. The man whose soul had traveled the spirit path was still alive. The man who showed no vengeance in his eyes when they met in the canyon below Scotts Bluff. But this was no place to be for the only white man he trusted and once thought dead.

The disturbance had the interpreter darting his eyes around the room. He cleared his throat and announced the headman's name. "We offer you peace Mato-Sunkmanitu-Tanka, known as Bear Wolf, from the Brule band of Sioux."

Bear Wolf and Julian exchanged glances, nodding to each other. The Sioux warrior thus far saw lies in the eyes of the soldiers who were dressed and ready for battle, as they had always been. Seeing the white man again reassured him the Great Spirit, Wakan Tanka, was among them.

Julian shifted his gaze to the fort's commander. "Major Van Voast, I'm Julian Marquette. I apologize for interrupting your important meeting."

"No apology needed. I'm glad you've joined us. It's good to see you're recovering from your injuries."

Julian sensed the major didn't expect to see him in the flesh and tried to make light of it. "Not quickly enough, sir."

He wheeled himself to the end of the table and looked down the planks of wood toward the Sioux brave. Bear Wolf picked up his chair and took his seat at once to keep from staring down at the crippled man. In his mind's eye, they were both equals, for they had fought their own battles with honor and suffered the ravages of hatred by others, not because they caused such hate, but because of who they were.

The process of negotiating a new treaty would take months or longer. Van Voast had his back up against a wall. If he didn't offer the chiefs a promise he could damn well keep, he'd have Washington breathing down his neck.

He swallowed hard. His shirt collar chafed his skin. Getting the late news about Marquette's link to the railroad left him no time to figure out a strategy before the tribal leaders rode into camp. There were no other options now. He'd have to marshal all his tactics of diplomatic guile before he addressed the thorny issue of the railroad's route through the Sioux's sacred hunting grounds. With his mind focused on striking the right tone, he opted to bring up the matter as though the route wasn't set in stone.

"It is our hope that Chief Red Cloud will come to our next gathering to talk about a new Iron Horse which is far off to the east. Today we welcome this honorable man who has truth of this great news."

Julian understood why the major invited him here. He acknowledged Van Voast as fast as he saw the fire erupting in the eyes of the tribal chiefs when Antoine Janis translated the Great Father's words into their Lakota tongue. But what was the major's next move? This wasn't the time to play cat and mouse with the volatile issue of the railroad, not when peace was at stake.

A glance from Van Voast motioned for him to speak. He missed his chance.

Man Afraid of His Horses tired of the white man's words of great news. Unlike Red Cloud, he agreed to sit with the army negotiators one last time. But his patience ran out. He stood up. His brooding eyes pierced through the hollow stares glaring back at him. What he said next drove straight to the heart of his fellow warriors.

"The spirit of Red Cloud is with us. I speak his words so you will see the lie you bring before us again."

I have listened patiently to the promises of the
Great Father, but his memory is short. I am now
done with him. This is all I have to say.

"We have heard before this day of the Iron Horse you speak of, and our people are afraid. The Great Spirit has told us the end is near. Our way of life will be no more."

Man Afraid of His Horses grew more indignant with every word he spoke. His resentment deepened with each step the white man took across their sacred land, and with the buffalo they killed, and with every Sioux brave, woman, and child who died from the disease they brought with them.

"And there *you* sit, with your faces that look upon us with no honor. You do not hear the Lakota voices cry out to chase the white man from our lands, for he marks the trail of the Iron Horse across our sacred hunting grounds! Did you think we did not know of this? And now you say you want peace with the Sioux."

He grunted in disgust and stormed toward the door with his fists clenched in defiance. Then he turned around and spat on the floor. His final words scorned the Great Father and his shameful ignorance.

"This is all I have to say."

In a rash move Van Voast didn't expect, Julian called out to the Ogallalla leader. "If the great Sioux chief will accept the apology of our government for acting without honor, perhaps he will listen to my words."

Man Afraid of His Horses crossed his arms and stood silent. The air grew thick with uncertainty, and the end of it all was only a few steps away. If the Ogallalla chief walked out the door, his Lakota brethren would follow as a sign of respect for their fellow tribesman.

Bear Wolf could not speak for the leader of his tribe, but Iron Shell would accept his words, even if he did not agree with them. He placed his hands on the table and waited. Iron Shell acknowledged him. He looked at the wounded man.

"Want to hear white man speak."

His voice was unbending, as though the existence or complete annihilation of his people rested on the words the white man had yet to say.

On both sides of the table, the tribal chiefs and soldiers gave Julian the same confounded look. Had Bear Wolf just offered a line of defense to the enemy? The Brule warrior and the railroad man ignored the stares and kept their eyes fixed on each other. There was another fight brewing. A fight to give peace one last chance.

Julian's mind raced unchecked while his fingers drummed on the arms of his wheelchair. Given more agreeable circumstances, he would've telegraphed Dunnigan and had him convene an emergency session with the railroad syndicate to analyze the route through Dakota Territory. But conditions deteriorated with the Sioux leaders and left him facing an impasse. He needed options, and he needed them fast.

His thoughts flashed back to his meeting with the company investors before he departed Boston for Council Bluffs. He had to stall for time. That was his only way out, or the rift of tension between the two great nations would shatter peace for good.

"Major Van Voast, I'd like to show the Sioux leaders their sacred hunting grounds on the territorial map." He traced a rectangular shape on the table as he spoke.

The major walked over to his desk and picked up a coiled tube from under a pile of papers. He strode back to the table where he unrolled the map before the entire assembly.

Man Afraid of His Horses did not expect any truth from the crippled man. But his courage startled him. He watched as Julian struggled and stood up—the unbearable strain crushing his arms—while he braced his body against the table with the brute force of his hands. The wheelchair jolted back and rolled away. A chasm of silence swept over the room, except for the sound of clipped breathing.

Julian locked his eyes on the Sioux chief.

"Come and see—the change I will make—to the new trail of—the Iron Horse."

A glimpse at the map confirmed his hunch. He spotted the gap in the Black Hills before he rode into Fort Laramie with Mariah and the lieutenant. That shorter route for the railroad was the excuse he was looking for when he wired his boss and explained why he came this far.

Dunnigan's reply was to the point. *Bad idea, Julian, unless you have a damn good reason.* Rerouting the track farther south, away from the Sioux's sacred hunting grounds in the Powder River Valley was damn good reason enough. He'd send a telegram to Dunnigan in the morning. There'd be hell to pay no matter what, but he called it the way he saw it. The deal was done.

Guttural noises growled deep in his throat as he fought against the dead weight of his body. His arms shuddered, like an earthquake unleashed in the room. Every breath set fire to his lungs and rushed air through his nostrils with the force of a gale he couldn't stop. Any second, he was going to implode. But he kept his eyes on the Ogallalla chief. He wasn't about to give in.

Man Afraid of His Horses stared in disbelief. His arms fell to his side. He stepped toward the gathering. At the table, he nodded to the white man who chased cowardice from the room.

Just as the Sioux warrior sat down, Julian's arms crumbled under pressure. He collapsed into the wheelchair the major held steady from behind. Pain streaked through his back with the shock of a lightning bolt cutting through him. He embraced it. He had a promise to keep with the Sioux Nation.

The soldiers witnessed one of their own surrender his position to what some considered savage Indians whose land was free for the taking as the white man saw fit. Van Voast surmised the rerouting of the railroad would cost the Union Pacific dearly, but he had to use whatever means necessary to persuade the Sioux leaders to sign a future treaty filled with new assurances.

He watched the tribal chiefs and their headmen walk out the door, then put his hand out to the Easterner and gave him a firm handshake. "Gotta tell you, Marquette, you're one hell of a negotiator. The army sure could use a man like you."

As the sun dipped low on the horizon, the warriors straddled their horses and gestured to the white man who made a great peace offering. They turned their Mustangs, guiding them to the north to ride among the wild buffalo in the untamed lands of the Powder River Valley.

Bear Wolf was the last warrior to leave the fort. There were words he left unsaid. Words that needed to be spoken. He mounted his horse and reined it in. They were eager to ride free again. He looked at Julian and saw a restlessness in his eyes. It was time to speak the Lakota words and tell him how beholden he was to the white man he would never see again.

"Pilamaya." His voice thundered with the might of an entire Sioux Nation.

Both men stared at each other, and both understood. In their parting goodbye, Julian realized he'd been given more than Bear Wolf's gratitude. Maybe he wasn't half a man after all.

CHAPTER 29

On The Precipice

*D*UNNIGAN *STOP* R*EROUTE* *track south of Powder River Valley Dakota Territory STOP Shorter route confirmed through Black Hills STOP Discuss details upon my return STOP Marquette STOP*

Julian heaved a sigh of relief after sending the telegram. At least Dunnigan wouldn't be in his face raising Cain after he read it. But he could already hear his boss yelling the question about what the deuce he was doing in Dakota Territory, and if he lost his imbecilic mind about rerouting the Transcontinental Railroad. Dunnigan didn't know the worst of it.

Outside the telegraph office, Ketchum stood on the boardwalk chewing on a strip of dried beef. Just as he swallowed the butt end, Julian wheeled up next to him.

"Much obliged for the wait."

Ketchum grinned. "You betcha. Don't mind takin' a break."

Julian squinted at the sun and shook his head. "Heck, it's already afternoon. I shouldn't have slept in."

"Naw. You're better off goin' easy on yourself. Don't wanna louse things up."

All the urgency Julian hauled into the telegraph office was overtaken by a good old appetite. Ketchum caught his look and pulled another strip of beef out of his shirt pocket.

"There's more where that came from."

They both got busy with not much talk but a lot of jaw action. Julian sensed a camaraderie between them he likened to his days growing up with Johnny back home in Cohasset, long before all this hell broke loose. He hadn't felt in high spirits for a while and polished off the best beef he ever tasted.

"Guess I should take it easy for the rest of the day. Got a long trail ride ahead of me." He was getting antsy with all the sitting around he was doing. The soreness in his back didn't help. If he could just stand up and walk a few yards. He leaned forward in the wheelchair, trying to shift the ache away from his backside.

Ketchum took notice. "Sittin' in a wheelchair can give any man the fidgets, that's for sure. I'll take you on over to your quarters." He moved behind Julian and grabbed the push handles, then flinched. His duty as a soldier was to report any activity the way he saw it, and what he saw looked bad. "Uh, hate to say it, but goin' to your quarters ain't such a good idea. You best be headin' to the hospital."

Julian reacted like he was laughing at a sick joke. "The hell I will. That's the last place I ever want to set foot in."

"Ain't that the truth. You might wanna have Doc look at your back 'cause it's bleedin' right where one a them slugs went in."

Julian's head slumped at Ketchum's remark. He was on the mend since he left the hospital. This was the first time his wounds gave him enough grief to warrant a once-over. He raked his fingers through his hair. The facts were the facts but not what he wanted to hear. Any sign of blood signaled a relapse, and that got him riled.

"Damn it—"

He eased back in the wheelchair and felt a damp patch through his shirt. No sooner had Ketchum hailed a soldier riding by on a buckboard than they loaded him onto the wagon bed and rode across the complex. He felt too weak to kick up a stink. The last thing he remembered was being lugged into one of the rooms when he passed out.

THE axles creaked under the weight from the water barrel mounted on the side of the wagon. All the supplies had been loaded up. The lone travelers weren't bound for Oregon with a wagon boss guiding their way. They were tracking east, not to Independence, but Omaha City.

A chance encounter with the doctor yesterday had Mariah scurrying about with not a moment to lose. Her body shivered from the early morning chill, yet her nagging thoughts grated on her nerves. She was troubled by what Julian had done. Why didn't he tell her he was leaving the fort? She never saw it coming, the incredible power of self-pity that was tearing him apart. Whether he walked again or not meant nothing to her, but she had to face the possibility he already said goodbye.

Standing on the porch, she shut the door to the place she once expected to call home. The click of the latch didn't banish the ghosts haunting her from the past. A breeze whirred off the High Plains and broke the silence of a new day, but she found no comfort in the solitude that came over her. She did not expect to feel so alone.

In the bustle of gathering her possessions and tossing them into the wagon, she lost track of her boots. The faint outline of the doctor's face, with his mouth pinched closed, hinted he was eager to get going. From where she stood, the sky appeared more dark than light. She sighed. Looking straight across the parade grounds would've given her a perfect view of the cemetery.

Riddler cinched up the saddle and glanced over Chakote's back. He kept his eyes on Mariah and what she was doing. A grieving woman needed time to figure things out, he guessed. As for the Boston man he took a liking to, there was no telling how friendly she was with him. He didn't much care. He saw it before, wounded soldiers who crossed his path in the battles of Shiloh and Opequon. Men whose lives he tried to save at a price too high for them to pay. A man wasn't much good trapped inside a pathetic body.

Maybe Julian was suffering the same fate. But the bullets were removed in time to save his life. Riddler would never dispute that fact any more than the Hippocratic Oath he swore to uphold in his duty to his patients. He shrugged and tied Chakote up to the feedbox. It was no use stewing over why his patient ended up paralyzed. He did all he could.

What he couldn't get out of his head was Mariah. In the time they spent together, he came to know her as someone who engaged him in intelligent conversation while they worked by each other's side. He saw she was a refined woman by the way she spoke and carried herself. She could have entered his circle of New York colleagues with ease and had them vying for her attention. No doubt, she was the most exquisite woman he ever set eyes on. With their journey to Omaha City, he'd have the chance to share her company again.

He caught up to her at the back of the wagon. "Mariah."

She looked up. "Yes, Dr. Riddler."

"Please, call me John." He smiled in a more sincere way than before.

"All right . . . John."

"You don't mind if I call you Mariah, do you?"

"No, of course not."

"I'm glad you decided to join us instead of waiting for a small caravan to head back East." His voice sounded genuine, as though she made up her mind only because of him. He covered his tracks. "My guess is you didn't want to stay here for much longer."

She gave no sign his assessment was wrong. Even if she did, the look in his eyes told her she made a wise decision.

He changed the subject. "Well then. First off, we need to stop at the hospital. I'll drop you off there and take the wagon to the stables and fill up the feedbox."

His remark had her blurting out a slew of questions. "The hospital? Is Julian back in the hospital? What happened?"

"Last night, when I was packing up my medical books, Samuel—rather—Dr. Johnson, told me your friend overexerted himself and returned to the hospital for an examination." He paused, waiting for her reaction. "He is just your friend, isn't he?"

It was an awkward question coming from the physician who saved Julian's life. His words felt too personal. "Yes, I suppose he's a friend. A close friend."

Mariah tried sounding nonchalant with her answer, but John was far more interested in looking into her eyes, as if he never saw the color aquamarine before. He stepped toward her. She stepped back and bumped against the wagon bed. Standing near him had her noticing his eyes too. That shade of cerulean was bluer than the western sky she came to know on the trail. In his gaze, she sensed he was trying to tell her something. She ignored the rambling thought. All she wanted was to see Julian.

The wagon pulled up in front of the hospital. She ran up the steps and dashed inside. The pungent odor of antiseptic hung in the air, stinging her nostrils. It didn't take moving heaven and earth to bring back those memories. They were chasing her down faster than she could outrun them.

She rushed from one end of the corridor to the other, searching for Julian's room. The last door was partway open. She peeked inside. Dr. Johnson was wrapping the last piece of bandage around Julian's chest. She didn't want to barge in and interrupt the patient who made her heart jump.

The door swung open. Dr. Johnson gave her a surprised look. "Good morning, Mrs. Lawton." His smile lifted his cheeks and pushed up his spectacles. "Please excuse me. I have a few other patients to attend to." He passed her and continued his rounds.

A sudden impulse swept her into the room. She shut the door. Julian's expression told her he wanted to be alone, but her instincts drew her toward him. She brushed her body against his as she sat down, just sensing his presence. Leaning closer, she whispered, "I've missed you."

He glared at her with a cold look in his eyes. "Admit it, Mariah. There's nothing left between us. So don't make this harder than it already is."

His words sent a shock through her, but she wouldn't have it. She stood up and planted herself in front of him, facing him head on. Her move was deliberate. Willful. Her gaze fused into his while she took her pretty little time sliding her dress up her thighs. She straddled his legs and eased onto his lap, then placed her hands on his shoulders, nudging him down on the bed. Julian needed more than a good talking to. Only he could quench the ache inside that left her yearning with every breath.

A tingling in her bare feet rocketed up between her legs and sparked a fire, liquefying the ice in his eyes. She had every reason to tease him, with all her feminine devices.

"I'll try not to make it harder than it already is, but I can't make any promises."

All at once, Julian's gaze lassoed her heart and set it pounding in her bosom. She came down on him and kissed him hard, triggering an avalanche that buried them tight in one embrace.

With each kiss, he murmured her name and set free his self-inflicted misery. His fingers followed the contour of her back, around her bottom to the warm indentation in between. But what he discovered that night hounded him again. He had nothing to give her. Nothing. Yet her kisses told him she didn't care. Over and over, she kept telling him she didn't care. For them, there was no place to be except together—for good. They had a lifetime of love to give each other, and it was time to start now.

He raised his bandaged torso and curled her body beneath him. Making sense of it all was a waste of time. Being apart was madness. He gazed at her and let his passion burst into words.

"You are everything to me. *Everything*."

He said it with no shame, as though he were a man who was made whole again. Each kiss he laid upon her lips hurled their need skyward. *Losing control. Letting go. Feels so right.*

Where Mariah felt the outline of his bandages, her touch was tender, but even that caring gesture aroused her. What he gave her before was just a taste of what she wanted now. She lifted her arms above her head and moaned to him.

"Love me, Julian. Love me . . ."

Anxious sighs grew deeper with their kiss as skin caressed skin. The rhythm of their bodies kindled a rising heat between them when voices echoed in the hallway and tore them out of their embrace.

Their breathing stuttered. Mariah whisked to her feet and shuffled her dress back into place. The doctor reentered the room. Her casual air carried on while she tended to the patient. She tugged Julian's shirt off the bed rail and draped it around his front, inching her fingers down past the top button of his pants.

Each touch they shared gave Julian his truth. Mariah didn't give a damn if he couldn't share all of his love with her. But the stranglehold wouldn't let go. He had to walk again, and feel everything again. He clung to the urge with every fiber in his being. The odds were against him if he gave up. Now he had every reason not to.

CHAPTER 30

Bound For Home

O N THE WESTWARD passage to Fort Laramie, the ver-
dure of the High Plains gave comfort to the emigrants,
despite the harshness they endured on the trail. But
the seasons had changed. The prairie faded. Blades of dry grass
hissed in the wind. Summer's hues of tan and brown were overtaking the landscape. Mariah imagined she was living another
life in another place. Yet this hardship was real again, even welcomed, if there could be such a thing.

What hadn't changed were the deep ruts along the trail. The
wagon rattled the cooking pots like the trail ride before, but the
sun blazed brighter, leaving no adobe buildings to hide in, just
the haven of her sunbonnet.

How strange it felt heading east, where clouds of dust were
visibly absent, except for an occasional caravan passing by. Silas
warned the pioneers about getting a late start out of Independence and crossing the mountains with the threat of snowfall.
It could be too late for those caravans.

As the miles widened the distance from Fort Laramie, old

memories reawakened, and one more than any. The memory of home. Mariah was going home.

Inside the wagon, Julian cursed the twist of fate that had him lying facedown in a makeshift bed. What became of him was from one man's doing. No turn of events could change his circumstances. But the overland trail made no exception for a man's condition, whether he was decent or rotten to the core. With all the upheaval from the rugged terrain, he figured the trail was hellbent on ripping his wounds open just so he could bleed to death. Every minute he put behind him, he mustered the strength to get to day's end. When the ground no longer rumbled, he rested.

Mariah sought out a place of respite after the long hours of riding. Along the banks of the North Platte River, a tide of cool air breezed off the water, reviving her tired frame. She kicked off her boots and lifted the hem of her dress. Something crackled in her pocket. She pulled out a piece of paper. *Heavens. I forgot to give it to Julian.* Major Van Voast entrusted the sealed note to her before they left the fort. But as he readied his platoon to escort a wood train back to camp, he left no indication of the sender's name.

She couldn't give the note to Julian. He fell asleep. Under the wagon, she spotted the saddlebags. *I'll put it there for safekeeping.* She tucked the note into one of the bags, then returned to the river and dipped her toes into the water. She recalled the blisters on her feet that stung like bees before. If only she could wish those memories away.

After making camp, Dr. Riddler noticed his patient nodded off in the wagon, and not a moment too soon. He'd been watching Mariah standing alone at the river's edge. His gaze riveted on her slender figure as he approached.

"You're a deceiving woman."

His voice startled her. She spun around, pressing a hand to

her bosom. "Dr. Riddler—" Her breath caught. "I didn't hear you coming." She puckered her brow. "Deceiving? What do you mean?"

"A sophisticated woman like you doesn't make a habit of unhitching oxen from a wagon. I must say I'm impressed."

She thought of Silas. "A wagon boss I once knew taught me a few things about riding the trail." She stepped out of the river but stumbled and lost her balance. A quick tug, and she was corralled in the doctor's arms.

"Why won't you call me John?" He grinned. "I won't let you go until you do." Her waist felt smooth. He imagined her skin just the same without her dress in the way. A little manly business could take care of that. He liked where he was at right now.

Mariah squirmed in his arms. There was no getting away from the doctor, or the odor on his breath. His embrace told her he was accustomed to getting what he wanted. She feigned a look of melancholy and spoke with a heavy heart.

"Forgive me . . . John." Her gaze drifted down to the flask bulging in his vest pocket. No thought at all went into the words she said next, only an urgency to keep talking, as if that would make their intimacy less awkward. "It's been difficult, you know, trying to bear the grief. Too many things happened at the fort."

John took her hand and brought it to his lips, and kissed it. "Maybe I can help you take your mind off these *things*."

The lovely widow's lips mesmerized him. He first took notice when she was fretting over the lieutenant before the soldiers hauled him into the fort's hospital.

He leaned in for a taste.

"Dr. Riddler—" She gasped. "What do you think you're doing?"

She tried breaking free and flustered him. He didn't take kindly to being interrupted. He came at her again. Her face veered away, sending his mouth into her neck. His muffled groans turned his body rigid against hers, a telling sign he hadn't been with a woman for who knows how long.

"You're drunk. Get your hands off me—"

A surgeon could ill afford making foolish mistakes. John did. He had a hold of Mariah's waist but not her arms. Did he think she would throw herself at him with reckless abandon? Her flailing got in the way as he groped for her bottom and pulled up on her dress. He growled like a wild animal come out of the woods with a fire in his breath reeking of whiskey.

"You know you want me. And I want your bare, naked flesh—"

Her resistance aroused him full force. He tried smothering her yelps with his mouth. A slap against the side of his face annoyed him. She cut short his dalliance, and worse, made his head spin.

Her blurred figure vanished from his grasp. He tripped up the riverbank in pursuit, consumed by the urge to subdue her. Just as he caught his stride and snatched the end of her hair, his outstretched arm froze in front of him when something solid slammed him in the forehead. He belted out a grunt and keeled over.

Mariah heard a voice calling her name. She stopped in her tracks and whirled around. Julian was leaning out of the wagon with a cast iron pan clenched in his hand.

He looked down at Riddler and back at her but couldn't hide the grin on his face. "Trouble with the doctor?"

"Julian— What did you do to him?"

"I'd say, from the looks of it, I knocked some sense into him." He tossed the pan inside the wagon and almost tipped over the candle he lit when Mariah's panicked voice stirred him from his sleep. His idle humor turned serious. "Did he hurt you?"

She hurried to his waiting arms. "He tried to have his way with me. It happened so fast."

Without a word, he guided her inside the wagon and laid her next to him. Her body trembled as he brushed the wisps of hair away from her face. "It's all right. I'm here now."

His touch soothed her. How she longed to love this man. She felt protected in his arms and knew she belonged there. But his tenderness overwhelmed her. She couldn't quell all the heartache from her past.

"It's been so hard . . . for so long. Hold me close."

And he did.

In his embrace, she didn't feel her life in turmoil anymore. She needed the balm of his compassion, and he gave it to her. The peace of nightfall surrounded them, except the wind soughing through the prairie grass, like the sound of hushed voices whispering all was right with the world.

By the candlelight, Julian cast her tears away. One by one, they vanished with his kiss. His every breath yearned to say her name and proclaim how impossible their love had been, but would never be again.

"My sweet Mariah . . ."

She let his name profess the same.

"Julian . . ."

His eyes beheld hers as his fingertips tumbled down her cheeks. He traced her parted lips and let his words touch them. "I love you." And then he confessed what he kept hidden all those years. "I've always loved you."

Passion's fever came over them and emboldened their kiss. Lips strained with the sensation. Their heated breath intensified. It was his love she tasted now—a love meant for a lifetime—and he gave it to her without precondition, not even to promise that she had to love him back.

A whirlwind of feelings rocked between them. Mariah's instincts took over. She stood up beside him and nudged her dress sleeves off her shoulders. The fabric slinked over her hips and puddled around her ankles. Not for one second did Julian take his eyes off her ankles. Yet even if he touched her there, he'd be done for. But her touch did him in. He spiraled into a free fall as her toes skimmed across his stomach. Just a tease, or maybe an intentional gesture, so she could straddle him and ease down on top.

And there he held tight to her starry-eyed gaze.

"You're beautiful." He nestled his hands in the hollow of her back. Skin like silk. He swore he was dreaming. "But you deserve more." His words echoed regret, yet his eyes kept on loving her. In all her splendor, she was giving him everything.

Her finger sealed his lips. "There's nothing more I want. You've given me your heart."

The bronze glow of his chest heightened the outline of his muscles and their power over her. She arched her back and beckoned him. He came up on his forearms and tongued her nipples, sparking a tightness below. She moaned, then pulled back and tugged the top button of his pants. He grabbed her hands and made her stop.

"Don't—"

His look told her his broken body was forbidden. He did not want to see disappointment in her face. But her words melted away what stood between them since that fateful day.

"Let me love you. All of you."

He released her hands, and the fear she would reject him, as he watched her unbutton his pants and saw her eyes grow wide. Slowly, she inched down, letting her breath caress his manhood. She explored its contours and the feeling it gave her, that part of lovemaking she never knew before. Every touch aroused her and awakened her life force. Every part of him left her breathless. She drew her hands up to his shoulders and arched her back again.

Julian had been there before, tasting the fullness of her

breasts, but the thrill felt new. All of her felt new. He fingered her bottom along the edge of her lace panty, then came round and fondled her belly. His touch excited when he found her warm place.

No movements rustled around them, only the distant howl of a coyote, calling out to the crescent moon.

He stroked her pleasure point. She whimpered. He quickened his pace and strummed her swelling fire while his tongue caught her tempo, flicking her nipples. In a fevered pitch, she crested higher, panting in short bursts. He kept her going. Then she shuddered out of control. She sang out into the night as her spasms quaked through her body, whipping her hair back and forth.

From her climax, she collapsed on top of him. Her entire being was suddenly spent. She drifted back to where they lay, and to the only sound she heard. The rumble of his heart. Beating. Beating. Alive.

With their bodies entwined and content to stay that way, the morning light came too soon. A kiss tingled her forehead. She stirred in Julian's arms where she felt loved beyond her dreams. The warmth of his body lulled her back to sleep.

Outside the wagon, a voice groaned. "What the hell?"

Riddler couldn't see straight. Whatever he ran into the night before whacked the daylights out of him. His head hurt more just thinking about it. He swore his skull had been split open and he hit the ground, ready to die, preferably in slow fashion. Maybe savages attacked him.

He bolted up, scouring the camp. The exertion of trying to focus hurled pain to the back of his eye sockets. He clutched his head with his hands and figured being scalped felt the same. Dazed, he stumbled toward the campfire, swaying left and right. Then he toppled over and passed out.

A gush of water smacked him in the face. He jolted awake.

"Hey, Doc. What does it take to get a cup of coffee around here?"

Riddler staggered to his feet as he palmed the water off his face. A bucket load of swear words teetered on the tip of his tongue. "You oughta be showing me a little respect for saving your hide." He scowled at his patient. "Or maybe you've forgotten I'm a surgeon and should be treated like one."

"Hold on a minute. You're the one who should be showing a little respect, to the woman you tried to seduce last night."

The sting of insinuation cleared Riddler's head fast. So did the welt on his forehead. The throbbing made his eyes go cross-eyed.

Julian chided him again. "Next time you get carried away with that flask of whiskey in your pocket, you better make damn sure you're drinking alone."

"Hey, simmer down. I crossed the line. I get it."

Riddler shrugged and raked his fingers through his hair. But he couldn't mistake the look in the railroad man's eyes, telling him Julian and Mariah weren't just friends. Being trapped in a remote outpost, and cut off from the east coast while he watched his surgical skills go to waste, he considered his encounter with Mariah a mere slipup. A minor miscalculation.

He knocked the dust off his sleeves, then tossed a few buffalo chips onto some tinder and lit a fire. As he waited for the coffee pot to heat up, he listened to his patient describe something odd which seemed too late in coming yet offered no explanation otherwise.

"Just now, when I dropped myself down from the wagon, my feet took the brunt of my weight before I slumped into the wheelchair." Julian stared at Riddler across the campfire. "It felt like, well it's hard to explain, like somebody was jabbing needles into my feet. A second later, everything went numb again."

Riddler pondered the news, shaking his head. "Curious. Strange, but curious."

"That's not telling me much."

"I can't give you a precise diagnosis. The sensation in your feet baffles me more than why you became paralyzed in the first place. Dr. Johnson and I performed a meticulous operation."

Julian's patience wore thin with Riddler's ego getting in the way. "Look, Doc. The feeling came from somewhere, so don't go quittin' on me now because you think the job's done. I need a better answer than that."

"Well, I don't have one." Riddler picked up a rock and chucked it into a skunkbush. "Even if I did have a better answer, it doesn't mean anything out here. It's just a roll of the dice."

He parked his butt down and shoved his back into the groove of his saddle while his boot heels dug parallel lines in the dirt. A hint of sarcasm put a sharp edge in his voice.

"I guess there's no telling what can happen in a desert dungeon like this." He locked his arms across his chest and slapped a grin on his face. "Who knows, Marquette? Maybe you rolled a lucky seven. Maybe this is your lucky day."

CHAPTER 31

Mistaken Memories

MARIAH HANDED JULIAN the rumpled note. "I completely forgot. Major Van Voast gave it to me when we left. I hope it's not urgent." Her voice pitched higher. "Is it?"

Calculating lines creased Julian's brow as he read the telegram. The news distracted his thoughts of Chimney Rock and crossing its path a few days earlier. The towering spire marked how much time passed on their journey and the measure of time that remained on the trail to Omaha City.

Before leaving Fort Laramie, he mapped out their course heading east, along the route he took from Council Bluffs, not the route Mariah followed from Independence. His decision was the right one for another reason. The telegram.

"My business partner wants us to rendezvous with him."

Mariah scrunched her nose as she chewed on a piece of bread, tasting the charred bottom. She swallowed the lump and a mouthful of coffee. "What kind of rendezvous does he have in mind? We're out in the middle of nowhere."

Aside from the bank loans Julian negotiated with Mariah's

father, he never told her about his work on the Transcontinental Railroad. "Charles Dunnigan oversees the Union Pacific Railroad. The telegram says he'll be testing out part of the track with a new steam locomotive. We're supposed to meet him at the end of the construction line, somewhere due east of the fork in the Platte River." He paused for a second and sized up his thoughts. "We've got a lot of riding ahead of us."

Mariah handed Julian a chunk of bread from the skillet. An apologetic look masked her face. He took more than the leavened bread as he swept her onto his lap. The wheelchair creaked under their mutual weight.

His bold move surprised her. She smiled. "Do you remember, last winter at the cottage?"

"I do remember."

"Those memories seem so long ago. A long time ago . . ." Her voice faded.

She recalled their evening supper and the warm biscuits they shared. A far cry from the scorched bread she just offered him. That memory rekindled the sadness she once felt, seeing Julian for what she thought would be the last time. But now they were together, and their forbidden love inexplicably turned sublime.

Julian curved his hand along her neck and drew her lips close to his. "I want us to be together. For good." He sealed his words with a kiss.

The eagerness of her lips intensified his longing. Every minute she was gone from his side was time spent with no purpose, just wasting away, for all he wanted was to cleave to this arresting woman until his dying breath. His restless kiss made him unsteady and left him hungering to give her more. If only . . .

His heart was on fire, and her passion fueled the flames. He gathered her in his arms as the bit of bread fell to the ground. From the time he first saw her, he knew. From the moment he first heard her voice, he was convinced. In his world, he was obsessed with his dream to forge a rail line across America. Then Mariah walked into his life and brought the railroad man to his knees.

How he wanted her then. But love was a risk he'd never taken and rejection a bitter pill he never swallowed. Where sleep and death were like old friends, love and pain were much the same. In the end, his one obsession left no room for love.

Though President Lincoln understood his allegiance to the Transcontinental Railroad, much had changed since Julian's brush with death. His love for Mariah grew mightier than his railroad. His crippled body magnified his need as their moans echoed against their lips. Maybe he was destined to take those searing bullets, to bear out his real reason for living. His reason for loving her now.

"Come away with me . . ."

There was no stopping it, this thing called love. It came barreling at them with the power of a locomotive careening out of control, its destination unknown but its force undeniable. And then he uttered his love song. The rhythm of his voice made her weak as he traced the soft lines of her face indelibly into his memory.

Far off in every direction, the panorama of the plains stretched to the rim of the sky. A land so vast and staggering to conquer for a wagon the size of a speck, lumbering across its sweeping expanse. But the slow pace of the oxen, thudding their hooves on the hardpan, only added to the struggle of each grueling day. Nothing was going to make the wagon go any faster, or get them to the fork in the river any sooner.

Anticipation for reaching the end of the trail had tensions mounting, and most of all with the doctor. His muttering grew louder by the hour. He wasn't going to keep his opinions to himself for much longer. Each day put him up against more of the same monotony. A tedious wilderness that just wouldn't end.

By midmorning, Julian called out for a halt to the wagon. An obstacle in the distance blocked their path up ahead. Sunlight reflecting off a glassy surface created a disruption on the horizon. A mirage shimmering in the haze. The heat rising off the prairie played tricks on the eyes and made the imaginary seem real. But every mile closer, the mirage grew bigger and brighter, and then split in two. They reached the fork in the Platte River.

The spring rains had long ended and made the river crossing easier in shallow water with a gentle current. Once they reached the other side, they watered the oxen and pressed on. The landmarks guiding the pioneers on the Oregon Trail disappeared behind them. Chimney Rock. Courthouse Rock. Jail Rock. They stood as beacons of hope for a new frontier yet to come.

Riddler paid no mind to the mileposts they encountered. The endless trail ride pushed him to the brink. Starved by the scant meals churning his gut, all he thought about was his life back in New York. Though he served the army during America's greatest time of need, the consecution of events brought on by the War of the Rebellion put him right in the middle of a hellhole called Fort Laramie. It was only out of his loathing for the place that he commanded the fortitude to keep going. Not even the wind's incessant aggravation was going to stop him.

"It's enough I have to stomach the victuals and be forced to sleep in the dirt every night," he bellyached, "but this dust is about to make me go blind!" He spat out a mouthful and cursed.

The wagon changed course, veering from the fork in the river. Julian peered through the canvas opening and steadied his eyes on the terrain. With no rock outcroppings or the river as their guide, dead reckoning their route was his only option for intersecting the railroad line. Miles of barren land gave no clues how far west the track was laid. He rubbed his eyes and kept scanning the horizon.

Out there somewhere was the Transcontinental Railroad, and so was his future with Mariah. All he wanted was what he said to her. He wanted her to come home with him to Boston.

Leaving the river behind, and their source of precious water, they rode straight into the heart of the devil's plains, a sweltering landscape where the hot sun beat down on them, mile after relentless mile. Even the winds were tamed by the stifling heat.

A deep rut along the trail hurled Julian backwards in the wagon. His head bounced off the canvas, jolting a pang down his legs. He grimaced. The sensation of needles pricked the bottom of his feet. A second later, the pain stopped. His legs felt heavy, like they turned to stone. He waited. Nothing happened. Maybe it was all in his head. He let go his frustration when Riddler bellowed across the plains.

"There! I can see the train!"

Julian pulled himself out of the wagon and leaned against Mariah. He squared his hat and took in the sight ahead of them. His thoughts converged. The ordeal was over, and that meant a new beginning. He looked at Mariah's hands gripping the reins. All the hardships she endured he saw manifested in them.

He let out a breath. "We're almost home, Mariah. We're almost home."

She brushed the sunbonnet off her head and gazed at him in disbelief, unable to grasp the end of what had been her life turned upside down.

"I can't believe we're really here."

As the miles dwindled, the steam locomotive came into view, burnished and coal black, emblazoned in scarlet and lines of gold. Closer in, they saw the number *119* inscribed along its side. It was an imposing sight, and they stared at it awestruck. The naysayers with their bulging pockets branded the railroad idea absurd, but Julian forged ahead despite the shortsighted reactions. He could still hear the uproar.

How the hell do you plan to lay thousands of miles of track across the entire country? And what about lumber? Damn it, Marquette, you can't get trees to grow fast enough for the railroad you wanna build.

The more they undermined his vision, the more driven he was to see it through. He'd hire a hundred more track gangs if he could, just to get the Transcontinental Railroad built. The sight of the smokestack belching clouds of steam was proof enough the naysayers were wrong.

His eyes swept from the front of the cowcatcher to the railcar at the rear. Ahead of the locomotive, clamor erupted at the end of the line. A band of sledgehammers clanged against the rails, in unison with the work crews chanting in song. The sounds were a sobering reminder of how much backbreaking toil lay ahead. Only when the Central Pacific and Union Pacific merged their tracks would Julian concede his job was done.

The wagon pulled up alongside the train. A man stepped out onto the railcar platform. His stout figure and topper were unmistakable. It was Charles Dunnigan. The business partner Julian admired for being a man of his word had kept his promise. For his part, Julian had some explaining to do.

"Damn good to see you, Marquette. Damn good, I say."

"Mr. Dunnigan. It's been a while, sir."

"We've got some business to catch up on. No time to waste." Dunnigan pointed in the direction of the steam locomotive. "Mighty beast, isn't it? Just delivered to the railroad yard last week. Made its first run from Boston to this exact location." He looked at the man responsible for their rendezvous out on the borderlands of Nebraska Territory. "Impressive work you've done on the railroad. I knew you had it in you." He arched his eyebrow. "Just make sure you finish the job, or we'll both have hell to pay if you don't."

Dunnigan had a way with words, and Julian counted on him to speak his mind. But their reacquainting was interrupted when Dunnigan's daughter appeared on the platform and maneuvered her way in front of her father. Seeing the Belle of Boston standing there in her emerald dress took Julian by surprise. Their last encounter wasn't a pleasant one. Her teasing smile and the way she drew him in with her eyes told him she'd long forgotten. What could he do but tip his hat to the woman whose lips he once tasted?

"Hello, Annabelle."

It wasn't like her to ignore his attentions. Another curiosity caught her eye. She spied the windswept woman sitting beside him. Nothing about the lady impressed her. She narrowed her eyes, searching for any threat. How could a woman with tousled hair and tattered clothes be a threat out here in this godforsaken place? She dismissed her suspicions. Someone else was on her mind.

Julian had indeed called Annabelle by name, but too many unfamiliar faces left Mariah unsettled. Perhaps the woman was an acquaintance or confidant, someone whose concern for Julian was so great she needed to travel this far to see him again. No matter her intentions, Mariah recognized the face of deception when she saw it. Nathan taught her well.

Dunnigan gestured to Julian. "Take what you need and bring it on board. Callahan and Trinity will drive the wagon on to Omaha City and meet us there." His voice filled with gusto when he looked at his hired hands. "Men, get moving!"

Their departure was cut short when Julian asked for help. Amid the commotion, nothing was said while everyone boarded the train.

Annabelle eyed her next move. She wormed her way between Julian and Mariah and sat down. Oh, the fuss she made fluffing her dress all about until she had Mariah nearly buried underneath it. Her little trick worked. Mariah crossed the aisle and took a seat facing the doctor. His grin let her know he was amused by all the nonsense.

Despite his daughter's shenanigans, Dunnigan had plenty of questions for Julian, the most pressing being that wheelchair in the corner of the railcar. But he grew more perturbed with Annabelle controlling the conversation.

"Jule darling, what on earth happened to you? I'm devastated to see you this way." Her gloved hand curled under his arm as the other hand primped his vest. She cast a hasty look at the disheveled woman whose name she still didn't know.

"I had some unexpected bad luck a while back. I'm over the worst of it, thanks to Dr. Riddler."

Annabelle tried corralling Julian's gaze, but his mind was far off, marveling at the sound of the drive wheels grinding against the iron rails beneath him. The shimmy of the train made him feel alive. Like every nerve in his body was electrified. Then it hit him. Annabelle was up to something. He glanced at Mariah. His expression magnified her anxiety and the question written on her face. When was he going to put a stop to this charade?

Charles rolled his eyes and bristled at the lack of consideration he was getting. "I say, Julian, there's no time like the present. We have some urgent issues to discuss. Your telegram about rerouting the railroad, for one."

Annabelle ignored her father and looked askance at the doctor. His ruddy hair and sunburned face, marred with dirt, made him seem quite the brute and not the physician Julian made him out to be. Her opinion of the man waned.

She fastened a spurious smile on her lips, but it soured when Julian's eyes wandered away from her. *What can you possibly see in that woman?* She glared down her nose at the unkempt creature, reminding her of her proper place which amounted to nothing more than living in the servants' quarters. As such, she should consider it a privilege to be in the presence of those of higher status. The look in Annabelle's eyes made it clear. Whatever the woman had to say would not be worth listening to.

"Jule darling, you don't have to worry about a thing. When we get to Boston, I won't let anyone take care of you except *me*." She leaned in with her plump red lips and said, "I do have a knack for spoiling a man. But you already know, don't you?"

Mariah felt the heat rising in her face. The air grew so thick from Annabelle's gloating, she almost choked on it. *If you say "Jule darling" one more time, I just might throw up all over your pretty little green dress!*

Dunnigan's daughter came out of the shadows and robbed Mariah of her chance to come to terms with her harrowing past, and what it did to her. She was a changed woman, and her mind needed to sort out the one thing that bothered her most. Who had she become? Being torn from her life in Missouri by a jealous husband obsessed with power was more than she could fathom. But Nathan was dead, buried in a distant place. A place she could never erase from her memory.

Her emotions welled up and engulfed her. She dug her fingernails into the seat. This wasn't the time for losing her composure in front of Julian and these strangers, and most of all the woman who put her on edge. Yet her instincts kept hounding her. It was no accident why she felt alone. Something about Annabelle seemed familiar. The clever ploys she used to get her way, and how she manipulated others to suit her needs.

Mariah hunkered down, waiting until Annabelle flashed her another look. She had to be sure it wasn't the color emerald green she spied in those eyes, but rather that hue of forever blue. Nathan and Annabelle would have made a perfect match. Almost too perfect. The cunning game was on again, cloaked in petal soft skin and laced with fine perfume.

CHAPTER 32

Cloven Hearts

*J*ULIAN WAS TRAPPED. He couldn't blame Dunnigan. As much as his boss considered him a favored son and heir apparent to the railroad, Charles wanted his daughter married off. But when Julian refused Annabelle's advances at the estate, he didn't just put her in a bad mood. He jeopardized his railroad. And, more than anything, he wanted this railroad. Now matters became more complicated.

The moment Annabelle waited for was staring her in the face. She relished her little victories. Those lovestruck suitors, whose faces she couldn't remember, bored her to tears with their affections. What was the harm in making them her puppets? All she wanted was some amusement. Love wasn't important. But behind her games of the heart hid an unmarried woman whose age would soon make her undesirable by the high society she prized most. In truth, it was Julian she prized, the man whose railroad meant more to him than her hand in marriage. How preposterous.

Her voice purred against his cheek. She, too, had him

trapped. His condition was most unfortunate yet a delectable situation. Being in the company of both Julian and her father gave her the chance to take whatever she wanted, even if it was the one thing that mattered to Julian most.

All her conniving added to Julian's aggravation, upending his attempts to talk with Mariah in private. The minutes kept slipping away. Every bit of truth he shared with her was turning into lies. Within the confines of the railcar, his fortunes were chasing him down, leaving him desperate to reassure Mariah of his intentions and why he entertained Dunnigan's daughter. If he could just tell her his success with the Transcontinental Railroad rested on the shoulders of his boss, and appeasing Annabelle was necessary to protect his dream. But his past actions came back to haunt him and threatened the woman he loved. The woman he would have died for.

Mariah stepped outside onto the platform. She had nowhere else to go where she could collect her thoughts and ground her senses. Not a moment later, Annabelle swooped in and shut the door behind them.

Her sudden absence had Dunnigan huffing through the bristles of his moustache. "I say, Julian, it was not my intention to bring Annabelle along." He made his confession as a way of putting an end to all the distractions. "But you know how unrelenting she can be. After so many failed engagements, I'm beginning to wonder if she'll ever get married." He stroked the grey hairs fringing his upper lip and studied his apprentice. A burst of confidence perked up his eyebrows. He let on what he was hinting at. "You'd make a fine son-in-law. Fine, indeed."

The podgy yet amiable codger only had his daughter's best interests at heart. He had no idea how far Annabelle would go to make her next engagement her last.

Julian nodded to his boss, then shifted his gaze to Riddler, looking for a way out. But the doctor had stretched out and fallen asleep. His thoughts were consumed with the railroad and the situation confronting him. If he'd only finished the project, Annabelle's game would be over.

He stared at the railcar door. What was going on outside? His instincts made him panic. Annabelle already spun her web of deception, and her next victim just stepped into her trap.

Out on the platform, the noise of the locomotive converged with the grinding wheels on the tracks. Both women stood side by side with their eyes fixed straight ahead. Neither one looked at the other.

Annabelle's voice chimed above the din. "It's not my business to know why you've been traveling with Julian." She turned and faced the plain woman. "Uh, what did you say your name was?"

"Mariah."

"Well, *Mariah dear*, in case you're wondering, when we reach Omaha City, I expect you'll be needing to hurry on home. After all, there's no reason for you to spend any more time with Julian, if you know what I mean."

Mariah glared at Annabelle and snapped back. "Where I choose to spend my time concerns me and no one else."

"Yes, of course. You're absolutely right. But you've forgotten one thing. You see, Julian is—well—practically my fiancé, and it wouldn't be right for you to be, how shall I say, *in the way*."

She tried sounding sweet-tempered with the news of her engagement, lest it be misconstrued as unwelcome. Yet the drama unfolding before her eyes satisfied her immensely. The crimped mouth. The tightened grip on the handrail. The spurts of breathing that turned Mariah's skin pathetically pale. It was more than she could have wished for, and almost more than she could bear to look at.

Annabelle's words cut deep. Mariah rebounded and shot back with narrowed eyes. "I don't recall Julian ever mentioning your name."

Her quick retort caught Annabelle off guard. She batted her eyelashes, hunting for words. "Men don't tell all their secrets, you know, especially when it involves another woman." She tilted her chin up and curled her lips. "Besides, Julian *will* marry me, or my father just might take back his precious little railroad."

The clicking of her fingernails on the metal rail echoed a clock ticking away time, as though someone's misfortune was about to be realized. Her ladylike sparring let her have the last say. She aimed straight for the heart. "Now, you wouldn't want to see a brilliant, handsome man like Julian lose everything he's worked so hard for, would you, deary?"

Just stew over that one, Mary, or whatever your name is.

Mariah heard enough about Charles Dunnigan to know he wielded clout with the Union Pacific. But why didn't Julian tell her Dunnigan controlled his personal life? She didn't want to believe anything Annabelle said, yet her alleged engagement to Julian came as a shock. Her mind was tangled in doubt. Every reasonable thought escaped her, except one. She had to get out of Annabelle's way, and get out of Julian's way too.

The door slammed shut. A rush of air whooshed against her face. She lost her grip on the handrail, teetering near the edge of the stairs. All around her, the desolate vista closed in and would not release her, until she let go of the hope that steadied her all this time. *Nothing can save us now.*

Her breathing stuttered. The weight of another curse heaved the last gasp out of her lungs, leaving her helpless to stop the ensuing vertigo. She was on the verge of passing out. The railroad tracks whizzed beneath her as the air roared in a vortex, ready to sweep her off the face of the earth.

In the midst of the whirlwind, a pair of arms encircled her waist. She tried breaking free. "Leave me alone—" Her body swayed. She reached for the handrail, but her knees gave way and she fell suspended in the stranger's arms.

Words hummed against her cheek. "I guess you don't care much for riding the train, do you?"

That voice. His embrace. The doctor came to her rescue.

She caught her breath. "No, I suppose not. I don't know what happened." Their last encounter by the river made her feel uneasy, but she clung to him a little longer.

John rested his chin on her shoulder, sensing she wouldn't run away from him. "The noise is deafening out here. Let me take you inside." When she turned and faced him, he saw in her eyes she was grateful for what he did. His caring was genuine. "Are you all right?"

She nodded. "Yes, I think so."

"Hold on to me, just in case."

And she did.

Through the glass porthole in the door, Julian only saw Annabelle's gestures. Mariah's reactions eluded him. Then she walked inside the railcar, holding Riddler's arm. The hero saved her because he could. It was as if the doctor knew every dark secret about his past. Now he was taking full advantage of the situation, plucking Mariah from his grasp like a sweet portion of fruit dangling from a tree. Riddler's triumphant glance had him writhing with resentment.

Mariah took comfort in John's concern for her. His attentions kept her eyes turned away from the others. Just as well. There were no more questions needing answers. The truth had come out.

She tried quelling the sensations in her fingertips, and the masculine places they once explored. Those memories had her clinging to this moment that Julian might come to his senses and tell her his love wasn't a lie. But all he could do was stumble over his usual formalities.

"Are you . . . doing well?"

She despised his words and glared at him. Her look turned him to ice. And Annabelle sat there, exactly where she wanted to be. With her dirty work done and her prized possession won, she looked more relaxed than ever.

"Jule, darling." She thrust herself in front of him and severed his gaze of the trite woman. "There's no need to fret about the girl. I'm sure she'll be *just fine.*"

THE train reached the end of the line. So much happened since Julian first set out from Omaha City. How fitting the end came for him where it started. All of it gone wrong—in a heartbeat. His thoughts consumed him. The man driven to build this railroad just watched his world disintegrate around him without him lifting a finger.

As the train slowed to a halt at the depot, he gave a blank look at the commotion outside. Omaha City bustled in a frenzy of activity. The new bridge crossing the Missouri River transformed the face of the town. Throngs of people hurried everywhere. Not a soul stood still. Lines of loaded freight wagons headed west out of town while one stagecoach after another rode in and rode out. Brawls from the saloons tumbled out onto the road, kicking up dust and a flurry of fisticuffs. Not much different than Council Bluffs on the other side of the river.

What changed was the sight of the train. The townsfolk gawked at the locomotive. White puffs of steam belched from its undercarriage and permeated the air with a kind of magic, casting a spell over the land. A promise of one day traveling to California. The spectacle created a blockade of curious onlookers inspecting the Iron Horse.

Julian cursed under his breath. There were too many people, and too many distractions. Despite the chaos, he couldn't let Mariah get off the train. He never acted without a plan and worked alone to control the outcome so others wouldn't meddle in his affairs and muck things up. But he underestimated Annabelle. *Gone to hell. All of it.*

Neither Dunnigan or Riddler returned with any hired hands for the wheelchair. Annabelle voiced her displeasure and stomped off the train. Julian turned to Mariah, but she was on her feet ready to leave.

He caught her wrist. "Don't go. I need to explain."

Her hand was throbbing. "You don't have to explain anything. I've already been enlightened by your fiancée."

He clenched his jaw. "Don't believe anything Annabelle said to you. It isn't true." Mariah's distant gaze told him what he didn't want to face. She was saying goodbye. He tugged her closer. If he didn't, he was certain she would walk away from him for good. "You have to believe me. I'm telling you the truth."

She looked at him and saw nothing of *their* truth. It was already shattered. She freed her hand and retreated from his side. "I want to believe you, but you've left me no choice."

Maybe the ache would go away if she fell into his arms again, and felt his strength and his love. But it had turned forbidden. She despised him for what he did, and for what he destroyed between them.

Riddler peered inside the railcar, gesturing to Mariah. "It's time to leave. Mr. Dunnigan's making arrangements for your passage on the next steamboat to Independence." His news was abrupt. "He sent a telegram to your father. He'll be taking the train from St. Louis and will meet you there." He realized he interrupted something and cleared his throat. "I'll wait for you outside."

Mariah feigned a smile. "Thank you, John." Her voice cracked. "I'll be right there—"

Riddler nodded and disappeared into the crowd.

Escalating tension in the railcar had Julian holding tight to Mariah's gaze that offered him only emptiness in return. In a desperate move, he pulled himself up and braced against the seatback. He looked down into her eyes, telling her this was their last chance to fight for each other.

"Mariah—" He sucked in a breath. "I love—"

She pressed her fingers to his lips. "No. Don't say it. *Please* don't say it."

He slumped into the seat.

She plodded toward the steps leading off the train, but then stopped and turned around. Only heartache dwelled there. The finality of it all had her clutching her bosom. There was no more to say. Just the usual formalities.

"I'm sure you'll do a fine job finishing your railroad."

In an instant, she was gone.

CHAPTER 33

Holding On To Nothing

THE HEADY AROMA of baked bread smelled of home. It felt good to be home again. Mariah placed the loaf into the basket with the other two loaves she bought at the bakery on Carondelet Avenue. The excuse she gave her mother about craving the crusty bread let her slip away from the house for a while. As a child, she walked the path to the bakery many times, holding her mother's hand on one side and Fanny's on the other.

Strolling back to the waiting carriage on the outskirts of town gave her the solitude she longed for and a chance to breathe the fresh air. But her spirits faded when her mind fell trapped in the place she couldn't escape from these months past. Every thought led her to think on, dwell on, and struggle to be free of—him. Even the scent of the bread carried her back to the open plains and to a campfire that scorched another skillet of bread. Those memories found her in Julian's arms again, sheltered by his love. A love she once believed in.

Her return to St. Louis had come at a high price. All she pined for on the overland voyage to Fort Laramie was to be home again at the estate. But seeing the mansion reminded her of how naïve she was, and how unfaithful others could be. Her tumultuous life did nothing except bring her back to where it all began.

A warm breeze rippled the frills on her dress sleeves. She shivered like she was bitten by a cold December wind. Yes, she paid a high price, but it was because of Nathan and what she endured for the sake of him.

Thudding boots. Blistered feet. Sunburned hands turned to leather, and cracked lips that smelled of lard. Had the figment of a pioneer woman sprung from the pages of a diary filled with perilous tales of the Oregon Trail? If only she could transcend all the loss and pretend it never happened. She so wanted her past to be someone else's bad dream.

By late morning, the air turned muggy and the long walk to the carriage ravaged her strength. It seemed even the elements were trying to break her down. *How can I go on this way?* The questions kept coming. *Why did you have to love me, Julian? Why?* She knew the answers before she even asked herself the questions. She could only go on if she kept on loving him. There was no denying it, as much as she tried to forget him. She would always love him, and he would always be a part of her.

With Julian out of her life, she had to find solace. Of that she held out hope but of the consequences she was certain. *To love a man who belongs to another promises a future alone. There can never be someone else.*

Shadows cast by the brick buildings gave her respite from the sun. An impulse made her turn onto Bellefontaine Road. Her spirits rose at the thought of seeing Benton School. Then the Florissant Café came into view. She was reliving that day when winter's chill numbed her cheeks and a blanket of snow crunched beneath her feet as they strolled together, arm in arm.

It was deliberate, walking into the café and sitting down

at the same table with her back against the absent fire. She imagined every aspect of Julian's face glowing in the firelight. He was a man she never dreamed could exist, a man she tried not to love, but she let him into her heart anyway.

You are, and always will be, the only woman I will ever love. If I am destined to leave this world a lonely man, my heart will not be, for you will always be with me.

Always, Julian

The crumpled piece of paper she found tucked in her coat pocket the day she arrived in Independence came with her all the way home. But Julian's professed love lingered as mere words. Oh, how their mighty passion had fallen.

She raised the mug of hot tea to her lips. The drink was deemed an odd request when she ordered it, yet she needed to keep the memory alive, and close, for a little longer. She rubbed her fingers against the mug and felt the strength along his jawline, and the intensity of his embrace. His passionate gaze blazed so true. His love for her. The forbidden love they dared not speak of. He was more of a man in her wanting eyes—the only man she longed to love—even now.

She walked out of the café. A tear strained down her cheek and cooled in the breeze. Such sweet memories.

The children were gone and the hallways empty at Benton School. Mariah reasoned it was for the best. Though she would have welcomed the affectionate hugs and chatter from her students, her emotions thus far proved too unpredictable. In time, she'd see them again. She was better off being by herself in the classroom.

As she paused beside the coatrack, her body quivered. Julian was there, standing behind her, drawing her coat over her shoulders. The desire overwhelmed her then to turn around and fall into his arms.

She stepped back and bumped the corner of the desk. A deafening silence closed the door on her past. She curled her fingers under the handle of the breadbasket and left the classroom. *It's time to go home.*

SINCE the day Mariah's father brought her home from Independence, her mother found it difficult talking with her daughter. Chatter about her visits to Lafayette Square and the latest gossip over afternoon tea wasn't drumming up any small talk that might encourage Mariah to get out of the doldrums.

Mother coaxed her outdoors for a change of scenery. Muted tones rustling in the garden permeated the air. Spangled butterflies danced among the cardinal flowers as water spluttered into the fountain. The scarlet glow of dogwood berries stood out against the backdrop of a blue sky.

Mother's eyes grew wide. "Goodness. I forgot to tell you."

She divulged her own bit of gossip about the grand ball she was planning at the estate. Her friends relished the idea of getting a Renwick invitation. And what better way to lift her daughter's spirits.

"I've been thinking, Mariah. It would be good for you to start mingling again." Her voice softened. "Perhaps it's time to put your past behind you."

Mariah savored the fragrance of the Damask rose pressed against her lips. She always closed her eyes for an instant when she inhaled the scent. The blossoms were one of her most vivid childhood memories, running along the garden paths bordering the flower beds. She wasn't ignoring her mother now. She just didn't want to interrupt the serenity drifting over her.

A smile formed on her face. "Of course you should have a grand party. I think that's a wonderful idea."

"You must promise to help. Your father won't have anything to do with it."

Mother refused to give up. Mariah had to find purpose in doing something. Anything. It was for her own good. She couldn't bear seeing her daughter so unhappy from the ordeal she endured since early spring. Maybe she needed to stop pretending Mariah would become the woman she once was. She cupped their hands together, cocooning the rose in between, and gave a look only a mother could give her daughter.

In her eyes, Mariah saw her mother carrying the same burden of loss she did. She was looking at her own reflection, seeing the truth she could no longer deny and the ache she could no longer hide. Mother and daughter together sharing each other's sorrow, yet conceding that time and love would someday heal the heart, at least enough to go on.

Mother blurted out her feelings. "Oh, my precious child. I know how much it must hurt. But you have suffered more than I ever have." She recalled the scandal Edmund told her about the day he brought Mariah home. "I know Nathan stole your father's money. Your father has a way of uncovering the truth, even if it disgraces the family name. I'm just sorry you got mixed up in all of it."

Mariah lost her grip on the rose. Mother held tight. She had more to say on the matter. "Your father won't talk to you about the affair because his pride has been wounded, knowing Nathan forced those soldiers to break into the house and commit the crime." Then she revealed the most painful truth of all. "He trusted Nathan as if he were his own son. He's absolutely devastated."

The news stunned Mariah. She never wanted her parents to find out how her life changed since her wedding day. Now her husband's deeds exposed her darkest secret, clouding her mind in memories. But like the warmth of the rising sun lifting a blanket of fog above the Mississippi, a glimmer flickered in the shadows and brought answers to light.

It was the evening of their farewell party. She overheard a conversation outside the library window. Two soldiers were talking low about her husband's private affairs. She was too startled by the news to hear their next revelation. *It must have been about the crime.* Still, one question remained. "Why did they steal the money?"

Mother stared at her in disbelief. "Your father told me what he feared most. Nathan devised some sort of scheme to buy votes for political power. Someone by the name of Moonlight was caught red-handed with the stolen money. When he confessed, the army notified our governor. Can you imagine? All this news has been such a shock. Such a terrible shock." She sighed. "It's true Nathan was an ambitious man, but his lack of moral fiber led to his undoing. Despite how hard you might have tried, you couldn't have changed him, or saved him."

Mariah shook her head. "I just can't believe I was so blind. Even when I had a second chance."

A bewildered look swept over her mother's face. "What second chance?"

Mother could not have known about Julian. There was nothing left to know about the man Mariah trusted with her heart. All was in the past where it belonged, hidden away in the empty places she struggled to keep to herself, no matter her own heartache, no matter the cost.

A light sparked in her mother's eyes as though the gates of heaven parted from above. "It's Mr. Marquette, isn't it?"

Mariah's emotions tumbled out of her mouth. "Oh, forgive me, Mother. There's so much I haven't told you. I didn't want you to worry and suffer on my account because of my own foolish mistakes." Her shoulders wilted from the weight of what happened. "You've lived through such unbearable sorrow since Fanny died. I didn't want to be a burden."

"My dear child, I never knew how you felt."

A family broken by death could not see the fragment of each of them that died too, for the yearning was so great to turn back time and live life the way it used to be. In her daughter's eyes, Mother saw the missing piece of Mariah's sorrow for her sister she never saw all those years ago, amidst her own grieving. And, she saw the pain her daughter kept hidden for the sake of her marriage to Nathan. Blind love was not easy to see as much as facing death was not easy to accept.

Mother steadied her gaze. "We all have to mourn at some time in our lives. But you must live your life on your own terms. Even if you make mistakes, you need to be the woman you were meant to be."

The wisdom of Mother's words rang true. Mariah hugged this sweet and knowing woman with all her strength. They held each other and let go their worries, for only then could the healing begin. With their arms entwined, they strolled back toward the terrace.

Mother spoke again. "I do remember seeing you and Julian walking together here in the garden. When I peeked through the dining room window, I had this sense that something was different between the two of you. Even at dinnertime, I saw the way you looked at each other across the table." She paused, deep in thought. "You know, love isn't a force you can control. It has a will of its own. Love just . . . happens. And when it does, it is an intensely beautiful thing."

But her words only offered more heartache. What she saw in the depths of her daughter's eyes broke her heart. Had she misjudged Mariah's sadness as the grieving of a wife for her dead husband? A wound opened up. No, she was grieving for someone else.

"What is it, my child? Please tell me."

Mariah squeezed her mother's arm. Her steps faltered. She was standing on the brink of the abyss where hope abandoned her. How could a woman keep on loving a man without him by her side for the rest of her life? *I never told you. Oh, Julian, I never told you that I love you. I will always love you.*

CHAPTER 34

Hidden Hell

"I CAN DEAL WITH it myself." Julian snapped at Riddler as they rode in Dunnigan's carriage to Massachusetts General Hospital.

"Damn stubborn, aren't you?"

"Call me whatever you want, Doc. I don't need your help."

Riddler stared at him with a deadpan look on his face. He'd seen his patient closer to death than he deserved to be, and too close for his own good, but he never saw this kind of reaction. The man had a streak of willpower running through him, an obsession hellbent on crushing the crippling beast, no matter the odds against him.

"I'm here in Boston for one reason. Your condition. To put it bluntly, if there's any chance you can walk again, you *are* going to need my help." He turned up his chin. "And if you don't want it, I don't care. Either way, your paralysis still baffles me."

The doctor rambled on with his medical gibberish. Julian tried to make sense of it, but the longer he listened the more he stewed. "Just give it to me straight, for crying out loud. All your mumbling about theories doesn't do me a damn bit of good if I can't understand a word you're saying."

Riddler tugged on his neck collar as he cursed the place which left him with no medical explanation for what went wrong. "Fort Laramie didn't offer me the luxury of trying to prove a theory. That wasteland of a hospital left me with two choices for my patients. Amputate or die. Lucky for you, Dr. Johnson and I saved your hide *and* your legs."

His frustration mounted just thinking about the outpost. Lines creased his brow, and his crossed arms shoved him deeper into the seat. Then his eyes lit up when Boston's landmark hospital came into view.

"God, it's good to be home. It's not New York City, but I'll take Boston over Fort Laramie any day." He squared his shoulders and looked at Julian. "First order of business. Once you're checked in to your room, I'm going to need time to analyze your problem. Medically speaking, that is."

"You always have a way with words—and women. Don't you?"

"You're never going to let up on me, are you? It's irrelevant anyway, unless Mariah's concocted some kind of magic potion to make you walk again."

Riddler's words cut deep, but Julian had it coming. Mariah was just a memory, worlds away from the Oregon Trail and their time together in St. Louis. He beat himself up good letting Annabelle manipulate Mariah with her lies. If Dunnigan hadn't been there, he could have put Annabelle in her place and kept his railroad project out of it. Now she was reveling in her coup de grâce that put all her pawns exactly where she wanted them. She took advantage of a perfect situation, knowing it could lead to a perfect marital arrangement.

The cold truth sank in, and Julian made Riddler the target. *It's your fault I can't walk. You made me a cripple.* All the blame fell on Riddler's shoulders, even losing the woman he was foolish enough to let go.

"Listen, Doc. I didn't ask you to follow me back to Boston, and I sure as hell didn't ask you to meddle in my affairs or try and win over Mariah's affections. As for magic potions, I don't need any." He tightened his fists, waiting for a fight, but stopped short of lunging at the doctor and punching him in the face.

Riddler threw his hands up. "Take it easy. I'll admit I've had my eye on Mariah from the first time I saw her. So did the other soldiers at the fort. And who could blame them? She's the kind of woman you dream about at night and never stop dreaming about."

Then he saw, plain as the sun at midday, what the railroad man couldn't hide anymore, and it filled him with envy. "You love her, don't you?"

Julian clenched his jaw at Riddler's blunt scrutiny. He darted his eyes out the window. This wasn't the time for lovestruck confessions. It was none of Riddler's business anyway.

Riddler had more to say concerning the well-being of his patient, and it wasn't doctor's advice. "Mark my words. Mariah is the least of your problems. I've known women like Annabelle, and you'd be wise to watch out. She's capable of tearing you apart and destroying that railroad of yours right along with you."

BY week's end, Julian's schedule was upended with grueling leg therapy and strict convalescing. Each day kept him fixated on his rehabilitation and made him grow more distant. The isolation set in. With no end in sight to his regimen, his fight to walk again bordered on the maniacal.

Riddler dispelled the notion that he prescribed therapeutic

torture for his patient, no matter how loud the cursing echoed down the hall. But the risk he was taking with Julian's treatment was necessary. He had to know how far he could push him. He had to know Boston's prestigious hospital would prove him right. The time he wasted at the fort didn't rob him of his consummate skills as a surgeon. He was still an esteemed physician who commanded everyone's respect.

There was another pressing matter he couldn't ignore. Dunnigan was expected back from Washington any day and would be fuming over his orders to keep Julian in the hospital indefinitely. There'd be another fight brewing. He had to be ready.

AFTER returning home, Charles noticed a difference in Annabelle's demeanor. She was in a good mood and spent almost no time in the house. Whatever she was up to, he welcomed the change. Gone was the aggravation she caused him when she had no one else to annoy. Not that he wanted to wish her prospective fiancé any aggravation of his own, but he was convinced if any man could handle his daughter, Julian would be the one.

With all of Annabelle's comings and goings, he didn't tell her about the invitation he sent to Dr. Riddler. The thought was foremost on his mind when the housemaid pounced in front of him. Livy held out her hand and gave him a sealed note just delivered at the front door. He huffed, juggling his satchel and walking cane.

"I was about to set out for the office."

"Yes, sir. I can see that. Beggin' your pardon, Mr. Dunnigan. The young man at the door said it was urgent."

He surrendered his belongings to her waiting hands and snatched the note. "Right. Well, running a respectable railroad is urgent too."

Another interruption had Annabelle bursting through the front door. She stood beaming in the grand foyer, as if a concourse of suitors were requesting the honor of her presence on the dance floor. In a gust of impatience, Charles stomped into the drawing room and plopped down in the overstuffed chair. She swept toward him.

"Daddy, why haven't you left for work yet? It won't be long before I have afternoon tea with Penelope and Elizabeth, for heaven's sake." She puckered her brow. "What on earth are you doing in the drawing room? A guest in your own house? Why that's absurd."

A bit more ranting. She's almost finished. Wait for the breath.

"Is that a note in your hand? Who's it from? Do tell, Father, do tell." She gasped.

"To answer your last question first, the note's probably from Washington. Railroad business, I expect. As for my present whereabouts, I elected to sit down in the chair closest to the front door so I could make haste and return to work promptly. I'm running late as it is."

He glimpsed the seal on the envelope and tucked the note into his breast pocket. Annabelle didn't need to know he lied to her. But that urgent correspondence triggered his suspicions. Bad news from the doctor could only mean he didn't want a face-to-face confrontation. *Well, he's going to get one.* He stood up and walked over to Livy. She hadn't budged an inch. He grabbed his satchel and walking cane and marched toward the door.

Annabelle eyed his troubled expression. She ran up to him and kissed him on the forehead. With all her life's cares tended to, she coddled him at every turn, especially if he seemed worried. He was all she had for family, and anyone who brought discontent upon him would have the wrath of Annabelle Priscilla Dunnigan to answer to. Forever, if need be.

"Now, now, Daddy. I'm sure the grand Union Pacific Railroad won't miss its brilliant *King Charles* because he's a little late."

Her praise turned her father's scowl into a slight grin. He gave her a peck on the cheek, and together, they walked outside. Just as he stepped into the waiting carriage, he popped his head out the window. "Goodness, I nearly forgot, Annie. I sent an invitation to the doctor from New York. You do remember him, don't you?"

She muttered, "I suppose . . ."

"Well, I thought it best to invite him to stay with us while he's helping Julian. He might be joining us for dinner tonight." The coachman snapped the whip. "Tell Livy to set the table for three!"

She waved to her father, then made her way to the kitchen and gave notice to the cooking staff about their guest.

With teatime still an hour away, she sashayed into the study and plumped down into Father's elephantine leather chair. The feel of the animal hide put her in a sultry mood. She caressed the armrests, breathing in the scent. A pirouette in the chair twirled her around to a view of Boston Harbor where her mind drifted off to thoughts of Julian. *When, oh when, will you be mine?* His accident dampened her spirits, but not enough for her to worry about his injuries. *Why would the doctor come to Boston unless he knows my Julian will fully recover?*

The radiant sun filled the room, softening her features. She opened the window and settled back into the chair, admiring the fountain and the shimmering water that sparkled like diamonds. A cool sensation tingled her skin. But the plinking of droplets into the basin masked another sound outside. Her daydreaming carried on until the humid air stifled her thoughts.

"I can't bear it. The heat is dreadful. Utterly dreadful."

She could be unreasonable when she wanted to be, especially if it required the slightest effort on her part. Sitting there, she kept staring at the curtains while she unbuttoned the top of her dress and slipped the combs from her hair. No sooner had she run her fingers through her tresses than a thud startled her from behind. She spun around and spied a shadow lurking in the doorway.

"Who's there?"

For an instant, she thought it was Julian by the way the figure leaned against the door frame. Of all the men she was acquainted with, no one stood taller than he did. Just as the stranger eased into the room, her body slouched in disappointment.

"Oh . . . it's you."

"Your warm welcome is more than I expected."

Dr. Riddler's words gave a rhythm to his swagger as he strode up to the desk. Annabelle turned the chair around and blotted him out of her view. Her disregard of his presence didn't surprise him. What she said next bowled him over.

"Close the curtains, *Mr. Riddler*, and be quick about it. The heat is tormenting me."

It was only fair she treat the visitor like the other men she toyed with. She reached back, hugging the corners of the chair, and waited. Nothing happened. She whirled around and narrowed her eyes at him. Why didn't he bow to her demands?

"Please offer my gratitude to Mr. Dunnigan for his invitation. I'll be making arrangements elsewhere. Good day, Miss Dunnigan."

Annabelle's jaw unhinged. She sat there aghast by his remarks as he left the room and slammed the door shut. His appalling behavior set fire to every inch of her body.

She bolted up from the chair. "Why, the nerve of that man. How dare he speak to me that way." She threw open one door after the next and stormed after the doctor poised to board the carriage. "*Mr. Riddler!* Since you are an invited guest of the Dunnigan family, and *I am* part of the Dunnigan family, it is unacceptable for you to walk out on me. I'm not done talking to you yet."

Riddler saw the disdain in her face. Her conduct proved him right. But he wasn't going to back down. "A woman of your standing should have the good sense to address me as Dr. Riddler. And secondly, I only stopped by to accept Mr. Dunnigan's dinner invitation. I have no intention of heeding your beck and call. You can use your servants for that."

He stepped into the carriage without another glance at her highness, standing there with her hands bearing down on her hips. He'd never concede defeat to a woman like her, and he wasn't about to start now.

CHAPTER 35

No Turning Back

UNNIGAN READ THE NOTE and almost tore it in half. Every word aggravated him. The doctor had the gall to insist no visitors were allowed while Julian stayed locked up indefinitely. He set off for the hospital at once, mumbling at the unthinkable. *Dear Annie will be devastated when she finds out.* The devotion of a father for his daughter put Annabelle foremost in his mind. A promising suitor was at stake. Then panic set in. *Good God. The railroad.*

His thoughts converged on the prospect of an impending failure of the Union Pacific. And to think he just informed his boss that Julian was back on the job. *Doctor's orders be damned.* Julian had a railroad to run. But first he needed to figure out a way to get him out of that prison of a hospital. Holding on to a few scraps of hope was all he had.

It was midafternoon when he arrived at Massachusetts General. He delayed a scheduled meeting with his railroad partners until his return. Julian's recent absence could no longer be overlooked and would have him facing a lot of questions. His worries mounted. *All I need is for President Johnson to quash the Pacific Railway Act and shut down the railroad, and I'll be done for.* His proclivity toward impatience took hold when he thought of Annabelle again, and her preoccupation with all things holy matrimony. For her sake he hoped, in the midst of this mess, a marriage was still in the making. His sanity depended on it.

The corridor leading to Julian's rehabilitation room posed another obstacle for him. His walking cane was a constant reminder he wasn't getting any younger. The future of the Union Pacific rested in the confidence he placed in Julian as his successor, and that certainty turned to doubt over his present circumstances. Who the hell was he going to count on now? An undigested portion of lunch growled in his stomach when Dr. Riddler appeared at the end of the hall.

"Good to see you, Doctor. Where's Julian?" His blood thumped against his stock collar. "I need to see him. Immediately."

Riddler sauntered up to him with his hands fixed to the lapels of his black lab coat. He offered a handshake, but his welcome was ignored. "I didn't expect your visit to the hospital." He readied himself with another fib, then thought better of it. "If you're here to discuss Julian's condition, there's nothing to talk about."

The barrel-chested industrialist used his stature to its fullest extent and conveyed who was the mightier man. Testing his temper was a bad idea. The conversation would be far more pleasant if the doctor complied with his orders.

Riddler crossed his arms, drawing a line of defense between them. Dunnigan flashed him a look, saying he was going to wait all day, if he had to, for Riddler to get out of his way. The doctor took a wide stance and dared him to do just that. A grumble reverberated through greying whiskers as Dunnigan heated up the conversation before it even started. It was time to have it out with the ruddy-haired physician.

"What do you mean, there's nothing to talk about? I want answers. Do you understand? I've got too much bureaucratic pressure from Oliver Ames to sit back and wait for Mr. Marquette to walk out of here. As President of the Union Pacific, Ames knows Julian is my man on this railroad, and he will undermine my ownership if I don't give him a satisfactory explanation." He pounded his cane on the floor. "Simply put, Doctor, I need Julian's brilliant intellect back on the job, not his legs."

Dunnigan made his point. Riddler wasn't flinching. "I already explained to you in my letter that Julian's prognosis is poor. But I won't let him out of this hospital until I'm certain he can or cannot walk again. In the meantime, you'll just have to wait."

"I can't wait, damn it." Anger flushed Dunnigan's face. "There's only one other living creature I know who is more obstinate than you, and she's my own flesh and blood." His chest deflated in defeat. "So be it." He shot back one last importunate glance. "Rest assured, I will hound you each and every day until Julian is released. You have my word."

He tapped his cane against Riddler's lab coat for added emphasis. The gesture didn't make him feel any better. He wasn't the kind of man to use threatening words, but this sudden turn of events made him a worried man. He shrugged and dropped the subject.

"Did you get my invitation? I told Annabelle you'd be coming."

Riddler stepped close enough to the railroad magnate to be considered insolent. Something had to be said. "Your offer was generous. I'm obliged. Unfortunately, I had an unexpected encounter with your overbearing daughter which necessitated a change in plans."

"Unexpected? Overbearing?" Charles furrowed his brow, puzzled by the doctor's remark. He didn't plan on chitchatting about his daughter.

Riddler wasted no time giving his assessment of the situation. "I'm a man who speaks his mind. As a physician, I have an obligation to tell my patients the truth. As for your daughter, I can only say I considered her to be rude. I mean no disrespect, Mr. Dunnigan."

"None taken. I appreciate your candor. I've learned to tolerate Annabelle's moods, though her intentions are sincere. Her mother was much the same." His voice faded at the thought of his departed wife and how much Annabelle reminded him of her. He gave Riddler a hasty slap on the back and pulled his mind out of the past. "I've got to get going. Important meeting at the office." He tipped his chin up and looked the doctor in the eye. "Do join us for dinner. And remember, my offer still stands if you'd like to stay at the house. I'll stop by and pick you up around six this evening. Agreed?"

Riddler didn't hesitate. "Agreed."

The matter was settled. Charles nodded. At least he won this round.

Riddler watched one of Boston's richest men don his top hat and walk the long corridor out of the hospital. A grin framed his face. He didn't expect to find himself in such well-suited company.

Julian agonized over his recovery. He put up with Riddler barking orders at him, but all his efforts promised more of the same. A man just as crippled as the day he was shot.

Sweat gleamed on his chest. Tension creased his brow. He gripped the crutches and forced his legs to take the weight of his body. Flaccid muscles proved how futile the task was, heightening an urgency he couldn't suppress.

He growled through his teeth. "Move, damn it!" The crutches wobbled. His body pitched forward. He threw his weight back but went too far and collapsed into the wheelchair.

As he stared ahead into empty space, he kept brooding over his plight. If he could just see Mariah again. He figured she had time to think about things. When was he going to face it? She was done with the gambling man who never knew when to quit. And this time, he went too far. He lost her for good. The secrets. The deceit. What he did to her disgusted him more than the agony of being a cripple. It sucked the life out of him. *I deserve this.*

Riddler entered the room and broke his thoughts. "You're done for the day. Reward yourself with a steam bath. I sent the attendant for a towel and your clothes." He glanced at his pocket watch. "I have to go. Your boss has invited me to dinner." He didn't notice Julian's face clouding with resentment.

Shades of night altered the light in the evening sky, but time didn't move an inch. Every second slowed to an hour, and every hour to an entire day, leaving Julian more frustrated with his condition. His anger mounted at Riddler's concern over his own affairs and his absurd decision confining him to the hospital. Enough was enough.

"To hell with this. I never should've listened to you. I feel like a prisoner in here."

Riddler expected the backlash. "You don't have a choice. If there's any chance for you to walk again, you need to stay put."

"Stay put? All I've been doing is busting my ass in this place. And for what? I haven't felt a thing since we came off the trail."

"Nerve damage is out of my hands. I've already explained that. But if you give up, we lose."

Julian almost gagged on his spit. "What do you mean, *we lose?* I'm the one who's a cripple." He slammed his fist against the wall and belched out a grunt. "You know what I think, Doc?"

Riddler didn't want to know but asked anyway. "What?"

"I think you're fulla shit."

"Now hold on a minute—"

"No, you hold on a minute. I think you're just using me for some kind of experiment so you can pat your damn ego." He felt the urge to punch Riddler square in the face when the doctor chided him.

"This isn't about my ego. Maybe it's your ego that's getting in the way. You're the one who wants to walk again, not me." Riddler regretted his remark, but he took the matter of his ego personally.

"I've had it with you and your high and mighty medical theories. All your talk's been just talk. I'm done. Understand?" Julian threw his crutches on the floor. "I'm not staying locked up in here another second unless you give me one damn good reason why."

Riddler looked him in the eye and told him straight. "You want a damn good reason? Well, I'll give you one. Annabelle."

It was the best he could do. He had nothing more to say.

THE carriage rattled along the cobblestone street up Beacon Hill. Dunnigan and Riddler talked politics and the railroad business, topics Charles spoke passionately about and John took note of on the train ride to Omaha City.

They arrived at the estate where both men repaired to the parlour before dinner and continued their conversation. They were soon interrupted by Annabelle, awaiting her father's escort into the dining room.

A fleeting glimpse had Annabelle turning her nose up at their guest. She couldn't resist her displays of impoliteness. Yet she danced with utmost delicacy between silent insults at the doctor and a daughter's doting on her father. Little did she notice, her performance had John snickering under his breath.

As the evening ended, Charles sipped the last of his brandy and set his glass down on the side table. He sighed. His entire day wasn't a waste. John did come for dinner and agreed to stay at the estate. What better way to keep a close eye on the man who stood between him and the fate of his company.

He gazed at his daughter through weary eyes. "Annie, be a good hostess and entertain our guest for the rest of the evening. I've had a long day." He looked at John. "Do join me in the morning. Breakfast is at seven o'clock sharp."

"Yes, of course. I need to get an early start myself."

"See you at seven then." Charles gave his daughter a hug. "Good night, Annie."

When her father was out of sight, Annabelle fastened her eyes on their guest. "Your room is upstairs on the right, *Doctor*. I'm going to bed."

As she turned toward the staircase, John grabbed her arm and stepped in front of her. She glared at him, flabbergasted.

"What do you think you're doing? Let go of me."

He had no intention. "It's clear you and I don't like each other, Miss Dunnigan, so I'll overlook your childish behavior in the interest of keeping the peace."

She took his comments as an affront. Was he trying to make her mad? She snapped back. "Get out of my way. I have nothing to say to you."

"But I do." He let her have it. "I think it's time you found out the truth about your fiancé."

His words stung. The heat rose in her face. Without warning, she yielded to him and asked, "What truth?" She had to know. "I say, Dr. Riddler. Tell me now."

He let her go, hesitating with his response. "I'm afraid . . . I have bad news. Julian will never walk again."

Annabelle's mouth dropped open. She stood staring at the doctor as if she fell into a stupor. But she was an unpredictable woman. As often as she bent the truth, she acquired no talent for seeing it either. That left her temper to decide.

Her eyes lit up. "You're a liar. I don't believe you."

"You don't have to believe me. But know this. Once a man becomes paralyzed, there's no turning back. Not even for your fiancé."

She cursed his idiotic answer. Julian *was* going to walk again. She would see to it with every selfish bone in her body.

John hinted at another shocker. "There's something else you should know."

What was it about this doctor that drove Annabelle out of her mind? She despised his manipulations. He had no business trying to ruin her life and the life of the man who belonged to her.

"I've had enough of you and your nonsense."

"Call it whatever you want, but Julian has quit the company. He's done with the Union Pacific Railroad."

John's tidings sent a tremor across Annabelle's face. Her body started swaying as though she overindulged from being too merry. He pitied the helpless look she gave him and felt a pang of guilt settle in his stomach. He did more harm than he thought. He didn't expect her bleeding heart. She was hurt. He drew her close so he could say he was sorry. They needed to make amends and start over. Just then, he caught a whiff of her perfume. The heady scent drooped his eyelids. He stood there dazed and didn't see it coming. Her hand lunged at him and snapped his head sideways. A kiss on the cheek would have been nicer, but he wasn't looking for nice anymore.

Annabelle ran toward the stairway and dashed up the steps. John's heart jumped out of his chest. He chased after her, mounting three and four stairs at a time. The sound of her breathing goaded him as he pursued her down the hall. He was on the verge of overtaking her when she vanished. Her bedroom door reared up in his face. He forced it open and snatched her in his arms.

She lashed out. "Let me go—"

His hand muffled her mouth. Her anger unleashed. She tried slapping him again. He bound her in his grasp and held her against him.

"Is this how you treat—all your guests—Miss Dunnigan?"

"Only rogues like you—"

John was done playing games. He dragged her on top of the bed and pinned down her arms. The gentleman and his respectable ways had left the room. "Don't fight it, Annabelle. You know you want me—"

Every ounce of fury writhing her body turned him hard. He tore at her bodice and gaped at her breasts. Emboldened by the sight, he took a taste and started rocking against her.

Annabelle's eyes glazed over. The ceiling blurred. A flux of arousal left her helpless to quell the heat that robbed her of all her petty desires and all her scheming plans.

John didn't have a clue what raged in her mind. He stopped long enough to silence the explosion bulging in his pants while he moved his hand under her dress and found what he was looking for. He spread her legs wide and gave her his remedy, claiming his woman in one, deep, thrust.

Their battle for domination left Dr. Riddler the victor as Miss Dunnigan submitted to him without reservation. She needed him. And he needed her.

CHAPTER 36

Waiting Until Forever

ARIAH GAVE HER father one of her girlish grins as she straightened his neck tie and curled her fingers under the silk lapels of his evening suit. So much time passed since she last did that. She relished the moment, letting her thoughts drift back to a time when life was uncomplicated and her heart untouched by the dark nuances of love.

Standing by the arched window at the end of the upstairs hall, Edmund saw the faraway look in his daughter's eyes. It clouded his mood and made him curse her deceased husband. Keeping his sentiments to himself aggravated the twitch in his eye, as though he already told the world he was stewing over something.

What's done is done. He misjudged his son-in-law, and Mariah suffered the consequences. She deserved better. He placed his hands over hers, letting his big heart console her. But he pondered her gaze longer than he should have. His twitching eye gave him away. Pent-up feelings came to light with sudden haste.

"There's no sense in beating about the bush, Mariah. It's just—well—I've never been good at saying the words right." Then the anger marched out of his mouth. "I am sorry that the man, whose name I will never speak again, has put you through such misery. And the whole money fiasco. Good God, I took him to be an honest man. A man like myself. But I was wrong."

Since they returned home, their cursory smiles and light-hearted talk got them this far. If only Daddy could sit his little girl down on his lap again and take her cares away.

Father's regret left Mariah troubled. "You shouldn't blame yourself for what happened. It wasn't your fault. We can't change the past any more than we could change those we once knew—or thought we knew."

"You're right. The past is in the past. I can't imagine the dangers you would have faced if Mr. Marquette never found you. I'm indebted to him for saving your life." His chest ballooned with exuberance. "Now there's someone I could count on. He's a man of his word, and his reputation is topnotch. My biggest bank loan to the Union Pacific Railroad was because of him. He is quite the negotiator, I must say."

Mariah's hands slipped from under her father's. He wouldn't understand the disappointment in her face she quickly disguised as indifference. It was best to avoid unnecessary questions about the clever negotiator and his reputation. Unlike her father, she misjudged Julian more than she ever misjudged Nathan.

"Well, Father, I think it's time we joined our guests. Mother has been planning this gala for weeks, and you know how much it means for her to see everyone enjoying the Renwick hospitality."

"Yes, you're right." He gave her a wink, a silent gesture of his love for her. How he adored her smile that lit up her face and turned his heart to putty.

As they strolled along the balcony overlooking the grand

hall, Mariah felt uneasy about joining the guests staring up at them. She held fast to her father's arm, seeking a place of refuge more than anything.

But what gave her comfort was the memory of that place of unfettered beauty and enormity, and earthshattering stillness. The land of the High Plains had forever changed her. She sensed it when she looked down at the polished bankers, and the ferryboat capitalists with their fur trading partners, even the senators and their insincere wives. None of them would ever understand the hardships of the common man who sought the promised land in hopes of finding a better life. She thought of Stella, a woman determined to improve her own lot and keep the dream alive for the sake of her children. Gazing at the crowd, she wondered if any of them possessed the fortitude to fight for what was right, in spite of their own privileged circumstances.

Above the grand hall, the chandelier glittered in a menagerie of crystal pendants, accenting the sapphire blue of her silk taffeta gown that concealed little of her shoulders. With each step she took down the cambered staircase, her eyes captured the light as sparkling gems.

The melody of Byerly's Waltz echoed from the ballroom while champagne cocktails flowed golden like honey. She swallowed hers in one quick gulp and set the glass on a side table. Getting tipsy with another drink might have calmed her nerves, though it wouldn't stop the unavoidable mingling coming her way.

The heir of the Camden dynasty strutted toward her. She hadn't seen Hugh since her farewell party in early spring, but ignored his recent invitations asking her out for a Sunday picnic.

He bowed and kissed her hand. That dreamy look left no doubt of his intentions. He curled his mouth into a smile and settled in. "You are the loveliest, Mariah. Stay with me and talk. I haven't seen you in months. We need to get reacquainted."

"I'd love to talk, Hugh, but perhaps another time."

He didn't make it easy for her. A passing tray of champagne caught his eye. He snatched two cocktails and offered her one. They toasted their reunion, clinking their glasses together.

"Well, I won't let you go until we dance. And I'll only take *yes* for an answer." He swilled his champagne and set the glass on another tray.

How could Hugh possibly understand? What Mariah needed, he couldn't give her. The feeling of the boundless frontier and the open sky, setting her free from the confines of mansion walls, and people and their shallow notions.

He whisked her away in his arms and carried her across the dance floor in a whirlwind of flowing gowns and suit tails. An evening of gaiety hummed in the air, intoxicating everyone with excitement and laughter. But not Mariah. The embrace from another man brought back too many memories.

The music stopped. She fumbled the glass, still in her hand, and said her goodbyes. She had to get away from his brown eyes. She did not want to remember.

Ahead of her loomed the door. A way out.

But there was no escape, only the shock of what she saw between her and the front entrance. Her body froze. The champagne glass slipped through her fingers and shattered on the floor, spattering its bubbly liquid.

It was Julian.

He stood there under his own strength, tall and wickedly handsome. His gaze fused into hers with a passion, unmistakable, telling her he'd never again let go of the woman he traveled so far to find. Time stood still. Noises faded around them, except the sound of his footsteps and the ebony cane that eased him closer to her.

He fell lost in her aquamarine eyes, putting an end to the wait he thought would last forever. He hated forever, for it meant a life without her, and a love worth nothing more than the dust on a cowpoke's boots.

Love could be a stubborn thing, yet patient if one believed in its tenacity. Julian needed time to tell Mariah why he came back. If she could just listen to what he had to say. But he never got the chance.

He felt the sting against the side of his face and was stunned at her baneful act. Now all of St. Louis could judge Mariah's unladylike deed as a change in mood overcame the guests who were anxious to whisper the gossip, long into the night, and on the carriage ride home.

Mariah fled from the crowd through the glass doors and onto the terrace. Julian's heart raced as he followed her in pursuit. He caught up to her and stopped short, afraid she might run away from him. The evening light carved a soft silhouette of her figure. Even with her face turned away from him, the pain of his presence weighed down on her shoulders. He couldn't stand seeing her that way. He moved closer to where she stood against the balustrade.

"Don't leave, Mariah. I need to explain. Please give me a chance."

She heard the pleading in his voice and despised it. But he had to tell her what burned in his heart all this time since they parted.

"Forgive me."

She spun around and looked daggers at him. "Forgive you? Is that why you came back, to ask for my forgiveness?" Her temper set fire in her throat. She did not want his answer, any more than she wanted to set him free from all his lies. "I don't need your apology. All I need is for you to leave!"

The ire in her voice made her tremble. She couldn't bear the sight of him. Her hands covered her mouth, stifling her breaths. A flood of emotion swept over her. She bolted from the terrace down the steps and onto the garden path. Then she disappeared behind the mansion.

Julian tossed his cane on the ground, out of frustration and anger toward himself. He raked his fingers through his hair and set off through the grove of maple trees. As he lumbered along, gaining momentum in his legs, he searched for her up ahead, knowing he'd be forced to stop her, even if it was against her will.

Beyond the mansion, he scanned the estate, listening for any subtle movement. A noise roused his senses. He approached the horse stable and opened the door. Inside, slivers of light shining between the vertical planks of wood etched lines on the ground, distorting the images he couldn't make out. But sounds were easier to discern, especially her weeping.

He exhaled into his sleeve, cloaking his steps as he edged toward a horse shifting in a stall with its long neck encircled in Mariah's embrace. When the horse turned its head, he saw in a moment of distraction, the face of the beast who guided him across the plains.

"Chakote . . ."

Mariah reacted to his voice and dashed toward the stable door. He lunged and caught her arm. She tried breaking free.

"You should have never come back—" She lashed out. "Leave me alone!"

Julian couldn't think straight. He locked her in his arms. But the more she resisted, the more it hardened his resolve. It had been so long. Too damn long.

She threw her fists against his chest. Her voice teetered on hysteria. "Go back to your harlot! I don't ever want to see you again. Get out of my life!"

He pressed his hands against her back and tugged at the seam of her dress. The hooks popped open. But she wouldn't let up. Her writhing inched the gown down around her ankles. Then their bodies tumbled onto the mounds of straw below.

All of Mariah's anger, built up inside, suddenly gave way to a deep-seated hunger when she looked into Julian's eyes and realized he was telling her to just let go.

"Let me in, Mariah. Let me make love to you."

This was their time to lay bare their struggles and share all the love they possessed, for what they once dreamed of had found them at last.

With a trace of his fingers, Julian felt the outline of her breasts through her chemise, and he remembered. He couldn't hold back. Her body beckoned him. Their worlds collided as they plunged headlong into a desperate kiss.

An upwelling of passion had Mariah fighting for every breath, frantic to catch a wisp of air to keep her delirious and dead set on quenching her need.

She wrestled Julian's tailcoat and opened his shirt. His physique left her stunned at how well built he'd become. His muscles flexed in full view and drew her eyes down to the dark line of hair that disappeared below his pant line. She was spellbound and wanted more by the way her lips parted and called his name.

"*Julian*— I've missed you, *terribly*."

He dusted her lips with petal soft kisses as he skimmed his hand up the curve of her thigh to what tempted him beyond his reach. His touch set her afire and made her lose control. A shudder quaked between her legs. Seeing her release left him restless to take her higher. He caught the rhythm of her spasms, sliding his fingers in and out, when she climaxed again.

There was no more waiting. No more fighting to stay alive. He parted her chemise. Her nipples stiffened at his touch. Slowly, he eased over her and teased them with his tongue, drawing each one into his mouth all the while spreading her legs wide with his own. Hard and fast, he held steady as he looked into her eyes, so he could see all of her consuming all of him.

Susan Rounds

He thrust his manhood into her wetness and felt it spike. A groundswell rippled through him. He quickened his pace and pumped inside, sensing the end almost near. *So tight.* His body moved against hers with all the pleasure he could give her. A lifetime of love streamed from his eyes, a sweltering love he could give her now.

"It's been—so long—"

His voice strained with the words. Every part of him gave her more and pushed him closer to the breaking point. He wanted to make it last and make endless love to her, but her passage burned hot and enveloped him in a wave of fire. He erupted inside. All of his pent-up need. All of his steadfast love. Their ecstasy was a passion he never felt before, and for Mariah, it was a place she never found love, until now.

They let go their rapture into the night air. Mariah lifted her hips and let Julian go deeper into the realm of desperation, triggering a drumfire of sensations as he watched her breasts quiver to his pounding beat. His eyes gleamed with every surge, keeping him solid and pumping hard, until they careened into the abyss in a staccato of moans that shattered their past.

With their weakened bodies entwined and embracing all they shared, this moment was like no other. And it was only the beginning. A beautiful and everlasting beginning.

CHAPTER 37

The Past Washed Away

*T*HE SCENT OF rain lurked in the night air. Breezes shifted into powerful gusts and creaked the walls of the stable. Chakote banged his hooves against the stall at the sound of thunder in the distance. Bad weather was moving in. Julian's mind flashed back to that squall in Nebraska Territory, and when he found Mariah. The ruckus of the wind meant little time was left to get to the cottage before the sky opened up.

Thunder clapped again. Julian stared into Chakote's eyes and steadied him with his voice. "Easy does it, boy. We've been through storms like this before."

Chakote felt his master's hand stroking the contours of his coat as it glinted a silvery black where the full moon cast its light through the cracks in the walls. Another boom ruptured the sky. He snorted and threw his head back. The stall gate swung open, and the tug of his halter guided him out. He gestured with an affirmative neigh.

Julian drew close to Mariah sleeping under the cover of his

jacket. He kissed her forehead and whispered, "Wake up, my love . . ."

The murmur of his voice created an imperceptible stirring, yet that aspect on her face told him she had no desire to wake up. He had satisfied her fully.

With the brunt of his weight bearing down on his left leg, he gathered her in his arms and headed toward the stable door. He lifted the latch. The wind hurled the door open. Mariah roused from the rush of air. He hoisted her sideways onto Chakote's back, then straddled behind her and made tracks over the grassy knoll.

Jagged bolts of lightning streaked overhead and unleashed a mighty rumble, pitting Chakote's courage against the reins steering him into the shadows. The brooding clouds shifted in and out of the light from the alabaster moon, giving a glimpse of the cottage up ahead.

Raindrops spattered against Julian's face. The bad weather caught up to them. He huddled over Mariah and snapped the reins, spurring Chakote into a canter. Just as they reached the cottage, the droplets coalesced into rain.

He swept Mariah inside and carried her into the bedroom where he nuzzled her under the bedcovers. In the main room, he silenced the shutters banging against the outside wall. The deluge clattered on the rooftop like no ordinary storm, at least not for the Boston man who swore he was living through another High Plains downpour. He tossed a few chunks of wood into the fireplace, then lit a match and watched the flames rise up while he braced himself against the mantel. Looking down into the fire warming his muscular frame, he fell deep in thought.

The ordeal was over. He shook his head, in denial he was still alive, as he skimmed his fingers over the scars on his back. The wounds reminded him of all the bad that happened, but he would never forget all the good that came of it. Their love had been tested by forces greater than the two of them, and now it brought them to this place. Julian and Mariah finally came home.

A passing glance more than two years ago couldn't erase her from his memory. Last autumn, he saw her again. Her smile. Her face. There was no going back. But all they could hold on to was their forbidden love. Through all the insanity, they kept believing in the impossible. Now, everything became possible.

As he reflected on what the night already gave them, he was quick to pass judgment on what he did. Had he braved the depths of his love for Mariah? She gave him a love so profound, he wondered if all he had given her was enough.

The clamor in the sky disguised footsteps behind him, but not the touch that pricked his spine. He fixated on the voice.

"Don't move."

A tug on his shirt collar peeled the wet fabric off his back. The breath on his skin tightened every joined tendon in his body. He closed his eyes and took in the thrill. Every synapse in his brain sparked on high alert. Every touch told him she was in control, because she wanted to be.

Mariah's body pulsed against his, triggering a sudden urgency. Her past came back to haunt her, not for its heartbreaking consequences, but for how it cheated her out of a part of her life she could never take back. This moment intensified her need.

She drew her arms around Julian's front and stroked the muscled terrain of his chest as her lips slid down his back and tasted the rain. The sensations made her wish, with an unrelenting fervor, that she never met Nathan. While she stumbled over her own misguided love, Julian waited. So much time had been lost. Wasted time, daring her to make up for it in one solitary night. What burned inside yearned for affirmation of the passion hidden so deep, she feared it would suffocate her if she did not release it. Julian set fire to her soul. He made her believe in love again.

From where her lips and hands touched him, she embraced his reaction. She could tell by his controlled breathing he was fighting like hell not to take over. But she had to know how long he could hold out, until he couldn't. Perhaps her foreplay was testing him too soon. Or not.

She fumbled his belt buckle. Down to the floor it fell with a clank. She pressed her breasts against his back and heard him say her name. Still, he showed no sign of weakening under her sensory overload. The more he resisted, the more she aroused him, pushing him to the brink where she demanded his ultimate possession—his supreme gratification point.

Her hand slipped down and surrounded his shaft. She was stunned by how it felt and responded to her touch. With her other hand free to please, she palmed his stomach and felt it flex. Like when he made love to her before. The surge of rhythms made her body join in and sway against him.

Julian held fast in a death grip on the mantel. He locked his eyes on the flames, knowing he'd combust if he looked down and watched what she was doing to him. All at once, she stopped and moved in front. He pursued her eyes with his, trying to steal her power of possession over him and use it against her. She wasn't ready to surrender. Her knees gave way, and she came down on him.

He couldn't temper the pressure throbbing in her mouth. Her pace let him know how far she'd go to prolong his torment. To the end, if need be.

He belted out a groan. "You're gonna make me—"

In one motion, he eased away, before it was too late, and laid her down on the rug. Gazing at her, he was overcome by her insanely beautiful figure. Her sheer nightgown revealed her body glowing in the firelight as the lace drawstring dangled between her breasts.

She skimmed her hands down her front and parted the gown. A little tease was harmless, wasn't it? Lying there naked wasn't. Mariah let it get out of hand. She lured his gaze past her belly button, and farther down, where she found the slippery nub and flicked its peak. Her spasm excited, and her body twitched. She went higher. Julian couldn't stop her. He didn't want to.

Her lips parted and she exhaled, "*Come* with me—"

His look made her blue-green eyes flash electric. "With pleasure, my love. With all my pleasure."

She spread her legs wide and beckoned him. His rigid tip dipped into her essence and joined with her finger, doubling her delight. Every breath she fought to take drove his erection to her opening. Then her fire drew him in.

He thrust inside. The vestiges of his resistance tested his mettle like never before while their eyes fueled a need that rose sky-high, cresting their voices through the claps of thunder. Mariah's body shuddered and pushed him over the edge. He pumped with a fury until his potent fluid released, causing a chain reaction which had them both riding a tidal wave cascading in a frenzy of emotion where two lovers stormed as one. Their bodies fluxed in heightened contractions, prolonging their ecstasy, never-ending. The splendor of the night belonged to them as they collapsed in each other's arms with their entire beings spent.

To be joined so perfectly had them tasting love's tenderness between them when the heat of their bodies sparked a flame into the embers of nascent passion.

It was happening again.

Julian barely moved when his stiff rod emboldened him with a newfound intensity to deliver an encore performance of the most virile kind. Mariah made it so damn easy for him to lose control and take whatever he wanted, and take it all for himself.

He pulled back just enough and kept his tip pulsing inside her entrance. Enough to make her beg for him. He had to be sure, in her most desperate moment of desire, all he was about to give her was enough for all he was about to take.

The look in her eyes turned him hard to the core. Years of hunger spilled from his lips. "God, I need you—"

Her voice teetered on reckless. "Take me now. Take me—"

He thrust in deep and saw her eyes open wide. She threw her arms around his neck and rolled on top of him. He went deeper. A short shrill burst through her lips. She drew her knees up and straddled him, bracing her hands against his shoulders. He came up on his elbows and met her halfway. Out of the corner of his eye, he glimpsed the firelight reflecting her silhouette on the wall. His eyes riveted on the erotic sight like he was part of some dream. The sudden movement of her shadow clipped his breath. She was riding him.

His hands gripped her thighs while her body undulated against him. He couldn't stand it and answered back. Not even the racket raging in the sky suppressed their moans that catapulted their tempo and made her breasts shimmer. He rocked her hips and penetrated her to her deepest pressure point. He had the insatiable urge to make her scream.

"You're so—*wet.*" His hot member throbbed with every beat. His voice cracked on the precipice. A violent crescendo was seconds away as he fought for any remnant of self-control. "Tell me you want it. Tell me—"

Mariah looked down and saw his shaft sliding in and out. "Yes, oh yes—"

A whiplash of sensations erupted between her legs. Her back curved like a crescent moon, and her hair whipped back and forth, again and again. And then she screamed.

Julian heaved his being into her and ignited his fiery love. He rode out the quake surging inside while his eyes pierced her soul and proclaimed how madly in love he was with her. Their climax took them higher into the realm of the unknown where their bodies trembled together. Out of breath. Out of control.

The heat of their passion subsided and lingered in their embrace as their sweet love drifted over them. All they heard was the sound of the crackling fire mingling with love's sighs.

Their hearts brought the heavens to their feet, for the night was young and they found their mutual experimentation too hard to resist. They had not made love in a darkened room, in a soft featherbed, where they could hide under the lily sheets and make their own kind of rolling thunder. It was all so surreal, and it felt so right.

There were no more misgivings. No more need to try and stop the hands of time and make up time. Life had to be lived on their terms, and now it could be, for their lasting love would make it so.

Remember tonight, for it is the beginning of always.

- DANTE ALIGHIERI

Chapter 38

The Tenacity Of Love

*S*WEET SEPTEMBER. A new awakening. A journey of more than a thousand miles, and a lifetime to love and be loved. As it should be. As it was meant to be. Only Julian and Mariah could fathom where their future would take them. Even then, for them, it was a profound mystery. Every moment they were together was magical and unpredictable, and filled with unspeakable passion. As it should be.

On this voyage, Mariah was leaving home for the second time, but it was of her own choosing and her own heart's desire. The bonds of true love tied her and Julian eternally together, and they knew all their past struggles made their love stronger for all time. Nothing would tear them apart, and of that they were certain.

The twists and turns of Jerusalem Road, winding its way along the carved banks of Cohasset Harbor, stunned Mariah beyond words. She never knew the feel of the open sea and its startling beauty, and never imagined, one day, it would come to be her new home.

Through the carriage window, she inhaled the scent of the

ocean air and admired the placid waters lapping onto the rocky beach. In the distance, the bay opened up to the majestic Atlantic, like the gaping maw of a crocodile. Seagulls squawking above the harbor swooped down and plucked the morsels cast off from the bobbing fishing boats filled with their day's catch of mackerel. It was all so new, so wondrous, and a telling sign that she belonged here.

She nestled her side in Julian's embrace and felt the warmth of his protection. It was the one token of his love he gave her when his heart could not give her more. She touched the aragonite pendant on her necklace, enchanting his view of her décolleté dress. Unspeakable gratitude welled up inside. Had Julian not found it before they left Fort Laramie, she would have thought her sister's gift lost forever. Thinking back, she knew Fanny had been right all along. *Keep it close to your heart, my little sister. It will always lead you home.*

The one question Julian wrestled with, more than any, was asking Mariah about leaving St. Louis again. Too many memories of a marriage gone bad might have tracked her down and placed another curse on her. A curse bent on destroying the love they fought so hard for, and could finally share. But those thoughts wandered among the forgotten now. He saw her answer when her gaze met his. It was all there, every bit of truth she believed, every bit of happiness, and the certainty that her willingness to start a new life in this place was because she wanted to, and for no other reason.

"I will never grow tired of looking into your eyes, Mrs. Marquette." His whispers lit a spark and melted her heart.

"And I will never grow tired of you, my darling husband." Her eyes always kept him wanting as they brimmed with desire.

He brushed his lips against hers and felt her weaken in his arms. His power over her made him love her all the more. Her kiss left him just as weak as their moans grew sensual in their utterance with every exhale of their breath.

Mariah's longing sent a rush to her fingertips. She couldn't resist the feel of his hair with its rich lava hues, and the nape of his neck that swayed so sublime and heightened the intensity of their kiss. They let it deepen the need hidden between them as they fell trapped in the dream once almost ended in a heartbeat. But the end never came, not when the impossible became possible.

A command from the coachman halted the carriage and left them dazed. Mariah returned Julian's forever look with an ineffable sweetness, reassuring him she was here for good.

He smiled. "It's time." He guided her down the step and waved on his driver. "Take the carriage in, Albert. We'll walk from here."

"As you wish, sir."

Albert dismounted and swung open the iron gates, then climbed back onto the coach box and ushered the horses through. The clatter of hooves faded away. All was silent around them.

A whisper of air whirred softly through the entrance, telling Julian his moment had come. The tides of change stood before him, and his chance to reveal the testament of his undying love for Mariah. When she first walked into his life, she was unaware of his attentions. What dwelled deep in his heart had been overshadowed by the turmoil in her life. But he could not deny how he felt, and how much he was in love with her. Now he could show her that his love was not in vain.

He took her hand and led her through the gateway anchored by pillars of stone. At the center of each gate, an ornate emblem caught her eye. Curious, she traced her fingers around it, pondering the patterns.

"Julian, what is this symbol?"

"It's the Marquette coat of arms." He paused and thought of their future, and all the questions she would have, and all the answers he wanted to give her for the rest of their lives.

"It looks very imposing. And the colors, the greens and blues, do they mean something?"

He smiled at her inquisitiveness. "They speak to the Marquette legacy, and to our character and beliefs. The color blue stands for truth, and green signifies loyalty in love." He held tight to her hand and drew her near. "And for me, those colors remind me of the splendor of your eyes . . . and my fidelity to you."

Mariah felt a door opening and a facet of her husband's past unfolding before her that she never knew about. She listened as he revealed more of his family's legacy.

"The knight's helmet represents the soul guiding the body. The way one should journey through life."

"And the curved leaves surrounding the helmet. What secret do they reveal?"

Above all, the leaves in the crest drove straight to Julian's heart, for they embodied the essence of what she meant to him. "Those are the leaves of the woodbine, and they speak to the kind of love that doesn't injure what it clings to."

Mariah caught her breath and was overcome with emotion. She could see it in her husband's eyes, every aspect of his honor, and she believed him.

And then she said, "I know."

Muted sounds from the harbor drifted through the trees while they walked among a smattering of aspen, willow, and alder. As they rounded a bend in the road, an unexpected sight came into view.

Mariah stood awestruck. Her voice echoed disbelief.

"Julian—" She gasped. "I can't believe—it's beautiful."

The expression on her face was a wonder to behold and one Julian thought he might never see as she gazed at the chateau appearing before them. He fought to keep his dream alive and built this palace for his queen. For Mariah. He laid the remaining stones before he set out on his journey to Dakota Territory.

Mariah's eyes lit up with joy at the breathtaking sight. There was so much to take in. A sudden urgency came over her. She called to mind the French inscription above the Marquette crest.

"The writing on the gates reminded me of my family's French legacy. I never knew it's your legacy too." One mystery remained. She had to know. "Tell me what the words say."

Julian curved his hands around her waist where they came to rest in a close embrace. "*Pour Mon Vrai Amour.* It means . . . *For My True Love.*" He uttered the words that dwelled in his heart for so long as his eyes kept on loving her. "My hands and my heart have built this chateau for you, my sweet Mariah. All for you."

There were no words to convey the power of this moment and the skipped beat of their hearts, or the realization for Mariah of how long Julian had loved her, and how determined he was to keep his love for her alive. But only if they kept believing in the impossible, and if he remained, until the end, a patient man.

In their arms, they held each other so tight, they both could barely breathe. Their gazes coalesced. The heat of their mutual breath ached to be joined again, to become one again, yearning to be trapped within their kiss, so, so near.

Their lips quietly quivered, in anticipation of the words, everlasting words, suddenly exhaled and forever sealed with one destiny that now belonged to them—for all time.

"I will always . . . love you."

I love thee, I love but thee, with a love that shall not die.
Till the sun grows cold, and the stars are old . . .

- BAYARD TAYLOR

SUSAN ROUNDS has always been fascinated with history and other cultures through her travels and living in Europe during her childhood. Exploring fairytale castles sparked her imagination. Her adventurous lifestyle led to a career in aviation flying to Asia and Hawaii as a Flight Service Manager on the Boeing 747. Susan's passion for historical romance draws on many of her life experiences, inspiring her to write about the enduring power of love. She and her husband have two sons they're very proud of and call northern California home.

Visit Susan online:
susanrounds.com

Sign up for Susan's newsletter:
susanrounds.com/join

www.ingramcontent.com/pod-product-compliance
Lightning Source LLC
Chambersburg PA
CBHW051123190726
48290CB00006B/1661